ZombieGirl Ωmega

CONTENTION

ZOMBIE GIRL OMEGA – CONTENTION

BOOK TWO OF THE ZETA WARS
O. T. Riesen

MARA PUBLISHING

Published by Mara Publishing
www.marapublishing.com

ISBN-13: 979-8-9872034-2-2

Developmental Editor: Fiona McLaren
Cover Design By: George Cotronis
Printed in the United States of America

BOOKS IN THE *ZOMBIE GIRL OMEGA* SERIES
BY O. T. RIESEN

INITIATION
CONTENTION

✿

For D & K:
My first,
My last,
My only,
My everything.

☾

☾

To Chris:

The center of my ever-spinning,
always-expanding universe,
simulated or not.

"No, I cannot escape death, but at least I can escape the fear of it—or do I have to die moaning and groaning too?"

—EPICTETUS

The Zeta Creed

Zero tolerance for threats to humanity and its livelihood.

*I shall defeat my enemy on every field of battle and never surrender,
Though I may be the last of the Zeta.*

**Eradicate all evil through strength of force, cunning,
and determination.**

*Through self-discipline, I will outlast all those who oppose
a safe and free humanity.*

True to myself and my comrades.

*I shall perform my duties with deference and unquestioning loyalty,
To the United Forces and all with which they stand.*

Acceptance of all responsibilities and the qualities expected of me.

*I will execute any and all directives conferred upon me,
With fortitude and steadfastness.*

Prologue
THOSE YOU STAND FOR

EAGER BEGINNINGS

Approximately 10 years after the widespread incursion of Zee.

[OMEGA]

Ba-bump.

Ba-bump.

My pulse hammers like a war drum, each thunderous beat synchronized with the rhythm of my stride. The loose dirt beneath my boots becomes a conquered terrain, the impacts from my treads full of raw determination. My HUD—a honed lens of technological precision—dissects the world into a crystalline tableau of tactical awareness. Breath enters and exits in measured streams captured and replayed in a sensory feedback loop. A chaotic orchestra of potential threats and innocuous whispers threatens to intrude on my awareness, but it dissolves against the steel-edged concentration of my unit. We are a singular weapon. Our focus—a blade that cuts through the noise, rendering everything else insignificant.

A matching set of dark fatigues cuts ahead of me, sprinting in long, fluid strides just to my right. Another team member keeps close to my nine, a few yards behind. Three more complete our advancing line, our bodies forming a precise diagonal formation. A tactical spread engineered to eliminate any visual or physical obstruction to our engagement. This isn't a new experience for me, running this brutal gauntlet, nor is it my first time with this team. Yet, for all our practiced movements, we've never managed to succeed here.

Gritting my teeth, I continue to push the limits of my upgrade, seeking a metaphorical wall that I've yet to hit. Matching my team's pace and flow has transmuted into muscle memory driven by survival. Five squad members were culled during the first half of advanced training due to gross incompetence. Good riddance. The loss of that dead weight won't burden me. Nor do I want any of those fucks with me outside of base when my life and those on my squad depends on their aptitude.

With a huff full of mist and heat, we round the corner as a single organism. A crumbling wall of brick and mortar looms, simultaneously out of place and meticulously placed. Its height prompts me to switch my rifle grip to a single-handed one, freeing up the other hand to vault. Three other exhalations follow mine, including a fourth that breaks the melody, faltering and cursing. They audibly struggle with the impediment, and my estimation of them falls as well. That'll make six down after today's test skirmish.

Savage satisfaction ripples through me at the thought of one less hindrance to the mission. One less potential point of failure. A smile cuts across my face—razor-sharp and invisible behind my helm. No one will witness this moment of pure, clinical joy that I allow myself.

"Keep up, Delta! We're not retrieving your mangled corpse when all of this is over. The Zee can have it." Theta's voice loudly resounds through our open comms.

The sharp bark of command lights the fire of Hades under Delta's considerably lagging rear. This isn't the first time that she's been called out since we were assigned to the same unit, and I'm sure the assessor will finally make the needed call to nix her this round. She's too awkward a soldier to make up for whatever extraordinary gift she claimed with the upgrade. It's readily apparent she never anticipated doing anything physical in her life. She'd be better off planted firmly behind a desk to allow her lower girth to grow. Okay. Now I'm just being a bitch.

"*Screw you, Theta!*" Delta counters back hoarsely.

I know I'm not the only one who catches the fear encapsulated in her furious reply. I chuckle, sizing up Theta against my position— a linebacker personified with arms like telephone poles and a midsection that could stop a truck. The guy's so massive I could probably slip into a single pant leg. He's dominated our training and is currently blocking my path to the top spot. I may have once been content to fade into the background. However, I now wrestle with an unfamiliar hunger to lead. To dominate.

Another quirk of the Zeta upgrade, I suppose. Those of us who opted to become United Forces super soldiers did so of our own volition. The promise of a means to fight back against the Zee— to not just outlast them—proved too great a temptation for many. If transforming my lifelong tendency to blend into an almost primal drive to stand out is the cost I face, so be it.

As we round the last empty structure before engaging our enemy, I pull my mind into that less emotion-based place of decision-making. This drill may be intentional and a mostly controlled setup, but these are still actual, functional Zee we're engaging. As unpredictable as any rabid animal. Not to mention, who knows how fresh they are or how well-fed.

Screeeeeeech!!!

There's no time to react as a shrill and ear-splitting sound echoes from above, followed closely by a shadow dropping at the speed of free-fall. Spurred on by gravity, the formless shape flies dead on toward our leader. It's an incredible thing to witness—the inertia of a human body impacting with another from four stories above. I wince at the thud of impact for Theta's ugly mug even as I push myself into a sprint to his downed position, slowing my momentum at the last minute to assess the scene. A downed and broken Zee can still be a lethal one.

The fallen creature remains sprawled on top of our current leader's unmoving form, twitching spasmodically. Its remaining eye, veiny and pink from blood, rolls toward me from its position, but beyond the quiver of muscle, nothing else moves. I suspect it severed its spine upon impact. Either that or the trainers are particularly sadistic and thought lobbing a half-dead Zee from on high was a great workout variation.

As I drop into a crouch, scanning the building tops for more falling Zee, the others finally decide to catch up. I'm quick to throw out a hand, gesturing for them to halt and get low. This exercise may not be the same simplistic rehash it's been. With the rest of the crew holding, I cautiously make my way to the intermixed pile of Zeta and Zee.

The creature clicks its teeth together over and over, uselessly biting the air as it strains to take a piece out of me. Flipping my faceplate up, my nose crinkles at the first wash of aroma flowing forth from the Zee.

With a light kick aimed at the ankle closest to me, I call out, "Theta? You still with us?"

I pause, waiting for a response, but none is forthcoming. Glancing at my comrades for ideas, they offer little more than a half-ass shrug. Figures. Shrugging myself, I opt to give Theta's booted leg a more solid thwack with my steel-toe. That gets a response.

Theta moans long and loud as he feebly rouses. Without forethought, he attempts to right himself from his prone position, curling upward without first assessing his surroundings. The moment he shifts his considerable mass, he collapses to the ground with a sharp cry.

"Theta, hold up!" I call, trying to gain his attention.

I attempt to prevent the approaching train wreck, but I'm not fast enough. He ignores me and reaches for the lower half of himself and the source of his pain. What he encounters is an additional body strewn atop him. One that simultaneously realizes that a potential meal is equally within reach.

"Wuh? *Shit!*"

Crouching down, I quickly reach across his downed form and swat his flailing hands away. It's easy enough to do with him as weak as a baby Zee.

"Theta, stop freaking out. You've got a Zee on you, but it can't do much. Let me…" I stow my weapon and reach down, preparing to shift the living carcass off him.

Apparently, that was the wrong thing to say. In an instant, our squad leader does precisely what I was hoping to avoid. He writhes under the Zee's weight, a frantic mix of attempted escape while attempting to knock the unknown invader off. Subsequently, he puts me in the line of fire.

"Aw, fuck me!" I curse, eyes rolling skyward in a prayer. Now, I have to avoid the creature's disease-ridden mouth while protecting the idiot. Growling in frustration, I turn to find who's closest.

"Epsilon! Help me out," I shout over my shoulder, using every available limb of mine to pin the moron in place.

"You got it!" The stout Zeta soldier stashes his weapon before hurrying to my aid. Faceplate already flipped up, he drops to my side and asks, "What do you need?"

With his full face partially exposed and closer than I'm used to, I glimpse day-old stubble. Epsilon is an unexpectedly competent soldier. With a thicker build and soft edges, you'd think someone so cheerful wouldn't be capable of the work we're expected to do. He's gained a bit of my respect thus far. I'll give him that. He's damn quick for his size and handy in a skirmish. He's also not too bad of a shot, though it's evident he's never held a gun before now.

On the other hand, I have been handling a rifle since I was eight, much to my mother's supreme disappointment.

"Grab Theta's arms. They're getting in the way. Sit on him if you have to." I nod at his upper half, which I've attempted to immobilize with an outstretched leg. "I'll pull the Zee off him and toward me. Drag his ass away when he's clear. Got it?"

He grins broadly, a well-chewed toothpick poking out to the side as he does. "Not a problem."

Boots shuffle around us, followed by minute clicks of rifles at the ready. Our remaining teammates encircle our position and watch our sixes without being told. The squad awaits our move and any subsequent Zee, trigger fingers hovering in anticipation.

Epsilon shifts into position, and I'm grateful to release myself from the awkward side lunge I had landed myself in.

"Ready?" He asks. I nod once before giving a countdown.

"K. Three, two, one, *heave!*" I call out as Epsilon's wider form hauls Theta forward. Conjointly, I grab the supremely agitated Zee by its legs and toss the gnarl-limbed thing to the side of me. I underestimate my newfound strength and accidentally throw it a little further than intended. Of course, Delta has to duck as its body barely clears her helm. The creature slams into the wall behind her with great force, making a wet crunch upon impact.

Whoops. I really need to get the hang of that.

"Watch it, Omega!" Comes a snarl, echoing from the comms in my helm.

"Go fuck yourself, Delta!" I reflexively spit back. I must say that my parents would be unimpressed by my behavior if they still had the breath to care. I take the "talk like a sailor" bit to a different plateau.

I turn to say something inane to Epsilon, and Theta by proximity, when I catch movement behind my squadmate's hunched-over form. Shit, again.

"Contact!" I call, slipping my faceplate down and bringing the end of my rifle to bear on the approaching Zee. Without waiting for any command from our squad's current team leader, I drill three rounds precisely through the bulbous mass between the thing's skewed eyes.

"Oh, crud!" Epsilon scrambles back as the Zee falls forward and toward him, exit holes still smoking. "Theta, c'mon. All hands on deck."

He takes a few precious seconds to help the man sit up before pulling his weapon into position. All the while, Epsilon firmly plants himself between our injured teammate and the advancing horde.

I'm astounded when Theta pulls out, not his rifle, but a Ka-Bar from an ankle holster, holding it out at the frothing Zee as if that'll hold back their onslaught in any reality. As Epsilon begins taking shots of his own, something seems to crumble in our de facto leader. Instead of doing something marginally intelligent and helpful, like using his rifle, he drops the knife and curls into himself. Visibly trembling hands thrown over his head in an attempt to hide all two hundred and fifty-plus pounds of him.

I don't prevent my frown of judgment at his behavior. It's a bit disappointing but not altogether unexpected. It's better to have soldiers break down and lose it here than out in the wild, where an easy bailout is impossible.

Again, I curse not for the last time today and make a speedy assessment of our enemy. The horde isn't nearly as numerous as it initially appeared. Combine that with the fact that the UF wouldn't give us a challenge outside of our collective capabilities. As expendable as we are as soldiers, we're still Zeta, and that comes with a higher price tag and greater value to our bosses. In other words, we can take them. It's what we're made to do.

I open the team's general comms channel, which I've memorized by now. It's been the same through every iteration of advanced training. I'm going to salvage this operation, whether the rest of the team is on board or not…hopefully they're on board. I've only a few more minutes before the proctors pull the plug and consider this round a failure.

Moving toward the two pinned soldiers, I call to the others, *"Come on, guys, we can't leave them here. There are not as many Zee as we're being made to think. We can take 'em!"*

"Are you nuts?" That voice comes from either Eta or Phi. I can't recall which of those two is which. Never really cared to.

"Probably, but not for the reasons you're inferring." I snark back at him. *"Command wouldn't have given us something we can't handle."*

Not yet, at least. I can't help that afterthought. I've seen more than a few things thus far in my UF training that don't warrant blind trust in this institution. I have no doubt there's a more extensive agenda unbeknownst to underlings such as myself, but that doesn't help matters at present.

"*Fan out,*" I state with all the confidence I'm imbued with. "*Delta, take the right wing. Phi, the left. I'm going up the middle to help out the other two. Eta, cover me.*"

"*Roger.*" Comes a calm and immediate reply. Surprisingly, it's from Delta, of all people.

I pause my firing in astonishment as she pulls up short beside me and takes a wing position. Shaking off the initial surprise, I don't wait to see if the other two comply. Probably not the best idea on my part. Who knows if either of them would shoot me in the back—accidentally or intentionally?

I drop to a knee and work to take down the Zee, picking my targets from the center of the fold, closest to Theta and Epsilon. Delta does the same for her side, as does Phi, who's now joined our triage line. There are close to thirty Zee left shambling in ragged, jerking waves toward us. However, with our organized firing, we're having little difficulty holding the line and clearing their numbers.

"*Eta. Cover me. I'm going to help Epsilon move Theta.*"

He grunts in reply but seems to change his mind as I finally receive a gruff "*Roger.*"

Not for the first time, I have the nagging suspicion that he's not so keen on taking orders from a woman. Faceplate hiked up, I take the last few steps and nearly get a blade to the throat for my carelessness. Theta's pupils are blown wide as I catch the swinging arm with its knife in tow. He doesn't seem to process me for a moment, but as he blinks again, the fog lifts, and he stares back dumbly.

"Omega, what?"

"Hey there, Theta. How's the leg? Still not working?" Slinging my rifle behind me as I speak in a relaxed tone, I pause to toggle through my helm's settings via gauntlet and ensure my peripheral alert is engaged. I'm not getting surprised by any more stray Zee. I've had enough entertainment for the day. The other soldier still hasn't answered my questions, and I risk a glance at Epsilon. He sees me momentarily glance his way and nudges his chin toward the lower part of Theta's left leg.

I lay a hand gently on his shoulder while assessing what Epsilon has marked. "Theta?"

"*Mah ___*," he mumbles unintelligibly, chin tucked into his chest.

"Say that again?" I try to lift him up to understand him better and get a good look at his face.

"My knee," he repeats glumly, but at least more understandably.

Blood drips from a broken nose, and a lower lip filleted open by his own teeth. I imagine Theta's face took a good part of the fall, along with his left knee. I can tell from the angle of it that something's not where it should be. If it weren't for the kneepad, I'd be witnessing some inside stuff on the outside.

"Eps, got a sec?" I shift my shoulder under one of Theta's arms, and Epsilon rushes to comply, mirroring me on the other side. I notice that Theta helps us by putting exactly zero weight on his bad leg. Hell, barely any on his good one, either.

Epsilon snorts, his canary-yellow bangs catching the light as I gape at him, askance that he finds anything about the entirety of this situation amusing. I guess he reads something in the tilt of my helm because he shakes his head in deprecation but still smiles.

"Sorry. Nothing funny about any of this, but I think you couldn't have picked two worse people for hauling our squad leader." He nods to me, then to himself.

I narrow my eyes skeptically before recognizing Theta's awkward lean. He's the tallest of our teammates at six feet and seven inches, and is supported by the two shortest members of the squad. Epsilon probably only has a few inches on me height-wise, if that. Width-wise is a different story.

The irony surprises me enough for a quick bark of laughter to escape unchecked. It's a shock for both of us, I think. Epsilon's grin broadens in response, boyish cheeks dimpling along with it.

"See. That wasn't so bad, was it?"

"What wasn't so bad?" I mumble glumly as we begin our laborious and exceedingly awkward shuffle. It's an embarrassing reaction for me, to be frank. I don't allow myself the luxury of coming off as anything other than stern or surly. The last thing that I want anyone to think is that I'm somehow agreeable toward others.

"Letting yourself enjoy this, for once." Epsilon remarks, his response full of cheek.

"Frankly, I don't know how you could find anything about our position wholly enjoyable. The entire reason we're in this position is because we're fighting for our very existence, as well as those of our fellow humans…"

"Should I be humming the UF anthem?" Cherry-red eyes half-mast, he gives me an expectant look to go along with his sarcasm.

I harumph, but I do see his point. There is a rush that comes with successfully taking out the enemy and firing some badass weapons without fear of punishment. I guess even working as a cohesive and codependent unit can hold value and appeal. All of the aforementioned appeals to a true soldier at heart. And who knows, maybe I'm best suited for this career path. I find *some* of my obstinacy and sharper edges have been filed down in the process of becoming Zeta. They're not entirely smooth but nowhere near as prickly.

"I had a momentary lapse in sanity, I can assure you," I comment dryly.

Not that it throws Epsilon off in any manner. Undaunted by my attitude, the short and stout man continues to grin brilliantly even as we lug Theta's heavy ass toward the simulation's clearly marked exit.

With no more bogeys on our radar, the exercise is complete for now. With a sigh and a thank you to the heavens, I briefly dip my head to the side, knocking helmet to shoulder guard and triggering one of several release mechanisms for the visor. With a hiss and pop, it slides up, and I take a deep breath of the sweat-laden air around me.

High above the steel-gray of the dual exit doors, an ever-present light, no bigger than a stoplight, has turned from red to green, indicating that the space has been cleared of threats. Funny, I bet they repurposed an actual stoplight just to save effort. They'll release us now. Hmm...now there's an interesting tangent. I wonder what would happen if we were unsuccessful in completing the exercise. Would they leave us here and see who survives—the soldiers or the Zee?

I shake off my errant line of thought and use the interlude to subtly analyze my surrounding teammates, looking for a clue as to where we all stand. The rest of the troop grumbles, not far behind Epsilon and me, as we make our way out, but there's less grumping than usual. I briefly catch Delta's eye, and she smirks at me, though not in the usual ugly sort of way. Eta follows her with a brief nod to me. That little exercise might have earned me the begrudging respect of a couple of my co-competitors. Not that I needed it.

What I need is to get through these exercises, pass advanced training at the top of the class, and get posted to an Alpha squad. In that order and within the next squad rotation. Hopefully, they're not heavily weighing assignments based on how we operate as a whole team in these exercises, or else I'm screwed. In my opinion, half of my squad needs to undergo another round of advanced training and perhaps even be kicked back to basic training. That and I could live without working under Theta's ugly mug for the rest of my meager existence.

On silent rollers, the doors slide apart, allowing us to make our great escape. Almost immediately, we're confronted with one of the base's medical teams. A group of five specialists waits to ferry any injured out. At least one stretcher has already been laid out in preparation. Theta becomes their primary focus, unsurprisingly. Phi also immediately veers off to approach them. I didn't realize his skinny ass had also been injured. That guy is better off in the backend tech area and not on the front lines. He tends not to say much beyond the minimum required. Phi's not aloof, so much as reserved.

With his shaggy navy hair covering the upper portion of his face, I don't get a good read of his expression. His arm is readily thrust out to one of the waiting medics. An unlikely injury from a Zee. More than likely, from the room and one of the multitude of things to climb over, through, or around. I'm sure that I'll find out about it later from Epsilon. He seems to know everything that goes on with these people. Goody.

Gingerly, I lift Theta's arm from its resting spot across my shoulders as Epsilon hurries to do the same. Together, we prepare to hand the wounded warrior off to the next available medical specialist. Without a prompt, a mountain of a soldier relieves us of our load. He seems particularly tall and broad, although perhaps everyone appears that way to me. That or his overall manner emphasizes his presence and makes him hard to overlook. Deep brown skin, the color of a well-roasted cup of coffee, is paired with bright, intelligent eyes that perceive all in a calm, collected manner. He says nothing but smirks, whether at our awkward trio or something private, as he effortlessly takes Theta's girth and eases the soldier onto the gurney. There is little talk between the two as the medic assesses his new patient's state.

Hands empty and with nothing further for either my teammates or me to do, I don't linger. With our assigned leader down and Phi following the medical team out, the rest of us opt to head to the locker room. After a good rinse, we'll proceed to a debrief with the test's proctors and possibly grab some chow. I'm tired, dirty, and I've got Theta's blood and who knows what else on me. All in all, not the worst day.

—Ω—

ACCOLADES MAKE THE WORLD GO IN CIRCLES

Water, a degree or two below scalding, sluices away the day's detritus, turning pink as it spirals down the drain. Not my blood this time—I've learned to be smarter than that. Although getting too close to a Zee's chomping jaws hurts, it thankfully does little more than that. No virulent contagion to deal with. Just pain. With my back to the rest of the open stalls, I allow my shoulders to relax and head to fall, chin momentarily resting against my chest. The showers are our small reward for enduring endless training exercises, and I savor every second until the last echoing spray cuts off beside me.

I wrap myself in a threadbare towel, tucking the rough edge of the towel snugly between a convenient line of cleavage before making my way back to my locker. Delta catches my eye across the room, her usual dismissive glance absent today. I'm too focused on dressing to dwell on it. Fresh gear awaits in my locker—one of the perks of being optimum Zeta advertising.

I'm just putting on the last of my kit when the locker room door swings open, admitting two stone-faced captains. Without a second thought, I stand at attention and call out the same to my other teammates.

"Attention!"

We snap to attention, regardless of the state of dress. We all stand stiff and straight, salute firmly in place. Respect and deference to rank have been drilled into all of us from day one. We all await the returned gesture and the subsequent "At ease" before following suit.

The higher-ranking officer consults an antiquated clipboard, flipping the top page up before announcing crisply to the general public, "Sergeant Omega Two Two."

"Yes, Ma'am!" I respond without hesitation.

"You've been requested to attend a review before the performance panel. Please follow us." The captain flips her paperwork neatly back in place before turning sharply and exiting, her cohort following silently.

Epsilon, shirt half-on, offers only a shrug as I hurriedly gather my remaining gear. The captains' polished heels click against the concrete as they lead me through sterile, gray hallways. I finish securing my armor as we walk, mind racing. I haven't screwed up recently—at least not noticeably. In fact, I performed well in our last exercise, taking command when needed.

I've never been an overachiever. My parents' endless prodding and extracurriculars never sparked any real drive. But something changed when I first glimpsed Alpha level. Their assignments, their hard-earned respect—it lit a fire I'd never felt before. While others like Epsilon seem content with the Beta Squad, I've been fixated on reaching higher. I want to be *that* soldier.

One more right turn down an equally nondescript hallway, and then the captains stop before a traditional hinged door. Unusual in our electronic facility. The smaller of the two soldiers opens the door without ceremony and gestures for me to go inside first. Neither of them moves to join me, so I straighten up, pull my shoulders back, lift my chin, and do my best to think like an Alpha, giving them a brief nod before entering.

Beneath the coarse material of my gloves, my palms itch like mad, obnoxiously moist with sweat. I'm not typically a person who gets nervous, but some scenarios can provoke a level of anxiety in me. For example, being put in front of a panel responsible for your foreseeable future. Staring at the faces blankly looking back at me, I don't recognize a single individual in the lot. This is unexpected, as our base, while not particularly small, has minimal staff fluctuation unless you count the occasional soldier who goes AWOL.

Three men and two women sit ramrod straight, all buttoned and pressed into crisp suits of charcoal, their shoulders and breasts adorned with various ribbons and medals, their heads topped with dark, glossy, peaked caps. Their insignias make my Zeta gear feel woefully inadequate. All seasoned military. All are far older than I.

"Sergeant Omega. Do you understand why you have been brought before us today?" One of them speaks without a preamble, but I'm not paying close enough attention to catch who at first.

For a moment, I consider how best to answer him before opting for the brief and honest route.

"No, Sir. I have not been informed."

His expression doesn't shift to show surprise or emotion. In hindsight, his question might have been more rhetorical than anything else. That assessment appears to be accurate as he continues in the same drab, monotonous voice.

"Your testing proctor thought to inform us directly of how you performed today, under duress and with a team leader wounded. It has come to our attention that your performance has been consistently exemplary, particularly in comparison with that of your squad. You have demonstrated excellence in skills that we seek for our ranks."

Well, this is news to me. I know I'd improved, but not to that extent. He continues in this vein, oblivious to my thoughts.

"Given what your record shows from your training and exercises, as well as how you have conducted yourself in stressful situations, this panel feels it is within its right to recommend you for the

Alpha squadron." He allows for a momentary and dramatic pause before adding on, "As a Staff Sergeant."

The floor tips precariously beneath my feet. Shock doesn't even begin to describe my current state. There's an icy slush gliding down my vertebrae, which seems at odds with the flames suffusing my head and face. The correct label escapes my lexicon. Elated? Confused? Nauseous?

The woman on the far right of the panel speaks up from her seat. Her voice is low and soothing, but no less firm.

"We believe that this recommendation is in the best interest of the United Forces. Do you agree, Sergeant?"

"Yes, Ma'am." Too quick, too eager.

"And are you prepared to lead an Alpha squadron?"

"Yes, Ma'am. I've been preparing for this from day one." It's the truest thing I've ever said. The first time in my life that I've felt this burning need to excel.

Her mouth twitches into what might be a sort of satisfied smile at my answer. However, it's so fleeting that I've little time to confirm what I saw. Leaning back into the arch of her chair, she steeples her fingers in front of her face, regarding me critically as though a specimen under a spectrometer.

"Very well. You will report to Personnel at 0800 tomorrow for your assignment and equipment."

"Yes, Ma'am. I'll be there." Straightening up even further, I barely suppress the pleased grin that wants to break across my face.

The gentleman from before speaks up before I have the chance to move.

"We expect great things from you, Sergeant Omega Two Two."

I salute crisply and exit, barely containing my triumph. Tomorrow marks the beginning of everything I've worked for— or so I thought.

—Ω—

ZOMBIE GIRL OMEGA – CONTENTION

Act 1
GHOSTS OF THE PAST

NOT WITHOUT PIE

Present Day

[OMEGA]

I am unsurprised by the angry red lines streaked in parallel tracks down the length of my forearms. Their phantom pain, lurking beneath my gauntlets, has followed me since the Zee gifted them to me earlier. I was sure to return the favor by caving in its misshapen skull. Thoroughly.

I've no qualms about fulfilling our core role in this theater. Leave no remnants. Erase all traces of these humans-become-monsters. It's what the Zee demand of us. To do anything less allows the door to remain ajar to future pain and suffering. The marks that remain, physically and mentally, are telling and potent reminders of what's at the other end of our rifle.

The human mind and body have definitive limits. It was the siren's promise to conquer them through genetic engineering that seduced humanity and doomed us all. We discovered too late that there's a threshold coded into our species. Cross it, and everything that makes us human—consciousness, identity, soul—is eradicated, leaving a hollow void. What's left isn't just mindless. It's an abomination. Zeta squads like mine are here in the middle of fuckall for one reason—to end the Zee.

I've witnessed soldiers fall to their inner demons after killing former countrymen, friends…and family. They question whether they have abolished lives that could have been saved one day. Fixed and made right. That there might be a different finality to this madness, yet undiscovered. Or, perhaps, already in existence but unreleased and undisclosed.

The rumors of a cure are always floating around, but I've learned to tune them out. False hope is a luxury none of us can afford. Survival is what matters now, and I've gotten damn good at it.

A wide swath of tan and gold bleeds unendingly in all directions as my team lounges unhurried and unconcerned in the open desert. Their chosen R&R spot is no more than a few yards away from me. Each one of them is a survivor in their own right. Chi handles her explosives with the same grace she brings to combat, her sharply cut violet hair somehow never astray through it all. Nothing rattles her—a gift in our line of work.

Omicron towers over us all, his broad frame housing a skilled medic and a fearsome fighter. His stern bedside manner matches his combat style, though right now, his carob features are softened as he listens to Mu's animated chatter.

That girl could talk through an apocalypse—and has. Our youngest member might at times be overwhelming with her endless energy, but she's the finest sniper I've ever seen. She's made it her mission to "fix" my mood whenever it drops too low for her liking.

Rho completes the quartet, all six-and-a-half feet of him sprawled nearby, his mechanical arm catching the afternoon sun. Between his marksmanship and that perpetual grin beneath his goatee, he's both my most reliable soldier and my biggest headache.

And then, there's Tau.

After our recent sortie present, Tau, the Alpha soldier, sits as the lone introvert amongst my team of unfiltered and think-out-loud speakers. He's situated himself as far away from where the rest of my team is as he can, Japanese features pinched tight in misery. If he were less of a prick, I'd join him in commiseration. I'm not a lover of people by any measure. However, the Alpha is not one of mine. I don't want him, and we don't need him.

After a harrowing rescue of his lone, sorry ass, my unit is on strict orders by United Forces command to bring him back, intact, to the closest UF base. We're stuck with this bitchy, steady drain on our resources until then.

Regardless of his unexpected interjection into our otherwise well-worn dynamic, my Beta Squad and the plus one are...managing. They need to be as cohesive as possible. It would be counterproductive and a hindrance to our overall mission if we cannot function as a unit. The sum of the parts is *not* greater than the whole.

With his shaved head tucked down into his bronze poncho, my better judgment would lead me to ignore Tau and his stick up the ass. We don't owe him a lick. However, he's still Zeta and, ergo, loosely one of us. I've no alternative but to incorporate the guy into my team's general mix, at least temporarily. We're not failing any future assignments due to hums of discordance within. Not under my command.

As is typical of our encounters with the Zee, it was nothing more than a brief dalliance, with no harm done except to the local enclave of cannibals. It did, however, expose the glaring fact that our new squadmate isn't the best at following orders. Now, it's probably a difficult transition from being the one to lead to being the one to follow, but I don't care. Like, at all.

There's always a push and pull between soldiers that can't be helped. What do you expect when you combine diverse personalities, total isolation, and a complete lack of privacy? We're all hyped up on a not-so-sexy cocktail of adrenaline and Zeta-modified genes, doing our utmost to stay alive while saving the world. Or, at present, preserving what remains of *The Silver State*.

Rubbing the hidden red streaks along my arms one last time, I force aside the morning's exertion against the tiny Zee cell.

Combined with the midday heat of the open desert, I'm not good company at present. However, there's no sense in dwelling on minor deviations in life when there are more important things to focus on.

The smooth and sand-dusted boulder behind my shoulder blades releases its collected heat into my body. The subtle warmth soothes and grounds in its purity. I could have been a Chuckwalla in a previous life, for how much the simple pleasure of sunning against a stone delights me.

With a casual check to the right, over my shoulder guard, and toward where my cohorts sit, I dare to do something quite secretive and devious—a departure from my nature. *Truly.* Sliding a gloveless hand beneath my dusty poncho, my questing fingers seek the crinkle of man-made plastic hidden in a deeper belt pouch. With the utmost devotion, I cup the sacred and formerly stowed goody in my palm.

Saliva pools in the corners of my mouth at its mere sight. Without hesitation, I unwrap the precious package and take an exaggerated whiff of its contents, heightened olfactory senses assaulted by cloying sweetness. I'm sure I look like a damned fool sniffing the fuck out of an oatmeal creme pie, but you can't even begin to understand the lack of pleasingly good things left in our world. If a well-aged package of artificial sugar, cream, and plausible oatmeal is my slice of heaven but not yours, walk away and keep your unwelcome opinion to yourself.

With musings of nirvana in mind, I take a tiny nibble from the rounded edge of my wee cookie pie and nearly moan at the sensation. The sweetness. The chewiness. Oh, and that chalky cream that almost instantly dissolves on the tip of your tongue. Bliss, pure and simple.

"Hey, Omega!" Rho's unwelcome bellow plunges my body into an arctic freeze, as it seizes in no small amount of fear and alarm.

Consequences be damned, I forgo any savoring and shove the cookie in its entirety into my mouth and down my gullet. The compact mass expands from some fourth dimension within my throat, blocking any attempts to chew and swallow its squishy contents. Now choking, I hit my chest lightly (no shattered sternum for me, thank you) and manage to dislodge and swallow the remainder of my sad little treat.

A dark sorrow descends upon me at its loss, even as a cursory glance confirms my adjunct second's casually loping form heading my way. Without invitation, he drops down next to me, dust puffing up as his bony ass smacks into the ground. Waving my free hand to dispel the small cloud, I go to chastise him, only to be abruptly cut off by an open cigarette box thrust into my face. Without hesitation, I grab one of the proper death sticks, popping it between chapped lips.

Rho smirks but gratefully says nothing. Considerately, he lights the end of my smoke before dropping both pack and lighter into one of the upper pockets of his vest. With a grateful drag, I enjoy the slight burn before giving my attention to Rho. His russet hair is more tousled than usual—more than likely from recent helmet wear—and there's a minor cut swelling on his lower lip.

"Is that Zee or Chi?" I nod to the new mark on his mouth.

"Hmm?" The gunner goes cross-eyed trying to glimpse the surface of his face. Reaching his fleshy left hand up, Rho delicately feels around before wincing as his fingertips come across the mini wound.

"Oh. It must have been one of the Zee. I haven't had time to piss off Chi yet. Or Omicron, for that matter..." Rubbing his chin, Rho considers that particular fact.

"*Don't* even think about it." I growl around the end of my cigarette, finger pointed sharp as a dagger at his long nose. "I've finally got everyone calm and compliant. Don't screw up my Zen by starting shit."

"*Oh-mega.*" Rho drawls. "You being calm and collected is a fantasy. It takes less than me to derail that dream." His tone, accompanied by a slight head tilt and a smirk, is simultaneously sympathetic and patronizing.

With fists clenched, a guttural sound rises from deep within me. Unwilling to be riled up by his antics, I turn and give Rho my profile to talk to while summarily avoiding eye contact.

"Is that all you came over here for, Rho? To be an ass and cause problems?"

Hands held up in defenselessness, the taller gunner leans back, face contrite, and maybe I believe him. *Maybe.*

"No, Megs. Sorry. Really." Eyes dropping to the loose dirt beneath us, he idly drags fingertips through the stuff, leaving slightly curving lines reminiscent of my arms. After a moment of this distraction, he mumbles something I don't catch.

"What? Speak up! Quit wasting time and spit it out." Cranky me is in full effect now. Rho apparently takes note of that fact as he's quick to repeat himself, and clearly this time.

"I was just saying that I thought Tau did pretty well with that last horde of Zee."

I give him a dubious expression at that, and he verbally backpedals a little.

"Not that I didn't notice him distinctly NOT following orders. It's more that he obviously has some skills and talent beyond your average Zeta soldier."

"Is that so? That couldn't possibly be why he's an Alpha, right?" I bite out.

"Yeah, I get your point. But he's here now, and we might as well make use of him. The guy's a great asset if we can get conformity from him."

"If we can." I allow. "I don't think he wants to follow my orders, let alone become a part of our team. We'll be lucky to make it back to base without him going AWOL or me killing him."

I'm not too fond of unknowns, and squirrelly Zeta soldiers certainly can be tucked into that category. At a minimum, understanding his drivers and motives will help me anticipate his actions more effectively while protecting my team, if necessary.

"Yeah, about that…" Eyeing Rho's facial hair-heavy profile, I wait for another smart comment. "What does happen if he goes AWOL under our watch? Are we supposed to 'hunt him down to the ends of the earth' and all of that? Have you seen the frickin' sword he carries? Holy shit, I'm not crossing that. I don't do swords."

"Why yes, Rho, I did notice the six-inch, leather-wrapped katana handle jutting out over his left shoulder. I mean, really?"

Sarcasm flows forth in tidal waves, and Rho's experiencing its impact, crashing forth with the utmost gusto against him.

Scratching my head in irritation, I peripherally notice the rasp of my finger against dry skin. Man, what I wouldn't give for one minute under a UF shower. There's a good reason I left behind the long locks of my youth when I became a soldier. I need function over form. Not that I'm trying to win some kind of beauty pageant around here. Granted, my haircut is woefully inadequate in practicality compared to Omicron's shaved head. Still, it works for me, for what it's worth.

Solitude wholly lost, I break my seating arrangement and push myself to stand at the entirety of my short-ass height.

"Alright. We've got mission prep to do. Might as well brief the team while we're all together and settled. You coming?"

"Yes, Sarge." Grinning, Rho stands, brushing his lanky butt off before extending a titanium hand toward the leading group. "Shall we?"

Shaking my head in exasperation, I nod at the twerp to go ahead of me and do my best to match his long strides with my shorter ones. Is there a single damn thing in this world that doesn't reinforce my size or lack thereof?

As we step soundlessly into the wobbly ring formed by the remaining four, I discreetly assess them all. There are no obvious signs of injury or discomfort. To be safe, I still ask, "Any casualties accrued from our little skirmish?"

Rho's hand shoots up eagerly like an excitable preschooler, compelling me to clarify explicitly.

"That is beyond the permanent damage to Rho's future modeling career."

He slumps down as the others chuckle in good humor. Well, others, minus the reticent Alpha. The guy needs to lighten up if he's going to survive the trip back to base.

"None?" I confirm before pressing on. "Okay. Our next mission is coming up, so let's get a few things straight." From my gauntlet, I tap through a few different screens before selecting the correct mission file to share with the team. "SITREP says the site was overrun, then abandoned, with no Zee activity noted in the area. It should be ready for reclamation and rebuilding. We'll remove any stragglers we come across and secure the site ten miles out. Fencing materials should be placed along the eastern border."

All heads bend over their gauntlets to read through and consider the mission specifications. If there's a time for questions or concerns, it's now. There won't be another chance to methodically go through requirements and scenarios while we're engaged. That's not how it works.

Turning to my scout, I single her out first.

"Chi, I need you and Mu to retrieve and work on the setup of the barrier fence."

Looking to Omicron next, I continue my assignments, "Rho and Tau will clear, starting at the southern border. Omicron and I will start from the northern end and do the same."

A slight shuffle from the right captures my attention. The gunner isn't happy but is holding back any griping, for once. A bushy eyebrow lifts, and I stare him down, giving Rho a moment and the means to give in. Light red eyes, almost amber in hue, flick briefly to Tau's form before flicking back to mine.

Ah. Rho doesn't want to lose face in front of the new guy. Perhaps the Alpha will come in handy if it encourages certain individuals to refrain from immaturity or utter stupidity. Hell. I'm not particular. I'll take a reprieve from either.

Our newest addition misses the side play, too focused on whatever has pinched his face as though he's going to hurl.

"Your plan wastes time." Tau interrupts, tone harsh and raised.

"*That* is my call, and it's our mission." I correct, equally caustic.

"Pairing off will take longer than if each soldier completed their task individually. Or does this team *require* companionship to successfully execute on their work?"

The last part holds such a haughty breath, as the Alpha sneers, though it's not aimed solely at me. This is why I don't work with Alpha soldiers. Fuck this.

"This team is following proper protocol to ensure that not only will we get the job done right, but we'll do so in the safest manner possible. Do you have a problem with that?"

For me, it's the right call to make, but that's not going to matter much if Tau deems me an incompetent squad leader and decides to take command for himself. As a Staff Sergeant, he outranks me, and it's within his right to do so. Of course, he risks my team deciding as a whole that they'd rather face punishment back at base rather than follow his lead.

That heated look nearly boils over as the soldier's face flavors into a vivid beet red, eyes narrowing to dark slits. But then, unexpectedly, his expression relaxes into one of stone-faced continence, offering nothing.

"No, Sergeant." Is his flat response, almost spiteful in its lack of emotion, nor acknowledgment of what preceded it. An entirely different form of 'fuck you.'

After a minute passes without further forthcoming, I deem his lack of response adequate and dismiss the soldier from my immediate concerns. Speaking of wasting time, I have better things to do than argue tactics with a petulant boy. I continue to address the team as if the last few minutes hadn't occurred.

"We must be exceptionally thorough in our assessment. I don't want any surprises here when the new homeowners arrive.

That means going through every building, every structure, from top to bottom. Absolutely any place those GD Zee can hide or get stuck in. If you find more than a couple, call for backup and don't engage. Is that understood?"

"Yes, Sergeant." They all chorus like some elementary schoolers, save for Tau. Frankly, they act like children...apart from Omicron. I'm guessing Om's more so one of those 'old soul' folk.

Speaking of which, our calm and controlled middle appears to be off-center at present. I'm momentarily taken aback when I notice how hard and unyielding his expression has transfigured into. It's a strange state for Omicron to be in. Not that it's entirely abnormal for my team. We're all prone to bouts of introspection, anger, and insanity, though not always in that order. Have to own up to that.

No, this feels different—empty and foreboding in some foreign way. If it still lingers after we wrap up this mission, I'll take him aside and prod for what he's willing to offer. In the meantime, I've got cats to wrangle and potential Zee past their best-by date.

—Ω—

DESOLATION OF THE SOUL

A monotonous landscape of inconsequential taupe passes by as we advance toward the site. I wish seeing the same damn thing over and over would make it easier to deal with the monotony, but it hasn't. The end of civilization can be underwhelming. And depressing, if you missed that.

Now, I've developed a healthy numbness to this world, but not all aspects. I remember what our home was like. Seamless buildings in ever-shifting hues that self-adjust to their environment. They stretched as man-made trees toward the sky or sprawled out over acres of land, creating an ecosystem of their own. The elegant weaving of highways and skyways connected major cities and supported all manner of vehicles.

Despite the mass of noisy, self-absorbed sentient beings going about their lives, it wasn't so bad. When you consider the Zee, what we had was alright. Assuming we make it another generation or two, what remains of this world will exist in a faded imprint—overturned cars, defunct technology, entire cities vacant of life, and, of course, real-life monsters.

With the freeway arranged in its usual cluttered disarray, we take off-road routes to avoid the worst of the congestion during our commute. Skirting this close to the remnants, it's never the time to drop your guard as the Zee tend to collect at cross-sections of humanity. There's probably not a considerable horde, but the stragglers don't give up easily despite their bodies decaying and falling apart around them.

A ping from my beast's display notifies me and my team that we've only another twenty miles left before we reach our destination. Not that you would think there's anything of value out here with the mix of deserted highway and empty desert surrounding us. The sectors closest to ground zero are the most devoid of anomalies. Low to no Zee means a simple 'clean and secure' assignment to prep this locale for redevelopment and eventual resettlement.

I can picture the UF-sponsored billboard they'd put up. A smiling couple, with rows of carbon-copy homes in the background. *"Future Site of Safe Living, Brought to You by Your United Forces."* Missed my true calling as a marketing person. Who in their right mind would live here?

It's actually not my first visit to this particular sector. During my earlier deployment as a Zeta soldier, I, along with a small group of new recruits, was tasked with reconnaissance in this area. I was still a trainee and under general UF instruction at the time. This place looks the same as it did back then, barren of anything resembling life or usefulness. We barely ran into any Zee then, which was disappointing, and I can't imagine we'll encounter any now.

Not that I'd voice it to the others, but this is an enormous waste of time—both ours and the collective energy of the UF. I get the desire to clear out the undead bastards ravaging the remaining, mostly alive populace. Honestly, I do. But who'd want to live here? The few outposts of survivors I've come across are high-walled and layered with all manner of security. Civilians aren't allowed to venture outside of their settlement. Only UF soldiers and staff. It's not exactly living it up, but I guess it's living in its own right. Who am I to judge?

Releasing a deep sigh, the warm air from outside pulls through my mouthpiece's filter. At least it smells and tastes clean here. I don't get to replace my filters often enough, so at a certain point, everything starts to carry the same flavor of stale sweat and dust. The bonus is at least most of it's mine.

An insistent beeping calls out from my bike's scanner, instantly drawing in my wandering thoughts. I queue up the comms and hail the others.

"Looks like a few bogeys coming up, team. Fan out and take them down. Reduce speed, but don't stop. Let's see if we can deal with them on our way in."

"Copy that," Rho responds promptly.

Grinning to myself in delight at the prospect of a bit of side hustle, I follow my instructions and slow my All Terrain Cycle, or ATC as we like to call them. Acronyms make everything better. Calling up one of our seldom-used toys, the front of my bike shifts apart slightly, allowing a pair of gnarly-looking muzzles to set their sights on the target ahead. Corresponding data flows across the face of my helmet's HUD, showing everything, from wind speed to total distance and rate to target.

The others, I imagine, are doing the same in preparation. After all, it's fairly standard practice. I could allow my bike's system to autotarget and fire, but where's the satisfaction to be had in that?

Instead, I breathe slowly and evenly, thumb hovering over the primary firing button embedded in my handle's grip. I await that perfect, precise moment of alignment. The orange changes to yellow, then almost immediately to green, as I depress the button with all due concentration and vigor.

A line draws before the half-naked Zee, leading up to its stumbling form before cutting straight through it. It goes down boneless in a heap as I ride by without pause. Another four of his buddies meet the same fate, courtesy of my squadmates. *And then…*it's over.

Hmm, I was expecting a bit more engagement time.

"*Well, that was regrettable,*" Chi comments blandly.

"*No shit.*" Rho agrees. "*Not sure that was worth the rounds.*"

"*Well, I at least got to knock one down!*" Mu remarks brightly.

The remaining two soldiers in our group refrain from participating in the chatter. The absence of Tau's voice is unsurprising but isn't indicative of a lack of involvement. I'm confident that line of fire number three came from him. Tau's rigid profile has been avoiding any extraneous interactions with the rest of the team since I countered him. It'll probably take an inordinate amount of strength to pull his head out of his ass at this point. That matters little for the time being.

Which leaves Omicron. Stealing a quick look his way, his lack of engagement is noticeable, as jeering and whining over the comms are hallmarks of my team. I wonder what's going through that soldier's hairless dome. There's a heaviness in my gut telling me something's off with Om. I won't claim to be an expert at reading him or humans in general. However, I have lived alongside Omicron for years now. You can't help picking up on certain behaviors.

In no time, the high-pitched whine of our electric engines lower into a softer squeal reminiscent of some small animal getting thoroughly trounced. Two from our unit break away before we hit the city limits, following the sand-coated road that borders part of this site. Chi and Mu speed off toward the opposite side of the town, focused and on task. It's time for me to be so as well.

Upon crossing into the former suburbia, the streets suddenly close in around us and our slowing beasts, forcing us to enter single file. Most roads are one-way, with very few allowing more than a single lane of traffic in each direction. Small Town America, indeed. Our first order of business is to find a good parking spot.

It doesn't take long to locate what seems to be a decent place to stop and dismount. More than two routes out and plenty of open space to see a problem before it's upon us. Not to mention the lovely, clear shot back to the highway if everything goes tits up.

"All right," I clear the rasp out of my throat before continuing over the open comms. "Let's park by the gas station sign."

The remainder of the team complies without further instruction, keeping a decent buffer of space between the bikes. The last thing you want during a hasty getaway is to get in someone else's way. This part of the process is a no-brainer. Any clean and clear op always starts the same way and is muscle memory for all of us by now.

With our ATCs shut down and locked to the world, I slowly lean back from the handles, giving a good stretch to release the tension accumulated across my shoulders and upper back. Being in the same hunched-over position for any amount of time is a bitch. Grabbing the underside of the helm, I disengage the main latches that join it to my collar one-handed and pull it off across my face in a single motion.

Aah. Unfiltered oxygen for my brain. At last. Letting the warm breeze greet my sweat-dotted flesh, I inhale deeply, tasting what lingers in the low wind. There's the oil and rubber from our bikes and dust, followed by fainter tones of rusty metal and old wood. Most importantly, there is no scent of rot or decay.

After a complete rotation to take in our surroundings, my eyes linger on the large and attractively scrawled "*Welcome to...*" sign affixed front and center of one of the businesses, faded and partially broken. What the...*seriously*? The sign's present state isn't so far gone that the partially worn-off name is unrecognizable. Yet.

I'd recall that name from any of the UF's historical records.

It's hard to forget the place with the dubious honor of being Ground Zero for the Zee outbreak. How the hell did we land this mission? It hardly seems the type assigned to a Beta Squad. An Alpha team, for certain, or even the rumored Sigma level, because of how high-profile it is.

Well, it's not my job to wonder why. Ours is to do as we're ordered and secure one more piece of the world for those with a functioning brain. This place, this era, ceased to exist a long time ago. It's hallowed ground—an unremarkable little hamlet that never knew what would begin here, catch, and spread like a West Coast wildfire, eviscerating anything its flames reached while leaving its ash to suffocate the rest.

The ugly rumor is that the change happened so quickly that no one was spared. An entire population became victims or victimizers. What a horrible end to an otherwise uneventful and idyllic life. I shake my head at my grim thoughts, returning my attention to why we're here. The mission. It's always about the mission.

"Okay. Rho. Tau. Take the western part of the site, start at the outskirts and clear inwards. We'll come from the opposite, East to West, and meet you midway."

Deliberately making eye contact with both males, I press, "If you run into anything off—*anything*—you radio it in before engagement, if at all possible. You got me?" The last part is almost a growl and primarily aimed at the Alpha. Fuck if I'm dealing with any dissent from his quarter.

Crimson's wrath meets my scarlet, and I withhold a sneer as I await his capitulation. There's only a slight hesitation before he allows a small nod. At this point, I think I deserve a damn medal for putting up with his shit.

Before they move more than a half step away, I remark to their retreating backs, "We'll meet you back here in two. Keep your comms open. No hero bullshit." I hate heroics.

I lean my head to the side and produce a satisfying crack that dissipates some of the gathered tension. With the irritant and my de facto second heading steadily away, I regard my selected partner. Bright red crosses stand out prominently on each of Omicron's wide shoulder guards, making him even more difficult to miss with his 250-plus-pound frame.

Attempting for levity, I pat him on the arm with a heavy thunk, the hard jolt of armor-encased muscle ricocheting up through my arm. Ouch.

"Ready to ditch these guys, Om?"

Flipping his faceplate up, he gives me a tiny quirk of the lips.

"Sure, boss. Lead the way." His tone is subdued but genuine in response. He's at least acting like himself for the moment. I'll take what I can get.

Marauders and those hostile to the United Forces have the nasty habit of targeting our medics. The logic is that if they take them out, the rest of us will eventually follow. Probably not so far-fetched a concept. I have a lovely map of repair work from Om on just about every limb and surface. Some internal, as well. They're simply less obvious.

Side-stepping his low mood, I offer a soft but open smile—something I can't help but do just for him.

"Alright then. Let's move out."

—Ω—

TO SEEK THAT WHICH IS SOUGHT

The first ten minutes of our somber patrol leads us directly to the middle of town. The outer walls and windowpanes we pass are liberally coated in burnt orange dirt. Countless seasons witnessed by this shell of a town are captured in each progressive layer of grime. Precisely squared sidewalks, gently arching lighting, and long empty planters line the cut pathway of the street.

While this wasn't a major city before, the smooth pavement under my boots differs from the broken asphalt and overgrown streets we usually find. The storefronts display modern facades with hand-painted signs and artistic logos, perfectly aligned with the UF's vision of humanity's ideal future state. Once secured, redevelopment will begin, followed by civilian settlement. The town will exist once again, just with less autonomy.

The quality and care evident here speak of serious wealth, though money proved worthless after the Zee outbreak. Much like my schooling and personal coaching, they now amount to nothing. The UF recruiters never asked about my credentials or pedigree. They needed warm and willing bodies with basic cognitive function. They'd handle the rest.

I chuckle at my dark musings and glance back. In this complete silence, it's easy to notice when someone's mind has drifted. Omicron lags, uncharacteristically distant and withdrawn. I wonder what's troubling him beneath that placid expression. I've never seen our medic this dejected, not even when he was first assigned to my team.

Let me be clear: surviving takes its toll on everyone, Om included. We all carry our burdens. Important dates, such as birthdays and anniversaries pass by, unmarked. What we remember are the violent deaths of loved ones.

These ghosts drive our mission—ensuring future generations won't endure what we have. At least, that's the hope.

Splitting my attention between my partner and our immediate surroundings isn't the smartest choice. Have you ever known anyone to be successful at multitasking? Regardless, I persevere with all my sensors on, head and eyes tracking constantly. Searching for any deviations—anything that doesn't belong.

What momentarily captures my full attention is not a Zee or even my partner. Across the street, a baby blue convertible lies halfway out of a mechanic's garage. It sits there poised as if its owner stepped inside for something brief, leaving the car in limbo. That beauty has got to be more than a century old and not lacking in curb appeal, in spite of the perpetual filth caking the town. It happens without my will or intent—I whistle. And loudly.

Immediately, there's a phantom thwack between the shoulder blades by my one-eyed drill instructor. The resulting chill isn't unwarranted. Rifle raised, I quickly turn a full circle, expecting the worst before finally stopping on Omicron. His face is turned to me, and the expression I'm bestowed with is a mix of disbelief and *'Are you really that stupid?'*

Sighing, I meet his dumbfounded stare with a shrug and a wince.

"Sorry, Om." I hitch my thumb behind me. "I wasn't expecting that."

His brow twitches in skepticism, but he dutifully glances behind me and takes in what captured my inner teenager's attention.

"Hmm. '69 convertible. *Nice.*" There's the kindred love of a good car embedded in that warm tone.

"Yeah, I used to have a poster of one just like it as a kid."

"Really?" He may be vaguely intrigued or probably simply humoring me.

"Yeah. I was never a boy band kind of girl."

With a snort, he shakes his head, smiling mildly in indulgence. "That I'm not surprised by." With a nudge to the shoulder that could probably upend me without Om trying, he attempts a bit of levity. "I'd be more shocked if you had some secret sparkly pony collection."

"Wouldn't you like to know?" I draw the words out, eyes narrowed in suspicion but revealing neither the joke nor the truth of the statement.

Unscrewing his canteen, the big medic ignores my teasing. As he takes measured drags, there's an unspoken prompt for me to hydrate as well.

In between swallows, he unequivocally declares, "I have no desire to know what kind of 'creepy shit' you got into as a kid."

Shrugging off the comment and subsequent smirk on his part, I take my water ration without fuss. A carrot to him for breaking his funk. At that first instant, when your mouth is renewed with moisture, the water feels utterly perfect and cool on the tongue. I barely hold back a moan. I guess I was a little dehydrated.

With a satisfied "*aah!*" I finish off my gulp and screw the cap back into place. With no small amount of longing, I bid my dream car a fond farewell.

"I'd love to know who got to drive that car."

"A man who worked his whole life to own it." Om's response is immediate. His deep timber falls flat once again, the abrupt switch almost taking me aback. The verdict is delivered with a cutting kind of certainty that doesn't match his detached look.

O-kay. Back to failing in the morale department. Scuffing the rigid toe of my boot on the loose ground, I try to think of something. *Anything*! Some fraction of thought to grasp onto firmly with both hands and offer to Om. Maybe I can haul him out of the pit that he's falling into with it. However, my capacity to empathize with others is severely lacking. That particular trait of my mom's didn't successfully transfer to my genetics.

In the muzzled silence that follows, we continue our steady trek across the intersecting streets. Scanning buildings and outcroppings for anything amiss, though there's little that requires further inspection. The place is adamantly dead.

"You know that sweet shop we passed?"

Lost in my internal self-flagellation, I blink back to reality at Om's now mellifluous voice. My mind plays a quick game of mental catch-up as I try to recall which of those grayed-out shops would have passed for a dessert store.

"Yeah, what of it?"

Omicron tilts his head back, blood-red eyes taking in the azure sky, stretched above in a great expanse of floating ocean.

"That place had the best scones outside of a bakery in Scotland."

My heart stops for a breath, and then two. A slow and hard thump follows, lodging somewhere between my chest and my throat. It explains so much. Entirely too much. It just goes to show how little you can know a person even after sharing space for so long. Swallowing past the sudden dryness of my mouth, I do my best to recover from my lapse.

"Really? What made them so special?" Hopefully, that doesn't sound too forced.

Smiling softly, he directs his gaze at me, practically two feet beneath his standard line of sight.

"Well, see, the baker had a real talent for any baked good. You could give her any recipe, and without fail, she would make it even better."

"No joke?" I feel the beginnings of a grin in response to his latest personality turn—his mood is that infectious.

"Yeah, no joke. The baker—she was a casual genius like that. Came by it naturally, though, I guess." Omicron's voice pleasantly rumbles as he expounds on his baker, face softened. "Her dad was a famous chef on the East Coast. She'd come out here to make a place and a name for herself."

This conversation is the most Omicron's said to me or anyone else since we first received the orders for this mission. There's more depth woven into these unhurried words, and three guesses as to why. The first two don't count. I feel a bit of a fool for not figuring it out sooner.

"Good thin' I was just comin' off of Active when she showed up," he continues, lost in his memories. "Else, this would have been a lot thicker."

The medic slaps his definitely flat and solidly muscled stomach appreciatively as I consider the two pieces of information he's now shared without solicitation.

"So, you were military before?" I cautiously pry, choosing the less loaded route, hopefully. I'm worried I'll spook this strange apparition mimicking our medic. Not losing that faraway look, his smile strains against its sorrow.

"I was. At the end of my service contract, I reentered the civilian realm into a trade I was already familiar with durin' my time in the Army."

Maybe it's an old comfort to Om to return to being a soldier. I guess I'd inadvertently accepted that Omicron's never been bothered by the rules and regulations issued by the United Forces. He's played his part without complaint or trouble. I've heard plenty of tales of soldiers from previous times who had difficulty being civilians in a non-war zone. No concern about that nowadays.

"Which trade? Physician?"

"Hah!" He barks out a loud, belly-shaking laugh at that.

"Try mechanic. That was my gig, and I was damned good too."

"Wow, I don't know whether I should be encouraged or fearful of the next time I'm bleeding out."

Smirking my way, he confides in a secretive manner. "It probably doesn't hurt to be a little of both. Mind you, the crash course in medical trainin' was courtesy of the UF. They needed more first responders than engineers in the ranks. For me...it gave me somethin' else to focus on and forget."

"*Bravo team checking in.*" A loud, very male voice cuts across my comms. The volume is high enough to cut off the medic's reminiscing.

Unsurprisingly, distraction arrives late in the form of my de facto second.

"What's your status, Rho?" I absently rub a smudge on my rifle, succeeding only in smearing it more along the metal.

"*Not much to report, Sarge. We haven't encountered any hostiles or friendlies, or well, anything.*"

"Nothing?" That's interesting. Come to think of it, we haven't seen any fauna either. Rho probably picks up on the incredulity in my voice, responding more to it than the actual question.

"Yeah. Exactly! No cat, mouse, bird, nada. Zip. Zilch. Shouldn't there be something alive around here? It's not like this place is a nuclear wasteland."

My thoughts drift inward as I rub my chin in contemplation. Not encountering any life form is out of the ordinary. Even that hell hole that we unearthed Tau out of contained local wildlife and had strays running around. There's something we're missing. I can feel it like a hard jab to the gut.

"We're experiencing the same. Keep your head in the present and finish the job. We should be wrapping things up in an hour or so on our end. Let me know if you do find anything living. Got it?"

"Yup. Rho, out!"

The sigh bubbling around in my chest is released in a great plume. Omicron gives me an amused look but doesn't comment any further. I wasn't exactly looking for action, but I didn't want to kick my heels wandering around a lifeless town either. I'm sure there's a healthy middle somewhere in there.

I quietly contemplate Omicron's expansive back, swathed in the same drab taupe poncho as mine. I'd say he's back to piloting on automatic. Now more than a little miffed at my ineptitude at empathy, I drop it for now and opt to check in with the rest of my squad. There's no sense in wasting a lousy mood frivolously.

"Team Charlie, what's your status?"

As I await a response, my gaze drifts toward the cloud-dotted blue sky. I'll avoid my Omicron-watching for the time being. I can only imagine what kind of existence this place once offered. It's serene here despite all the broken things.

Chi responds quickly enough, although Mu is equally quick to try to talk over her.

"Chi, here..."

"And Mu! Everything is going really well."

There's a gusting sigh from Chi's comm. It's one that typically precedes my scout about to lose her shit with some unfortunate soul. Mu must be pushing it in the camaraderie department. Perhaps not my most well-thought-out pairing for this assignment?

Another pregnant pause. I can only imagine the look Chi's inflicting on our sniper.

"As I was saying. We are almost halfway done with the setup. The terrain is relatively flat and lacking in major obstructions. We have also not encountered any Zee or have come across any signs of their presence."

Nodding my head along, although no one on the other end of the line can see. There's definitely a consistent theme of this being a true dead zone. Small miracles.

"Alright. Continue. We'll head your way once we've completed our sweep. Assuming we find more of the same nothing, we can probably be there soon enough to lend a hand."

"That would be most appreciated."

"You got it. Omega, out."

Releasing a sigh, but back in the present, I take stock of our shift in surroundings. With half a mind, I've inadvertently followed

Omicron's casual stroll to the brick walkway of a two-story tract home. A narrow front door stands partially open. Royal blue paint chips curl away from wood that's warped from years of whatever weather has passed through here. The rust-colored dust of disuse coats everything.

A crisp mix of dirt, leaves, and brambles crunches and crumbles under my tread. Scanning the front face of the house, there's no doubt where Omicron has led us. I don't bother stopping the medic—there's no point to it. He needs to do this, and I can respect that.

As he forces the door wider to admit his much broader frame, it creaks loudly, mournfully echoing into the stillness within. I brace myself as violence and death always lie in wait where it's least expected. However, all remains quiet and unchanged by our intrusion.

Once across the threshold, we enter into a simple foyer no bigger than a ten-by-ten-foot space. The tiled area doesn't contain much. A shoe rack is on the left, and an umbrella stand holding a lone umbrella sits against the wall opposite from it. Small picture frames blank of their digital content are strategically placed here and there, leading to a lone painting lined with pure black, white, and red strokes.

Two cranes arc elegantly toward each other, conveyed through single brush strokes, in the thrall of their dance. There's joy there, but also some unnamed sorrow. I'm no artist. I simply know the imagery captures your attention and speaks to something more profound. Its placement is first in the home, where all will see and none will miss it. I'm not insensitive enough to pry, though. It's not my place or my business. I'm also unwilling to break the quietude that's been in effect since before Omicron stepped foot in this town. A reunion of sorts for him and his ghosts.

—Ω—

WHAT HAS BEEN LOST

"My son was five," Omicron speaks slowly and so softly, I lean in to catch the words as they escape reticently from his lips. "He was at home with his mom when it happened. They were gettin' ready for dinner. They'd greet me at the first sign of my car in the drive, like always."

"It was the same routine: 'Welcome home,' followed by hugs, kisses, and maybe a few giggles from Eli."

The medic breaks off, and I swallow past the hard lump in my throat I didn't notice before. I want Omicron to continue, for his sake, but a selfish part of me would rather be somewhere...anywhere other than here at this moment in time.

"I don't remember why I stayed late that day. It was a Friday. I had a good gig, workin' on cars, like in the service. I wasn't wealthy, but I made enough to put us in a good home and ensure that our family was always fed, clothed, and happy. Eli went to the local preschool a few days a week to give Jess more time to focus on her other passion."

"Didn't notice at first. Then weird stuff started happenin' outside the shop. It could've been just some drunk or homeless folk actin' up. But nah. Was way worse than that."

"I was headin' out when something crashed through that big old storefront window. Glass everywhere. All those screams from outside came pourin' in. Someone from our church was lyin' there, twitchin' like they were having a fit. Their eyes...blood-red and drippin.' It wasn't just vacant—it was empty. Seen enough dead faces in the war to know what I was lookin' at."

"They got Cal first. Good man. Owned the shop after his daddy.

He had just cracked some terrible joke before sendin' me off for my rare Saturday break. When he went down, I tried to help, but… I knew. Then I saw there were dozens more outside. People I had known for years, actin' like wild animals, tearin' through everythin' and everyone."

"Had to get home to Jess. She and Eli were waitin.' My car was behind the grocery store, right in the thick of it all. But being the star runnin' back in high school wasn't for nothin.' I could still be a fast motherfucker when I had to."

"Ran faster than I ever did before. Duckin', dodgin', and stayin' low when somethin' wrong came around the corner. Couldn't let anythin' stop me from gettin' home."

The medic stops, holding a breath he seems to forget to let out. I know what's coming. We all do.

"Didn't matter though. The door was open when I got there. I was too late."

By this point, his face is drained of all color, skin lightening to almost the same shade as mine. Not that I'd ever consider myself fair-skinned in any sense of the word. I watch as he wipes his hand slowly across his face, dragging fingertips firmly across his eyes and then a little under his nose. I'm sure this isn't easy for Omicron to relive, and I'm loath to interrupt him and break this tableau that's going on between us.

"They were here when I got home." The medic nods at the two forms hidden under a blanket on the floor. "Without the comforter, of course." He smiles faintly, the act placing delicate lines around his generous mouth. "I put it there later. Had to."

Based on the sharp edges where the shoulders and hips are and the direction of the legs, the larger of the two is wrapped snugly around the distinctly smaller one. Their last moments left them huddled together in each other's arms. The blanket covering them must be from Om's son's bed. Faded pictures of starships and asteroids, with little astronauts in their spacesuits, decorate what once must have been a soft, fleece cover. What's left of it is a muted blue-gray and coated in dust mites.

"I got what got them." His voice turns cold and brittle, like a ragged shard of stalactite waiting to sever from its grip and impale someone. I don't think I've ever heard our medic speak this way. There's no depth in that hollow tone. "Bastard's in the kitchen millin' about not doing a damn thing. Took my entire universe from me—*my life*—and it didn't care. Couldn't care."

His voice cracks as he takes a moment to regain control, his breath trembling. "I took my Little League bat—there's not much I ever threw away—and beat that fucker until not a piece of it so much as twitched. It didn't do any good. They're still dead."

He shakes his head, heavy with grief. That pain, I can't help but empathize with, to the extent that I'm capable of. In some ways, I guess I was lucky. I never found out what happened to either of my parents. My dad, well, some suits showed up at our front door. Left us with an offer of support, a check, and a flag. That was it.

I lost both parents that day. My mom fell apart after that. I guess I wasn't enough to keep her here. I never did find out exactly how her end came. I wasn't there. Should I have chosen to stay instead of running away? I don't know. I'm still on the fence regarding that.

With Omicron, I don't wonder if he regrets not being there when these two died. Not just because of a desire to save them from such a wretched fate, but perhaps also because he didn't want to be the one left behind.

Regardless of past failings, we need to move on. Cautiously, I clear my throat.

"Om, we still have more ground to cover."

I don't want to cut Om short of his healing, but time is ultimately our driving force. The Omicron that looks at me is not the man I've come to know, for sure, but he's also not the person he was before. I guess he's trapped in that void of in-between. This place, here and now, is where all of his strength and anger originates, fueling the pure hatred he holds for the Zee. There's enough destruction to this home to feed that fire for a very long time.

That expression undoes me. Here is a man, a soldier, who never asks for anything. Has been a solid rock for not just me, but the entire team. One who gives but never takes. That, more than anything, makes the decision for me.

"But," I relent. "We can stay here a little bit longer. There's still time before the others will need us."

His face contorts in concentration as if he's genuinely thinking hard about this.

"Yeah, I'd like that. Just a while more?"

I'm not even sure that he perceives me entirely as he makes the request, but that doesn't bother me. Instead, I find a relatively empty spot on the ground and make myself as comfortable as possible. Taking in what I see of the space of his home, but not violating any more of this sacred place than that. I attempt to understand from this brief glimpse of Omicron's past who he was and what life might have been like for him. I don't even know his real name. I think that's a special kind of fucked up.

—Ω—

FROM ENDING TO BEGINNING

The minutes grow as shadows upon the wall, time passing inexorably but slowly. I'm patient, figuring that the rest of the team can do their job without my nannying. I am reluctant to halt something that seems desperately needed, even as responsibility sinks its teeth into me to drag me back to reality.

All at once, the silence is broken by the distinct crackle of my comms. It quickly broadcasts through my neckpiece, echoing mournfully through the thick veil of silence shrouding this lifeless dwelling. Casting a brief look at Omicron, he raises his eyes briefly to mine before returning them to his interlaced fingers, hanging limply over the dust-coated floorboards.

Trying to avoid disrupting the space any more than I have, I snag my helm from its spot on the floor, secure it over my head, and quietly exit the room. Well, as quiet as one can with all my gear rattling around like some spirit of Christmas past.

"Omega here. What's up?"

"*Hey, Omega. It's Rho. We're just about done here. We didn't find anything except for a half-dead chihuahua running around. This place is a ghost town.*"

Oh, if he only knew how true that is and whose ghosts in particular. I don't bother to reply with that, though. It's not my place to share it. I'm only privy because I happened to be in the wrong place at the right time.

"Okay. Got it, Rho. You and Tau return to the bikes and meet up with Chi and Mu. Give them a heads-up that you're coming. Omicron and I are just about finished here, too."

"Sounds good. We'll see you there." My second cuts off his transmission with no banter or stalling, apparently more than ready to be done with this assignment.

I take a spare moment to tap in with the remainder of the team while I think about it. Queuing up Chi's code, I wait for her to answer. There's a minute or so of low buzzing as I stand by for my call's acknowledgment and acceptance, and then the line finally chirps.

"Hey, Chi. It's Omega. How are things looking in your neck of the woods? Rho and the Alpha are done."

There's a hiss of static followed by a low curse that has me raising an eyebrow.

"Having a little trouble there?"

Another curse, this time probably aimed at me, before the spy responds less than congenially.

"Forgive me, but this thrice-damned mesh insinuated itself into my hair and refused to let go."

I stifle a chuckle, not wanting to set her off. However, imagining Chi's perfectly straight locks wrapped in wire...well, can you blame me? What the scout does to cope with hygiene limitations in the middle of nowhere is *fascinating*.

"I guess you can always do an additional round of deep conditioning when we get back, right?" I muse, picking at some crud stuck fast to my left glove.

"Do not tempt me, Sergeant." Comes her growled response. *"I am more than happy to leave this fruitless endeavor to you and indulge in some well-deserved self-care."*

"All right. Let's not get all crazy. Everybody else is done, so we'll be heading your way. ETA is probably around fifteen to twenty minutes. If there's anything left, we'll help you to finish."

"That is incredibly gracious of you since we are almost done." She unenthusiastically replies.

Mu's chirruping tones faintly admonish Chi in the background, obviously having overheard her statement. The sniper has probably reached her limit with her partner's attitude, but will still endeavor to maintain a 'positive' atmosphere.

"All right, I'll see you shortly. Omega, out."

After ending the call, I'm swift to slide the hunk of metal off my head, grateful for any time not spent inside my helmet. It's unbearable at the best of times and worse when the ambient temperature is anything above warm.

Turning to go to where I left Omicron, I find he's already waiting for me at the landing. He's still too quiet, though perhaps it's more of a thoughtful introspection than depressed withdrawal. I dunno. I could be reading into things, but his face seems slightly less pinched and drawn. Maybe this was cathartic for him—a closure he's been missing. Only time will tell, as cliché as that is, but all we have is time. And each other, which is equally cliché. I think I'm just full of clichés today.

"Hey." I give him the smallest of smiles.

"Hey." Om returns, equally low-key. "I'm ready to head out, Omega."

Eyeing him, I feel compelled to ask, "You sure? We have a little more time."

He shakes his head. "I'm ready. I'm not comin' back here."

I let him lead the way to our bikes. He knows this place better than I ever could. Before I step entirely away from the house, there's one last thing that I feel compelled to do. Momentarily turning back, I hook my fingers into the ornate, rusted handle, pulling the door closed. I hear the latch click into place, even with the warping of wood and metal to time. There's no need to leave it open.

—Ω—

ACT 2
SAILING WITHOUT A COURSE

EMPTY MUSINGS TO GROOVE BY

Approximately 10 years after the widespread incursion of Zee.

[OMEGA]

The walk from the training complex to the barracks is brief, though my mind barely registers the journey. Enclosed by a whirling storm of thought, I find myself navigating through the United Forces facility on autopilot.

The stark transition from winter-cool corridors to desert heat hits me like a physical wall, bringing with it the sharp tang of sunbaked concrete and metal. This area of space we occupy is preternaturally empty of life, other than us Zeta soldiers. No birds cross the sky's threshold, and there's no undercurrent buzzing of insects. There are only Zeta soldiers and some cursory staff, enclosed and sectioned off from the world behind walls too high to scale and a single, well-guarded gateway. Even our footsteps are muted here as if the very space swallows all sound.

I hadn't intended to end up at the barracks, but here I am, standing among the rows of neatly pressed bunks with precise right angles. The familiar scent of gun oil and laundered uniforms fills the space, mixing with the metallic undertone that permeates every UF building. My attention immediately fixes on a lone soldier performing maintenance on his cybernetic limb.

With careful movements, he painstakingly works oil into each panel and groove, leaving the immaculate silver of his arm gleaming brightly. The soft whir of servos accompanies each movement as he systematically tests the joints. His eyes are drawn off to some neutral place, his regular protocol lulling him into a quiet or perhaps disquieted state. It's entirely at odds with how he usually comports himself. The arm itself is a stark piece of machinery—no attempt to disguise its purpose as a weapon, unlike the flesh-toned prosthetics I've encountered before. All hard edges and exposed components, its utilitarian lack of humanity designed to intimidate.

I can tell from the coil of this soldier's muscles and the way he holds himself that he's no weakling. He would be a challenge, although I know I would still best him hand-to-hand, false arm notwithstanding. All I would need to do is remove the arm from the person. However, there's not a lick of hostility or confrontation in his countenance. Instead, there's this weird openness to him that throws me off every time. I suppose he could be faking it, but I've yet to find anything to the contrary. For now, I file his presence away as an unknown quantity.

When he notices me, the soldier's serious demeanor vanishes instantly, replaced by that signature wide grin of his. The fluorescent lights overhead cast harsh shadows across his sharp features. "Hey! Omega, right?"

I nod, mutely waiting for whatever follows his robust greeting. Undeterred, the one I know to be 'Rho' continues.

"How was your last sortie? I saw the rest of your unit come through a bit ago. Well, most of them. With you gone, along with your team leader and that other guy. Phi? Your team looked down in size. Like the Zee might have won the day."

I nod again, somewhat unsettled by how closely he seems to track my unit. I couldn't tell you a single member of the unit he's assigned to. Before I can question his surveillance, he launches into a series of concerned questions about my well-being.

"How come you weren't with the others earlier? You're not hiding some horrible wound, are you? Avoiding Medical?" His eyes scan me with genuine worry rather than the usual male appraisal I'm accustomed to. The gentle hum of the climate control system fills the pause between us.

"I'm fine," I bite out, uncomfortable with the attention. Small talk is not my thing, either.

"Oh, that's good." Continuing in more of a whisper, the auburn-haired man leans forward as if to impart some significant secret to me. "Frankly, I think people are scared of one of the medics there. He's wrapping up his residency, but I hear that his bedside manner makes you hope for speedy sedation."

He leans back, pleased with sharing such a juicy bit of gossip.

"Not that he'd ever grant it to you, even if it's your dying wish. But you didn't hear that from me."

As if I care.

"No." I grit it out. "I was summoned for a review panel."

His playful demeanor shifts. "Seriously? Were you reprimanded?"

"More like they're looking to submit me to the Alpha pool," I admit reluctantly. My words echo hollowly in the nearly empty barracks.

"Holy shit! That's awesome!" He stands abruptly and takes a few long strides toward me. His enthusiasm manifests in a congratulatory shoulder slap that sends me stumbling slightly. The sound of his mechanical arm servos adjusting to the movement is unnaturally loud in the quiet space. I use the momentum to reinsert some distance between us.

"I need to check on Theta," I state resolutely, not waiting for a reply before making my escape.

The echo of my boots striking against the polished concrete floor follows my retreat. Rho's friendly goodbye and promise to "catch up later" trail me out. I've no intention of following through, but something tells me he'll find a way to continue our conversation regardless.

—Ω—

NORTH IS A MATTER OF OPINION

Present Day

[OMEGA]

A breeze softly pushes against the exposed skin of my face. Shuttering my eyelids, I let the heat and air swim around me in gentle ripples. It pools at the juncture of my throat and swirls in lazy eddies along the nape of my neck.

I shouldn't complain. It's a welcome relief, honestly. I'm just so dry. Like, holy crap. Is there any moisture left in my body at this point? The desert might as well be using me as a sippy cup. Taking a brief pause in my internal whining, I undergo another round of over-analyzing, weighing the merits of dipping into my on-hand water ration early. Am I really this dehydrated, or has my brain hijacked my higher thinking, feeding my cyclical thoughts further?

The sound of trickling fluid hits my senses just right, initiating a Pavlovian response. Perhaps if I hadn't been so focused on my thirst, my lizard brain wouldn't be so keyed up. Then, I identify the sound's origin. Frowning deeply to the point my mouth may fall off my face, I turn abruptly from my position and vacate the area. The punctuated stomping of my feet does little to mask the continued stream of something I'd prefer not to mention, let alone the accompanying smell. Stupid enhanced senses.

"Fuck you, Rho," I shout over my shoulder and keep walking, much to his bewilderment. Well, that seals it. I'm in serious need of some headspace before I contemplate drinking anything. My heavy tread lands me squarely back by the bikes and the remainder of my team… plus one. I tack on the last individual to my thought processes, as if he were some underwhelming addition to an insectarium.

Chi is correct, and please don't let that phrase ever pass from my chapped lips to her slightly pointy ears. I need to get over my personal and personnel issues with Tau. It doesn't help our situation any. The unhealthy focus also draws attention away from far more imperative matters.

Speaking of the demon, I catch a flash of lilac hair as the aforementioned scout flicks her long forelocks to the side and strides purposefully toward me. While I naturally inflict my weight in its entirety onto the innocent ground as I step, Chi...*floats*, for lack of a more eloquent way of putting it. It's a question of which came first, Chi or her abilities? It's inarguable that the upgrade changed all of us irreparably. However, I'm unconvinced it introduced entirely new capabilities to us. In my wholly unofficial and unscientific opinion, I believe that our change was directly influenced by aspects of ourselves that we already possessed.

Let me explain.

I was *not* She-Hulk strong pre-Zeta. That would have been ridiculous. However, I could lift and move objects that, for my size, people would have initially dismissed as impossible for me to do. So, who is the truest form of the individual? Zeta Chi and her hare-footed stealth, or pre-Zee Chi, who may have been equally slick and sneaky. Was I inherently built to be strong, and the Zeta process somehow emphasized it?

There's a lot to consider, and frankly, I don't have the mind or the patience for it now. I'll consider the deeper meaning of the Zeta upgrade when I'm less focused on what's smacking me right in the face. Maybe next time I'm hanging at one of our bases, I'll pose the question to the local eggheads. Give them that obtuse train of thought to chew on and digest.

A snap of fingers in my field of vision brings me back to the present and away from my inner pondering. My scout regards me shrewdly, unimpressed as always. Of what specific part of me, I'll never know. Nor do I give two fucks. Somehow, my presence causes her unconscionable boredom and endless exasperation. Eyes flicking briefly to hers, I smirk even as her thin lips tighten into a stern line.

"Need something in particular, Chi? Or is there nothing more dignified to apply yourself to?" She doesn't bother gracing me with an answer.

Turning her head and eyes deliberately elsewhere, she deigns to impart her reason for approaching.

"Mu completed decoding the latest set of coordinates for the supply silos. If you are finished staring at the desert, I suggest we move on from this place." Her calm, smooth voice grows a little crabby as she finishes nasally, "The dust is killing my eyes."

And here I would have placed bets on her complaining about her fair skin and the high noon sun. I'm certainly objecting to it, but it'll go no further than in my head.

Rolling my eyes, I shrug a single shoulder and feign nonchalance. There is little reason to stay where we're at unless the resupply depot is beyond a casual daytime trip. I have zero desire to run our ATCs in the dark. That kind of gross stupidity is asking for a problem. Either death by drop-off or Zee ambush. Hell, maybe marauders, too, if they're feeling ambitious.

Craning my neck to see the taller femme against the sky's brilliant blue, I ask, "And how close is the nearest silo? I've yet to get an approximation of the mileage from anyone. Hell, not even a general direction."

Chi goes from indifferent to mildly irritated with the slightest shift of the hips. I'm not sure which state of her I prefer at this point. As she crosses her slim arms, she aborts a glance at the sniper's position. Even in that brief eye contact between the two, something is passed. Apparently, this subject has been a part of some ongoing conversation between them.

With a gusting sigh, she rolls her eyes and opts to answer me. "The nearest noted outpost is approximately two hundred miles east of our current position. The more direct path will bring us through what the maps indicate is a fairly high-walled canyon."

My expression lowers as I take that in. It's further away than I anticipated, and it's not the best route. *Hmm.* Flashing back up to Chi's face mid-thought, I can tell she's holding something back. Well, that doesn't work for me.

"What is it?" I bark, throwing her off whatever game she's playing.

Leaning back a little, she glances at the ground, then skyward. Exasperatedly, she imparts the missing piece of her report.

"There is potentially a closer depot—perhaps no more than sixty miles from us. The difficulty is that it is listed in Mu's hard copy manual but was not mentioned in the latest information brief from HQ."

Out of habit, I scan our area, but am met with the same empty plateau stretching endlessly in all directions. Sixty miles isn't that far in this terrain. I know it's genuinely not as vacant as first appearances would imply. There's plenty of hidden wildlife and, more than likely, a smattering of Zee here and there. It wouldn't be the worst thing if we had to backtrack because the depot is defunct. However, it would mean an unscheduled overnight stop wherever we end up to avoid traveling to the outpost in less-than-ideal conditions.

The desert's been lacking strong winds the last week or so, and the dust storms we're routinely assaulted by out here have been non-existent. No loose dirt means that it's easier to keep the skins of our bikes clear of debris and at optimum efficiency for solar absorption. It also means it's been hot.

"It isn't that far to the offline depot." A pleasant voice chimes in from behind us as Mu joins our pair.

Mu's light step hardly makes an impression on the ground. Her short blue locks are shorn even closer to her skull than usual. Probably Omicron's work. He's not just handy with a scalpel. Give him a pair of scissors, and you'd be surprised what the man can do. And yeah, don't look to me as an example. I don't let anyone else near my hair, thank you very much.

"Yeah...?" I hedge. The sniper typically doesn't involve herself with these kinds of pittance decisions unless there's something for her to gain.

"It's also still along our path back." She turns her gaze toward the supposed supply building as if she can perceive it amongst the yellows, tans, and random green blobs from this distance. With the sun almost at its zenith, Mu has to raise a thickly clothed arm to shield her light-sensitive eyes. The motion sends a brief curl of cardamom in the air surrounding her. I've no clue where it originates from, just that it's something I associate with Mu.

I turn to see if Chi finds the other female's behavior equally suspicious, but she's studiously avoiding my gaze. That, or she's developed a sudden and thorough fascination with the back of her glove. Okay. Now I know something is up with these two numskulls.

The tick begins in my right temple and rapidly spreads to a pulsing sensation throughout my head, then to my hands.

"Alright, spit it out already!"

The words spew forth in a quick burst of annoyance without my consent. My hands add to the mix, flashing out to emphasize. I've never been the patient sort.

Chi gains the cool look of a fox bearing down on a hen house. Sly in demeanor as she parks her ass right next to mine. Too close. Like, front and center in my bubble, dammit.

"The fuck?" I exclaim at her proximity.

"What if I were to tell you," she croons in the sweetest tone I've ever encountered from her singularly snide self, "That the last list of goods for this particular depot includes Semtex?" Her perfectly straight and blindingly white grin is on full, magnificent display.

"And 7.62 munitions." The younger sniper pipes up, bouncing in place on her heels. Far too cheerful for my tastes. "Like, crates full. At least, there should be because no one has been through this sector from UF in a while."

I stare blankly at the pair of them. "Doesn't that set off a red flag to either of you? The UF isn't in the habit of leaving behind anything of value."

"Value, such as UF-brand conditioner," Rho adds to the now group conversation, saddling behind me to add his brand of peerless stupidity. I catch sight of Omicron and Tau moseying over and all but throw up my hands.

"How about you?" I gesture absently to Omicron. "Do you have something you'd like to chime in on? Perhaps a gift that this magical depot has also whispered to you on the sly?"

At least he has the common decency to shake his head in the negative.

"Nah, I wanted to see what the histrionics were about over here. However, if we're placin' our wish list orders, I could use a restock of any medical items. We take any more of the type of hits we had recently, and we're S.O.L."

I blow out a disgusted breath, bangs feathering out momentarily with the slight breeze. Head dropping down, I concede that this minor decision is not a big deal and may go a long way toward building synergy among my team. Yes, I used that thrice-damned word. Just goes to show you how low I've fallen.

"Fine. Whatever. Just keep it brief."

Harumphing, I push myself up and away from the center mass. This physical closeness and faux camaraderie leave me anxious for personal space.

"Let's get this train moving. As you all have nothing better to do, we might as well be hanging out at the depot."

I don't have to look to know I'm the unfortunate recipient of a pack of manic grins. There are negatives to leading a moderately unbalanced team of soldiers.

Heading toward our bikes, I pat myself down as I stride, checking for anything amiss with my gear. My mental checklist imitates an actual physical inventory, and all checkmarks go off without a hitch. Moving on, I inventory what we've on hand and realize we've run low on a good portion of our usual staples. Mainly, it's the result of the added Tau-shaped aberration in our routine. It also doesn't help that our missions took us further west than we're typically assigned to.

Normal supply depot runs are done to restock munitions and food supplies. Comparing what we've used versus the meager amount we had to begin with, the disparity between the two states is vast, like the Grand Canyon's vastness. I am hoping, against experience and common sense, that this will be as quick a refill operation as possible.

Hooking a leg over my bike, I practically slam my helmet back into its proper place in my haste to get moving. There's a rapid set of clicks as it automatically seals and secures top to bottom. This side trip shouldn't be more than a brief dalliance.

—Ω—

YOU CAN NEVER HAVE ENOUGH ORDNANCE

The landscape we move through is relatively smooth as we follow the underused remains of an old scenic highway. Miles of warm grays and browns, dotted with dark green clumps, span in all directions, undulated by rocky, rolling hills. Based on the data for the area, we don't expect to encounter any major Zee cells in this vicinity. There wasn't enough of a human population previously to begin with, and time would've whittled that number down substantially. Famous last words, I guess.

It's not long before we're going at a good clip. The wind streams steadily around my ATC and me as the scenery slides by. I don't have to tell my team how to arrange or pace themselves. Their normal formation is a given. Tau is the only oddball out and has the dubious joy of acting as the caboose.

As the leader of my team, I prefer to be at the front of the column. I lead from the front. Tau could claim the position, and I'm surprised he hasn't. Given the string of comments I've received, you'd think he'd be eager to prove how much better he'd run things. I'm glad he hasn't, though, regardless of his reasons. I'm not the best follower. Particularly of assholes.

As I distractedly track our steady and monotonous route with half a mind, I contemplate the next target on our extended tour home. Or as close to home as any of us has now. We had filler assignments left for us to complete before being redirected as a resource to save Tau's pathetic ass. We were almost finished with our regular six-month deployment. Hence, the low supply levels and general bitchiness of the team. The bonus of being this close to the end is that we should be able to make quick work of our assignments and get back to base in a reasonable amount of time.

"Ten minutes out from location," Mu relays calmly through the comms.

Returning to the present, I realize that most of the trip has passed with little incident and equally little of my focused attention. Not my best work, but at least nothing serious occurred between there and here. Redirecting my attention to what's directly in front of our collective faces, I make out the supply depot.

It's easy to identify once you know what to look for. An old farm silo, except shorter, stouter, and a good deal uglier. The entire thing is painted a matte grayish-tan in an attempt to imitate the surrounding sandbox and not stand out to the casual eye. The camouflage might have worked if it weren't the only object taller than a scrub. Its domed top is slightly more than twenty feet high, with a footprint spanning around fifteen feet in diameter. Not impressive in appearance by any standard, but it wasn't put here for aesthetics—the UF isn't big on those.

If an unauthorized person or thing gains access to one of the supply centers, the resulting alarm's pitch is horrifying. That sound will attract every Zee within hearing distance with its siren call. I also wouldn't put it past the UF to take more drastic measures if the break-in warrants it. Random missile strikes aren't unheard of.

As we near the silo's dull, curved outside, I slow, taking a wide arc around its base while looking for the entry point. There's only one way in and out of these. Short-sighted, considering the best time and place to be ambushed is as you funnel out of a narrow door, single file, with arms otherwise occupied. However, if the design has worked thus far, there's a good reason to keep it.

After a few loops, I finally locate the subtle arch that frames the entry point. It's on the western side, with the 'door frame' barely distinguishable from its outer walls. That feature is probably intentional on the designer's part. It's hard to break into a place when you can't find the door.

I release the throttle enough to come to a complete stop, no more than a handful of feet from the entryway. The high pitch of other engines idling off follows me as my team comes to a halt next to me without a word. We've been doing this for so long that it's pure habit for Mu and Chi to dismount and guard our six—rifles at the ready. The remaining three are not yet off their bikes, but they're just as aware of our surroundings. Believe it or not, it's not often that we do this. There's no need to with smart planning.

Sliding off my beast, I issue an order to Rho, although it's intended for everyone. "Wait here."

Popping off my helmet, I search for the elusive, subtle panel to let me in. Gaining access is relatively simple due to the various UF technologies embedded within me. Anyone who enters or exits this building will be scanned, cataloged, and their details transmitted via satellite to United Forces headquarters. It'd be a mistake to try breaking into one of these suckers if you're not supposed to. The UF doesn't share.

Deliberately, I trail my fingertips along the edge, an inch at a time, until I find a perfectly circular protrusion no larger than the pad of my thumb. It sticks out about a centimeter and is smooth and flat, resembling a button but not depressible. Holding said thumb to that spot, I wait patiently until a quiet click sounds, and the door slides open with a whoosh. A plume of dust and some other unmentionable smell is released into the air, but thankfully not of rot or anything suspicious. Merely air that's been kept to itself for too long, courtesy of a closed ventilation system. I must remember to avoid getting trapped inside unless I have a hankering for being entombed.

Stepping into the silo, the hard heels of my boots resound against the solid floor and echo all the way to the top. My eyes follow the sound to the very pinnacle of the structure, where LED lights have automatically come on, flooding the interior with their artificial glow. Row upon row of shelving reaches from about a foot above my head to the near-surface of the ceiling. In four equidistant spots, a set of railed ladders runs the length of the interior like some cylindrical library.

I don't care how well-made the framework of this structure is. I'd hate to try to get something off the top shelf. The middle has been kept blessedly empty, with nothing impeding the central column of open space. There's more than enough room to accommodate my entire team. However, I stop Rho and Tau before they come through.

"I need you two to hang outside and take the second go-through. Keep an eye out for anybody sneaking up on us while we're all stuffed in here like rats in a trap."

Rho looks about to argue, with his faceplate flipped up in preparation for a probably spectacular argument for his side of things. I halt him quickly with a hand up.

"You'll get your chance as well. I want Omicron to have more time to assess supplies and not be rushed with his medical refill."

My de facto second harumphs. "Well, that's all great, but why do Chi and Mu get first dibs?"

Shaking my head, I ignore the question. "Just stick to guard duty and keep us in the clear. We won't be long."

Tau raises an eyebrow as I pass him, but thankfully, doesn't contribute more to the conversation. Having our team's sniper, and scout-slash-demolition specialist adequately equipped trumps simpler infantry needs any day. I'm content to let the other two run through their crazy list of wants if it means they leave happy and satisfied. So long as it doesn't overload our bikes or leave me having to answer HQ for any more stupid decisions than I already do.

Squaring my shoulders, I step inside, waving to the others to continue as they pause to see if I want something from them. Once in, I pause briefly to take more than a cursory glance around. At least in this silo, somebody was thoughtful enough to put signage beside each area, categorizing the neatly arranged supplies. Each UF-sanctioned object has an ID reader embedded in it. You must have a valid ID to remove any supplies from the depot without triggering the alarms. The method roughly works, although assigning and checking out each piece of equipment to a single individual with the entire team using it is annoying. Micro-managing at its finest.

Mu skitters around excitedly, pulling vacuum-sealed containers of ammunition for her compact semi-automatic sniper rifle, or CSASS, because that's a fucking mouthful. I can hear her chattering away the whole time to somebody. Probably Chi, although I can't see her or hear any response. She's likely up on one of the higher shelves—no ladder is required in her case. The woman is part spider monkey.

Instead of getting involved with those two and being further distracted, I tune them out and focus on the personal hygiene section. On my way there, I pass Omicron, his back to me, methodically checking expiration dates on pill bottles in the pharmaceutical section. He's muttering something about inventory levels, his eyes narrowing at some labels in either ire or annoyance.

"Gettin' low on Rho's meds again," he says without turning, more to himself than me. "Weather's goin' to get colder. That interface pain will be actin' up."

He adds Gabapentin and Lyrica to his list without looking up. I'm far more familiar with these medications than I ever was pre-Zee. Implants like the gunner's come at a price. I pause at that, frowning.

Rho never complains about the cybernetic arm, but I've noticed him favoring it more lately, particularly during the night watches.

"Still that bad?" I ask quietly, glancing toward the entrance where I'd last seen the gunner. Omicron gives me a knowing look—he's been managing Rho's pain longer than I've been in command.

"Cold weather's never kind to nerve endin's, especially where metal meets flesh. The difference in temp between day and night doesn't help either." I nod, making a mental note to keep an eye on my second as the cooler months approach. It can be damned cold in the desert.

"Omega," Omicron calls out, not looking up from his inventory checklist as I almost round the next corner, "Remind me to requisition more Lyrica when we get back to base. Not much left here."

"You got it." I'm quick to agree. Rho's arm is one area in which he tends to either downplay or dismiss entirely.

Upon returning to my original mission, I find what I'm looking for relatively quickly and grab three nearly identical bottles. One is soap, one is shampoo, and the other is conditioner. Yes, given the choice, I prefer not to use a combination shampoo, conditioner, and soap, thank you very much. There's not that many bottles left, but I say nothing of it to the others. Let them hash it out when they get around to it.

Speaking of which, I manage to locate my scout now that she's back on ground level with a handbasket, similar to the ones you'd find in a grocery store, but far more foreboding. The violet-haired femme has happily loaded it with all manner of things that probably go boom. It's scary when you have a bunch of explosive ordnance piled together haphazardly. I hope she knows what she's doing. Leery, I work to keep her on the polar opposite side of where I am, to be safe.

I skip over the bike maintenance area for now. Rho is the primary mechanic and all-around fix-it-guy on the team, though Omicron tends to fill in the gaps for him. However, Omicron can't be everywhere all at once, fixing everyone and everything.

Beyond our hardware, I've found that the gunner also has a keen understanding of programming and is quite at home fiddling with the code of our machines to either fix or improve them. I've no idea what his background was prior to the present. It's another personal bit of information to be avoided for now and maybe broached over a future fireside chat.

Even with the filters and ventilation as good as they are in the silo, there's a fine layer of dust coating every flat or semi-flat surface. Running my fingers along one shelf, lines follow the trails my fingertips create. There hasn't been anybody in this structure for quite some time. Again, this isn't surprising given the location, but it's still odd for the UF to allow it to languish. There are plenty of supplies here that could be recycled for use at other stations.

Shaking my head at the thought, I continue crossing supplies off my list of needs, grabbing as I go and piling them into the empty duffel bag I had grabbed on my way in. All of this, I do with great haste. I'd prefer not to linger here any longer than is necessary. As soon as I'm out the door, I'll send at least one of the remaining guys in to do his thing.

Behind me, the higher-pitched chatter of Mu and Chi continues as they fill their coffers. Omicron is somewhere to my right, humming contentedly to himself, a marked change from a couple of weeks ago. I allow myself a small smile at the languid atmosphere enveloping my team at present. I hope that it lasts a little bit longer.

—Ω—

FULL SPEED BEHIND

All in all, the supply run doesn't take nearly as long as I'd anticipated. For my team's overexcited behavior, the soldiers were relatively professional and completed the task in under forty-five minutes. Rho was a little grumbly after finding that all the fine haircare products had been swiped. I'm confident somebody's shampoo and conditioner will go missing from their inventory shortly. At least I'll be comfortable knowing who I must bludgeon if I end up being the unfortunate mark.

With the side trip successful, I need everybody back on track as fast as possible. We have less than a month to return to base with Tau in tow. My father always said, 'On time is late,' a motto my family lived by until the end. I don't want to miss our check-in time for any reason, even if it's due to the UF's poor planning. We've been out here longer than we should have. It's our job, and we do it well, but sleeping without being on a hairpin trigger would be a nice break in the monotony of things.

With little to impede our current trajectory, we ride along on our cycles at a good clip. The sagebrush and cacti flow by in a watercolor streak of green-gray. I've no clue what kind of cactus any of them are. I vaguely recall the term "cholla," but I don't know where I picked it up. I just know there are a lot of damn spiky things in the former state of Utah, and most are best left alone.

By rote, I scan as we go, seeking anomalies and anything that cries 'trouble.' The air is already at a point where the sun's heat has raised the temp thoroughly. Even with the built-in fan in my helm, I might as well be in a convection oven. I might request a more northern assignment next time we're back at HQ. We've been doing the southern run for years now. Then again. They deal with things like snow and dense forests. Mountain lions and bears, too.

"*Omega, we have an incoming transmission from base.*" Mu's voice cuts through the buzz of the fan motor and the hum of my ATC, crisp and professional.

Shit. That's an unwelcome surprise.

"Okay. Have the base hold until we've come to a full stop. It'll be easier to transmit if we're not on the move."

Even as I finish the order, I'm rescanning the terrain around us. We're pretty much in the open, which is both a good and a bad thing. We'll see who or whatever comes our way, but they'll also have a clear line of sight on us for some time.

"Team, slow and hold at my position." I throw out to the entirety of the team's channel. I select a random, fluffy thicket of underbrush as my parking spot and wait for the others to arrive at a standstill beside me. As I release the catch on my headgear and capture my first breath of unfiltered air, I'm unexpectedly hit with a mix of bitter and spicy smells. I don't know what to compare it to, but nothing about it appeals to me. Some of my distaste must be evident on my face as Chi raises an eyebrow from where she's facing me.

Turning her very symmetrical nose to take a delicate sniff, she seems to confirm something for herself before sharing it with my pea-brain.

"It is the sagebrush. The heat encourages the leaves to release their oils. Assuming that was your intent, you picked the best place to achieve full exposure."

Rolling my eyes, I don't concern myself with replying to her dig. Instead, I work to appear less affected by the local flora and take one last look at our surroundings before refocusing on the task at hand. It's best to become acquainted with the lay of the land, even if we're not planning to stay here all that long. I prefer to have a strong sense of where best to engage an enemy if it comes to it.

In the meantime, I wave Mu over to myself as she brings the backpack that houses our High-Frequency or HF radio unit. She also has a VHF version for those unique situations where our team works collaboratively in the field. But it's a rare occasion for that to occur for us. The HF unit fills the need ten times out of ten, provided we don't have any interference in the upper atmosphere.

Without being told, the sniper and comms specialist places her gear on the back of my ride, carefully setting up the individual pieces of radio kibble. She glances upwards, more out of habit, I imagine. It's not as though she can deduce a solar flare from our location, particularly in the middle of the day. Still, I don't bother saying anything. Instead, I impatiently wait for her to queue up the appropriate channel and pass the handset. This Mu does with much less delicacy.

I digress, though. Handset in my grimy clutches, I clear my throat before depressing the button to receive whatever HQ is throwing at us.

"Omega Two Two here. Proceed."

"*Sergeant Omega. We've identified a site along your route that requires data extraction. Your team has been assigned to retrieve all pertinent records from the location and return them to base camp. Based on your last recorded position, we assume you can complete the task within a 72-hour window from your currently projected route.*"

I glance up at my assembled team. No one seems surprised by the new assignment, but it's more a matter of curiosity that we're being allowed to handle data. Typically, Beta teams like ours are assigned to physical cleanup tasks rather than more sensitive ones, such as information retrieval. My eyes linger on Tau's stern face for a moment too long as I consider the real possibility that his presence is the culprit. We apparently require Alpha-level babysitting to be trusted to accomplish classified work.

I roll my shoulders and sideline the thought. There's no sense in getting all riled up over petty things. We'll do what we're ordered to without fuss and do a damn good job while we're at it. Beta-level, my ass.

"Roger that, Command. Order confirmed. Transmit all specifications, and we'll add it to our to-do list."

Okay, the comment at the end probably wasn't necessary. Chi's raised eyebrow would agree. Hopefully, they missed that.

"*You will receive the transmission once our call ends.*" Command replies with zero indication that they caught or cared about my snark. The speaker plows ahead. "*Maintain radio silence until the extraction has been completed. Do not broadcast your coordinates in any manner. Command, out.*"

I'm taken aback by the abrupt end of our call. Throwing the inanimate comms unit a suspicious look, I play back that last order. A body shifts in front of me, and I look up in reaction, this time catching Rho's eye. His abnormally serious countenance adds to my concern. We're never told to cut off communication and transmission in the field. Even when we pursued Tau, communication was handled like any other under-informed task we had been assigned. Radio silence means not broadcasting our location to the UF, but it could also mean fear of someone else picking up on our comms. I have the icky, nagging sense that we won't like the shit we're about to step into.

"Receiving new mission specifications." Mu intones, almost in a drone. Her brilliant blue irises follow the bold lines of text that linearly populate the four-by-eight-inch screen in front of her as she vigorously transcribes the details into her notebook.

All in-the-field missions are provided once and only once. Due to the nature of our comms devices and a lack of fancier technology, we're relegated to writing everything down verbatim as it transmits. Oh, sure. You can request a re-transmission, but it reflects poorly on your unit, as if we're incapable of following base-level expectations. I'd also wager HQ means to keep to their comms silence.

I wait as Mu crouches beside my bike, watching the screen with avid interest as it scrolls through line upon line of content. I imagine it wouldn't be too difficult to have the comms store the transmitted data, but that's never been the case. The UF likes to avoid having any communications accessible or retrievable by parties that shouldn't be privy to them, including other Zeta teams. In that sense, we function in a bit of a vacuum.

Thankfully, Mu is not nervous about being the focal point of everyone's attention. She's relaxed enough to bob her head to some unheard song, deep blue locks bouncing with the movement. I can tell she's just about done as she gives a happy hum, the tip of her pink tongue sticking out to the side in concentration. With a gust of breath, she sits up and smiles broadly at me.

"All done. Wow, that's a lot of details they've included. Not our typical assignment."

She hands me a notepad filled with her crisp, narrow print, and I do a quick scan to get the gist of what we're being asked and where it's landed with us. Blessedly, Mu likes bullet points and list format, so her writing is much easier for me to parse out the significant bits of info. I stop mid-read. Back up a couple of lines and re-read. That can't be right.

"That can't be right." Whoops. Outside voice, again.

"What is the problem?" Tau asks from his space, well behind everyone else. Of course, he's using his quiet, authoritative voice, so I have to give him my immediate attention to actually catch what he's saying and not be forced to ask him to repeat it like some nimrod.

"There's no problem," I respond curtly on reflex.

I finish my initial speed read, as I'll review the order more thoroughly as we get closer to our target. Not looking up, I expand a bit in explanation.

"The site is called out as a former UF base, but I don't recall ever seeing it listed anywhere."

Forgoing better judgment, I hold the pad out to my nemesis, curious to see his interpretation and whether I'm wrong. With a single eyebrow aloft, Tau leans in to accept the innocuous notebook from me without comment. Something passes in his eyes as he grasps it, and I'm quick to release the end of the book.

Stepping back, his head dips down immediately to read the provided mission specs. I can feel the weight of the gazes from the rest of my team. I guess if I surprised myself by 'asking' for the Alpha's examination, my team is probably shocked. No matter. What's done is done. Tau's shorn charcoal head pops back up a few minutes later, apparently satisfied with his perusal.

"I have not come across anything regarding this location either. Perhaps it was intentionally unlisted to ensure security." He begins, hesitant in his judgment, but becomes more solid by the end, as if convincing himself more than anything.

Taking back the notepad from his outstretched hand, I feel inclined to add.

"Or to ensure secrecy." Shaking my head, I try to dismiss the not-so-good feeling that continues to linger like an off taste on the tongue. "Never mind. We've got a job to do, people. Let's knock it out and get home."

There are a few hoots from the team as they all disperse back to their bikes. The comms specialist is once more tucking away her gear for the next time we need it.

Terrific. Access a secret, defunct base with zero communication or support, and who knows what kind of trouble is waiting for us? That sounds like a recipe for disaster.

—Ω—

SOMETIMES FORCE REQUIRES FORCEFULNESS

Approximately 10 years after the widespread incursion of Zee.

[OMEGA]

Head down and feet on automatic, I plod ahead, mindful of my footing but little else. The sounds of a scuffle reach my ears before I can identify the source. In these soldiers' barracks, skirmishes are commonplace, minor enough that the brass typically overlooks them. No sense in punishing warriors for living up to their nature. There wouldn't be many left in the ranks to serve as cannon fodder.

A pair of fresh-faced Zeta soldiers hurry past. One's arm brushes mine, and he turns to speak—but my look stops him cold. His jaw snaps shut with an audible click. It's partly my demeanor, but more likely the insignia proudly displayed on my shoulder plate that freezes him in place. My size doesn't make me immediately intimidating, but I've learned to carry myself with authority. That, coupled with the knowledge that I can lay out any of these people without breaking a sweat, bolsters my confidence.

He whirls away, shoulders hunched and head tucked, nearly bowling over his partner in his haste to retreat. I ignore their hushed exchange, focusing instead on the commotion ahead. The conspicuous absence of onlookers suggests this isn't something your average bystander wants to witness, even peripherally.

My hackles rise. I maintain my pace but can't help quickening my steps slightly. Rounding the next building's corner drops me momentarily into blessed shade, a brief respite from the already blazing morning heat. Summers here are hell, and it's not just the daily regimen. It's the complete absence of vegetation—not even the artificial kind. This place makes Death Valley look lush. I should know—I visited there more than once in my previous life.

I halt abruptly at the next corner, still shrouded in shadow at the junction of four buildings. Before me stands a group of five. Their scent and pulse mark them as Zeta, like me. I can't explain how I know—perhaps it's their bearing, their breathing, their heartbeats. I've never invested the energy to figure it out.

The situation crystallizes instantly. Four of them wear Alpha-quality uniforms, while the fifth, cowering in their midst, sports training gear. Probably from my batch, maybe younger, but definitely unranked and unassigned. She radiates apprehension.

That's two strikes.

My body moves before conscious thought kicks in. Head down and eyes fixed on the ground, I trudge forward as if blind to the five bodies in my path. The collision is spectacular—I plow through their center mass like a bowling ball. A rough shove meets my shoulder, followed by an indignant cry.

"Hey! Watch it!"

I affect surprise, head snapping up with obviously feigned amazement. "Oh, I'm sorry. I didn't see you there."

They tower over me—all of them a good head taller at minimum. I'm forced to look up, though I hate to. They're carbon copies of each other: similar crew cuts, patchy facial hair, Alpha insignias—and matching sneers. I catch the moment they size me up and dismiss me as just another trainee, and a small one at that.

A scoff precedes the attempted rebuke. "Fuck you looking at?"

I tilt my head, giving him a deliberate once-over before letting an unpleasant smile surface. "Some jackasses in my way."

The ringleader's expression plummets from condescending to murderous. Perfect. His buddies shift uneasily, eyes darting to their leader for cues. I hate sheep, and these muscle-bound ones are no different from any other I've encountered. The young woman, until now frozen in horrified silence, straightens and tries to intervene.

"It's okay. We're just having a discussion. There's nothing to worry about."

I turn to address my would-be rescuee and falter as vivid blue eyes capture mine. Her heart-shaped face holds me transfixed, those strange eyes unlike any I've seen on base. I shake off the momentary spell with a derisive snort.

"Didn't look like 'nothing' to worry about. These ass clowns giving you problems?" I jerk a thumb their way.

Though taller than I, she shrinks into herself, trying to diminish her presence. They've clearly been at this a while. My irritation spikes.

"It's okay. Just a misunderstanding. I'll...it'll be alright. Don't worry about me. Please, continue on your way."

I shake my head, eyeing the seething Alpha beside me. "Yeah. How about not?" I raise my voice. "How about you guys fuck off, and we'll go our separate ways?"

The leader explodes. "Don't you dare try to order me around, you puny-ass trainee!"

I chuckle. "Trainee? Really? That's the best you've got?"

"How about stupid cunt!" comes a cry from behind, followed by the telltale whoosh of an incoming blow. I slip sideways, catching the arm as it passes over my shoulder. Using the soldier's momentum, I send him flying. He crashes spectacularly into a pile of crates, wood splintering on impact.

Hopefully, I didn't break too much of him—I've been trying to dial back my strength.

"Fuckin' bitch!" Another Alpha charges, hands outstretched, while his friend draws a cheap collapsible baton. Not like my quality one—his would snap like a toothpick in my hands.

I let Grabby Hands catch my shoulders, but duck as Baton Boy swings. The weapon connects with his friend's throat instead, producing a choked gurgle as his grip goes slack. He drops, clutching his neck and gasping.

"*Oh shit!* Sorry, dude. You okay?"

I complete my movement with an uppercut to Baton Boy's solar plexus. He drops his weapon, curling into a groaning ball.

A right cross catches me before I can gloat. It connects solidly with my chin, throwing me to the ground. The attacker pounces, raining down punches. I get my arms up to block most, but a few slip through to my face.

"Stop it!" The woman tries to pull him off, but he shrugs her aside like an annoying insect. His elbow catches her jaw, sending her sprawling. That's all the opening that I need—I plant my foot against his chest and push. Something crunches beneath my boot, but I ignore it as I launch him off me.

He doesn't fly as far as his first friend—I really did try to hold back. There's no sense in further depleting our already limited Zeta numbers, not even the jerks.

Groaning, I ease up. My face and shoulders throb, peppered with stinging points of pain. My stomach aches dully, undecided about joining the complaint department. He must have landed more hits than I realized.

A slender hand appears before my face. I follow the arm up a matte gray bodysuit to find my would-be rescuee smiling hesitantly. A bruise already darkens along the girl's jaw, meeting a long vertical scar—a mix of cut and burn damage, the skin showing that permanent shine of old burn wounds. Despite it all, her expression radiates kindness.

"Here. Are you alright?"

I accept her help. "I'll be fine. That idiot didn't get too many good hits in." She grimaces at the groaning bodies strewn around us.

"Look, get out of here. This mess is my doing. You weren't even here, okay? These guys won't admit what they were up to, so you're in the clear."

"That's not what matters!" Those blue eyes shine with unexpected hero worship.

"It's no big deal. Anybody would have done it."

She shakes her head firmly. "Not like that. Someone might have said something, but they'd still walk away. You didn't have to, but thank you." Her smile blazes with genuine warmth.

It's the kind of smile that leaves an imprint of contentment in its wake. I've grown unaccustomed to such things lately. A spark of warmth flickers inside, but I snuff it out. No room for sentiment or attachment here.

"Just forget it, okay? And maybe avoid situations like this? I can't be bailing your ass out again."

She sniffles but nods and thrusts out her hand. "I'm Mu!"

I shake it once, carefully neutral. "Omega."

Her face lights up like I've handed her winning lottery numbers. "Okay, well, thank you, Omega! I hope we see each other again!"

"Yeah, likewise," I grudgingly reply, dodging the oncoming friendship bus. What I just did probably earned me some solid enemies. Maybe worse. Well, shit.

—Ω—

NOT ALL WHO WANDER ARE TOURISTS

Present Day

[OMEGA]

Our new marching orders push us further north than planned. It's not the worst development, but it leaves me less time to study the terrain and review prior field reports. These reports are crucial—every team documents their encounters, locations, and points of interest. The writing in and of itself can be atrocious, but if suffering through someone's painful prose keeps us from becoming something's dinner, I'll endure it. And contribute my own monotonous monologues, as required.

We avoid the freeway despite it being the most direct route. Instead, we snake along parallel surface roads—risky, but I want these last missions wrapped up before any potential fallout can occur. That, and the desert sun is murdering my complexion. Our path winds us up one side of what passes for a hill out here—more of a mountain anywhere else—and down the other. The endless switchbacks do our approach and mileage no favors.

This stretch of Utah is pockmarked with quarries and mines, relics of a bygone era. The quarries are relatively new, whereas the mines date back to the early settlers. We were well on our way into an age where mining asteroids would've been more profitable than scratching at the Earth's depleted veins. But then came the Zee.

The sun bathes the sky in rich violets, reds, and brilliant tangerine—well past when I'd planned to stop. We'll need to make camp soon. Basic needs, such as security, take priority before the complete darkness of a moonless night envelops us.

I hail our logistics expert. "Chi, we need to settle down soon. Any structures around here, over?"

Chi's our default navigator—she has an uncanny knack for deciphering archaic callouts and abbreviations.

The comms crackle with her low-toned response. *"Not much out here. Few abandoned structures."* She hums thoughtfully. *"Probably nothing suitable... Oh, wait."* A pause. *"Yes, that should be sufficient. Some tourist locale."*

"A tourist's place?" I ask incredulously.

"Omega." My name is released in a sigh, dripping with patronizing patience. *"Do not presume. It is more of a roadside attraction for a small town. Single building, from what I can tell."*

"O-kay, that sounds more useful."

"It will be. It is removed enough to provide adequate coverage."

That settles my nerves somewhat. Gnawing my lip, I acknowledge we can't afford to be picky. "Send me the coordinates."

The system chirps as a flashing dot appears on my console screen. Not far—just up the hill. Isolated, with nothing else around, as promised. During our exchange, I've fallen behind from my team. In my defense, managing a seven-hundred-plus-pound bike while scanning for threats and reading displays stretches even my multitasking abilities to the limit.

"All right," I broadcast to the team. "We've got our night's accommodation." I tap a sequence on the console. "Transmitting coordinates. We'll slow our approach five minutes out. Need to confirm it's clear before we settle in."

No objections—they're either too tired to argue or simply conscious of the setting sun. The final stretch steepens dramatically as we climb. The pavement here is worse than usual, a maze of puzzle-piece fissures from more than just the Zee years of neglect.

A flash of gray catches my peripheral vision as we near the entry point. It's gone instantly, but I don't doubt what I saw. You learn not to. I brake hard, sliding the last ten feet to a stop. My raised hand brings the others to a halt, engines cutting out in quick succession.

I sit tall, focusing on where I caught that movement. Even without enhanced visuals, I can make out a Zee wandering in its own private hell. Dismounting, I keep my eyes locked on the target. Adult male, evident from its naked, emaciated form. Its skin is pulled tight over a diminished frame, mottled with moss-like patches of darker green, interrupted by yellowed bone jutting through. It hunches, dragging lifeless hands along the building's wall.

I adjust my helm's zoom. There, a second head appears beside the first, equally vacant and devoid of intention. Milky cataracts cloud its eyes, lids rimmed with unidentifiable filth. Neither seems fresh, but they're still mobile, which means they are likely *very* hungry.

I back up slowly to the team, never breaking my observation. "Okay. I've got two marked up there. Guarantee there are more Zee inside. I'd call them mid-grade. We'll take this by the book."

To the rear pair: "Omicron and Chi. Position yourself on the western side, behind the building. Watch for runners."

"Mu. Tau. Take the eastern section. Eyes sharp." Before I can complete my assignments, the sniper surprisingly interrupts me.

"*Wait,*" Mu interjects softly. "*Maybe...maybe you should pair with Tau instead.*"

Her tone is airy and contemplative. I have the notion that if I could see her face, there'd be that faraway look that means she's *seen* something she deems crucial. Well, we don't have time to debrief, and I need everyone focused on the immediate threat.

"Noted," I reply firmly. "But we stick to the plan. Stay alert, and it won't be an issue."

Mu protests no further, chin tucking down slightly. I catch the Alpha's helmet turned her way in consideration briefly, before immediately returning to starting position, facing forward.

"Rho and I will approach from the west, head-on. If anyone spots anything, alert the team immediately. Do NOT engage unless necessary." I make eye contact with each member. "Let's assess before we commit."

They nod, comfortable with this aspect of our work. I trust their capabilities. Even Tau's.

—Ω—

SHOULD HAVE LISTENED TO MU

Tucked into position, I resist the urge to glance at my companion as he shifts yet again. This is always the tricky part of any assignment. With my team out of sight and continuous communication suspended, I've become that restless mother longing for her wayward children to return home safely.

Though my squad may have the collective behavior of preschoolers, they're still technically adults. Adults with lethal weapons and the impetuousness to use them at will. And here I am, back in worried mother mode.

Ignoring the need to fidget, I tear my eyes from the empty scrub before us to check my right gauntlet's screen. Before taking cover, I'd called up a live feed of team positions—including our Alpha asshole add-on. Each neon-orange blip represents a Zeta soldier or at least their subdermal beacon. All warm bodies appear accounted for and properly positioned. Should hear from them any moment now.

Right on cue, my comms light up, and Chi's dulcet tone comes through clearly.

"Omega, we are in position, over."

"Roger that, Chi. We're here, waiting for the last team. Hold your position until my command."

"Will do, Omega. Awaiting."

Nodding to myself, I reach across to tap Rho's forearm. Flipping my faceplate up as he mirrors the motion, I lean in close. "We're waiting on Mu and the Alpha. Should be in place by now."

Rho frowns, considering. "What's keeping them? They've had enough time to confirm."

"I'll give them another few, then push for confirmation. No sense having our asses hanging out waiting to greenlight a ten-minute op."

"If you say so. Not sure those two were the best pairing for this." The last bit comes out barely audible as his focus drifts.

Eyebrows in my hairline, I prod him. "What makes you say that? Mu's strong at range. Tau's better up close. Should balance well."

He offers a one-shouldered shrug, still avoiding my gaze. My ire rises with the urge to smack him. The material of my glove crinkles as I clench it, counting to ten and breathing deeply. Before I can decide whether to pursue violence, a frantic broadcast cuts across all comms.

I barely register it's Mu's channel before her voice breaks through. *"Contact! We're in it and need support. Ahh—"* The line goes dead after that sound of mixed exertion and pain.

Eyes wide, I jump on the line. "Mu! Status! What's happening? Where's Tau?"

Static answers. I waste no time hauling myself and my second to our feet. Mu's voice returns between ragged breaths.

"He's gone. A small horde jumped us." A gulping breath. *"He went after the stragglers."* She cuts in quickly as if reading my thoughts. *"I don't think he knew there were more. Probably assumed I had the last few Zee handled."*

"Let's go," I tell Rho before switching back to comms. "Mu, we're en route. Are you injured?"

"Well..." Her hesitation speaks volumes. *"Uh. I may have hurt my head when I got knocked down. It's all a little fuzzy."*

Growling, I slap my faceplate down and gesture Rho forward with my rifle. "Hold position. We'll be there soon."

"Roger that, Omega. I'll do my best."

As we traverse the uneven ground, I switch channels. "Chi. Omicron. Get your asses to Mu's coordinates as soon as possible. She's under attack, and Tau's who-the-fuck-knows-where."

"You got it, Sarge. Five minutes max." Om's first to respond.

"Roger. Omega, out."

No need to warn them about Zee. If part of the team is engaged, the rest can't be far.

My breath comes hard and fast, but thank God these helmets don't fog. Still, condensation makes the inside stuffy and damp. Rifles high, we round the corner just as Mu kicks a Zee clear and reaches for her weapon to fire at more incoming threats. The upper half of her helm lies a few feet to her left, more likely knocked off than removed, though it'd take a hell of an impact to manage that.

The fact that she was likely pinned moments ago sets my teeth on edge. With two quick shots, I put new holes in a nearly naked male Zee. His sagging belly stops mid-roll as momentum dies, lumpy skull hitting the dirt with a wet thud.

Rho targets a smaller female Zee to my right. His first shot goes wide as she dodges unexpectedly, but follow-up rounds through his scope drop her. I wince before I can stop myself—the body's too small, dressed in daisy-print overalls.

A glance at Rho shows him frozen, likely staring, though I can't see through his helm. Doesn't matter how often we do this—killing Zee kids never gets easier. Sighing, I move to where Mu sits dead center in the dust. Rho follows, scanning for threats, but I'd bet Mu handled most of them, judging by the bodies scattered around.

Crouching, I examine the gash above her right eye, tracking it into her hairline. Rho stands guard, his helm tilting briefly to assess Mu's injuries. Blood and darker matter mat her hair, a fresh line trailing down one sharp cheekbone.

Teeth gritted at my sniper's condition, I grind out, "Where's Tau?"

Mu opens her mouth, but crunching gravel cuts her off. We swing around, weapons ready, until Chi's sharp whistle identifies them. Ignoring their abrupt entry, I turn back to Mu and have to snap my fingers to break her attention from Rho's hovering presence. He remains oblivious, or pretends to be, to her fixation.

"Mu, which direction did Tau go? How long ago?"

Recognizing every second wasted could result in a dead Alpha, I shove Rho's organic shoulder hard enough to stumble him. I ignore his indignant *"Hey!"* But the motion serves its purpose, and Mu snaps out of it.

The almond-skinned sniper winces, squinting through a partially closed eye as she points over my shoulder. "Full speed that way, about five minutes ago."

With a grunt, I glance behind me, calculating. Tau's headed for the mining area's center—exactly where I wanted to avoid, with its deep gravel pits. Strategically speaking, it's dumb as hell.

Groaning, I rub my helm, cursing pig-headed soldiers and poor decisions. "O-kay. He was following some Zee?"

Mu nods slowly, partly because Omicron's now administering first aid while firmly shoving Rho from his space. I address Chi at her guard position.

"Chi, stay with Om. Watch his six while he patches Mu. Be ready if I call." I turn to my gunner, dusting off his pants.

"Rho, you're with me. Let's see what's left of this asshole to save."

Grinning, Rho taps his resealed helm twice. *"You got it, boss,"* comes clear across comms.

Faceplate locked, I ready my rifle and take off toward where I'm certain Tau's gotten himself into the worst possible situation. Something to razz him about later—assuming his head's still attached. If that's the case, I'll be happy to finish removing it myself.

—Ω—

I DITCHED MY LAST EFFORT

[TAU]

Guilt gnaws at the edges of my focus as I pursue the remaining enemy, leaving the sniper, Mu, at our position. Doubt flickers through my decision to abandon the female soldier, but despite her youthful appearance and bright demeanor, I find myself unexpectedly confident in her capabilities. She mirrors the rest of this strange team I have been forced to join. Capable. I did not anticipate that a Beta-class squad would demonstrate such competence. They function seamlessly, even accommodating my unintended presence.

I push myself harder in pursuit of my targets. My heart's uneven pulse might be from exertion or latent anxiety—either way, it is irrelevant. I separate mind from body, focusing solely on the Zee horde's trajectory. I will eliminate every last one. I must.

I should not have survived after my last mission, not in the state I allowed myself to fall into. That remains my greatest shame, my most profound agony. How to make amends for their loss…perhaps there is no way. Perhaps my kamma is to suffer their memory until I am ash.

A cluster of three Zee turns as one when I round a dilapidated structure. I neatly sidestep both the weathered wood jutting outward and their outstretched claws. Pivoting with precision, I plant my feet, turn, and execute three perfect double-taps between each Zee's bloodshot eyes. I do not wait for their corpses to collapse. My boots are already following the remaining Zee, mind drifting in a strange reverie as I continue the hunt.

Once I had recovered sufficiently, the pull toward oblivion lessened as my thoughts cleared. I spoke privately with Omicron at the time, expressing gratitude for his care. Nu would have enjoyed working alongside this medic. His competence reminds me of her, although she was always more...boisterous than I preferred. Her outward behavior as an Alpha-level medic often grated on my nerves.

"Tau, report! What's your position?" The Beta squad leader's voice cuts through comms, loud and brusque. I frown at the interruption to my focus.

"I am in pursuit of the horde's remnants. I will return to my position once I have disposed of them." My tone remains as civil as possible while concentrating on priorities. Something about this woman aggravates me, not like Nu, though. She is loud and brash— unsuited for leadership.

Phi, on the other hand, operated like a well-trained pit bull. Someone you unleash when brute force and disregard for consequences are required. This Omega is like neither of them. Not remotely.

"Negative! Get your ass..." I terminate the transmission. Undoubtedly, she has something acerbic to contribute to my decision, but I remain resolute. I did not become an Alpha squad leader at the UF's whim. She would do well to remember that.

My audio sensors detect the raspy moan of a Zee not far ahead. I grit my teeth and accelerate, though not Sigma fast. He was beyond my league, a college sprinter before becoming a Zeta soldier. The enhancement only magnified his natural ability, unlike mine. I have always worked harder to achieve what others accomplish effortlessly. My life has consistently presented challenges requiring additional effort to excel. Why my abilities developed as they did remains a mystery.

I duck my head and sprint harder. My path narrows between two towering piles of loose soil and rock. Rounding the final bend,

I dig in my heels, skidding to an abrupt halt. My slide nearly carries me headfirst into an idle horde. I immediately recognize these are not my original quarry—their numbers and individual characteristics differ entirely.

A line of sweat traces down my face, running beneath my chin. I have no time to address it. Biting my tongue, I step backward, movements slow and deliberate. I need distance to engage properly. This encounter is too close.

Then comes my next error. The ground beneath my heel suddenly gives way. I plummet down a slippery slope, rifle tumbling from my grip. I hear it connect with the ground—safety engaged, thankfully. My descent ends abruptly at the pit's bottom, weapon clattering uselessly beside me. This ineptitude becomes ridiculous. I curse harshly in my father's tongue—something I would never have dared in his presence.

I was too fixated on the Zee and failed to assess my surroundings properly. I am never this careless. I cannot continue losing focus. This entire situation has compromised my performance. Wincing, I feel hundreds of jagged gravel bits pushing through the glove and gauntlet. Not severe, but aggravating.

A scuffle and snarl from above draws my attention as loose rock scatters over the edge, spattering against my helm. Looking up, I attempt to leverage into a crouch, but the ground beneath fights my every movement, threatening to swallow me into unknown depths.

Solid footing is fundamental in combat. Teeth gritted, I sweep my hand along the ground, seeking my rifle, eyes never leaving the pit's edge. Without looking, I feel when I have located it and quickly extract the weapon from its partial burial. My position is compromised—the walls are close enough that I can nearly touch both sides. Insufficient space to engage effectively if Zee descend.

More debris rains from above. Three creatures now circle the edge, moaning and rattling, trying to determine how to reach me. Not reasoning—their consciousness is long gone—merely bodies recognizing an obstacle. It matters little as one jostles another, sending the third tumbling down toward me.

Cursing, I drop to one knee and track its descent. My first two shots find home in its skull, the third missing. No matter—the creature will not rise again. But now the others understand the path. With hoarse cries of hunger, they move forward as one, fixated on my form. Behind them come answering calls and screeches. More will follow.

If this is where I meet my end, I vow with each breath to take as many of them to hell with me as possible. I am not easy prey. On this, they can be certain.

—T—

COLD DISHES AND COLDER RECEPTIONS

[OMEGA]

The path ahead narrows. A long tunnel of gray and tan. The world condenses to the sound of my breathing, rough and harsh. Rho's boots and mine pound in echoing tandem, only my enhanced senses guiding us forward. The road transforms into a high-walled gorge that seems to close in with each heartbeat. My breath synchronizes with the rhythm of my feet.

This reaction...I don't know why I'm having it. No, that's a lie. I understand why it's happening. The question is, why for him? He's not from my people. Not one of mine. He's not Epsilon.

As I reach the final scaffolding, an open expanse unfolds before me. Narrow pyramids built entirely of gravel and rock rise precariously beside man-made valleys. A stale, musty scent hangs in the air between the steep pits, partly from the lack of vegetation. These rocks have been sitting exposed to the elements for God knows how long, devoid of human intervention. Grunts and harsh exhalations echo around us, punctuated by what might be foreign curses if I focus hard enough.

With sudden clarity, I realize Tau has somehow found himself at the bottom of a pit bordering one of these precarious piles. I recall playing in similar spaces as a child when my father worked near a construction site. Workers constantly shifted dirt from one area to the next—it seemed pointless then. I remember climbing one such pile and discovering exactly how unreliable that ground could be. In his eagerness to pursue the enemy, the Alpha must have paid insufficient attention and ventured too close to the edge.

At least he's still alive—a plus, I suppose. It'll allow me the opportunity to dispose of him myself later, and boy, do I want to. I slow as I approach the rim, carefully toeing my way to the edge. Peering down, I find exactly what I expected: the Alpha soldier braced at the bottom, surrounded by at least seven Zee. He's doing an admirable job keeping them from devouring his scrawny ass, but his footing is limited to the narrow pit bottom. The Zee, oblivious to their surroundings, push and climb over one another to reach their prey. Even those sunk to their knees—one to its thighs—remain fixated on their target.

Upper helm flipped up, Tau's face is flushed, exertion mixing with anger and a healthy dose of fear. His footing shifts slightly, nearly sending him backward. He takes a knee instead, bracing himself as he fires point-blank into the nearest creature's forehead.

Dropping to my knee, I sling my rifle from my shoulder and take careful aim. When I have a clear line, I drill two holes into the nearest Zee's cranium. Tau's buzzed head snaps up, identifying his unexpected assistance.

Rubber soles compact loose ground at my six. Glancing over my shoulder, I find Rho has finally caught up, prepared for battle, though slightly winded. He stops just at my six, surveying the scene below before releasing a low whistle.

"Wow. Tau got himself into a real good mess, didn't he?"

I can't help but snort. "Yup. It would appear that the Alpha took a wrong step or ten."

Chuckling, the gunner crosses his arms and tilts his head to examine our trapped comrade. Drawing out the first syllable, he asks, *"Sooo...what are we going to do with him?"*

I hear the clipped edge in Rho's voice—he's just as irritated as I am. The Alpha's lack of cohesion nearly cost us Mu, who holds far greater value to this team than he ever will. I know Tau's running out of options and time. As irritated as I am, I've let him wriggle on his line long enough.

"I guess we save his dumb ass. Again. No point wasting our effort just to let him die from stupidity. Although it would be fitting."

"*Agreed,*" Rho mutters.

"Alright, let's pick off some Zee and get him out."

It's second nature now—line up, select a human-shaped target, shoot to kill. My younger self would find this utterly twisted the ease with which I take lives. As I place the crosshairs just above a swollen lesion on a Zee's temple, I'm disconnected from the action. My finger squeezes the trigger, but that's simply mechanics. I watch the bullet exit the back of its head. A reaction. No remorse for the absence of emotion.

Our shots fly true as we knock down the small horde like dominoes. It's simple enough from our vantage point. Of course, when things go too well, the fuckening inevitably rains down. A shrill screech echoes across the expanse. Startled, I glance above my M4 to find a swarm of enemies clambering up the hillside several hundred yards opposite our position. They're approaching from a completely different direction—might have been holed up in one of the mine shafts. More than one horde. Damn. Another oversight.

"Fuck!" I curse with appropriate gusto. Rho echoes the sentiment.

Turning grimly to my second, I bark, "We need to get him out now!"

Patting myself down, I realize I left my extra gear with the ATC. "You got a line?"

Rho checks himself before shrugging apologetically. Slapping my faceplate, I scan our surroundings for a solution. The last thing we need is twenty Zee sliding down to join Tau's party. My answer appears quickly—the rusty end of an unraveling metal braid jutting from the grit.

"What's that?" I jog several feet to grab and yank at the metal cord, almost as thick as my wrist. Some kind of cable, likely from a winch or crane. Not bothering to find the other end, I heave against it, drawing out several feet of coiled metal in rapid hand-over-fist motions.

Without pausing, I call to Rho, "Here, throw this down to him."

Shouldering his weapon, Rho streaks past my peripheral vision, calling down to where Tau waits among the corpses.

"Tau, get clear! Back up to the opposite side. I'm going to throw you a rope."

I can't see from my position, but Tau must acknowledge somehow, as Rho returns immediately. If I'd asked the same, I'd have received a far different reaction. The gunner grabs the end I spotted and steps away. This cable is anything but light. If my second happens to smack the Alpha in the face with it, that might make this day worthwhile. I watch the freed length go taut as Rho delivers it to the trapped soldier. My relief is short-lived.

"Shit! Not enough."

"How much 'not enough'?"

The taller man rejoins me, tugging on the cable just below my grip. *"We need about ten more feet. Good thing he's not you. We'd need even more."*

Grunting understanding while ignoring the jab, I continue pulling at the buried cable. Charcoal filings and orange rust rain onto my gloves in confetti-like flakes. Thank god I'm not bare-handed, though I'm still not looking forward to the state of my palms afterward. My shoulders and back strain from the awkward, hunched position.

Predictably, the damn thing catches. I yank hard, nearly dislocating a joint. "It's stuck!" I pant. "I can't get any more length."

Sudden silence follows. The absence of exertion makes the mental pause behind me too noticeable. Rolling my eyes, I grind out, "Really, Rho? How old are you?"

A gasping squeak follows as he suppresses laughter. Between breaths, he chokes, *"Do you...realize...how many thoughts...I have to... to ignore...right now?"*

"Do you realize how hard I want to hit you right now?"

He sputters, *"Hard!"* releasing a few gasps. Being stuck with idiots like this at the world's end must be karmic retribution. I must have been a real asshole in my previous life. Or maybe early in this one? Hell, I still am.

"Shit!" I abandon the fruitless effort, rubbing my helm as thoughts jumble and reassemble. My unfocused eyes land on the beginnings of a good (bad) idea. Without a word, I backtrack along our path. My solution presents itself neatly, half-embedded in the ground and twice as long as I am. Smiling in satisfaction, I don't bother asking for help. Completely unnecessary.

Finding a gap for my gloved fingers between dirt and creosote-laden wood, I wrestle the railroad tie from its resting place. Rho raises an eyebrow, arms folded across his poncho, keeping a prudent distance.

Grinning ferally, I call down, "Tau, back away from the cable."

His muffled reply comes in negative tones, still reluctant to follow my direct order even when it's to save his ass.

Peering down at him, Rho chuckles, "*Just do it, dude, or you'll have both Megs and the Zee to deal with.*"

More grumbling rises from below, but I focus on my task. Curling my forearms beneath the tie's bulk, I heft it overhead, turning back toward Tau's position as the cannibals' cries intensify. Rho's attention shifts to the approaching threat, rifle raised as he prepares to guard our exit.

"Incoming!" I yell over the pit's edge as the gunner opens fire. I glimpse Tau's eyes widening comically as I boost the beam overhead. He scrambles backward, likely scraping himself on the opposite wall. With an almighty heave, I launch the 200-pound tie. It sails, plummets, and embeds itself into the gravel at his feet with extreme prejudice.

The moment it impacts, the slender Asian man scrambles up its treated side. He leaps the last couple of feet to grab the steel cable. I seize the length nearest me and haul him up and out, lifting what feels like a featherweight until he shoulders over the loose lip. The Alpha braces himself on all fours as I sit down abruptly to recover my expended energy.

With Tau out of immediate danger, my rage comes roaring back in full force. The Alpha and I have unfinished business.

—Ω—

COMMON SENSE IS NOT OPTIONAL

The pulse under my hand quickens—fast and hard, like a frightened hummingbird trying to escape my tightening grip. I allow Tau's hanging weight to increase the pressure on his throat. Two sets of gloved fingers claw uselessly at mine, attempting to protect that vulnerable spot but failing to pry me loose.

His dark eyes find mine for one held breath, and without warning, he ceases struggling against the immovable force that is me. His submission is unexpected, to put it mildly. Perhaps he's finally grasped his position—understood that I could efficiently separate his head from his shoulders if the mood struck me. As I passively scan the smooth planes of his face, my mind burns through a backlog of responses and subsequent actions.

Despite everything racing through me, I do the responsible thing and release the Alpha, waiting for him to regain his breath. Frustrated by his foolish actions and utter selfishness, I use this moment to take stock of the current situation.

We'll need higher ground with clear lines of sight. From the gray tint of the sky, sunset isn't far off. We can't go without a secure perimeter—we've encountered too many stray Zee in this area. I'd hate to add to the body count and ruin local statistics through carelessness. I recall Mu's cut and bruised face, that line of red tracing down her cheek. She needs a solid night's sleep to kickstart her healing.

Our kind always benefits from rest after a physical altercation, beyond the usual advantages of sleep. A lesser-known trait of Zeta soldiers is how drastically our healing accelerates following deep sleep. We won't be one hundred percent by morning, but Mu's face will barely show a scratch. Tau will be healed, too, disappointingly.

Turning fully to where Tau ineffectively brushes dust from the fiery bronze of his uniform, I detect that same lingering emotion. What does he fear? Certainly not his death, forgotten in a gravel pit. Then what?

"What?"

I blink out of my reverie, startled. Crap. Did I say that?

Tau stands before me, still as a deer caught in the open before a predator. He watches me as though I'm something unpredictable, poised to flee or fight depending on my next move.

I realize belatedly that I've been staring intensely while spiraling in thought. My flipped-up faceplate has made that all the more obvious. Whoops.

Snorting, I shake my head and relax my stance before returning his gaze. "You done yet? We need to get back to the team." My tone is casual and disinterested.

He doesn't immediately respond, scuffing a toe in the packed dirt, smudging his Alpha boots with dried orange clay.

Patience exhausted, I shake my head, thoroughly fed up with his sulking and troublemaking. I waste no more words—I've said what needed saying multiple times. Whether he listens is on him. There's nothing more I can do. I step back before turning to head toward the others. I'm not worried about their current state—I'm within easy broadcast range and running distance. If anything had happened, I'd know by now.

For a brief second, I see a flash of torn flesh and a bloodied facsimile of a smile. Gritting my teeth, I push against the mental imagery and the scent I know is impossible to detect. Mu's fine. The asshole too. My team remains intact. No need for unnecessary bouts of anxiety.

And yet...thinking about something to control emotion doesn't make it a reality. Likely the opposite. Thoughts drive actions, ending in consequences that are both predictable and not. I'm still carrying this emotional backlog nearly a year later.

With a deep inhalation that flares my nostrils, I draw one long breath. Hold it while counting methodically to four, then release it with equal measure. A modicum of stillness buzzes between my ears. I don't dare repeat as Tau reluctantly joins me. The last thing I need is the Alpha catching me doing box breathing. In fairness, I'm trying to sidestep an anxiety attack, and calming my mind is most effective.

As always, I push forward, rifle ready but stance relaxed. I'm confident we've removed immediate Zee threats, though never entirely. These creatures won't be eradicated—the hordes are too mobile and nomadic without resorting to extreme measures and substantial collateral damage. See the former U.S. coasts for prime examples.

Who's to say a new batch isn't meandering in right behind the previous? I never allow myself or my team to fall into complacency. I can't imagine feeling utterly safe and at ease anywhere, ever again. There's too much wrong with our world, which we encounter daily.

I press on, eager to rejoin my people and assess Mu's status. She's undoubtedly received Omicron's undivided attention while we were occupied. Any malady will have been efficiently addressed.

"I...apologize."

The unexpected statement—severe yet soft—jolts me from my thoughts. Looking sharply at Tau, I realize he's the only possible source of those words. I stop and turn abruptly, movements jerky in my haste to deliver a scathing retort. How dare he?

"You're sorry?" The words are practically spat out, and my

simmering anger boils over at his nerve. Nothing as rudimentary as a verbal apology will absolve his mistakes. Staring hard at him, he seems unsurprised by my reaction. If I'm being generous, he anticipated it.

Calmly, as if I hadn't spoken, he continues. "I should not have abandoned my assigned position. Nor should I have left my partner without support."

I say nothing, waiting to hear what follows, anticipating some spectacular excuse. Sometimes, the best approach is to leave the rope and stool out to see what happens. I've been trying to get this idiot to toe the line and not endanger my team at a higher risk than their daily exposure. Himself, too, though that's barely a secondary concern now.

He looks down at his hands and rifle. A deep line forms between his slender eyebrows as his eyes narrow inward. "I know better. I am better than this. I saw those Zee and I…I felt…I could not just ignore them and let them escape. All while awaiting backup that was only yards away."

"And yet, that's precisely what you needed to do." I coldly intone. This lesson won't be downplayed or sidestepped. It must be learned the hard way, it seems.

His expression shutters before his eyes open and fix on me. His face shifts to a healthy mix of pissed off and offended. Whether it's aimed at me or his internal thoughts, I don't care. I'm just warming up.

"You know better than most that following straightforward orders in the field is essential. Without it…" I take a steadying breath to banish the mutilated face, staring blankly from my mind, and refocus. "If we leave each other unprotected, we can't expect to survive this." My eyes narrow, pleading that he finally gets it.

"We won't survive this."

He grits his teeth, clearly not wanting another lecture. I catch his chest puffing as he prepares an equally vehement retort. It's on his parted lips and very nearly released—but then his eyes close, head turning as he releases a long exhalation. Perhaps I'm not the only one using calming techniques.

A brief intermission in the tension between us presents an opportunity—maybe the one chance to level with him and establish at least a temporary cease-fire to those suicidal tendencies. If not to protect him, then to protect those he's inflicting himself upon.

"My team has lived through a great deal. No different than others in our position. However, their survival and well-being—theirs alone—are paramount to me. Not much matters beyond them." I step nearly chest-to-chest, though mine is almost a head lower. Face-to-chest then? Irrelevant. I continue. "We will guard your six as we do each other's and ensure you reach base camp through whatever power and ability is ours."

My voice hardens to steel lightly coated in velvet. "In turn, I need you to protect my team as if they're your team. Grant them a similar priority and place their lives above yours." Drawing back slightly, I regard his still form. "It's what I need from you."

There it is. Laid bare before the Alpha and placed in his court. What comes next, no amount of blackmail or manipulation will help to attain. I hate the loss of control and vulnerability, but I need a genuine commitment from him. It's a risk I have no choice but to take.

Of course, my comms—and therefore my team—chooses that moment to make contact.

"*Yo! Omega.*" Rho broadcasts clearly and loudly through my helmet speaker.

"Where are you and the plus one? Mu's patched up, and Omicron says we're good to jet. It's getting dark."

Sighing at the gunner's mixed timing, I raise an eyebrow at Tau. He watches me with unnerving intensity, his clean-shaven face ardently severe. Not that I've witnessed levity from him before— the man wears stoicism like a martyr's pine cross.

"Are we good?" I ask, leaving no doubt about my meaning.

I set aside petty issues and general disgust with the situation. All I want is a real answer, something I can depend on for my team's safety. Without confidence that he'll protect them, the journey back to base becomes another unknown.

His eyes meet mine piercingly, gauging the depth of my question and the integrity behind it.

"I will respect your authority over this team and command." His voice is low and calm, but conviction resonates through those few words. He starts to continue, but turns aside. His gaze softens in introspection before returning to me. "And I will protect this team and guard them with my life. I will treat them as the cadre and brothers in arms that they are."

I let the quiet sink around us, filling spaces where questions might arise. For now, I have no choice but to believe this soldier.

"Good," I reply softly. "Then there's no need to say anymore. If this ever happens again, there's nothing to discuss. I take care of threats to my team swiftly and without hesitation."

I leave him with that truth. I've given enough second and third chances—there will be no more. If he can't keep his promise, I'll meet mission standards without risking my team. Count on it.

—Ω—

ACT 3
SLIPPING THROUGH THE HOURGLASS

WHO CHOSE WHOM

Approximately 10 years after the widespread incursion of Zee.

[OMEGA]

Someone is staring at me.

No, scratch that. They're attempting to sear a hole through the shaved side of my skull, Clark Kent style. I know who it is without looking.

Staring down at the thick brown-gray puddle of what should be beef curry, I contemplate drowning myself in the muck. Not that it would help. There's not enough liquid, number one, and too many bodies nearby, number two. Statistically, some fool will play good Samaritan and save me before I can make good use of the slop they call a meal.

Huffing at both the weight of my soul and the annoyance of my stalker, I abandon the pretense of shuffling the few perfectly cubed, meatless beef chunks around in the gravy. I place my fork down with a deliberate clang, brace my hands on the dinner tray, and abruptly turn to face the source of my ire.

"Yes, Epsilon?"

Despite the near-growl of my question, he smiles in that goofy, carefree way I've come to associate with his general state of being.

"Hey, Omega. How'd the board review go?"

Gritting my teeth, my fingers flex against the metal tray, nearly bending it inward.

"As if you didn't already know, you gossipmonger."

He's the picture of innocence and light, complete with curled locks of golden hair. I'm sure there's a halo above him and choir of angels singing somewhere.

"Hmm? Oh, I've heard a few things. Mostly from Phi, of course."

His eyes dart left and right in mock suspicion before zeroing in on me. Leaning heavily forward, mouth partially covered by the back of his hand, Epsilon whispers quickly.

"Apparently, he's dating one of the secretaries from Personnel. They saw the request for you and then the assignment recommendation after your little interview."

Rolling my eyes skyward, I lean away from Epsilon, my interest evaporating. I release my death grip on the flimsy tray. Now that the urge to hurt someone has passed, there's no point in restraining myself. If it returns, there's also no point in stopping myself.

"Good thing personnel matters aren't, you know, private or anything?" I frown disapprovingly, miffed at him for fueling the gossip train. And for getting into my business. Especially that.

He grins, unbothered. "Fair enough. Then again, truly private matters with personnel aren't exactly what goes on inside an air-conditioned boardroom, right?"

My frown deepens in confusion. "What are you getting at?"

Epsilon's cherub-like face transforms with a downright devious smirk that suffuses me with dread.

"Well, a little bird may have shared something they happened across. Something involving a group of Alphas and maybe a couple of trainees? Might have been one pair that fared better than the other?"

I stiffen briefly, trying to hide my immediate tension and pounding heart. The blonde grins unrepentantly, catching whatever tell I gave.

"Bingo!"

I shake my head, whether in denial or disbelief, as he continues.

"Hey, don't look so shocked. If you weren't such a big, bad, scary Zeta soldier, you'd probably have more friends congratulating you right now. Actually, you might have gained some admirers anyway, even if you weren't keen on it."

The news is both troubling and disappointing. I slump, abandoning all pretense of aloofness as I lament my shattered privacy and self-imposed isolation. Pinching the bridge of my nose against an impending headache, I warily regard the toothy soldier beside me.

"She shouldn't have said anything."

"She who? Mu?" he asks curiously. "Nah, she's not the type to kiss and tell. Mu's a really nice gal. Smart. Maybe a little too kind for this business, but she's a good sniper. I've seen her in action. Makes most of these doughboys look like they've never handled a rifle on the range."

"No, you had a sort of shadow, apparently. An unintended one. Somebody at the wrong place at the right time—or the right place at the wrong time. Take your pick." Epsilon catches my dejected posture and the misery radiating off me. "But don't worry! Your secret's safe. It won't go further than me or them. They shared, so I'd give you a heads up."

"Why?" I ask despite myself, perplexed. Why would he care? Especially if he's not planning to report me or use it for leverage later? The latter still remains a possibility.

"So I can be prepared."

"For what?"

"You know…to watch your back. In case there's trouble. My informant figured I'm the closest thing you have to a friend around here. And I have to agree."

Epsilon has lost some of his initial eagerness and jubilance. He sits patiently, waiting as I process my thoughts. What comes out isn't what I intended to ask.

"Are we?" I ask, concerned that I've magnificently failed at being unapproachable. Also, why would he consider me a friend? I've never used any words beyond necessity with him, certainly nothing of value or kindness. He cocks his head, a slight smile creasing his features as he regards me softly.

"Yeah, I'd like to think so. I mean, you're still sitting here, right? And you haven't even punched me yet."

I turn back to my meal to hide the heat suffusing my face.

"An oversight I'll remedy shortly, I can assure you," I mumble. I don't need to see Epsilon to know he's smiling at me like a fool again.

"Well, at any rate, you did good. Real good. But watch yourself, okay? Not everyone here plays by the rules."

I scoff, now that we're back to familiar territory. If there's one thing I know, it's how the world works, particularly regarding rules and rule-breakers. I typically fall into the breaker category, not the abider. This whole following-orders thing is a new phase of my life.

"Your warning's noted. I'm fine. I can take whatever gets dished out. You don't need to concern yourself with my business, okay?"

That last part comes out cold, but I'd rather not drag a straight shooter like Eps into whatever base politics that I've instigated. I'm still hoping this will all be forgotten by tomorrow.

Sighing in what sounds like disappointment, he shakes his head, golden curls flopping before returning to their exact original position. In a single movement, he pushes away from the table. I watch blankly as he rubs his face before fixing me with a look.

"Just...be careful, all right? I know you're strong, but that won't always be enough."

He says nothing more as he slides off the bench. My eyes follow his retreat as he makes a beeline for the nearest exit without looking back. He doesn't push through the dense, chatting crowd—they notice him with smiles and greetings, clearing a path unasked.

Frowning, I note that he's left his food tray behind, untouched by the looks of it. Staring at my own, I'm no longer sure what to think. And I've completely lost my appetite for any of this mess.

THAT'S NOT ALL SAND, IS IT?

Present Day

[OMEGA]

My de facto second has decided to vocalize his disagreement with our new assignment at great length to anyone in earshot. I'm sure Rho is trying to be helpful and supportive. He flat-out is not. Of course, our temporary and well-opinionated teammate decided this was the perfect time to break his self-imposed silence and initiate an argument. I've been trying to ignore their back-and-forth, but it's nearly impossible when they're airing grievances over the team comms channel.

"...*it's the last place we need to be going. I don't get why they don't send an Alpha team.*"

Rho's tone has taken on that high-pitched quality that emerges whenever he's irritated. Surprisingly, that's an infrequent occurrence for him. Regardless, it grates on my sensitive hearing and already shredded nerves.

Tau's rejoinder is equal parts clipped and pointed. I notice his vocabulary severely minimizes when he reaches the fraying end of his proverbial rope. At least the Alpha's response is quieter than the gunner's. I don't think I could handle two obnoxiously loud whiners.

"*It is sensible to send a team deployed nearby to handle the request. Most teams are likely on assignment and not in ideal proximity.*"

Rho growls low, and I can picture him jutting his chin out—an infrequent affectation I've witnessed only a handful of times.

"*How close we are is only part of the equation. I don't know about you, but we've exceeded our deployment well over what's normal. It's been long enough.*"

Tau's tone turns indignant.

"*We serve the United Forces in whatever capacity we can, and this assignment is merely data retrieval. Nothing I would consider complex or tedious.*" There's a momentary respite for us unfortunate bystanders as the Alpha prepares to extend his tirade. I, however, am finished.

"Okay. That's enough out of both of you," I bark, overlapping the start of Tau's next point on his mental bullet list.

Both fall unexpectedly quiet, though I suspect that's more from surprise than intention.

"*This mission is simple enough even—*"

"I said, we're done!" I cut off Tau before he can start again and reignite Rho. I can't stop and face either of them, so I'll have to make do with yelling. Loudly.

"We've been given our orders, and we will execute them to the best of our ability. It's on the way, at any rate."

"*Sort of...*" Rho mutters loud enough for anyone with a functioning cochlea to hear.

"AND this is a good change from our typical mission set."

A flash of orange draws my attention to the ATC's dashboard, temporarily derailing my train of though. For a split second, I could swear one of the sensors lit up. I hazard a glance while keeping the remaining ninety-five-percent of my attention on the terrain ahead and beneath my tires.

There's nothing to see, though, and I dismiss it as a trick of the sun as it climbs toward its daily apex. The land around us has transitioned from hard-packed dirt and rock of the high desert to layers of pure sand. There's not supposed to be a desert here, at least not according to our maps and historical topography. It's yet another anomaly to consider when I have the bandwidth to do so.

Exhaling audibly through my nostrils and the open comms, I rein myself in.

"Okay. Can we keep it civil and, more importantly, *quiet* for the next half hour? You two have caused enough of a headache."

"*Hear, hear,*" Om cuts in, voice booming.

"*If you please,*" Chi adds sharply.

"*And thank you!*" Mu is the last to join the prevailing sentiment.

"*Fine. Whatever.*" The gunner sulks while his antagonist mercifully refrains from further commentary.

Sighing to myself, I return to the monotonous Zen of riding a high-end piece of state-of-the-art machinery through the middle of nowhere. The air registers a pleasant eighty-five degrees, skies clear and awash in a breathtaking crystalline blue. Almost the same color as Mu's eyes, if I'm looking for a local comparison. Of course, these soothing thoughts can only last so long. To be precise, exactly five minutes pass between one incident and the next.

Simultaneous to my bike's primary panel lighting up, a shrill alarm broadcasts in identical tones through everyone's comms. The resulting din is deafening and disorienting.

"Chi, what—" I begin to ask our resident scout-slash-navigator, only to stop myself mid-question. The answer looms before us, prominent and impossible to miss. A towering wall of sandy brown advances on our position. I've never seen a *haboob* in person before, but I've heard it described in idle chat by other Zeta soldiers with an incredible sense of dread and horror.

"*The HECK...?*" Rho's baritone rises in panic before his channel cuts out, ceasing mid-broadcast with an ominous crackle. The rest of the team follows suit, leaving the hollow echo of a dead comms line. With the looming wall of sand and debris bearing down, I lack time for anything but a desperate shout, hoping the others will understand.

"MOVE!!" I throw my ATC into a tight U-turn and push the electric drive to maximum torque. I'm prepared for most threats as a Zeta soldier, but apparently not everything.

In my side mirrors, I catch sight of the team neatly following my improvised exit strategy. There's nothing more I can do to brace us for the looming threat. The first wave crashes into our ATCs with enough force to nearly wrench the handlebars from my clenched fingers. Innumerable sand particles pelt every exposed surface, leaving nothing unscathed. As undulating violence visits us in relentless swells, visibility reduces to vague taupe and gray shadows. Even with my helm sealed tight, I swear there's the disconcerting crunch of sand between my molars.

My ATC, which was running smoothly moments ago, begins to falter intermittently, its solar-electric drive struggling as particulates clog the cooling vents and abrade exposed components. Our bikes are engineered for harsh environments and capable of operating in sandy, gritty areas for extended periods. But not like this. They're not designed to withstand a concentrated airborne assault of microscopic projectiles, nor are their riders. The rest of my team fares no better. As our formation disintegrates, my power cell protection circuits engage, shutting down the drive system as a massive coil of wind and sand rocks me sideways.

Eyes closed, teeth gritted, I feel countless granules of sand pelt my body. The relentless winds buffet me from all sides. My tenuous grip barely holds until, at last, the handlebars wrench free, and I'm flung elbows-deep into the loose sand coating the ground. My visor offers zero visibility, and all tech buzzes, fritzes, and falls utterly unresponsive. Removing my helm is NOT an option, though I may as well be suffocating within its enclosure.

It's nearly impossible to gain any movement, let alone forward progress, so I brace myself against the deluge on hands and knees. I finally struggle upright onto two feet, though the ground beneath seems determined to swallow me. My boots, hell, my entire legs disappear under half a foot of shifting desert.

Attempts to turn slightly and search for anyone or anything, get me nowhere. My efforts halt when something heavier than myself—though thankfully not as heavy as a bike—smacks hard into my front and sends me sprawling. For a brief moment, my helm takes my head for a ride as it hits the ground and rebounds. Something firmer than loose sand meets the back of my skull with jarring force.

Sluggishly, I flop around like a dying fish before managing to turn over and attempt to stand again. Palms flat, I brace against what should be solid ground but am shocked when it suddenly yields beneath me. My support vanishes, and I'm no longer in the storm.

A gray maelstrom of whirling sand and air engulfs me momentarily, then gives way to absolute silence as I plummet through shattered safety glass. The storm's roar is all but cut off above me as I crash through the unyielding darkness below.

—Ω—

PATCH JOBS

Light flickers into being. Hazy at first—nebulous in its random scattering. Lazy white resolves into starbursts of blue, drifting and merging to form a more solid expanse of color. My enhanced vision finally registers what I'm gazing at through the sizable, jagged hole in the vaulted ceiling—a tiny slice of cerulean sky beyond the dust-caked glass panels arching overhead like a distended rib cage.

Memory kicks in, trying to reconstruct how I ended up flat on my back, staring at nothing. The sudden throbbing in my head forestalls any attempts at a proper assessment. Wincing, I attempt to push myself upright, but even with my above-normal strength, pins and needles cascade up my arms. The chills that follow are familiar feedback from my body responding to an impact. It's not the first time, or will it be the last, of that I'm certain.

A shadow falls across my face, and my combat instincts flare before recognition hits. A few seconds pass as I stare dumbly at the goateed man gazing down at me until my scrambled synapses finally ID him as Rho.

"You with me now, Megs?" A sliver of a smile quirks up the corner of his lip, though his usual smartass demeanor is notably subdued. Probably because I haven't attempted to clock him yet. At present, it's a 50/50 consideration.

"Uh…yeah," I manage, attempting again to become vertical.

A solid arm loops around my lower back, supporting me the final few inches to a sitting position. My equilibrium lurches, and I have to shut my eyes against the wave of nausea that coils in my stomach like a shifting cobra. An odd numbness continues through my fingertips as I try to brace myself.

"Take it easy there, Omega. Thanks to our little tumble, you've got a decent concussion to go with that head wound. Good thing that skull of yours is reinforced, or the landing would've done more than knock you about."

I attempt to glare at his smiling face, though the effect is probably ruined by the bandage I can feel wrapped around my head. Rho's always been heavy-handed with field medicine. Either I scared him worse than usual, or he's being deliberately obnoxious. We all underwent the same combat medic training in Basic and Advanced.

Pulling off my right glove, I gingerly probe the rough edge of the nano-fabric along my forehead. The tender spot underneath suggests a goose egg that'll last a day or two, even with my accelerated healing. If we manage to find Omicron and the others, I'll never hear the end of it. The big man's protective streak is worse than Rho's.

Once my senses finish imitating a scrambled egg, I take in our surroundings. Floor-to-ceiling display windows line a manufactured cobblestone path, their surfaces almost completely blacked out by dust except for scattered fingerprint-sized spots of robin's egg blue. The layout is unmistakable—we're in an early-century mall, now buried beneath the newly formed desert above.

"What's our status?" I croak out once I'm reasonably sure I won't upchuck on my teammate.

"Severely screwed?" Rho's raised auburn eyebrow probably mirrors my own. I channel my displeasure into a deep frown, and he breaks our staring match with a low chuckle. "Communications are dead. Can't get a signal through all this concrete and steel. No sign of our bikes either."

He gestures at the rubble-strewn space around us, his lean face drawn with exhaustion. I wonder how long he's been down here alone with my unconscious body and his anxiety.

"The others…?" The words come out tighter than I'd intended.

"Just you and me down here, far as I can tell. Couldn't exactly go exploring with you out cold, but unless they landed somewhere else in this maze…" He trails off, worry evident in his tone. I feel it, too—a void where the rest of the team should be. Their absence pulls at my subconscious. It's strange how physical separation affects us.

"That's good," I mumble, surprising myself. But it's true—being trapped down here with Rho is bad enough. The last thing I need is Mu confined in an enclosed space. I know all too well how she handles that.

I'm still processing how our twenty-to-thirty-foot plummet through the roof didn't result in broken necks or spines, even with our modified bone structure. At least I no longer have to listen to Rho and Tau's endless bickering. According to Rho, I've been out longer than a few minutes, though my chronometer's too blurry to confirm.

A worn canteen appears in my line of sight. I take it without hesitation, gulping down several mouthfuls of precious water. I don't question its source. I'm grateful to soothe my throat, which is as dry as the wasteland above. After capping it, I wipe my mouth with my gauntlet's rough material.

As the fog in my head recedes, I focus on a more detailed assessment. Despite being almost completely buried, there's still reasonable light filtering through the damaged ceiling—hazy, like looking through stained glass, though that might be my compromised vision. There's no way to tell if the light corresponds to the midday sun I last saw.

"Obviously, we're not getting out the way we arrived," I say, pointing toward the ruined ceiling.

The gunner quirks an eyebrow at my statement and chuckles. "Yeah, unless you've developed some new modification I don't know about, we're going forward, not up."

I smile despite the sharp spike of pain. "Oh, I've got skills, but flight and super jumping? Not quite yet. Working on it, though."

"Yeah, you do that," Rho responds with a wink, humoring me.

I tap the comm unit at my collar, but I get nothing but static.

Rho shakes his head. "No good. We're too packed in here."

"Sure enough." I huff, processing our situation. Getting separated and stranded wasn't part of the mission parameters, but our priority is clear—get ourselves out and reconnect with the team. Waiting for rescue isn't an option.

"Alright, this is a waste. Let's go."

"Hold up, Megs. I don't think you're ready to move just yet."

"I've survived worse, ya...*you* know?" The stumble in my words doesn't help sell my case.

"Yeah, I know that, but you should still take it easy."

Strangely winded, I pause to take a deep breath, lungs expanding with barely a hitch. They're functioning better now. Between the combat stims and elevated pain tolerance, I'll manage. Though I need to check Rho over soon—I wasn't the only Zeta who took the plunge. Outwardly, he seems intact, but he probably landed on something softer than I did. Having two-hundred-plus pounds of modified soldier land on you would explain some of my extra aches.

His words percolate into my packing fluff brain as my body catalogs its complaints. Much as I hate to admit it, it looks like we'll do what Rho suggests for once. But only for a few minutes—what dropped us through that ceiling went through the rest of my team as well. Who knows if they fared any better just because we can't initially find them? And in this concrete tomb, we're sitting ducks if anything unplanned decides to follow us down.

I lean back against a dust-covered column, fingers absently checking my sidearms. At least they're still secure in their holsters. "Five minutes," I concede grudgingly. "Then we move out."

Rho's knowing smile says he expected nothing less. "You got it, boss. I'll start scouting our immediate perimeter while you get your head on straight."

I watch him move off with practiced silence, his cybernetic arm gleaming dully in the filtered light. Five minutes. Just enough time to get my body responding properly and figure out why my gut is screaming that we're not alone down here.

AS A LEAF IN THE WIND

A thinning veil of light trickles through the gap far above, a remnant of our unintentional descent. From my short-term observation, I notice with growing dread that the opening has already diminished in size. The uppermost portion of the ceiling has an upside down "U" shape, allowing sand and scrub to pile alongside it. It won't be long before this place is indistinguishable from the surrounding wasteland, lost once again.

Boneless, I sprawl on the mall's floor, I'm half-tempted to make dirt angels as I recoup. That impromptu nap killed some of my convalescence time, and I'm already feeling better than when I first awoke. It's not precisely A-game territory, but I'm a solid "C" for sure. Maybe even creeping up to B minus the longer I lie here, if I ignore the persistent tingling in my right hand.

Touching the throatpiece of my comms, I try yet again to get in contact with the outside world. Oh, and the rest of my team, if it's not too inconvenient.

"Hello? Anybody reading me, over?" Pure, clean static meets my quiet request.

"This is Omega Two Two. Does anybody read me, over?" I try hailing a little louder, though not by much. We're unsure of our present situation, and I'd bet my last ammo clip we're not alone. I've come to anticipate as much.

Sighing heavily, I give up trying to reach anyone for the time being. Shaking my head, although not too vigorously, I carefully roll up, opting to be fully upright once more. Meandering my way over to my partner in isolation, I appraise the other soldier. Rho sits cross-legged, entranced by whatever he's folded his long-limbed form around.

Within a few feet, I can finally make out the device he's so engaged with. It's a salvaged signal booster, probably from one of our damaged comms units. He's split the casing open along its seams like a filleted chicken, his cybernetic fingers methodically disconnecting and reconnecting a mess of copper leads and circuit boards. The precision of his metallic digits makes him our go-to for anything requiring fine manipulation of electronics.

Tilting my head, I quietly watch his actions, unwilling to interrupt whatever meager attempt is made to resolve this situation. I'm also currently of little use to our escape with my partially functioning brain. Voyeurism is as good an activity as any. Of course, I can only be idle for so long. I'm not wired to sit still. No more than a few minutes have slipped past, but it's enough to bore me in place.

"What are you doing?"

At least, that's what I attempt to articulate. Instead, the result is more like, "*Whachu doin'?*"

Rho's auburn eyes flick up to me briefly before returning to his work. I catch the corner of his goateed mouth quirk briefly in amusement at my ineptitude.

"Trying to boost our signal output. If I can sync the frequencies from these damaged units and amplify through the primary transmitter, we might punch through all this concrete and steel."

"You can do that?" I ask dumbly, more than a little surprised at his self-announced ingenuity.

"Yup. Or at least I can attempt to. Most of these components are still viable. Just need to reconfigure the gain and modify the antenna array." Here, he gestures more broadly around him, and I realize I must have been out of it longer than I thought. He's had time to amass a small collection of electronics and gut them.

"I have some backups I can swap out if this first rendition is a bust. Beyond that...?" With a shrug, Rho trails off.

"Good to know," I remark. Bracing hands to thighs, I straighten up and peer again into the gloom bordering our slim beam of light. I haven't laid eyes on anything out of place in our peripheral, nor would I prefer to. If I had my druthers, Rho's device would shortly come to life, successfully hail our teammates, and within the hour, we'd be back topside laughing this off.

When does anything go my way, though?

Sighing more to myself than anyone else, I rock back on my heels, idly looking around for something to occupy me. Hmm...Nope, not a thing. Welp. Moving on. Smirking, I employ the whiniest voice that I have in my arsenal.

"Rho, I'm hungry. Let's see if the food court has anything hot and ready."

The lanky soldier gives me a dubious look. I grin back at him, although it may be entirely spoiled by the wad of bandages encasing my cranium. A few seconds tick by as he lays the same flat stare upon me.

With the silence stretching on, along with the discomfort, I'm compelled to clarify. "Kidding. We can hang out here a little more and move on when...er...I'm good."

Even as I state it, I'm not entirely convinced we can stay put for that long. I've attempted to ignore it so far—dismiss it as some head trauma-related nausea—but there's something about this place that has my hair standing on end and my right pointer finger itching for a trigger. The numbness in my hand isn't helping my growing unease. My long-held paranoia is not something to be taken lightly. I've survived in a world where living is a daily challenge.

Listening to ingrained instincts is paramount to survival.

My gaze strays again to the space surrounding us as Rho's low muttering fades to background noise. Tall, vertical panes of frosted glass line the central walkway floor-to-ceiling. At one time, I'm sure their effect was quite attractive. Now, with no backlighting, they serve to disguise if something is wandering around beyond them. Talk about cozy. There's a shift out of the corner of my vision. Turning my head to face the area fully, my eyes narrow as I search for its origin.

"Fucking shit-ass outdated tech crap…"

Rho's diatribe continues behind me as I carefully unholster my sidearm, eyes never leaving the spot. Safety sliding off with a quiet *schick*, I bring the weapon to bear. Another shifting of non-existent light, and now I know it's not my concussion causing a trick of the eyes.

"Rho…" I murmur to him. My hackles are up and more than a little on edge.

"This better frickin' work. I swear." His voice goes up in satisfaction, and I hear a resounding snap as he closes the transmitter's casing.

Too late, I turn to stop him from what I know will come next. "No, Rho. WAIT!"

My hand is outstretched uselessly toward him as he glances up at me in confusion, precisely when a cacophonous squeal of metallic feedback pours forth from the two tiny speakers. It almost obscures the howls that rise in response. Almost.

—Ω—

BLUE-EYED MONSTER

Can I say that it's sadly predictable when none of what I'd prefer to happen comes to pass?

Rho's completion of his modifications is the only thing that goes according to plan. Apparently, his first and second attempts at creating a working signal booster yielded absolutely nothing. The third try is wildly successful and nearly gets us un-alived.

I don't have to tell Rho to kill the device. He fumbles with the makeshift booster, attempting to shut down the awful racket and nearly dropping it in his haste. With a frustrated growl, he gives up trying to power it down correctly and smacks it with his flesh hand to silence it. Not that it does any good.

Now that the feedback loop has started, it doesn't seem to want to be stopped. Aggravated and more than a little on edge, I stow my handgun, shoulder my way to where he's still cursing and fighting with the device, and grab it from his hands. Unapologetically, I hurl the damn thing away from us with all my might. It arcs clear to the other side of the room before solidly colliding with the wall, bringing a shower of electronic components and blessed silence along with it in a puff of smoke.

"What did you do that for?" Rho yells at me, red-faced and irate.

I make a face back at him, fighting the tremors that threaten to derail my focus. Maybe not my brightest idea, but at least it handled the issue in the short term. We're out of options.

"I took care of a problem." I snap back as he glowers, but ultimately concedes. Still doesn't mean he's happy about the lost opportunity. The rumbling groans on a fast approach are more effective than anything in redirecting our ire. Rho looks as unsettled as I am, having arrived at the same conclusion. We're going to have undesirable company in short order.

With no time for further retort, I unsling my rifle, as does Rho, and both of us backpedal in unison as we prepare for the imminent onslaught of Zee. Without the full strength of our team behind us, we're lacking viable options. Add to that a complete darkness that makes it nearly impossible to tell where one passageway ends and another begins.

The first five or six of the Zee round the corner at a brisk gallop. They slide, colliding into already askew displays, faded signage, and each other in their haste to get at us.

Giving the full three-hundred-sixty-degree view a once-over, I notice for the first time a dried-up, whitewashed fountain further back from where we were previously settled. It's only a few tiers high, but it's broad enough that Rho and I can stand atop it, hopefully out of immediate reach. Throwing an elbow at the taller soldier's side, he yelps more in surprise than any real pain, and I nod toward the neoclassical piece of statuary. He seems doubtful but still nods his assent.

We book it to the hallway's long-dead centerpiece without another wasted moment. I make as if to climb up myself, the tips of my gloves hooking onto the rim of the stone bowl, but the gunner rolls his eyes. An impromptu step is offered from intertwined fingers, and I am quick to accept the boost. No argument here. As soon as I am on the first of the two tiers, I reach back and grab his wrist. Rho's longish form is up with me in one swing, and together, we climb the last bit.

Now that we're temporarily out of range of the local monsters, I work to regain some semblance of tactics. The first creature from the mob reaches our location seconds after we're safely perched. With a garbled cry, it stretches all seven of its fingers toward us, hoping to grab onto whatever piece of us it can get. From this close, I notice the swollen joints and missing fingernails clearly torn from their beds. For whatever reason, that particular fact bothers me the most in this mess.

Thinking beyond the next moment is difficult. My mind is still a bit muddled and, thus far, incapable of forming an intelligent plan of attack. Thankfully, Rho steps up without being asked. Nudging me from my reverie, he points down the line from us. At first, I'm unsure what the gunner indicates, but then I catch sight of it. Our new vantage point sheds a little more light on the space's layout. I can make out a junction no more than ten yards away. It seems to split at least three other ways and is opposite the direction from where our first round of visitors originated.

"Come on!" Rho calls.

Grasping the back of my poncho's firm collar, he pulls me quickly over and down the back of the derelict fountain. After a fast and awkward shimmy, we make a wide arc around the Zee, putting the graveyard of used machinery from Rho's early efforts between us and them. Our light fades, then disappears as we sprint for all our worth down what seems to be an empty passage. My feet move on automatic, pounding rapidly as we work to leave the growls, snarls, and thuds of unfriendly bodies behind us. Sound ricochets along the walls and high ceiling, releasing into the dark beyond and masking any approaching dangers.

As we round yet another corner, I have to slow my trek or risk falling flat on my face. We've only been on the run for around ten minutes, and my breath is already short. The numbness in my hand has spread up my forearm, and my muscles aren't responding with their usual precision. As it is, I can only gasp, "*Stop!*" at my partner's retreating back.

Pressing a hand against the cold metal wall, I attempt to bring my breathing under control. Gaping like a landed fish, I'm clearly not in my best shape at the moment. Even as I take precious minutes to get my body under control, I strain to hear any indication of our pursuers. For the moment, we appear to be in the clear. I can't make out anything following our impromptu sprint.

Now, with a clearer head and less impetus, I'm shocked to find light in this section of the mall we've arrived at. Squinting, I can make out a narrow strip running between the juncture of the wall and the ceiling. The light is faint, but it's enough to allow for the definition of the space. However, the minute you step out of the pathway's middle, the light exponentially fades until you're back to being immersed in oppressive shadow and darkness. It's noticeably cooler here, as well.

There's the crinkle of material and a light thud as Rho leans against the wall, which is responsible for my still upright state. Weapon nowhere in sight, he sighs and gives me a measuring look. From the narrowed eyes and slight frown he's sporting, I can interpret what's being left unasked and unsaid.

"I'm okay." I quietly remark.

For the most part, the statement is accurate. I feel better than I did a few minutes ago and have made a marked improvement since then. It may have benefited us to stay put longer, but that option was summarily removed from the table.

Gradually releasing a breath, I venture away from my support and find the ground stable and my vision clear. As the gunner fixedly assesses me, I do my best to ignore his attention.

"Let's move." I intone low, with a jerk of my chin.

Rho stiffens as if to counter me, but instead, he lets it go with a nod. More methodically now, we continue our careful trek into unknown depths. My mind jumps and wanders, hoping that Rho and I are right in assuming we're the only ones from the team that ended up here. What if we just left someone or several someones behind? Maybe worse off from the fall than Rho or me? What if they're in a different direction, a different hallway than the one we chose? Shaking my head in frustration and a tiny bit of misery, I can't allow myself to get caught up in the 'what ifs.' Not while we're in a risky situation ourselves.

With cautious steps, we wander down the halls, looking for signs of a way out and maybe a bite of food. I hadn't anticipated long-term separation from my ATC by thirty-plus feet of ground. In hindsight, perhaps I don't need to feel so bad about being this unprepared. I'm not a Scout.

At the next concourse, we're presented with five other paths. I'm reluctant to go anywhere outside the main drag, just in case. We choose the least chaotic-looking option to venture forth with. It branches off the central corridor slightly, leaving me somewhat uneasy, but not terribly so. However, there are fewer signs of damage this way, both by time and persons. Hopefully, that's a good thing.

I can't imagine that any one section is emptier of Zee than another, but it's remotely possible, given their tendency to cluster. More than likely, we haven't been heard locally yet, and I will do my damnedest to keep it that way. Even with the lack of issues, it does little to prepare me for the next surprise.

From one moment to the next, an empty stretch of ground becomes suddenly occupied. A sole being stands unencumbered and unmoving in the middle of the walkway. Backlit by overhead lighting, the individual stands a good head shorter than I. Shock has nothing to do with what I'm feeling. Rho's silence speaks volumes to his amazement. Of all the unexpected discoveries to be had down here, a lone, frizzy-haired nymph of a child is not one of them.

FINDINGS AND FOUNDLINGS

I'd been anticipating an encore with our usual foe in all their slobbering, mangy goodness. Hell, I bank on it being a regular occurrence. This kid, however, this girl…is so young. She can't be more than twelve or thirteen years old. I don't know. I couldn't tell you my own age at this point. Not that it matters anymore.

The child's long, jet-black hair would probably have been straight and shiny in a different life. Lovingly maintained by a parent, the same as her day-to-day needs. Right now, she's a ragged mess of a person. Her heart-shaped face is marred with all manner of things. It does little to cover the fingernail-thin scars scattered across her forehead, eyelids, and sunken cheeks that no kid should have. She's thin, almost to the point of being emaciated, and her skin has such a pale pallor that it's clear she hasn't been exposed to proper Vitamin D for quite some time. In spite of all that, she's cognizant. And human.

But what does that mean? How is she alive? Is it possible that there are others like her down here that we missed?

I'm still standing, mouth open and catching flies, when Rho gives me a not-so-gentle nudge to the side. Well, I suppose it would be my side if I were as tall as he is. As it is, he practically elbows me in the breast, promptly snapping me out of it. Throwing a much harsher jab in retaliation, I quickly grasp the situation and tamp down the myriad of questions for the most immediate one.

Leaning down to make myself closer in height to the girl, I ask in a perfectly calm and reasonable voice, "Hey there. Do you need help?"

I'll admit it's a brain-dead question, but I'm out of practice with survivors. We rarely deal with them in our line of work—just their leftovers. There is a protocol, of course. It primarily consists of transporting them to the nearest UF base or outpost, assuming they even want our help. There's also the big assumption that they're adults who can make rational decisions for themselves. It's been a long time since any child has been found, alone and unchanged, outside of UF-controlled space.

The girl startles a little, hunching down as wide eyes flick around nervously. I wonder if she comprehends speech. I guess I was a bit loud. Whoops. More's the fool with me and not the less-than-experienced child.

"*O-kay*. Are you alone?" Her lips press tightly together, but still, no response is forthcoming.

"Is there anybody with you?" I try again.

Head cocked and face oddly nebulous, she still doesn't appear to understand me. The seconds tick by, and then her eyes clear. Slowly, almost imperceptibly, she shakes her head. A moment later, she repeats the movement, her head turning side to side in a clear and definite 'no.'

"Right." I glance over to my gunner and get an encouraging nod. His expression is tight, almost pained, and I can see his cybernetic hand opening and closing rhythmically at his side. Something about this child has him on edge.

"Well, I'm Omega, and this guy standing next to me is Rho."

I smile to the best of my meager ability, trying to project a pleasant and non-threatening image. It probably would be a hell of a lot more convincing if I weren't a highly trained Zeta soldier suffering from head trauma and on the run from the Zee.

"Do you have a name? Like us? Something we can call you?"

She pauses in consideration, head angling slightly to the side like a dog. I think she's trying to work through what I'm saying. A small and dirty finger taps against her lower lip in thought. It'd be cute without the cracked and blackened nails.

A tap later, she stops, and a look of concentration pulls at her features. A voice, hoarse from lack of use, hesitantly offers, *"Meh-"*

Her brows pinch closely together as she tries again. *"Meh-guh."*

Her face screws up in frustration as it's apparent that's not what she wants to say.

"Megan?" Rho's quiet baritone offers, his voice suddenly softer than I've heard in months. There's an unexpected gentleness there that catches me off guard.

She visibly brightens before nodding vigorously. Score one for Rho.

"Megan?" I repeat. Her mouth pulls into a smile at my recitation of her name. I smile back reflexively.

"Hi. Nice to meet you, Megan." I greet, and not disingenuously.

There's something surreal about being close to an actual, honest-to-God child. I can't recall the last time I was near one. At least a living one. Shaking that maudlin thought loose from its foundation, I continue as if nothing's derailed my mental processes.

"Rho and I need to find our friends. Have you seen anyone else like us?"

The girl, Megan, gives a slow shake of her head, eerie blue eyes never leaving mine.

"That's okay." I soothe again, giving her another small smile. "Do you know if there's a way out of here?"

I practically clap a hand over my mouth after those words are voiced. Idiot. I doubt this kid would still be here if she knew a way out. At least, I would assume so, but maybe that's not entirely true. How would a child find their way out of a buried mall full of Zee, let alone survive?

Her face crumbles, and an out-of-place and pinched expression replaces it. I have vague recollections about smaller beings and what typically follows those kinds of looks. I don't do tears. That sort of thing pulls at a part of me best left to rust with disuse.

"Hey, don't worry. We'll figure this out." I search my memory for a distraction before being inspired. "Ah! Are you hungry?"

That she responds to, immediately nodding with such vigor that I'm afraid her head's going to dislocate from her neck. Isn't that an awful visual? Rumpled locks bounce on bony shoulders, along with her eagerness.

Rho steps forward before I can even reach for my vest, already digging through his own pockets. "I've got something," he murmurs and produces a small packet wrapped in silver foil. His hand trembles slightly as he unwraps it, revealing what looks like a compressed fruit bar.

"They're better than those chalk sticks you call food," he says to me, a forced lightness in his tone. Then, to Megan, he crouches down, offering the bar with his flesh hand. "It's apple and cinnamon. Real fruit, dried and pressed. Not the synthetic stuff."

There's something familiar in his movements, a practiced gentleness that speaks of experience. When Megan hesitates, he breaks off a small piece and eats it himself first, then offers her the rest. Smart move. Showing her it's safe.

Rifling through my own vest pockets, I come across the wonder that is our MRE bars. I hesitate, as although packed with all manner of 'good for you' stuff, they're decidedly not the most palatable option. The thin coating of chocolate only manages to mask any flavor or texture failings temporarily.

There's another option, though a teeny, selfish part of me doesn't want to share. Oh well. Why not? Reaching into the pocket next to my MRE stash, I withdraw one of my last oatmeal creme pies. The hermetically sealed cookie crinkles as I tear a line down the side and turn it out onto my palm. Circular, brown, and rather flat, it doesn't look like much. Imitating Rho, I break off a piece and hold it out to her, ensuring my movements are slow and predictable. The last thing I want to do is scare the kid.

With another hesitant smile, she gingerly reaches out and plucks the piece from my fingertips. Bringing it to her nose, she sniffs at it delicately, trying to discern its nature. Whatever cue she's looking for, the girl seems to find it. Within seconds, the piece is devoured, and, with great relish, she sucks the remaining crumbs from those dirty fingertips. A look of pure delight crosses her face as she savors what must be a treat.

As she enjoys the small gift, I glance at Rho, sharing a small smile with my oddly quiet companion. His expression is distant, but his eyes remain fixed on Megan with an intensity that seems out of place. I nudge him gently with my elbow, and he snaps back to the present, reaching into his vest until he produces another couple of candy bars, holding them within my reach.

"I was saving these," he says quietly. "But this is better."

With some awkward shifting, I unwrap both bars completely before handing them over to the girl. Megan noticeably opens to the offering of processed food. Her face is aglow under the filth and neglect as she grabs each foodstuff without hesitation. The novelty of us being scary beings has worn off quickly enough. That and she's probably a meal or ten shy of starvation.

After locating a spare water container, I shake it, ensuring there's something worth sharing, before unscrewing it and handing it off to our new buddy. The three of us quietly take a seat in that cramped space, backs to the wall, all crisscross applesauce. As Megan munches happily on pieces of dry calories between gulps of water, I work to get as much information from her as I can. Her words come out slowly and stilted at first, but gain momentum and complexity the more we go back and forth.

"Do you know where you are?" I ask.

"No."

"How long have you been here?"

"Don' know. Long."

"Are there any others like you?"

"Don' think so. Just mama."

"Do you know when you last saw Mama?"

Megan pauses, fingers midstream to her next bite while her eyes go distant. We wait patiently for her to recollect what must be a challenging request.

"Mama was here."

Okay. I think I get it now. "Your mama was here when you got stuck, right?"

Her dark head nods resolutely this time. The girl offers clarification without my prompting.

"Mama left me and didn't come back. The monsters came, and I hid." She stops her happy munching, crumbs scattered along her cheeks like dusted stars. With her face turned down and her voice so low, I barely grasp what she says next. "Mama's been gone a long time."

I share a look with Rho. His jaw tightens, and he looks away, swallowing hard. After a moment, he turns back and asks in that same gentle tone, "How do you hide from them, Megan? The monsters?"

The question is tactical, but there's something personal in his curiosity. His fingers flex again, the cybernetic ones making a barely audible mechanical sound.

Megan looks up at him, her expression surprisingly knowing for one so young. "They don't see good. I stay quiet and small. There are places they can't fit."

Rho nods, a ghost of approval crossing his face. "Smart girl," he says softly. "Very smart."

This place has likely been in this state for a while, given the extent of decay and the substantial accumulation of dirt and sand above. This means that this child has probably been trapped here for an equal amount of time. That would put her at, maybe, three or four years old at most when this happened. It's scary to imagine somebody so new to existence left alone in a corner of hell. No one to defend them, comfort, or talk to them. No one to make the monsters go away.

Perhaps it's not so unusual that she's survived. Being small, quiet, and quick has its advantages. She still would have needed to understand how to survive, especially if the Zee are as mobile as they were for us. Another oddity. Perhaps there were other survivors like her in the past. Ones who slowly but surely became fewer and fewer.

Rho clears his throat. "We should move soon," he says, his soldier's demeanor returning, though his eyes still linger on Megan. "Find somewhere safer to rest properly."

He reaches out as if to touch her head, then hesitates, his hand drawing back. The moment passes quickly, but not before I catch the flash of something raw in his expression. Old pain. Very old.

Regardless of all these unanswered questions, there's no way we're leaving her. With that resolve firmly in place, I smile more sincerely at her upturned face, going so far as to pat the matted mass of hair on her head. I imagine it's been a while since she's had anybody in her world who wasn't trying to devour her. That's one thing I can fix.

—Ω—

NIGHTTIME RITUALS

I'm reasonably sure there's something sharp poking me in the butt. I'm trying not to fidget. Truly, I am. My partner, however, seems entirely at ease in our decidedly odd settings. Well, there are worse things to endure for safety.

Shortly after making our small offerings to the Megan, we were led to this place through a series of aborted words and various hand gestures. Based on the size of the space and the kibble hoarded away, it's hers and hers alone.

The location is a wise choice for a child to make, with the entrance tucked ingeniously along what was likely a maintenance corridor. With its abbreviated size, twists, and turns, it's unlikely that any Zee could manage its path. At least, not without causing a lot of noise and disturbance, alerting the room's occupants long before they were in danger. Based on the leaning pile of cleaning apparatus coated in grayish-white dust, I'd wager this area was primarily for custodial staff.

I'm possibly proud to say I had little difficulty getting through Megan's private entryway. It simply required a temporary separation from my vest. However, we did make adjustments to get Rho's ass through, having to shore it back up afterward. Hopefully, temporarily widening the doorway won't cause us trouble in the immediate future.

I'm unclear how we'll manage it, but the kid's going with us, assuming we find a way out. She's been on her own for quite some time, and reintroducing her to humanity will be interesting. Not that I'm looking to adopt. In no way would I consider myself good material for motherhood.

The girl's intense blue eyes follow me as I finally give up pretending to be comfortable and stand up, albeit stiffly. My right leg drags slightly as I rise, the pins and needles having spread from my fingers up my arm and now creeping into my lower extremities. I shake it out, hoping Rho doesn't notice.

Stepping from one side of her space to the other, I finally take a good look at the room she's squirreled us away to. The space has a bright and homey feel, helped along by what can only be working electricity. Perhaps this mall is one of those places that was equipped with regenerative energy. That level of technology was primarily applied to more affluent areas. The irony of having such rare and exorbitant technology for a lone child's usage.

Megan has decorated the walls as high as she could throughout the long, slim room. Not that the walls are particularly high. If Rho were to jump up and down, he'd probably smash his head into the ceiling. It's a temptation to have him try. I could use the levity.

Various pictures, both framed and not, as well as stuffed animals, adorn the inset utilitarian shelving. Trinkets she's gathered during her excursions, I imagine. After another scan of the shelves, I notice that nestled amongst all of her childlike items are books on various subjects. The expected picture books are haphazardly piled together, along with what looks to be engineering and science manuals. The latter seems less likely, but I've encountered stranger things, I think.

What's more striking is the systematic organization. For a child who's been isolated for years, there's a peculiar orderliness to her chaos—books arranged by subject rather than color or size, tools placed within easy reach of her sleeping area, containers filled with water positioned near the doorway. Survival requires adaptation, but this level of methodical thinking suggests something more.

Frankly, I was surprised that she even knew her name to begin with, as there hasn't been someone around to care to call her by anything. Then again, who's to say it is her name? Thus far, the child has relied primarily upon gestures and body stance to express her thoughts and emotions to us. Despite that, it's apparent she knows words and speech. Perhaps she was old enough to have experienced interpersonal communication before everything went sideways. I doubt she's had another soul to communicate with, and the Zee are notoriously poor conversationalists.

From what she has been able to articulate, there's a reasonably sizable horde roaming the halls. Lately, she thinks she's run into fewer, as if their numbers have been steadily decreasing. I'd venture they've run out of whatever there was to consume around here. That still doesn't leave me with a good feeling. We've already witnessed far too many active Zee here that would require a steady food source. By all rights, they should have succumbed to rot and decay long ago.

The more time we're around her, the more I get an inkling that something's off with the kid. I mean, I get it that she's been in complete isolation, dodging who knows how many cannibalistic monsters without a savior or salvation in sight. But there's more to it I can't precisely say what, just that it's a feeling. For whatever reason, this child lived while everyone else died. Survivors are peculiar by default.

As I continue my idle musings while wandering, I spot a simple purple brush atop one of the shelves. Picking it up by its cool, smooth handle, I turn the small plastic item over. The whimsical flowers of its design have almost entirely worn off along the back as if it's been stroked regularly. Looking at the amalgamation of knots that make up Megan's hair, I kind of doubt that she's been using the tool as intended. But who am I to judge, right?

A small, pixie-like face tilts to the side as she watches me handle the item. Smiling as non-threateningly as I am physically capable of, I attempt to beckon her over. At a minimum, I can help her out with some of her bedhead issues. She hesitates at my invitation, clearly unsure of me and the brush. Not that I'd blame her. I wouldn't want anybody making my hair their business, either. I say as much to her.

"Heya, kiddo. I was thinking maybe I could help you out a little?" I nod toward the nest encircling her head. In some perverse way, I liked it when my mom brushed my hair out as a kid, even if her sorting out the recurring snarls along the underside of my mop brought tears to my eyes.

"You know," I continue as if she's responded, "My hair used to be as long as yours when I was younger. Maybe longer."

Her eyes comically widen as she impulsively reaches for my sheared locks before quickly aborting the gesture. Snickering arises from somewhere behind me, and I resolutely ignore it. Thank you, Rho.

"Yeah, I know." I continue, ignoring my current partner in crime. "I used to like my hair nice and long, too."

However, that's not exactly a functional hairdo when you're fighting Zee on a regular basis. One of the first things I did as a Zeta soldier was to divest myself of such frivolity. My mind briefly flashes to the wagon train girls with their ridiculous braids before I push the thought out of my head.

Megan stares at me blankly a moment longer before her expression transforms into a determined sort. With a firm voice, she states, "Oh-kay." Her pitch is no more than a breathy whisper.

Since she's still seated, I opt to plop myself down and gesture her back toward me and the space I've left between my legs. She hesitantly turns and crawls toward me, stopping just shy of where I sit on the ground. I do my best to be patient and encouraging, patting the floor in front of me in invitation.

"I don't bite much." I grin at her a little impishly.

Megan briefly considers me with another head tilt. I must pass whatever test is in her mind as she closes the remaining distance between us and sets herself gingerly in front of me. Her mass of hair is pushed over a shoulder and into my waiting fingers and the tines of the brush. Starting at the bottom, I gradually endeavor to separate gunk from strands. I do my best to ignore what the stuff in between is composed of as I work to avoid yanking or pulling.

After the first few minutes, Megan's shoulders fall from their hiked position, and her head obligingly leans against my strokes. Trust. It's what exudes from her now. This young thing has no one to depend upon or take care of her. Even with my psychotic team, there's reliance and dependability. As the brush slides through long black hair, I glance to where the gunner sits, quiet and still, lost in his contemplation of the room or somewhere far beyond it.

Rho notices my scrutiny and meets my eyes with an expression that solemnly asks, *What's next?*

I raise a shoulder, meaning *I have no fucking clue.* Shaking his head, he takes a bite from the bar of fruit leather he's had in hand since he sat down.

Once all the gnarls are out, I tap Megan's head lightly, eliciting a flinch before she regards me inquisitively with her vivid eyes.

"How about we do something to keep your hair out of reach of those pesky Zee?"

She smiles hesitantly and nods, perhaps interested to see what I will do.

My fingers fumble slightly as I separate her hair into three pieces at the top. The precise movements are initially challenging. Perhaps a bit out of practice on my end. Carefully weaving long strands into a hopefully tight braid, I kind of Zen out. It's not as though I've had somebody to do this to in a long while. I remember braiding my doll's hair when I was little, and later, braiding the hair of some grade school friends. High school, however? I would have been more likely to be dyeing someone's hair an ungodly shade of metallic pink or helping with a DIY cranial tattoo. So, yeah, it's been a while.

In no time, I've got a long plait tightly pulled from the back of her head, leaving a braid hanging just below her shoulder blades. At that point, I realized my lack of planning, coupled with my impulsivity, didn't account for anything to use as a hair tie. Frowning, I scan the shelves for something that fits the bill. Surprisingly, Rho comes to my rescue, holding out a small, black elastic to my questing hand. With a mumbled 'thanks,' I take the proffered piece and wrap it around the end of the braid tightly, once, twice, three times before releasing her hair.

"There you are," I say, with a light pat on her shoulder. "All done, and you're ready to go!"

Turning, she tries to get a look at the finished product. As she does, it flips from one side to the other, cleverly evading her sight. Chuckling and feeling a bit lighter in my chest cavity, I root around in one of her piles of stuff until I find something mirror-like. An old metal plate, perhaps sterling silver from a bygone era, that's tarnished black and slowly spiderwebbing inward along the edges, will do the trick. I hand it to her before holding the tail end aloft to allow her to see as much of my masterpiece as possible. Her response is well worth the time spent onboarding. A soft smile as she touches it tenderly, almost reverently.

Our night finishes with a bowl of simmered MRE bits, painstakingly chopped up to make a partially coagulated but completely edible meal. I'm unsure what else Rho might have thrown in, but anything can be made into a passable Zeta stew with the addition of suitable protein. Belly full, I tuck myself compactly into a corner, opting to sleep on my side. An abnormal position for me, but the situation requires it. Rho does the same by placing his back against the opposite wall, so in the end, he's facing toward me. His deep blue vest serves as a passable pillow.

Our current circumstances leave me hesitant to sleep. As it is, I allow myself to rest as much as possible while remaining alert. It's not that I don't trust the kid. It's the overall oddness of this situation. Rho seems to be of a similar mind based on the noticeable line of tension along his shoulders. He may be less concerned than when we first fell here, but his hackles are still raised like mine.

My sight loses focus, and the dimly lit room smears into various splotches of muted color as I give in to my body's fatigue and drift. My last clear thoughts are of my team and the fervent hope that wherever they are, they're safe. I stumble through a broken sequence of half-memories and fabricated illusions while sashaying in and out of a light doze. I may have had a dream about something important. At least, I'm left with that sense upon awakening.

Without a segue, adrenaline floods my system, bringing instant awareness along with it. My right hand fumbles for my weapon, fingers slow to respond as I try to curl them around the grip. The delay is subtle but alarming—I've always been quick on the draw. Consciously halting my body's natural progression, I take measured breaths to maintain the rhythm and illusion of my sleep while giving myself a chance to awaken fully. Eyes slit open only a fraction to let in the twilight glow encasing everything. The young girl's figure lies impossibly still in sleep. Soundless, inert, and so deathlike, I have to strain to catch a slight rise in her chest.

That settled, I switch my gaze to where my partner slumbers. Rho's garnet eyes are partially open, catching and reflecting the soft blue-white light of the room. I'm not the only one who heard something. The pressing question is, what is it? Then I reencounter it—scraping and scratching—like something being dragged against metal. Whatever monstrosity it could be, it's big and moving deliberately down Megan's tunnel. That's all the confirmation I need. With a slight nod to the gunner, my body tenses in preparation for a fast response.

A quick tuck and roll places me dead center in the room, both handguns drawn and ready, though my right arm moves a fraction slower than my left. The rustle of cloth and metal that follows my sudden movement halts behind my kneeling form. I don't waste time confirming Rho's placement or readiness. I anticipated as much. Our abrupt motion startles the third occupant of the space into wakefulness. I shake my head slowly, attempting to stave off any forthcoming sounds from the child. Not that I need to worry. She's not exactly your standard youth.

Megan shrinks into her pile of rags, eyes made more prominent by fright. A subtle shake of my head emphasizes the need for her to stay in place, just as I catch more shuffling. Eyes darting to one of the many vents that border the room, I try to gauge where trouble is most likely to strike from. This time, the sound's closer and less muffled.

A huffing noise has both me and Rho swinging around in sync toward the far end. Breathless, we wait for whatever is to come.

Weapons cocked and ready to rain down hell at a moment's notice. A few seconds pass, then a minute. Finally, the wait is over, and the grate closest to the girl's homemade tunnel opening pops open, allowing a large form to fall through and into the room. I take aim along my rifle's sight, an infrared dot lighting up the white and gray back of a...marsupial?

Without consideration, my rifle sags as I stare in wonder at the ugly snout sniffing around our space, utterly oblivious to the five-star danger it's placed itself in. I can't tell you the last time I saw a scavenger like this, particularly alive and well. Especially so friggin' close I could reach out and pet its matted white fur.

"Well, I'll be damned." The gunner murmurs, and I'm inclined to agree. "It's a 'possum."

"That's o-possum." A higher-pitched voice breaks in behind us. The tone, while still soft, is full of confidence and a wee bit of conviction.

I raise an eyebrow at Rho, and he does the same, barely holding back a laugh. I swallow my humor as well. I doubt if our charge would appreciate our mirth at this moment. Not as she stands there, stern-faced and deeply serious.

"You're right, Megan." I accede. "It's most definitely an opossum."

The creature turns toward Megan, its beady eyes fixing on her with what almost seems like recognition. She makes no move toward it, but her stance relaxes.

"Friend," she says easily, moving past us to retrieve something from one of her organized stashes. She pulls out a small plastic container and removes the lid, revealing what looks like dried fruit or scraps of some indistinguishable meat. The opossum approaches her without hesitation, taking the offered morsel from her outstretched palm.

"You've been feeding it," Rho observes, lowering his weapon entirely.

Megan nods. "Helps me. Doesn't come when they're around."

I exchange a glance with Rho, and the pieces fall into place. The opossum's appearance wasn't random—it's part of how she's survived. A natural alarm system, moving through spaces too small for Zee, its absence a sign to her of danger nearby.

"Clever," I say, genuinely impressed. "Very clever."

As the opossum finishes its treat, it turns and disappears back through the vent with practiced ease. Megan watches it go, then turns to us with those unnervingly perceptive eyes.

"No danger now," she states with certainty. "But soon. We should go when the light changes." She points to the overhead lighting, and I can only assume she's measuring the transition between days by the system's built-in night cycle.

Eyes narrowing, the child's casual words set me on edge. Is there a pattern to these Zee? I always assumed their movements were more random than not. I holster my weapon, flexing my stiff fingers to get the blood flowing. Rho catches the movement, his eyes narrowing slightly in concern, but thankfully, he says nothing.

Morning can't come soon enough. We need to find our team and get out of this concrete tomb. But first, we need to figure out how to bring Megan with us. Something tells me leaving her behind isn't an option—not just because of basic human decency, but because this strangely resilient child might be the key to our survival in this buried hell.

—Ω—

SHOULD HAVE BEEN A TECHIE

I squeeze through Megan's narrow tunnel, my gear pushed ahead of me. Better me first than Rho—there's far too much of him to get through here in a hurry, and I stand a better chance against any errant Zee.

Light filters in ahead, casting the wall in chartreuse. After a quick sensory check reveals nothing nearby, I shove my gear through the grimy plastic sheet that serves as a door and follow with my head and arms. The hallway beyond stands empty and predictably foreboding.

"All clear," I call back, voice just loud enough to carry.

I quickly rearm, the familiar weight of my vest and weapons grounding me despite the odd grip sensitivity I can mostly definitely attribute to my concussion. M4 at the ready, I scan both directions before detecting Megan's approach.

The girl exits like a ghost—silent and smooth, carefully avoiding contact with anything. Rho, in stark contrast, sounds like a rhino plowing through wind chimes as he struggles through the narrow passage.

"Can you be any more awkward, Rho?" I mutter as he finally emerges, red-faced and panting.

Megan presses close to me, her luminescent eyes scanning for threats. For a moment, they catch the light with an almost animal-like reflection. Odd. Even odder how well she's handling this darkness.

Rho says nothing as he focuses on reassembling his gear. Once ready, I signal our direction to Megan with quick hand gestures. According to her, there's an exit on the far side of the mall—one she's tried to use before but lacked the strength and height to manage.

With Rho and me helping, we all might stand a chance of escaping this tomb.

The air thickens as we progress, growing humid and heavy with decay to the point where I might as well be breathing through a sieve. Particles drift through our tactical lights like errant mist out of a ghost story. My modified vision struggles to penetrate the gloom, forcing me to rely on instinct and Megan's uncanny sense of direction.

Our movements are deliberate and cautious, pausing at the slightest hint of movement. The girl remains unnervingly silent— not a single childish sound escapes her. Survival has changed this kid fundamentally, reminding me of something I heard back at base about the children in UF outposts.

"*They're like shells, man,*" a Beta team soldier had said, eyes distant. "*They stand in corners watching but never doing. Freaked me out.*"

The shadows, deep and dark, can hide anything, including Zee. I keep expecting an ambush or attack from the direction of any one of the numerous vacant halls and doorways. Thus far, we've managed to move through unmolested. That could change at the drop of a pin.

An innocuous breeze with no origin passes by my face, kissing my cheek gently as it slides by, bringing along with it a stench far worse than anything I've encountered so far. Reminds me of that slurry of muck lying stagnant at the bottom of a pipe. That's not a good sign. It means rot, and a lot of it.

Proceeding left even slower than before, I'm confused when our path appears to be a dead end. Gritting my teeth, I'm about to comment, and probably not in the kindest way to our young guide, but my rifle's tactical light catches something several yards off. Moving the narrow beam more intentionally, it bounces off a partially eroded sign advertising God knows what. Squinting, it takes me a moment to realize the hall doesn't entirely end so much as T-sections. In my defense, at first glance, the lightless void gives a good approximation of unending nothingness.

Now, more sure of our adjacency and placement, I creep toward the juncture, pressing myself as close to the wall as possible. I venture a half step before the corner of my left shoulder guard halts my forward motion, momentarily catching against an unseen object protruding from the wall. My momentum stops a minute too late. I catch myself against the plaster as it crumbles with a sharp crackle magnified by the silence. Swallowing against a suddenly parched throat, I brace myself alongside the others, hoping the echo doesn't carry.

Eyes closed for a second. I willfully rein in my rapid heartbeat, slowing my anticipation as I look for any indication of what might lie ahead. For the time being, nothing Zee-shaped appears, so with a nod of my head to Rho, we raise weapons and continue our painstaking progress.

The second-floor railing rises hauntingly out of the gray, extending out on either side like limbs missing a central torso, only to stretch into the darkness before fading out entirely. The front and center are on an open mezzanine level. The vaulted space is reminiscent of where we began our journey, but different in that it lies entirely encapsulated by total darkness. It wouldn't be the worst thing if the lack of good lighting were the only issue. I, however, anticipate running into things down here on the far worse end of the spectrum.

Understanding arrives the moment I'm a few feet from the railing, and I hurriedly raise a silent fist, my partner halting immediately, along with the child trailing him. There are a lot of bodies moving around down there. A lot.

I can't yet see them, and hopefully, they can't see us, but man, I think we found where the rest of the mall crawlers went. At least the ones not heaped into piles of bones and filth along the outskirts of the space, awaiting the slow process of degradation. Now that we're directly confronted with the open space, all the mindless shuffling, groaning, and panting are amplified, bouncing along the crumbling, rust-smeared walls. It's almost overwhelming to consider what this noise level implies.

Practically holding my breath, I step back, inching toward my companions. I don't stop until my back impacts with the girl's more diminutive form, forcing her to press back until Rho stops her. I want to be sure as hell the silence does not carry our sound, or else we're going to be very thoroughly screwed.

"Rho." I hiss harshly under my breath. "There is a shit ton of Zee up ahead."

In our joined muted light, his eyes dilate behind his visor, glancing over my head as if he can somehow confirm it from here. Almost simultaneously, he frowns, but not for the reason I would expect.

"*Language, Omega.*" With a stern tone and tilt of his head at our cohort.

Rolling my eyes, I ignore his correction and continue with the more pressing matter. "They're below us. I think we're fine for now. They didn't see me."

Flipping my faceplate up, I catch the little girl's eyes as I direct my next question to her.

"Do you know if the exit is on the top floor or is it on the lower level?" I say with more force in my delivery than I intended. Stress will do that to you.

She shrinks back into Rho's larger form, clutching at him for a breath or two. Slowly and carefully, he places his flesh and bone hand on the top of her head, stroking her hair gently. The action serves to calm her down and settle me as well. Staring up at his raised faceplate, he gives her an encouraging smile. Almost shyly, she presents a small hand and points to the mezzanine space, which is more southern of our location and distinctly lower.

Crap. Well, that might explain why she hasn't succeeded in escaping. My hand goes to my forehead automatically before sliding down my disgruntled face. There is a genuine need to take a few deep, calming breaths before I venture forth a response.

"So...we need to get past whatever is down there to have any chance of getting out?"

It's more confirmation than a question, but still, she nods meekly in response.

"All right."

At this point, I need that mental break. Sliding down the wall until I'm firmly seated, shorter legs sprawled in front of me as I contemplate how the hell we're going to get out of this.

Tick, tick, tick. The metallic cap of my gloved fingers clips out a monotonous tune on my shinguard as I mull over what the fuck we are going to do.

Sighing as well, Rho gingerly steps away from Megan's cowering form, seating himself in front of me. Through the dark fringe of my bangs, I take in my quasi-second's understandably concerned look.

Arms and legs crossed, Rho considers me before his sharp profile turns to the source of the racket echoing hungrily down our long, empty hall. His multi-day scruff-covered jaw flexes involuntarily as he more than likely clenches his teeth, a look of deliberation gracing his hawk-nosed features.

Not for the first time, I take note of a faint, crooked line crossing the bridge of his nose. A noticeable break, long since inflicted, that always leaves me wondering when and how he gained it. Not since I've known him, so before then. Probably at least before Zeta, as the scar is pretty apparent, and our wounds tend not to leave much in the way of marks. I only have a question of how long before—prior to his arm, or perhaps at the same time?

I know he's thinking about the same thing I am. How do we get past a horde of this magnitude and survive in the end, preferably with all remaining limbs attached? It seems unlikely in my estimation. Or maybe that's coagulated pessimism eking out of my head wound, which has reasserted itself once more. In case I forgot, Rho is many things, even some of those good, but a medic, he's not. Not even a second-rate field medic.

With the obscene number of Zee occupying that space, there's no way Rho and I can get past those creatures without some serious hardware. But it's our only way out of here lest we want to end up like Megan—permanently trapped in an underground Zee mall, eating rat soup on a regular basis.

Don't get me wrong. Rho isn't the most horrible of companions to be stuck with at the end of the world, and please don't ever let me voice that aloud in his presence. He can be mellow, thoughtful, intelligent, and overall enjoyable to engage with in a snark contest. However, notable distractions aside, I may have a slight touch of claustrophobia, and this contributes to it in a not-so-good way. I'm also a dyed-in-the-wool hermit.

What I wouldn't give for an innovative way out or a sizable distraction. If Chi were here with her kit, I could rely upon her taking out a chunk of the enemy and producing a shiny new hole from which to escape. I estimate that at least a couple of hundred creatures are trapped in here with us. Granted, they're not in prime condition. They can't have had much to feast on lately, but they are still mobile and numerous enough, which will cause a real problem for us shortly.

My head dully throbs as thoughts spin in an unending cycle of 'what ifs.' It's bad enough that we're separated from the team and our newly acquired resources. I've avoided focusing on it too much, but at some point, we'll run out of ammo and food. There's a finite number of rounds to be expended, and I lack the confidence that they outnumber the Zee here.

Our best option would be to avoid an all-out confrontation and slip away discreetly. I'm a little fuzzy on that latter bit, having not laid eyes on the—at this point—mythical exit. As it is, I huff and irritably shift, yet again, getting an arched mahogany brow from Rho in commiseration, though nothing else of use.

I grumble mulishly, more to myself than those with me. "What's the chance there's an ordnance bunker hidden away in this mall?"

Megan's brilliant jewel eyes look at me questioningly and more than a little confused. I doubt "ordnance" is in her vocabulary. She opens her mouth to attempt some helpful reply, but I wave her off. An apology is already on my lips for saying something trite and of little value to our situation. Fully expecting a sardonic rejoinder from my counterpart, I turn to Rho only to find a thoroughly thoughtful expression on his countenance.

Frowning, I smack his unprotected thigh to get his attention. The resulting slap is obscenely loud in our gloom, and I hitch my shoulders up in reaction. Rho gives me a corrective glare, his lower lip jutted out, and I am quick to do the same in return.

Sighing, he lets it drop before leaning back and deftly flicking a pocket knife open, materialized from somewhere on his person between forefinger and thumb. In one smooth movement, he closes it, only to repeat the whole process in a steady loop.

"Maybe there's an electronics shop or something here? I mean, there's some unspoken rule that all malls have to contain at least one store with a bunch of noisy, flashy crap, right?"

Turning toward me, I realize that the gunner is mostly serious with his seemingly rhetorical question. I try recalling if we passed anything of the sort on our trek here. It's a bit of a stretch considering that when the Zee ran roughshod over this part of the country, most stores were merely places to sample goods and services. There wasn't an actual inventory in-store to speak of. I'm certain Rho is privy to this.

I scrape my memory for any details that might be useful. There's one that stands out to me, though I'm unsure why or what its value is.

"There was some kind of toy store two halls back. Could that work?"

The gunner lights up, slumped posture straightening and inadvertently emphasizing his height.

"Yeah! That'd be perfect. Give me ten minutes. Fifteen tops."

I try to picture the merchandise that might still exist there. Catching Rho's attention, I crook a finger to get him to my level.

"What exactly are you thinking of inside that pointy head of yours?"

"I'm thinking I can create some real craziness and, hopefully, buy us time to find our way out."

There are too many unknowns. I'd rather not have my second split off and run into who knows what trouble. It's bad enough having lost contact with most of my team. I can't afford to risk losing Rho, too. Frowning, I'm about to lay down the law and firmly disagree when Rho surprises me.

"Look, just stay here. I'll scope it out and see if there's anything worthwhile." Holding a hand up to forestall any reply on my part, he continues. "Have you ever hotwired an electric car? No? Okay, let me handle it."

Of course, that raises the counter-question, '*Have you?*' I debate arguing, more so for the sake of stalling than to gain insight into some miraculous solution. I know it's a wash, though. Rho's suggestion seems the most plausible at this point.

"Okay. Just, you know. Don't die."

—Ω—

WANTING SHINY THINGS

I feel each second pass as if I'm watching the face of an analog watch, the second hand jerking around in its predictable slow rotation around the dial. The absolute silence is killing me. That, or my nerves have finally blown out from the overall stress of the situation we find ourselves in.

Something softly alights against the back of my glove, and I start involuntarily. Megan stares back at me, face open and expressive. Her arm moves toward my glove, though this time, she telegraphs her movement slowly. Two smaller, dirt-blessed hands reach up to cradle my single fist. I don't know if she can feel the minute tremors that, for whatever reason, are sporadically assaulting that hand. The look she bestows upon me is imploring. I understand the expression and what she's trying to convey in such a simple gesture.

Sighing, I brush a couple of loose strands of hair from in front of her face, neatly tucking them behind the shell of a delicate ear.

"Don't worry. Rho is many things, but you can count on him to do the job."

I do my best to give her a reassuring smile filled with a confidence that I don't quite hold. Being a competent soldier can only get you so far in this business. The rest might as well be pure dumb luck.

Closing my eyes briefly, I lean back into the cool metal sheeting of the wall and reflect on that. Unbidden, a memory rises to the surface, crystalline but wobbly like a water droplet. It balances on the edge of my mind before letting go and solidly landing.

I was ten when I first saw it, gleaming in its display case in my father's study. The blade wasn't particularly ornate, just a military-grade combat knife with a serrated edge near the hilt. A Ka-Bar, as I would later learn in the United Forces. A fairly standard piece of military weaponry. All I knew was that I wanted it more than I'd wanted anything.

"*Every Guerra needs something dependable,*" my father had said, catching me staring at it. "*Something that never runs out of ammo.*"

"*Can I hold it?*" I'd asked.

He'd considered me for a moment, stern expression never wavering, then he opened the case and almost reverently lifted the knife out. "*Respect the blade. It's not a toy.*"

It was heavier than I'd expected, but it felt right in my hand, like it belonged there.

"*When you're older,*" he'd promised, "*it'll be yours.*"

I didn't know then that 'when you're older' would be after he failed to come home, and my world imploded.

Sliding out my Ka-Bar from its sheath along my leg, a slight turn reflects the meager light in our space. Even now, that feeling of emptiness in my heart where my parents once were is still there. It's never left. This knife was one of the few things I took with me. One of the only objects to survive from one life to the next. And my dad was right. In this game, we're playing with the Zee, there's no telling what can occur from one moment to the next. Having a weapon that never runs out of ammunition is key. But now, *I* am that weapon.

A scuff of feet has me jolting upright, rifle at the ready and aimed unerringly at Rho's center mass. In response, his empty hands slowly raise to shoulder height. A smile meant to disarm and reassure is firmly fixed in place. With a scoff, I settle down and lower my weapon, slinging it back over my shoulder and returning to my rapidly cooling seat.

"What took you so long?"

"Oh, you know. I had a little window shopping to do. And one thing led to another, so, well…*ta-da*!"

At that, he holds a mishmash of tech aloft. The item, in all its entirety, fits neatly between his two palms. I have no idea where he could have had it stashed when he first returned. I guess some things are best left to be a mystery.

"And what the hell is that?" My doubt is palpable, as is the letdown to Rho at my less-than-enthusiastic response.

"It's our new noisemaker. See, I got the idea from the radio earlier. I focused on recreating, then amplifying that same sound."

"Since it worked so well the first time?" He's kidding me, right? Rho wants to attract the Zee to us.

"Well, yeah." Shifting it around so that he can show me the device's opposite face—I wouldn't call it the back, per se. "See? I added this part here," he says, juggling the lump in one hand while pointing to a strange cylindrical object with the other. "To serve as a timer of sorts." We can set it to whatever delay we want, plant it elsewhere, and let the noise draw out the crowd."

My gaze wanders the hall, wondering where precisely we'll place Rho's miracle machine. I'm not keen on being in the horde's line of shuffle, even if it gives us the opportunity we need to escape. The Zee are notoriously unpredictable, and I'm unwilling to place any faith in assumed behavior on their part.

"Okay. One question." I hold up a finger in front of his face. His eyes cross and focus on it briefly before darting back to me.

"Shoot."

"Don't tempt me," I warn, voice dropping in not entirely an empty threat. One of these days, I might decide to.

"You know what I mean." He sighs, rolling his eyes with an added tilt of the head.

"Okay. Assuming that this device actually works, where the hell are we going to place it to avoid being trampled en masse?"

Rho's confidence falters for a heartbeat. Good to know I can still puncture his bubble of optimism. Then he's turning, hauling out a brightly colored mass of wires from a satchel I missed him placing on the ground.

"Been working on that," he says, fingers already weaving through the tangle. "We can hang it off the banister of the wing behind us."

"I suppose that could work…" I hedge. I might eat my words later.

"Could?" He prompts incredulously.

"*Probably* will work?"

Snorting, my partner stands up, a hand on his jutted hip. Doing a fair imitation of our currently absent and notedly sassy teammate. "You got a better plan that doesn't place us front and center in the buffet line?"

Shoulders hike up momentarily in a half-assed apologetic surrender. I know I'm being unhelpful. Frankly, I'm tapped out between my headache and the entirety of the situation…and I'm hungry.

I study his contraption again, finding myself reluctantly impressed.

For all his showboating, Rho's instincts in the field rarely steer us wrong. It's why he's still alive—why we both are.

"If you've managed to build something half as loud as that last one…"

Rho smirks, "Well, it shouldn't disappoint, but I can't guarantee how long the batteries will last."

That's unnerving. "So, any actual estimate on how long we'll have?"

Rho's auburn eyes flick up and to the right, humming to himself as he puts a bit more brain power into calculating it.

"One hour. Two tops. Assuming it doesn't meet an untimely death."

"Or us, for that matter," I grumble, slumping dejectedly. "Terrific. I guess we'd better find that exit in a hurry."

"Were we ever not?" Rho inquires, sarcasm dripping from the statement. I shake my head but agree that it's at the core of our overly simplistic plan. No gray area there.

"Sounds like we have our path forward." I interlace my fingers above my head, elongating my seriously compressed spine and getting both shoulders to pop.

Turning to where Megan still sits wide-eyed but unmoved and silent, I crouch to gain her attention. Her utter stillness is eerie, as is her blank expression and invisible focus. Brow furrowing, I reach out gingerly and give her shoulder a light push. A few slow blinks follow, and from how her face changes to something less doll-like, I can tell the girl's fully present again. No evidence as to where her mind had fallen so profoundly a moment prior.

"Hey, Megan. Are you okay?" Bright eyes blink at me owlishly, but the girl nods in agreement nonetheless. Her eyes stray to the far end, where our destination awaits, before swinging back to me.

Grinning, I choose not to remark on the girl's space out. "That's good. We have a plan. Just stick by me. Okay? It'll be fine."

She gives a relaxed smile, and I return it. I swear this is the most smiling I've done in years. Creepy if I think about it too hard.

The corridor behind us stretches like a throat, waiting to swallow us whole. Rho checks his makeshift timer one last time, nodding to himself. I can practically hear the gears turning in his head as he calibrates his plan.

"Remember," I whisper through our comms, "Five minutes. In and out."

He winks, though I barely catch it through his visor. "You know me. Stealthy as a cat."

"A three-legged one, maybe," I mutter, but he's already moving.

Megan tugs at my sleeve, her eyes questioning. I lean over to her level. "He's going to make a loud noise far away to distract the monsters. Then we'll run the other way."

She nods, seeming to understand more than a child her age should. Sometimes, I wonder what's going on behind those electric blue eyes.

I watch Rho's silhouette fade into the darkness, the bundle of wires and tech clutched to his chest like a precious gift.

—Ω—

AND IT COMES UNDONE

A soft crackle in my comms pulls me back to the present.

"*Package is set,*" Rho's voice comes through, slightly breathless. "*Making my way back now.*"

"Copy that."

Megan's small hand slips into mine, and I give it a reassuring squeeze. Her fingers are surprisingly strong for someone so small, and her grip is precise and unyielding.

The seconds tick by in agonizing increments. Three minutes pass. Then four.

"Rho, status?" I whisper, tension coiling tight in my chest.

Nothing but static.

"Rho?" A rare edge of urgency creeps into my voice.

"*Almost—*" His transmission cuts off abruptly, swallowed by a burst of interference.

"Damn it." I rise to my feet, pulling Megan up with me. "Change of plans."

I reach for my sidearm despite my earlier hesitance about using firearms. Rules change when teammates are at risk. The familiar weight settles against my palm, a lethal extension of my will.

Before I can move, the corridor fills with a high-pitched wail—not the sounds of the Zee, but something mechanical and piercing. The noisemaker has been activated, though whether it was by Rho's design or by accident remains unclear.

Seconds later, Rho comes sprinting around the corner, his long legs eating up the distance between us. His cybernetic arm gleams faintly in the dim light, hydraulics whirring almost imperceptibly as he adjusts his balance.

"*Time to go!*" he shouts, unnecessary given the cacophony erupting behind him.

I grab Megan and run, not waiting to see what follows. The sounds of shuffling and moaning intensify—the horde is on the move.

"What happened to the timer?" I demand as we round a corner, voice sharp but controlled.

"*Had to improvise,*" Rho pants, fingers tightening around his weapon. "*Got cornered by a stray. Manual activation.*"

We burst through a set of double doors into what once was a food court. The vast open space offers no immediate hiding places, just a graveyard of overturned tables and abandoned retail kiosks. Our footsteps echo across the tiled floor, and each sound is a potential beacon for the horde at our heels.

Megan stumbles, and I scoop her up without breaking stride. Her slight weight barely slows me down, though the muscles in my arm protest with an uncharacteristic tremor.

"You said this would work," I hiss at Rho as we duck into a service corridor.

"It is *working,*" he replies, slamming the door behind us. "*Just not exactly as planned.*"

Awkwardness aside, I push forward until I catch sight of an overturned kiosk. It's no more than a ten-by-ten, highly glorified box, but the angle it fell at leaves just enough room to jam some bodies under it. Hopefully, there aren't any under it to begin with.

"Here!" I direct my partner, sliding to a stop before the gap.

With firm hands, I push Megan underneath before waving Rho to follow. He backs in, barely clearing the gap between his girth and gear, the servos in his right arm whining as he contorts himself into the confined space.

The roar is now ahead of us and growing louder. Hundreds of them, maybe thousands, all drawn to Rho's noise maker. But for how long? Zee aren't known for their attention span, and once the novelty wears off, they'll return to hunting anything with a pulse.

Not a moment too soon, I slide my rifle in with a quick "Rho!" before shoving myself in feet first. I'm almost prevented from reaching the space, though my issue is less my overall body size. No, it's my friggin' front and the pair of things that cause more harm than good. With an almighty push against the floor, I clear the opening, halting when my body collides with another.

Large hands grasp my shoulders from behind, stabilizing me and preventing any additional noise or movement. In the pitch-black of the tiny space, I can make out where the two other occupants are sitting and how they are positioned. My breaths come as rapidly as theirs, panting like caged dogs awaiting an execution. I make no motion to remove my helm, even though I want to. Better to roast in it than risk attracting unwanted attention.

The parade begins, a macabre march of ruined shoes and fractured feet overlapping in their haste to get at the noise's source. The stench of decay seeps through even my helmet's robust filtration system, a cloying miasma of rot and stagnation.

Megan carefully leans away from her side of our makeshift den, where she landed closest to the parade of monsters. Every instinct she has must be screaming at her to move. I want her to as well.

But it's too late. We all know that. Instead, the girl denies that strong urge to put as much space between herself and death, and I, in turn, resist the desire to put myself bodily between her and our enemy. Rho's hand tightens on my shoulder briefly. A reminder not to do anything remotely ludicrous.

I don't know how long we huddle within those bare few feet of shadowed space. Time stretches into an elastic thing, measured only by the rhythm of shallow breaths and thundering heartbeats. We wait, listening as Rho's noisemaker coaxes every Zee with working hearing into its sphere of influence. One misstep by a Zee will land it at our doorstep, and there is no room for error. The device's wailing continues uninterrupted, and I'm grateful for that small thing going right.

It gets to the point where the rumble of bodies pressing by lessens, then altogether ceases. Oh, I can still hear them just fine. No enhanced senses are required to pick up on the thriving rave in progress around the bend from us. But at least our section now appears to be unoccupied.

Cautiously, I raise my left hand and tap on the knuckles of Rho's still-grasping one. I do it once to get his attention, which he replies to with a single tap to my shoulder guard. *'I'm listening.'* I follow with five more synchronous taps, pausing before I tap one last time, this time with a firmer touch. Solid. *'Five minutes, we go.'* He taps once again in confirmation before resuming his stillness.

Our gambit appears to pay off. No further beings wander our way, and our distraction continues doing its job. Gingerly slipping from under Rho's hold, I rock into a crouch where Megan sits balled up, arms around her knobby knees and head tucked down within their circle. She's attempting to make herself as absolutely insignificant as possible. I try not to startle her when I lightly brush an arm to gain her attention. Her dark head shoots up in surprise. Rubbing her arm to offer comfort, I stop and place my hand palm open, fingers splayed against her chest. I press lightly. '*Stay*.' I feel her shift at the silent order, nodding once in understanding.

Smiling, although it's lost on her between the dark and my helm, I creep toward our gap, carefully stretching out flat on my stomach, then flipping onto my back. Sliding the last few inches to the opening, I grit my teeth at the scraping of my gear, but it can't be avoided. There's no way in hell I'm taking it off. Eyeballing what I can see in the surrounding space, neither my eyes nor my sensors detect anything. Feeling braver, I push my head and shoulders out and gauge the area. Besides some drifting dust motes and the putrid stench of decay, there's nothing out of place. More secure, I pull the rest of my body out, holding a hand down to the opening as I keep a constant bead on the surroundings.

Rho obliges, pushing my gun into my groping fingers. Swinging the barrel around, I seek a target for it, but come up empty. Sighing in momentary relief, I quietly call to the other two, "Clear."

Belatedly, I realize the girl probably has no clue what I mean, but no matter. With Rho at least understanding my instructions and exiting, she follows without question. Beyond us, the frenzied sound of breaking glass and tearing metal tells us the horde has reached the noisemaker. They'll be occupied with it now, but I'm not waiting to see how long.

"We need to move," I say, ushering Megan toward the double doors. "Find a way down through the concourse to the first floor, then we're out."

Rho nods, his voice unusually serious. *"I saw something when I set the trap. Something...different."*

I pause, one foot into my stride. "Different, how?"

"The one that I ran into was standing completely still. It's why I didn't pick up on it. Like it was waiting...for something."

A chill runs down my spine, the kind of visceral warning that's kept me alive this long. "That's not possible."

"I know what I saw, Omega."

The banging on the service corridor door grows more insistent. Zee have never been known for their patience, and the ones that didn't follow the noise maker have found our scent. We don't have time for this discussion.

"Later," I promise. Kneeling slightly, I flip my faceplate up to whisper-speak to our charge.

"Okay, Megan. We're moving back the way we came to get downstairs to the exit. I'm going to lead." I place a hand to myself, then point to the gunner. "And Rho will follow. I want you to stay in between us, alright?"

She nods fiercely, her electric blue eyes locked onto mine with unsettling intensity. There's something in that gaze that doesn't match her petite frame—something older, more aware. I push the thought aside. Glancing up at Rho, I take in his roughened, dirty self. I imagine I don't look much better these days.

"Ready?"

"As I'll ever be." He gripes, wincing at the joke. Far be it from me to call him out on his poor attempt at humor. Now's not the time.

Without further conversation, we're on the move. I keep my steps light but quick, placing each footfall with deliberate care. I have no idea what we'll encounter and how well we can rely on our diversion. As we near the T-section, I slow, holding a closed fist up. Drawing closer to the wall but wiser about contact, I slowly stalk the rest of the distance, pausing every few feet to listen and feel.

At the junction, I can tell some Zee are upstairs with us. Their grunts and mindless shuffling remind me of a stray dog seeking some scraps in the trash. Although they sound further away, I'm not taking any chances. A glance around the corner confirms they're all lurking at the end of the hall, looming around where I imagine Rho's device currently resides. This subterfuge may work yet.

Opening a hand, I wave Rho and Megan over. The minute they're right behind me, we hurry down the open walkway parallel to the foyer. Making as fast of tracks as possible, anxious to get out of the clear, I'm happy to lay eyes on some odd formation jutting up from the bottom floor. At some point, I imagine it stood almost as tall as this building, centered on the lower level, reaching up toward the skylight. At present, its form is twisted and unseated from its foundation, and the metal and glass are askew and broken as it leans heavily against the balcony. But it's our way down, it would seem.

Throwing Rho a thumbs up, I jog the remaining distance to look over the rail and better judge the reality of our bridge out of here. At inception, I imagine it must have made for something eye-catching, particularly with light hitting those large glass panels. The remaining intact ones are about half the size of me and vaguely feather-shaped. They'll be more of an impediment for us with their slick surfaces and weak materials. Not the most reliable of handholds. The metal scaffolding encasing the glass plumage may do the trick instead. Each bar is as wide around as my forearm. I hope it will hold at least one person at a time. For starters, that person will be me.

Pulling myself over the railing but still, firmly on the balcony, the steel toes of my boot tips hang out precariously over the shaded oblivion below. With a careful shift, I settle the rifle between my shoulder blades before twisting around to gingerly grab the first set of horizontal bars I can reach. I take a moment to locate Rho's form, still on guard, and send him a quick comms.

"Okay. I'm giving it a go. If this holds, follow me down with the girl. If it doesn't, well…" Eyeing the distance between here and there, I figure I at least won't die, but it'll leave a mark.

With Rho's weapon still leveled and seeking a target, I catch the sharp nod of the gunner once in confirmation.

"Sounds good. Be safe. Pretty sure you're not supposed to fall on your head more than once a week."

Frowning, I almost rise to the comment, risking my death grip to give him the finger. Instead, I opt for the grown-up route, swinging my mass solidly over the guard rail and onto the structure. It creaks ominously, echoing loudly through the space, and I give myself a moment to adjust. The dust that coats every flat surface leaves the metal unsurprisingly slick. I have no time left to hesitate, though, and therefore, I push ahead. In this case, down into an even darker domain.

Through my helm, each breath rasps like some winded goat. I ignore it to watch the ground below me for any movement. Any. I'm not picky in this aspect. It appears that whatever latent energy kept the upper level lit and running doesn't extend to the downstairs. I'm ten feet out when my grip falters, and I slide another foot on a single hand before I can catch myself. Now breathing heavily, I scout the floor lying directly beneath my dangling heels via the crisp green of night vision. It's relatively clear of debris and wandering Zee, so I figure the hell with it and opt to take the shortcut.

"Dropping the last few feet," I inform Rho quietly, not waiting for his response before I let gravity carry me the rest of the way down.

Knees bent to absorb an otherwise jarring impact. I manage a seven-point-one out of ten landing—just a little wobble at the end, but not enough to disqualify me. Quickly, I pull my rifle forward and scan the space three-hundred-sixty-degrees around. My slow spin highlights more of the storefronts, which are mainly blocked by cluttered areas and upended chairs and benches. Probably a few tables of a sort thrown into the mix here and there, too. The utter silence is disquieting, as is the lack of bodies. There should be at least some sign of human remains. Skeletons, handbags...something. Gritting my teeth against what's become a familiar uneasiness, I hail my teammate.

"Okay, Rho. It's clear. Get your ass down here pronto with the girl. I'll cover you."

As I complete my statement, I scan the area for a higher point to watch his six. I settle for one of the overturned seating arrangements as the obtuse angle provides just the right point of view for my purposes and maybe a little extra height to boot. Briefly, I tap into the audio feed and increase its sensitivity to just this side of bothersome. We can't be caught off guard by something unexpected. Not now, when we're this close to making our great escape.

The awkward structure before me suddenly shivers, and a glance up its plane confirms the tall soldier is descending steadily. A smaller form clings like a limpet to his back, face buried into his poncho's folds, and I'm amazed at how well Megan maintains her death grip. Then again, given the twenty-foot drop at their backsides, it makes sense. My second seems unconcerned with the steep decline, carefully placing each hand and foothold. Watching him climb down, I'm envious of how effortless the man makes it look, even with all six feet plus of him.

I hold my judgment until he plants both feet solidly on the ground, bending enough to allow the more petite girl to slide off. Head half-cocked to the side, I say nothing as he turns to face me. Taking in my stance along with my silence, Rho prompts.

"*What?*"

"What, what was *that?*"

"*What was what?*" He sounds more than a little confused.

"That." I helpfully elaborate, freehand waving to the avant-garde mess of an art installation, then to his person.

"*Oh, yeah. I used to rock climb for fun when I was a teen.*" He states, unholstering his primary weapon as he scans the area beyond me, simultaneously taking in the new space.

"Fascinating."

It's not.

Dismissing the gunner in the next moment, I hop down from my perch before crouching in front of the child, waiting patiently in the almost absolute dark. Even without my night vision, she's unerringly focused on me. There's no way she should be able to perceive where I am in this oppressive black. Reaching out slowly, I grasp a bony shoulder and find that she doesn't so much as flinch.

"Hi, Megan. Are you doing all right?" I keep my tone light but my voice low. There's no sense in projecting our new location to the local populace yet.

She nods silently, intent on my unlit faceplate. Without making another sound, I hold my hand out to her on a hunch. Confidently, she places her smaller one into mine without being prompted. With a gentle tug, I stand, guiding her to hang on to me but remain slightly behind.

Waving over Rho, I wait until he's beside me to ask, "Any clue which way?"

Turning to stare down first in one direction, then another, he quickly pivots and faces the original path.

"*I think this is the right direction.*" He raises a single finger to point down the hallway furthest away from our entry point and the noisemaker. "*My helmet registers a change in temperature and some air movement. Based on what the kid showed us, the main entrance should be at this end of the level.*"

"Well, that's a relief." I allow my shoulders to sag along with the world's weight momentarily. Straightening up, I feel a renewed sense of purpose. "Let's go. Keep all your senses open and on full alert. We'll follow your lead."

"*Roger that, boss.*" I don't have to see the smirk to know the gunner's sporting it.

Moving Megan's hand to the back of my belt, I place it deliberately there, patting the material a few times before she takes the hint. Slender little fingers wedge between rugged nylon and the lower portion of the flak vest, grip solid. Nodding more to myself in satisfaction, I take a few steps until we're directly behind my partner. Tapping his shoulder guard to let him know we're ready, he nods once, and then we move briskly.

Rho faces one side of the aisle while I scan the other, switching occasionally. The gunner steers us around the worst damage for the most part while we scan continuously for anomalies. I've moved from amazement to distinct concern when the girl doesn't make a single misstep. There are no mistakes as she sidesteps every loose bit of stuff.

All that moves in this stillness are the three of us in our awkward train. Time and darkness stretch before, undefined in their obscurity. I don't know how far we travel, nor for how long. The only certainty I have is when my chemo filters register a change in the nature of the air surrounding us. Of course, there are more obvious signs as our steps slowly and gradually come to a halt.

Tilting my head back slightly, I observe where the high ceiling joins the arched endpoint of our journey. It's readily apparent that outside this part of the wall, the desert, left to its own devices, has all but consumed the front of the structure. The way is thoroughly encased, save for some errant pinpricks of light alluding to the outside world. At some point, several of the upper windows gave in to the outside force pressing upon them, allowing high piles of sand, rock, and other bits of nature's debris to spread from floor to ceiling. Time, water, and everything else have made it into a solid wall, but it's not impregnable. Not to this Zeta soldier.

For a moment, there's a lump in my throat that spreads through my chest, feeling akin to an inflating balloon. Until we were standing here, I lacked faith that we'd find a way out. Now that we have it, the result seems almost too easy. But you know what? I think I'll take a more leisurely route any time over our usual shit. Thumbing my faceplate up, I turn toward Rho. His broad grin greets me, apparently feeling the same rush of relief that's overcome my common sense in full.

"Alright! Let's get out of here." I speak as quietly as possible, though my disbelief threatens to pull a much louder cry of amazement from me.

My partner nods eagerly, turning to find a weak spot to work on hollowing out as an exit. I move at once to join him, but am stopped within that first step forward by a harsh tug on my arm.

Glancing back at Megan in surprise, I attempt to gently bring her after Rho's retreating form but find it akin to shifting a boulder.

The child can't be moved. Not will not. Can't.

—Ω—

WHY DIDN'T WE DO THAT FIRST?

The display of strength temporarily paralyzes me. Only for a moment, though. All that suspicion, those inklings of something being amiss with the child. They all merge and congeal into the knowledge that this girl is somehow Zee. No, that's wrong, too. She's more like us. Zeta. But how can that be? Rho's words from earlier cascade through my mind. The Zee are mindless—that's what makes them predictable. The thought of them working together, being led.

As the realization dawns on my face, it's likely put on full display for the girl. The smaller hand within mine turns and grips ever so firmly. Stunned, I attempt to dislodge her hold and find myself caught in a vise, unable to shake her off, at least not in a kindly manner. I could break the clutch, but I'd break the arm too.

"Megan." I remain resolutely calm, hoping to project the same calmness to her. "Let go, please."

Cold rage unexpectedly breaks across her doll's face as it pinches into a dark glare. Those brilliant blue irises dangerously flash as she shifts her footing and attempts to draw me more toward her position. Shit. This can't be happening.

"Megan." My voice rises unintentionally in a slight panic. I sense Rho shift in response to my tone and the warning vibes I'm undoubtedly projecting. He's probably only noticing now that we have yet to join him. "Megan, you need to let go. You're hurting me."

It's a partial truth. If I were a civvie, she'd probably have crushed a few bones in my hand by now. As a Zeta soldier, I'm made of much sterner stuff. I can also take much more punishment than this kid can dish out. Hopefully.

"You can't leave." She intones in perfect English but lacks emotional inflection.

I grimace but hold my ground. I may be able to salvage this.

"I have to leave. I have a team waiting for us. For you. You can come with us outside." I want to say where it's safer, but I can't bring myself to speak the words aloud.

"No! I don't want you to leave! You're...*different*. The others all listen when I tell them what to do. Why don't you?" Her wild eyes are imploring and earnest as if I'm some puzzle for her curiosity's sake.

The realization hits me like a physical blow. She's controlling them. Somehow, this child is inexorably tied to the cries of bloodlust reverberating behind her.

"I don't know what you're talking about, Megan. We've listened to you, haven't we? There's a lot we've shared with each other." She holds still a moment, and I can see her visibly parsing my words.

But just as quickly, that spark deadens, and her expression drops into a state of utter neutrality. It's as if someone has cut the power to her. It's also eerily reminiscent of the face she made earlier when she was so still and felt not altogether here.

"I won't let you leave." She finishes with utter finality, and I feel the chill of her words crawl up my spine.

"Rho?" I hedge uncertainly, with more than a little dread coloring my voice. He's at my side in a couple of strides, sliding to a stop directly next to me.

Without taking his eyes off the child, he murmurs to me, "What the hell is going on?"

Feeling partially insane, I reply from the corner of my mouth. "The fuck if I know."

"You have to stay." The girl ominously repeats, not registering Rho.

That may be my saving grace as he immediately seizes on her smaller wrist and pries fingers like bands of iron open enough for me to wrench my hand free. We both freeze as a long, mournful howl echoes along our floor. The silence afterward is stark in contrast. This disquiet lasts a heartbeat, then two. On the third, our ears are assaulted by a cacophony of cries in unison. Too many to judge an actual body count. I know, without actually seeing, that somehow the Zee have entirely forgotten our little diversion and are coming as one toward us.

Backpedaling quickly to Rho, I hook him around the waist with an arm and set more distance between us and the girl. My second, in all his asinine wisdom, seems to have realized the problem before I did. He's ready and willing to change our objective. Grabbing me by the arm, he doesn't hesitate to quickly remove me from the space and toward the end of the line. I have no idea what's being brought down upon us, but I do have an inkling that it's something that we won't be in a position to walk away from.

"Uhm. We need to get out of here. *Now!*" He all but yells, bodily propelling me toward the exit.

My gaze is finally broken from the third individual planted like a statue in our space. I scramble up the mound of debris, shoving fingers into whatever handhold I can. I scale the steep, crumbling hill, fighting for purchase. What Megan truly is, I'm out of my depth on. Every instinct I possess screams at me that she's the real threat and that we have to get away. Ultimately, I may be powerless to put an end to that danger. An untapped sixth or seventh sense chooses not to focus its collective attention on the utter wrongness radiating from Megan in surging waves.

With the tiny human posturing behind us, my partner and I do our best to remove the sloping pile of debris that impedes our escape. Concrete, asphalt, dirt, rock, and even some dead hedges are all mashed into one another and, through time's unending cycle, have become a solid partition. Wedging my fingers into whatever crevice I can, I look for purchase on the more substantial boulders in the vain hope of putting a dent in this mess. Even with the layer of protection afforded by my gloves, my nails disconcertedly flex and give as I work to tear a hole into the blockade. I can't find it in myself to care. We need to get out of here, and if the sacrifice is the dire need of a manicure, so be it.

Between my breaths and Rho's, I hear the Zee's approach peripherally. The sound climbs in ferocity, along with that dreadful stench. I made the mistake of removing my helmet to hear Megan earlier, so there's no buffer between my enhanced sense and everything else. Even as the noise level and the smell rise to an oppressive miasma, taking on a form of their own. I can't justify taking the extra time to put it back on from where it's hooked uselessly to my belt.

"Don't leave me." Megan's pleading words echo at our backs from somewhere far below.

It's a child's voice, but all wrong—too measured and calculating. As if understanding exactly what we'll respond to best. It's empty and cruel. She has yet to move, but even from where she stands, the intensity of her ire is unsettling. Rho's shoulders are hiked up as if doing everything in his power to avoid turning around. Fighting that compulsion is the same for me.

This kid will give me some new nightmares, and that's for sure. Hell, this whole incident will linger like one long, bad dream if we can make it out alive.

Rho takes a broken piece of pipe and wedges it into a crack, working to pry out a larger chunk and make headway on our hole. Desperately, I grab onto the end with him, offering my strength to force the mass over. The ache in my shoulders has yet to dull into something to be ignored, but I endeavor to push it to the side. I have no desire to tear something that will limit my mobility. However, it's better than dead.

Loose debris cascades around my wedged-in boot toe, partially burying it, but I press on, refusing to give in. Rho huffs, and I catch the sweat running down his brow from my side vision. He shifts his grip with a quick shake of his head to temporarily clear the fluid from pooling in his eyes. With the change in position, his right arm and the force it provides, combined with my inherent strength, are enough to free some of that goddamn rock.

"Watch it!" I shout, pulling Rho's taller form into mine as the boulder tumbles down, along with a lot more rocks and shit. Still no light, though. Cursing, I turn to scope out the next place to try for when a godsend voice crackles through the air, radiating from our helms.

"kssh...meg...kssh...a...hear...kssh...me?" Our radios blast to life, both Rho's and mine in synchronicity.

"Omega...Rho...can you hear me? Are you reading?" Mu's chipper voice has never been more beautiful than at this moment, singing through the air and the silence.

"Holy shit!" Rho says, and I can't help but echo with the same surprise. If we have their signal, it can only mean one thing—the team is nearby. At least close enough that they might be our saving grace. Backing away from Rho, I slide a few inches down the wall before grabbing a handhold to settle myself.

Flipping on the commlink in the lower half of my jaw, I don't bother with the pleasantries. "Mu. Fuck where are you?"

"*Oh my god, Omega! You're okay!*" Her jubilation echoes throughout the chamber. Loud and bright, and oh so happy to hear us. I can't say that I'm not feeling equally relieved.

"Mu, we're trapped underground. I don't know where we are to you, but we're finally getting a signal, so you've got to be on top of us. Can Om read our location?" I hear some background noise as Mu probably, hopefully, confers with the others. At least, that's my hope. I didn't bother asking if everyone else was alive.

She pops back on. "*Okay, Omega. We've been looking for you. Oh! We found your bikes. Omicron has his reader out. Just hold tight.*"

I roll my eyes skyward at that. What else are we supposed to do? Pull out some knitting needles and make a scarf.

"Yes," I grit back into the line. "Can you please hurry it up? We're about to be thoroughly dead."

Rho guffaws at that, but it's a relieved laugh, full of joy and not fear of our impending doom, so I let him get away with it. This time. Thumping his shoulder in commiseration, as well as to bring him back to the ugly present, I attempt to hail my demo girl while we wait.

"Hey Chi, can you read me?"

"*Yes, Omega. It is good to hear you two are still among the living.*" Grimacing to myself at how close that statement is to the truth.

"Yeah. For now. I'm assuming you're somewhere in the neighborhood above us. We're definitely in need of a hot exit, and now, or your previous statement will be moot."

There's a pause and some minor shuffling noises. I assume the scout has dismounted her ATC and already begun making preparations for a boom.

"*What are we working with?*" She inquires, all focus on business.

"Best guess, we're buried under a good seven to ten feet of desert. We're at one end of a decent-sized mall. The ceiling is approximately twenty feet high. Rho and I are barricaded in this mess. Everything's been compacted to all heck from time immemorial." I continue scanning the area we're attempting to dig out of, but my confidence in a self-directed escape is waning.

"*Sounds problematic.*" She pauses, although her mic is still active. I catch the mumbling of low voices before the demolitionist returns. "*Omicron has your position. We are almost directly above you.*"

I sag in relief before relaying the news to Rho. He doesn't pause in his excavation, but his expression speaks of a similar satisfaction.

"So, can you drill us an escape route?"

"*About that,*" she hedges. "*I do not suppose you have some way to shelter in place?*"

"Not particularly, unless we feel like shacking up with the horde."

"*Right. Well.*" Chi clears her throat in what I realize to be uncertainty. It is not the best impression from the person in charge of blowing up the space directly above one's fragile skeleton. "*I recommend moving as far from your current location as you can and having your dampeners on at full strength. I am going to do my best to contain the blast, but this is both sand and a solid surface I am pushing through.*"

"Understood." A screech echoes high and long down the hallway, just beyond where Megan still stands, affixed to the ground in the exact position that we left her in. Eerily still, and eyes positively glowing. Something about that gaze is compelling, almost as though she's trying to speak through it. I see her as if from a greater distance. Her tiny hand is clenched into a hard fist, veins bulging from the strength of that grip. For one so lean that you'd think a breeze could blow her away, she radiates power and authority.

My vision tunnels so that it's just her and me. Even Rho's presence directly next to me fades as I try to decipher what is going on in the girl's head.

"*Omega!*" A voice practically yells in my ear, jarring me out of whatever stupor I had fallen into.

"What?"

Chi sighs long and loud, more than irked about something. "*I said to brace yourselves. I am set up, and we are ready whenever you give me the go-ahead.*"

"You got it. Give us a minute to hide in plain sight."

"*If you please. Not to worry, I have all day.*"

Rolling my eyes, I jerk my head to the side. "C'mon, Rho. There's a hunk of pipe with our names on it."

Gingerly, both he and I shift to the wall a good ten feet back from our poor attempt at escape. We both do our best to anchor ourselves to the exposed plumbing. I take the extra precaution to hook my arm around it as well. The last thing I need is for my grip to falter right now. I have no idea if it'll work, but it's the lesser of two evils, right?

Now's an excellent time to refit my helm, and with a quick flick to close my visor, it seals tight. Pressing an external button along the side of my helm, the surrounding noise ceases, leaving me with nothing more than the whirring buzz of my helm's internal fan and my excited breathing. Turning to my taller partner, I pat the top of my helm twice and give a thumbs up. He repeats the gesture, and I don't hesitate to pull the trigger. We're out of time.

"We're ready. Do it, Chi."

"Roger that. See you on the other side."

There's a pregnant pause, possibly for dramatics and to ensure we dangle, but who knows? And then Chi speaks that thrice-blessed call.

"Fire in the hole. Fire in the hole. Fire in the hole."

Being beneath the effects of an explosion is probably one of the more exciting things I've experienced. It's also something I never want to have a front-row seat to again.

Having worked with Chi for many moons, as well as several other demolition specialists during my tenure in the United Forces, I've been around my fair share of explosive charges. Mainly with some protection, but there have been those rare instances when there was little between my fragile being and the aftereffects. I was prepared both mentally and physically for the initial concussion blast, punching into me with the force of a super-charged Omicron fist to the chest. The pressure clears my head and sinuses in one fell swoop. Rho and I were far enough from the explosion site, gear cinched on while braced against the wall, that the initial blast was adequately dealt with. The worst effect was a jostled rib cage and a rattled brainpan.

Subsequently, I watch in horror as our ceiling atomizes, leaving a gaping hole that just as quickly refills. Driven by force and gravity, debris cascades in a considerable wave of dust and sound. As close as we are to ground zero, we're all but enveloped with the shifting sands.

Our newly made hole is filled even more thoroughly than before, as parts of the ceiling decide they are quite done staying put in this mess. The portion of the wall we're leaning against shifts beneath my shoulder, and there's a moment I believe it intends to come down upon us as well. My brain finally kicks in, along with some cursory panic, as I see one of the beams overhead bend with the newly shifted weight. There's little choice for us.

Grabbing Rho by the arm, I haul him bodily into my space. A loose steel slat dangles temptingly at arm's length, so I snag it, on the chance that we might live through what comes next. With my stunned partner close, I thrust the sheet up against the debris, continuing to pile on.

Instead of succeeding in burying us up to our necks, it stops at the manufactured board held aloft above our helms. We're kept relatively safe, although I can't say the same for my shoulders. Dear God. I'm about ready to give in and let this thing have its way, consequences be damned. There is no choice but to hold fast. It's all that's standing between Rho and me getting flattened.

The pressure is immense as my spine is gradually compressed, centimeter by centimeter. I think Rho's trying to help, too, but it doesn't make much of a difference. With my ears ringing, I can't hear anything beyond the thuds of rocks and soil against our enclosure. I have no idea what happened to the Zee, or Megan, for that matter. I push that last thought aside as I don't want to deal with it. That girl—she shouldn't have been here. This whole mess shouldn't have happened, but again, I've more pressing matters to attend to.

I realize the rubble avalanche has ceased when no more loose materials land upon us. With more than a bit of relief, I painstakingly tilt the side of our sheet up where it's closest to the wall. The slight change in angle is enough to release the payload sending more dirt and crap falling as well as into the air. I try clearing my throat of the fine particles of dry sediment coating it. Dust particles fall like millions of microscopic leaves, polluting my nostrils, windpipe, and eyes. Even without our lights on, I can tell we're absolutely coated in it. The air's thick—almost damp in its cloyingness—the resulting cough is unavoidable. Rho's, as well. I hear him hacking up a lung right after I finish doing the same. Unoriginal.

Amazingly, with all that roiling and rippling of the floor, we're still held fast and tight to the wall. Of the two people on my team to be in this exact position, my de facto second-in-command and I are best suited for this task. Glancing above our heads to where my hand maintains its death grip on an exposed steel pipe, my partner's mechanical arm is similarly wedged in. Our gear appears a little worn, but nothing more than a few minor tears that can be easily repaired with some simple mending. Have I mentioned the UF gives great Home Economics courses?

Everything settles into an unnatural stillness, the area around us holding its collective breath for what's unfortunately coming next. A sweep of the ground not so far below, run through multiple visual spectrums, reveals nothing of consequence. There's no girl. No trace of her. Flipping my grubby visor up, I confirm with my eyes what every sensor I have at my disposal is telling me. My stomach twists with something I can't quite name—a nauseating cocktail of relief, guilt, and dread.

"Megan?" I call out despite myself, voice cracking. Turning to the gunner's dirt-caked bare face, I ask, barely above a whisper. "Do you see her anywhere?"

Rho shakes his head, his eyes scanning frantically through the debris field. "Nothing. Christ, she was right there." His voice cracks slightly. This girl got to both of us.

I force myself to look harder, ignoring the throbbing in my skull. Part of me wants to find her small form unharmed amid the chaos. Another part—the cold, tactical part—hopes she's gone for good. Whatever she was—whatever power she wielded over those Zee—it was dangerous. Terrifying. But her face...her damn face was still a child's.

"Maybe she..." Rho trails off, unwilling to finish the thought.

"I don't know what to think," I admit quietly, the words slipping out unbidden. "She wasn't what we thought." What I thought.

"She was still just a kid, Omega," Rho says, but the uncertainty in his voice betrays his own conflict.

Closing my eyes briefly, Megan's face swimming behind my eyelids—those bright blue eyes, the determined set of her jaw, the way she'd looked at me with such intensity. All angles and lines from a life lived on the edge of a precipice, but still youthfully innocent in moments—until it wasn't.

"Yeah," I finally reply, my voice hollow. "But she was something else, too. Something I don't understand."

"Hey," Rho's hand finds my shoulder, squeezing once. "Whatever she was, it's not on us. We tried to help her."

"Did we? Or did we simply use her to get us out?" The question hangs between us, unanswered and unwelcome.

Rho's expression hardens as he processes my words. "We both did what we thought was right. If she made it this far on her own, I'm sure she survived. That kid wasn't normal."

The certainty in his voice is almost convincing. I nod slowly, trying to believe it. Megan is more than a mere child. She's Zeta or Zee, or some horrible mix of both. An unnatural occurrence in this world. Whatever the case, we've stayed past the close and need to be gone before the horde of actual Zee residing here decides to explore the sights and sounds of our corner of the mall.

The thought has barely cemented in my mind before the cries begin anew. This time, they're louder and much closer than before. Our helms snap toward one another at the first echoes. With a shared look of trepidation, we both voice the same favorite word.

"Fuck!!"

I adjust my grip to pull myself higher toward the cracks of light breaking through dense layers of sand and rock.

"Come on!" I growl, struggling up the landslide toward our newly minted exit. Our boot treads scramble for traction on the shale-like surface. Every foot gained is lost to a half-foot slide as the wall crumbles at the lightest touch. My partner's larger form misses some hand or foothold, and my lunge to stop his slide is also nearly a miss as he almost slides through my grip.

Panting, I flex my right arm awkwardly as I inch-by-inch drag him to my level. I may or may not have been ready to lay into Rho as some warped stress-coping mechanism, but I'm sidetracked as a black coil of something smacks against the hard polycarbonate of my visor. Head shooting up, I follow the length of the rope to its beginning, where our sniper awaits not so far above, waving at us like a maniac.

"Omega! Rho! Grab on!" Her light voice broadcasts readily through our helms. I don't need to be told twice. I loop it around an arm and under my elbow, watching intently to ensure Rho does the same. There can't be any accidents or mistakes this time.

The screams reach us as bodies impact below with muffled whumps. Without pause, the creatures claw at the organic face of the hill while attempting to get at the fresh meal lying in wait just above their outstretched hands. In their mindless frenzy, they claw at one another, separating decaying flesh from bone as each tries to climb the unstable surface. As they do so, they inadvertently pull down the ground beneath where we're braced.

"Pull us out, Mu!" I command loudly and with perhaps a tinge of panic at the end. I've not made it this far to become a Zee chew toy.

"You got it! In three. One. Two. Three."

That's the quickest ascent I've been subjected to in my short life. Even with our combined weight on the line, we're hauled up and out like a couple of hooked bass. I brace myself moments before being forcefully pried out of the ground and dragged a goodly several feet. The sand and gravel are an unpleasant abrasion against my body, but I'm just happy to see the open expanse of sky above.

Laid out and panting, I lift my head to confirm that my second's escape is equally evident before unceremoniously flopping back in bone-deep exhaustion. Everything…it's been too much. Holy hell. I'm done.

With all of its billions of microfine specks, the sand I'm partially embedded in is the most comfortable thing in my world. Tilting my head slightly, I make out the sun's position in the sky. It's morning, not quite to that midday mark. Has so little time passed? It felt like another life was lived in there. Right hand fumbling for a second with the aftereffects of a whole lot of adrenaline, I shakily flip my faceplate open from when it must have fallen closed. The air, warm and dry enough to steal the moisture from the hidden corners of my eyes, rushes in and envelops me. One deep breath and then another clears out the lingering stink of that tomb.

The shuffle crunch of boots making their way toward my prone self warns me of incoming. A few seconds later, a colossal figure blocks my perfectly lovely view of the perfectly blue sky.

Tilting my head as best I can without entirely moving, I regard my shadow. "Omicron."

"Omega," he retorts. His smile is soft as he pleasantly rumbles my name.

"How's things?" Apparently, that explosion may have knocked a few more screws loose for me. Good thing I have an on-site medic...and here he is. A giggle slips out at that thought. Oops.

"Oh, things have been interestin'. Although I'd hazard not nearly as interestin' as for you and Rho." He nods a little way above my head and beyond me, where I assume Rho is equally laid out.

The medic's attention refocuses on me as he reaches to take my chin, gingerly turning my head with an evaluating look. No doubt he's taking in the haphazard fix-it patch to my skull, barely visible within the cushioned sides of my helm.

"So, what happened?" He cautiously questions, even as he gently shifts my head. Suddenly, it's really bright. Wow! Did someone turn up the sun's magnitude?

"Do you want the whole story or just the highlights?" I ask agreeably.

"Let's start with the basics. Like, what happened to your head?" One thick eyebrow shifts in expectation.

"I hit it." There's a pause. Maybe two, as he slowly blinks at me. Expression blank.

"Right." Glancing first skyward, then somewhere behind me, he calls, "Rho, if you can safely move, I need you for a minute."

"You got it." Is the gunner's immediate and exhausted reply. Contrary to the languid response, I pick up on a quick trot from the gunner as he moseys over to our location before dropping unceremoniously down next to us in a muffled whump.

He looks like shit, frankly. I can only now see some of the nicks and bruises he acquired during our time underground. I realize I never thoroughly vetted how severely he might have been injured. Especially as he just recovered from a couple of broken ribs. Damn. Something really was off with my head to have forgotten that.

"You okay, boss?" I'm startled out of my reverie by my second's low question. It's asked with a frown and a line of concern between his eyes. I have the distinct feeling it's not the first time he's asked me.

Tired of lying in wait under inspection, I curl my upper body up. I throw an elbow behind me to steady my torso as the world tilts yet again.

"Just dandy. I'd be better if you two stopped quacking." Wincing, I do my darndest to glare at him.

Grinning unrepentantly, Rho turns to Om, not bothering to respond to me. "She hit her head pretty hard when we fell through the ceiling. Can't say what against, but she was out a good half hour before I could get her to come around."

Now it's my turn to blink. Half an hour? It felt like a few minutes, tops. No wonder Rho was a little panicky when I initially came to. As the space around me wobbles less, I meet a welcome sight— my bike and Rho's, each hooked up behind one of the other ATCs and still in the land of the functioning. Small miracles indeed.

"I'm fine." I bite my lip as I shift to my other arm for support, rattling my brain a little bit more with the movement.

"Of course you are." Omicron's tone is heavily condescending as if speaking to a particular dimwit. "I'm goin' to go on a limb and guess you either aggravated your existin' head trauma with Chi's ordnance or added a second concussion to an unhealed first."

The corners of my mouth pull down severely as I don't particularly appreciate where this is going. The majority of the team has gathered around our small half-circle by this point. I even catch sight of Tau's shaved head over Mu's left shoulder. His back is turned, watching the space around us, but he's close enough to follow along.

Eyeballing my spectators, I don't bother hiding my irritation as I grind out, "Obviously, the Zee weren't able to follow us out if you're all standing around with your thumbs in your asses."

My hackles are up for some unknown reason. Perhaps it's related to feeling caged. Maybe not. We nearly died. I lost Megan. My head hurts. I rub my free hand against my forehead, belatedly noticing that at some point in the last few minutes, my helmet was altogether removed. I couldn't tell you how.

"Your head hurts." Omicron echoes. "Anythin' else?" He prompts, searching my eyes for signs of...something. I guess I said that part out loud.

I want to say no, but realize it's probably in my best interest to answer lest he decide to figure it out for himself. I have the terrible vision of Chi and Rho pinning me down so Omicron can poke and prod at me, to his dark heart's delight. Shaking the image loose, I refocus on the looming medic. Was he that blurred, to begin with?

Despite my not saying anything, the medic has picked up on something unspecified while gazing into my unintentionally vacant expression. After snaring the fingertips of his right glove between immaculately white teeth, Omicron tugs off the set, baring a myriad of small scars along his chestnut brown hand to the elements. That broad, smooth palm captures my jaw firmly, turning my head first left, then right, before prying an eyelid up with a firm shake. He hums quietly but says nothing.

"That's enough," I grumble, forcibly pushing up from my supine position.

Now, I'm pretty much done dealing with any shit for the day. I jerk my chin out of his grasp, and he allows it without comment. A quick arm out invokes a decent distance gap between him and me. My head pounds as loudly as a bass drum with the sudden movement, but I lack the will to care. I'm done feeling bad about this day and myself. It's nothing if not a waste of energy.

"Omega..." he begins, but I give him no opportunity to order or lecture. I'm the one who gives the orders.

Momentarily hunching over blurred knees and panting, I give myself a few seconds of grace before I'm back on two feet, reeling from the sudden vertical format, yet far beyond letting it prevent me from succeeding.

Omicron's hands are extended in preparation for catching me as his brows scrunch down, alongside a severe expression. The man doesn't like being dismissed when doing his job. I'll apologize to him later when I feel less like the object of a spectator's sport.

"Fine." Omicron snaps. Hands raised in surrender, though not entirely cowed by me. "But I will be informin' Base Medical about your injuries. They need to check for any potential long-term complications."

"Enough! Let's pull everything together and move out if we're done here."

Utter and complete silence greets my command. Jaw clenched, I regard the range of concerned and wary expressions surrounding me. All are looking toward me as if I'm some wild animal showing its teeth and claws, ready to attack at the wrong shift in person. They're not so far off. My fight-or-flight instincts are way up right now. Their concern is noted, but I don't give two fucks about it.

"Did I stutter? Move out!"

There's murmurs all around, but my team finally moves to comply with minimal fuss. Glancing back only once toward the empty breach in the desert, I can make out the faint sounds of bodies pushing against one another. Moans hollowly call from the depths in their unrelenting need for our bare flesh. Without further consideration, I turn and make my unsteady way to where my beast awaits. The chaos in my ears becomes white noise, and then...silence.

—Ω—

ACT 4
SHADOWS WE CANNOT FLEE

A QUIET MOURNING

"Hmm..."

The pause is unmistakable. A breath held fast in a throat, unable to escape. Switch flipped to combat-ready, my senses lock onto the anomaly like targeting systems. Every detail registers without my having to physically move from my sentinel position. In the dark and gloaming, I've become the unwilling guardian of those lost to their dreams—or nightmares.

There it is again. My head snaps toward the source—one of the team's tents. The rustle of sudden movement follows a stifled gasp as someone is ripped from sleep. The otherwise steady rhythm of slumbering soldiers fractures once more by what can only be a night terror. Selfishly, I'm grateful for the interruption to my own horror-filled replays of the past week. I've had far too many mental screenings of that child's face in various states—afraid and unhinged, then carefree and wicked. Which was the mask, and which was real?

Confident in my threat assessment and the lack of actual danger, I release a ragged yawn that seems to originate from my marrow. Rubbing my face, I wince at the scrape of the worn tactical pads on my gloves against my dry skin. It's damn near impossible to purge this level of exhaustion, especially when operating on a sleep deficit that would flatten a regular soldier. I'm surprised no one objected to me taking the night shift.

Within sixty seconds, I identify the source and release the remaining tension coiled in my muscles. Unsurprising. At least Rho managed several solid hours before the latest trauma announced itself. Minor miracle that none of the other hyper-aware Zeta have roused. Head tilted, I listen for a minute more, but my de facto second has gone quiet—doubtful he fell back asleep so quickly. More likely suffering in disciplined silence, as we've all learned to do.

A repeated pulse of pain lances along my temples, demanding immediate attention. The warning signs of a significant migraine I've been ignoring for hours. I was never prone to headaches pre-Zeta. Post-upgrade, they've become a near-constant companion. Hell, they're so common for our kind that standard-issue equipment includes heavy-duty ibuprofen—or at least, that's what the label claims.

I'm not indulging in conspiracy theories tonight. The ache sharpens into something that pulls a low curse from my lips. Grumbling in discomfort and overall crankiness with this godforsaken world, our assignment, my throbbing skull, and the ruins of memory, I opt for the chemical escape. Fingers probing through the dark, I feel along my tactical vest, digging into a dozen identical outer pockets until I retrieve a cylinder no longer than my thumb. I shake out eight hundred milligrams of whatever concoction UF's mad scientists cooked up. Chances are, it won't succeed in killing me before the Zee do. Hopefully.

Chuckling at my dark humor, I dry-swallow two of the salmon-colored tablets with a parched convulsion of my throat. Never mastered taking meds without water, especially the chalky ones.

There's a rustle of material—sleeping bag, going by the synthetic slide—this time from a completely different tent. The crisp snap of gear being locked into place follows. Company incoming. Checking my chrono, I note the time: twenty-four minutes until Tau's guard duty officially begins. Makes sense, he'd be up and ready prior to shift. Most Alphas would be. I would, too. However, that means spending extra time with his temporary squad leader and nemesis extraordinaire. Oh goodie.

As his tent flap folds back, the soldier emerges like a wraith, silently stalking to where I'm seated on the rise. A long-dead fire pit from the day's cooking has been my only companion until now. Without preamble, he positions himself on my side of the circle and takes a seat on the hard-packed ground, studiously facing forward and avoiding eye contact. I raise an eyebrow at the uncharacteristic behavior, but resist the urge to go on the offensive immediately. The night just got a little more interesting.

After a span of silence and stillness, Tau's eyes slide to me, but still, he says nothing. Through the quiet, I make out Rho shifting again in his tent. Even knowing I'm up and on shift, he'll likely stick it out alone. He isn't one for any company during these episodes, and I'm not one to push. Murmured prayer drifts through the stillness of camp. I might recognize the words if I strained to hear them better, but I don't. Can't. Some things are best left with the dead.

Returning my attention to the interloper, I have to acknowledge that the Alpha chose to join me when he could've avoided my presence until the last possible second. He certainly has before. Intuition suggests that a conversation is brewing. Perhaps my being here at the time of his readiness isn't a coincidence. For now, I say nothing, returning my senses to the watch while appreciating the small patterns of life flickering unimpeded around us. A whisper of a desert mouse darting swiftly between burrows. The hushed swish of owl wings cut through the night air somewhere above. The rasp of scaled skin sliding through loose sand as a snake methodically stalks its dinner.

All soothing in their normality. Our presence hasn't derailed the local inhabitants, nor has anything unnatural. That state is both relief and comfort. I'm content to wait however long Tau needs to gather his thoughts. However, when my shift ends, I'm heading for my sack, and God help anyone who gets in my way. I needn't worry about timing, as it only takes a handful of minutes more before he interrupts.

"*A-hem.*" The Alpha clears his throat mildly. Dropping my gaze from the constellations, I zero in on him. This time, he meets my eyes directly, no longer avoiding me.

"I want to...express my gratitude to you and your team for coming to save my team, retrieving me, and bringing me back to full health. You did not need to involve me in your dynamic as has occurred, nor show me the courtesy that you extended."

"Including the courtesy of a right hook?" I can't help but interject. I'm not quite needling, but everything hasn't been sweetness and roses with this guy. Actually, it's been the polar opposite until the most recent debacle.

A frown cuts sharply across his features, no doubt recalling the event and what preceded it. He's about to argue, or at least fall back on his previous disdain, but after a moment, he doesn't. Instead, he slides his hand from the front to the back of his shaved head, then front again. A gesture of frustration I've caught before. The scritch-scratch of skin over shorn hair is loud in the darkness. I wait curiously for more oddities, still in a pleasant enough mood for now.

"You and your team have strong personalities. Perhaps stronger than I am used to. I crossed a line that I had no business crossing. I have also underestimated you in the past."

He glances up, his entire demeanor trying to convey the genuine nature of his words. I imagine it's like swallowing broken glass for him—admitting he wasn't in the right. I nod for him to continue, resisting the urge to fiddle with something lest I be accused of inattention. He continues his monologue, voice calibrated to a low, precise volume.

"From what I was led to believe, Beta squadrons do not operate as yours does. They are a step above drafted infantry—front-line Zeta soldiers lacking in true skill and cohesion. I've seen your team behave as mine would have in similar situations, and I do not know what to think."

"Why? Where's the confusion?" I frown, puzzled about his direction.

Tau shifts, no longer facing me but giving a good view of his straight nose and sharp features as he turns to stargaze. From this angle, he's an entirely different person than when we first retrieved him. Granted, he was near death initially, but even after healing, he markedly changed. I wonder what effect being thrown in with my unorthodox team has wrought within him.

"I became a Zeta soldier to protect my family. I worked to join Alpha Squadron to honor them and prove myself worthy. From what I was told, being an Alpha is about being the elite and the best at everything. To accomplish anything meaningful and impactful, it had to be my path."

It's not the first time I've heard Alpha Squadron described that way. Makes me think there's a recruitment script circulating to convince everyone of their superiority. Recalling my past altercations with other Alphas, I know those interactions soured my opinion of that class of soldier. Though they've certainly made me work harder to prove myself better than them.

"But I have difficulty believing that now…"

"And it makes you question your place and if all the hype is worth it," I finish for him.

He gives me a penetrating look, eyes flicking between mine, reading something in my expression. A ghost of a smirk passes over his lips.

"Precisely."

Shrugging one shoulder, I let loose a slight chuckle, turning toward the unlit fire and giving myself something else to focus on. This conversation feels vaguely familiar.

"Let me share something I was told about ranks, roles, and life. It's about the individual. Who we are and how we choose to act influences our path and the effect we have on ourselves and others."

I don't receive an immediate response from the Alpha. Wasn't expecting one. The silence stretches, and I'm in a mood to let it. I've said more than enough for one sitting. My ears pick up the subtle shifting of a body, and I know without turning that Tau's looking at me. The sudden interruption of his low voice nearly startles me from my reverie.

"You seem..." Here, he pauses. Audibly selecting his next word. "...*mellow.*"

I snort. Can't help it. This time, I turn my head enough to see him from the corner of my eye.

"What? Did you anticipate a different reaction from me?"

His head tilts slightly, considering. "Perhaps. You and I do not exactly lead in the same manner."

"Yeah, well, I've dealt with enough unexpected shit lately. Puts things into perspective. Sadly, you annoying me doesn't rank high on my list right now."

"Ah."

"Indeed."

With a glance at my chrono, I see my shift is over, and it's Tau's watch now. With a grunt, I stand and stretch toward the heavens, attempting to release the slumped energy that's settled in my spine.

"I may be Beta Squad, but I've never let that stop me from giving it my all. If I don't, how can I expect my team to?"

Eyes narrowing, the Alpha says nothing, seeming to digest my words. I leave him with that final morsel to ruminate over.

"Enjoy your shift, Tau. I'll see you in a few hours."

With a lazy wave, I turn to make my way in the low moonlight through the staggered tents to my own, not bothering to turn and see if the Alpha takes what I've said to heart. I almost stumble over my own feet, with the realization that our conversation was almost pleasant.

—Ω—

NOT ALL THAT'S EMPTY SHOULD BE FULL

The building is no more impressive standing right in front of it than it was fifty yards back—entirely and utterly innocuous in appearance. It has the generic look and feel of any government office structure. I'd call it mid-century modern, but that would be giving it too much credit. It's more like a slightly glorified mud hut. Not the quality of architecture you'd expect to find in the late twenty-first century.

The space around it is devoid of anything remarkable. A barren parking lot of faded asphalt flanked on three sides by more desert and low scrub. There may have been trees planted along the curved concrete walkway leading from the lot to the front door at one time, providing shade and a token attempt at aesthetics. Without regular watering, they've withered into scrawny twigs jutting from the ground, adding to that homey feeling of abandonment that permeates this place.

Regardless, its entry is as secure as any other United Forces facility, which gives me a sliver of hope that we're not completely wasting our time. With a terse nod to Rho, I step aside, allowing him access to the main entryway. In situations like this, Rho's cybernetic arm is the simplest way to gain entry to anything UF-made. It functions as an all-access key far superior to any physical credential we could have procured or fabricated.

"Weapons at the ready," I command, my voice crisp through the comms. There shouldn't be any lifeforms here. Ergo, open season on anything that moves. No sense in getting caught unaware.

Rho works whatever cryptographic magic lies within his prosthetic, and there's a resulting creak of a lock disengaging from its rusted cage. But then, nothing. No motion or indication that what the gunner did was successful.

And so, we wait sixty seconds for something miraculous to occur. I suppose I should've expected complications. Nothing about this mission has been straightforward. Rho shrugs his shoulders in confusion while the rest of the team maintains their defensive formation, eyes locked on the entry point and a couple at our sixes for good measure.

"*It should be open,*" Rho states, uncertainty creeping into his voice.

Humming to himself in contemplation, or perhaps bewilderment, he places his non-cybernetic hand against the door, trying to peer through the thin slats set into the upper portion of the door frame. The moment he applies pressure, the door shifts inward with a metallic protest that makes my teeth ache. The hinges screech as Rho shoves it the rest of the way open, not even bothering with the second door. The first one was painful enough.

Our initial look inside is equally underwhelming as the exterior. The room is cramped, with a disproportionate amount of real estate allocated to a reception desk set against the far wall. Dust motes dance lazily in the dim light filtering through grimy windows—a space untouched for at least a generation, judging by the accumulated filth.

Beyond that, there's not much to be impressed by and no apparent reason to be here. It's as vacant of purpose as my de facto second's attempts at flirtation.

"Someone needs to open a window or ten."

Rho's dulcet tones echo around the circumference of the room, obnoxiously loud in the sterile space. For once, I'm not the one to correct him, either through reprimand or a flat-out death glare.

No, that honor goes to Chi as she deigns to cuff him upside the head. Rubbing the very short cropping of hair along the underside of his skull in offense, the gunner gives a muted *"Hey!"* before cutting himself off in a sulk.

"Maybe if you left your helmet on, as you are supposed to, it would not be an issue, Rho."

"Doubtful." He shoots back. "You can't tell me your filters are actually preventing you from smelling this?"

"Doesn't matter. Put your fucking helmet back on, Rho." I bark at his sullen look.

He's right, of course. The place has obviously been sealed far too long, with something organic and far beyond rotten held within. We're not off to a good start.

We haven't been in a favorable position since this mission was assigned to us. Actually, let me back up. Mu barely extracted any details from HQ command, let alone specifications on what to expect. Odd, but not entirely unprecedented in their handling of things. Once again, we're operating partially blind, and that could be either incidental or intentional.

The morning had proceeded at its usual pace, even after the unplanned early morning heart-to-heart with Tau. Mu was in the middle of trimming Rho's hair, as she typically volunteers to. I've yet to let her get close to my head with any sharp implement. What happened next only reinforces this decision.

Mid-stroke, her nearby comms unit went off loud and clear, startling everyone within range, including the comms specialist holding the clippers. With Rho's wail of pained dismay echoing through the camp, Mu switched priorities, forgot him, and answered the call. The gunner's pitiful looks in her direction were ignored, and Mu's focus remained wholly on whatever the person on the other end was conveying.

A few sharp nods of acknowledgment gone unseen by the caller, and she was urgently waving Chi and me over. We shared the same quizzical look before joining her. On a split channel, we both listened to an unusual and oddly secretive set of additional commands for our final mission before returning to base.

I felt my eyes widen at the Alpha-level assignment and couldn't help glancing over to Tau's stoic form in question. His presence might explain why we were being handed this responsibility, although he wasn't apprised of it, to my knowledge. There's not much else I can attribute it to except proximity to an Alpha.

Regardless, I provided my verbal authorization, consenting to the mission parameters. Not that I had any ability to decline. This order wasn't a request, but I'll be damned if we don't execute it flawlessly.

Taking in the barren interior now, I'm beginning to doubt my intelligence in not questioning their directive more thoroughly. Then again, maybe I'm wrong. I spot what appears to be an inset door panel behind the semi-circle of the reception desk. That's an interesting place for an important door.

Nudging Chi with my elbow, I indicate the panel, and she straightens when her visual locks onto it. Without hesitation, she stows her weapon before vaulting gracefully over the desk to inspect the small interface next to the door.

Upon approach, I find it easy to identify the biometric scanner. Chi confirms this by removing one of her sleek tactical gloves and placing the open palm of her left hand against the matte gray panel. Instantly, its display illuminates, and several electronic confirmation tones emit from the wall.

With a precision this derelict base should be incapable of producing, the inner doors slide apart to reveal a hidden inner sanctum. A rush of cool, dry air sweeps past, carrying a crisp, clean scent reminiscent of industrial-grade sanitizing agents. I'm grateful I made Rho resecure his helmet. For all we know, that could be aerosolized acid. Chi, though sealed, is closest in range and seemingly unaffected. Probably not acid, then, though the possibility of something lethal remaining here is high.

I run a fundamental chemical analysis through my helmet's sensors. Thirty seconds later, it reports back in the green with a bland *"no detected toxins"* readout. That's all the okay that I need.

—Ω—

HEARD BUT NOT SEEN

[MU]

Somewhat on automatic, I follow the others in a single file down the empty hallway. The walls, ceiling, and floor all appear the same, reflecting the flickering lighting like some out-of-focus dream. I keep my senses alert and ready, but I already know there's no one here. How could there be? It's been sealed for more than a decade. No one is coming in, and no one is going out. Just dead.

We turn right at the next junction and approach the door waiting at the end. A black sign, faded to a charcoal gray, is centered at eye level. A formerly white zig-zag line cuts it diagonally in half. That doorway should lead us down several flights of stairs directly to the central control room. It should. According to the schematics I downloaded, it should. But even before I follow the others inside and down, I know the room won't be what we expect it to be.

There's something wrong with all of this, and I felt it the moment I spoke with HQ. That soldier acted all wrong. He provided no details or explanation. No SITREP or basic understanding of potential threats. I know Omega thought so, too, but grim-faced, she accepted the assignment without pushback. Another strange thing. When we arrived and gained entry, the first area looked like an outdated government office lobby. Cue mystery door and an even more mysterious abandoned underground base!

The stairwell is nothing to write home about. Totally empty, like, in an almost sterile way, other than the few defunct cobwebs fluttering in the corners where the wall and ceiling meet. After the fifth nauseatingly twisting loop of staircase, landing, staircase, and landing, we finally reach the exit, along with a stale and musty odor. Not a moment too soon, either. I was beginning to get a little dizzy going in circles like that. Once again, Rho takes point and unlocks the innocuous gray door marked with another black sign—this one emblazoned with a white "6" to mark an otherwise indistinguishable level.

At least they were right about the proximity of the control room to the stairs. We literally exit, turn left, and bam, there it is. As we queue up to exit the stairwell and enter the main area, I crane my neck to take in another very empty hallway. It's so strange that there's, like, no signage whatsoever. I mean, usually, there are at least directional signs, room placards...you know...something to direct you to where you need to be. But Chi seems sure that it's the right door, and Omega is fine with her directions, so we wait in the sparsely lit hall as Rho accesses the final door.

Sighing but willing to go where I need to, I crowd into the now-unlocked room along with the others. Once I can see around Rho and into the proper space, this really eerie feeling washes over me. The emergency lighting lurking everywhere focuses more on what's behind the glass than the side we're on. A creepy green glow comes from everything. It's both strange and hypnotic, yet also familiar. Weird, right? Like I've seen the same light somewhere before. I don't know where or why I'd even think that, but I know this isn't the first time.

Does that mean we've been here before? Glancing to the sides, I check to see if anyone else is having a similar reaction. But no, nope. Not at all.

I mean, they're reacting, but more in the whole secret-underground-UF-lab-doing-questionable-things kind of way. Omega, as usual, seems more irritated about the lack of full disclosure than anything else. Maybe she expects these kinds of surprises by now. That's a little disheartening.

Chi begins working to gain access through the nearest console while Omega and Rho snipe back and forth about petty little things. At this point, I'm ready to tune them out entirely unless something positive and valuable comes from their side of the conversation. Doubtful, sadly. Sometimes, I think Rho likes to bait Omega when he has nothing better to do. Not helpful, Rho!

Frowning more to myself than the others, I nibble on the corner of my lip and accidentally catch the skin on one of my canines. I always forget how sharp they are. The nip draws blood, and the iron taste lingers on the tip of my tongue for a held breath. I can't escape the utter rapture that taste brings me. It's not right, and I know that, but I can't ignore the sensation. I can't, and I don't want to. That tiny droplet draws me out of the familiar weight of my body and the relative security of this space.

I blink, and the room opens.

It's from a different perspective, and I'm on the other side of the glass, blinking rapidly. I can't get rid of the thick goop coating my eyes and making everything so blurry. I try reaching up to wipe it away, but my arms are stopped short of their goal. Way short. And everything hurts so much. I tug again, trying to reach out and touch something, but whatever holds me, I can't move my hands any higher than my waist. I drop a shoulder, attempting to see what has me in its grasp. Even in the murky twilight, the bright colors from multiple lines of plastic tubing are obvious.

I can hardly move enough to follow their trails and find where they end, but I guess I don't have to. I know they're part of why I hurt and why I'm unable to move. At least where they're attached to my wrist and my stomach, too, I think, or maybe that's something else, like the constant burning stinging along the side of my face.

Where am I?

Where's mom and dad? Selvi and Rama? Eddie?

Where are they? Am I alone?

Squeezing my eyes as tightly shut as I can, I try to ignore everything else going on in this weird world I've woken up in. There has to be a better answer. My family wouldn't leave me. There's the burn of tears trying to form, but this gel stuff stops anything from leaking into it. Leaking. Wait, something is leaking. The world tilts wildly, and everything in my mind is upside down, including me. My body sways like a fish caught on a line, trying to escape as ribbons of seatbelt press against and bind me.

My neck aches as I crane to see Selvi hanging from his seatbelt in the seat next to me. He dangles, all four limbs dropped down akimbo, and red drips slowly—so slowly—through the dark curls matted to the back of his head. But there's more that's wrong. His neck is at a weird angle, and he's not moving.

I swallow against the urge to scream, even as heat seeps in around me. I don't hear Rama or Eddie. They were in the row behind me. And where's Dad? He was driving. The front windshield is almost totally gone, a vast hole gaping in the middle like some giant smashed his fist through it. Something long and sharp sticks out of the middle of the back of Mom's seat, along with a growing blob of dark maroon against the tan-colored leather. I can see a few of her curls over the shoulder of the headrest as she remains in place, unmoving.

The heat is becoming overwhelming. I'm in an oven getting baked alive. It's so hard to breathe, and when I cough, my insides feel like they're going to fall out. I need help. Why isn't anybody helping us?

Shoes and boots run around on the pavement just outside of the missing front windshield, but none of them come close enough to our car. Help, *please*! I don't know if I manage to say it out loud, but I'm thinking it. Screaming it. *Save us*!

With a jolt, I fall out of not one but two levels of waking dreams, or perhaps living nightmares are more accurate. The first is a bit murky, but I remember the second clearly. It's my only memory of the accident, the last one I have before waking up in a UF facility. I don't remember being asked if I wanted to be a soldier. I just... became *Zeta*.

I take a shaky breath and come back into the present, though not much has changed around me. I can't have been gone for more than a handful of minutes—not enough for anyone to notice. It's been long enough for Chi to be frustrated with her lack of progress in gaining access to the system. I can always tell when something's irritating her. Well, more than people generally irritate her. I suppose I'm not entirely sure Chi is meant to be on a team. She's regularly short-tempered and snippy to anyone in range. There's also a lot of sighing and eye-rolling as if the world around her is too much to deal with. It's funny because I tend to think that Chi has a better handle on life than the rest of us. I could be wrong!

Regardless. I know our scout can do it, and I say as much, even if she doesn't need to hear it. It can be beneficial to receive affirmations from others. I get that expected eye roll for my comment, but I see how she sits a bit straighter, and her grim smile of doom becomes almost a challenging smirk.

Omega's helmet turns my way, maybe in appraisal. It's hard to tell with no facial expression to go by, or words, for that matter. It'd be nice if our standard uniform didn't include our helmets. It makes it so difficult for us to read and understand each other. Well, more so than usual.

There's a gusting breath out from Omega, and then she disconnects the upper portion of the helm and pulls it off. Without looking, she neatly attaches it to its connector at her waist. Another sigh, but more in relief. A small smile is directed my way before she refocuses on whatever Chi is doing on the computer with a solemn face. The clickety-clack of keys being pressed succinctly in a neat sequence is hard to miss in this quiet. I don't think I've ever been able to type that quickly.

With Omega now unhampered, that seems to be the signal for all of us to do the same. Rho pops off his helmet with an audible suction sound, releasing a long *Aaahhh*, which Omega quickly jumps on to quiet him. I hold back a giggle as he mimes zipping his lips, although Rho obviously hears me somehow because he throws a wink and a dashing grin my way. I just want to melt or maybe not take off my helmet because then I can hide my face, which I know is quite flushed at the moment. I don't know how he does that every time. It's kind of embarrassing.

Pretty much everyone I've met has told me that my facial expressions are easy to read. The same as me, but I don't really care about it. I've got nothing to hide, and I've always shown how I felt. It's how I am, and besides, there are enough emotionally reserved people on my team that I can afford to be different.

I am unlike the other Zetas, anyway. And not just because of my blue hair or doing my best to be positive about...well, everything. It's my eyes, I know. They burn sometimes, like there's this heat behind them I can't escape. Eventually, it stops, but for that time, it's as though everything around me pulses with energy and life. I'm not sure if I'm describing it correctly. It's just...I can feel everything alive, and I really mean feel. Like their feelings. Especially powerful ones. And I can feel their life force.

If I try to initiate it on my own, like right now, it's not as strong, and my eyes don't hurt. The helmet off helps remove some interference as well, and I can sense Rho's agitation and Omicron's always-there anger, Chi's boredom, Tau's eagerness, and Omega's...*Omega*. She feels better than she has. I think Tau being with us has been good for her. She's really focused and intense, but now in an excited way and not anxious or sad. However, she does get mad at Tau for everything.

Speaking of which, Tau shifts his stance behind me. It's not the first time in the last few minutes. He seems agitated but is trying not to draw attention to himself yet. I shift enough to get a better look at where his attention lies. His face is turned toward the still-open doorway. Head cocked subtly. He's listening. Or hearing something, maybe?

Watching as intently as I am, I can see the moment he stiffens, holding his breath and body utterly still. I tilt my head a little as well and try to pick up whatever has him so engrossed. I can't hear anything beyond the breathing of the team, the light shifting of bodies in stiff fabric, and Chi's insistent typing. But the Alpha hasn't been the type to overreact or behave as if he's paranoid, so I'm going to guess there's something else going on.

"Tau," I call out to him softly. I know he won't appreciate the extra attention, but I think it's needed. He turns briefly to face me, eyes darting first to me, then Omega, and finally, back toward the hallway beyond.

Omega picks up on both of us, which is not what I expected otherwise. "Mu? Tau? What's going on?"

We have the entirety of her attention, but I think that's a good thing. Tau frowns, opening his mouth once, only to cut himself off and close it. His smooth features pinch as if he is figuratively chewing on something. He gains the confidence to continue and speaks in that low tone I can now pick up anywhere.

"I believe there are multiple forms moving down the hallway."

He stares intensely at Omega, trying to impart that he's not just hearing things, I imagine. Not that he needed to. I can tell Omega believes him without hesitation as well. It's strange for her, but I can't help feeling some excitement at the change. The fact that she's extending trust so quickly is a good sign, I think!

"Can you tell how many?" Omega questions quietly.

"No." Tau shakes his shaved head in a negative gesture. "There's too much in the way. My best guess is at least three or four organisms being careful, or at least not moving in a predictable pattern."

Nodding once more to herself, Omega's red hair emphasizes the motion as it flashes in the dim lighting. She turns and lightly places a hand on Chi's nearest shoulder, appearing to scan whatever she's managed to bring up before giving her a pat and leaning away.

"Okay. Keep at it, Chi. Mu. Omicron. Keep an eye on things here. I want your comms open." Turning to address the remaining two soldiers, Omega issues the rest of her orders. "Tau, lead the way. Rho and I will cover you."

He nods sharply before replacing his helmet, rifle raised, and exiting the room on silent feet. Rho nods as well and is quick to follow.

"Be careful," I warn Omega. "We don't know what's actually here, and I have a feeling that it's more than we're prepared for."

Our squad leader gives a half smile in response and blinks once in confirmation.

"Oh, I'm sure there's plenty down here we want to avoid. Be ready, Mu." She intones with a severity that I find troubling as she disappears outside the door and to the right, following after the other two.

The dark swallows them all up. I stand there staring at the void for a moment longer. I attempt to follow their movements in my mind, a sense of them extending out only so far before, first Tau, then Rho, and finally Omega leave my perception entirely.

Lump in my throat, I continue to watch the dark opening, hoping it's a big nothing. Even though I know that's nearly impossible. We're never truly alone. There are ghosts everywhere.

—M—

THINGS THAT GO THUMP IN THE DARK

[OMEGA]

I head after the other two, even as the skin between my shoulder blades twitches with Mu's fixed attention. Never fails. If I want to know when something's off with the team, all I have to do is keep an eye on Mu and, apparently, Tau's ridiculously good hearing.

If I wanted to be a brat, I'd say something along the lines of he has stellar hearing but is lacking in the listening department. I'll skip it this time and reserve that snipe for later. He's behaving at the moment, and it's always good to have a clever rejoinder on standby. I waste a handful of seconds pulling up Rho's and Tau's channels on my gauntlet to create a private comms link between just the three of us. With that minor detail settled, I jog to catch up until I spot my gunner's taller back and Tau's shorter form, a few paces ahead.

I allow a boot to scrape in warning as I converge on their halted position. Not that I needed to—their lack of reaction tells me they've already clocked my approach. It's easy to identify where our intended destination lies. The Alpha is fixated on the last door at the end of the hall. His bronze helm is turned unerringly toward it and hasn't shifted a millimeter in his attentiveness.

Opening our new short-range channel, I hail both of them.

"Status?" I ask, calmer than my climbing heart rate feels.

"There is a group of individuals in the next room. Based on their movement patterns, I believe they are human and appear to be searching the space. We are waiting for your order on how to proceed."

The Alpha is quick to convey before Rho can respond. Although my de facto second doesn't exactly stop or correct him.

It's something to consider later. For now, we need to deal with this unexpected and unpleasant discovery. Glancing at the door again, it's hard to miss the clear "SERVER ROOM" placard spanning the door's width. What are the odds that someone else would be in this derelict facility, on the same floor level, and at the same time as us?

There's no such thing as coincidence. The data that we've been tasked with retrieving can be the only culprit. It's unlikely there'd be any other Zeta here without our knowledge, as there's no reason for HQ to send a second team, at least not yet. Additionally, any UF-sent soldier would have access to the main system and wouldn't need to undertake the extra work of connecting and downloading information directly from the servers. That's not good.

"Chi." I cut over to my interim data analyst.

"*Yes, Sergeant?*" A short and irritated voice immediately responds. Apparently, all is not well on her end.

"We have intruders down the hall from your location. Server room."

"*Shit.*" She growls. "*I thought I saw notification flags about attempted unauthorized access. I assumed it had to do with my initial problems with this archaic system.*"

The Alpha has finally managed to pry himself away from observing the door, and based on the cant of his head, I imagine he's wondering what the hell is taking me so long to decide.

"I'm betting not. Any chance you can further block them from gaining access?"

"*Not without a lot more time than we have.*"

"Shit." I agree. "Okay. We're engaging. I'll let you know when we're clear. Keep at it, and let's be done with this."

"Roger that. Chi, out."

"Well?" Rho prompts no sooner than my two-way with the demolitions specialist cuts off.

"They're trying to access the same system we are. They haven't managed it, but Chi can't prevent them from doing so digitally. We're going to have to, analog-style."

"Sounds like a plan to me!" Rho crows.

Apparently, he's feeling the need to do more than stand here, thumbs up our asses. It's an unknown quantity who's on the other side of that door. That's clear. What's also apparent is that they're not on our side, and that second point makes the decision for me.

"Alright. We need to stop whoever's in there and secure this site. Tau—you take the lead, Rho middle, I'll follow. We remove them quickly and with utmost prejudice. Got it?"

"Affirmative." Tau's quick to respond. Rho nods.

"Let's move."

As one, we shift forward. Thankfully, there's no inset window in the door to give our presence away. The downside is we can't see inside either. At least, two of us can't. We're left relying on whatever obscure enhancement Tau's in possession of that lets him detect presence through solid objects. I've stopped questioning these Zeta quirks—just another thing the UF scientists never bothered explaining during our upgrade.

Said individual switches to a single-handed grip on his rifle as he lightly tests the door handle. Just as carefully, he releases it, leaving the door unengaged but not fully ajar.

"*It is unlocked,*" he confirms.

"Roger, proceed. Rho?" I nod toward the entry point, and he saddles up next to it, replacing Tau as the Alpha shifts to the side to enter first.

The gunner braces against the steel of the door before quietly counting down, "*Three...two...one.*"

Smoothly and without a hint of sound, the gunner pushes the door inward, a black space opening up before us. From the dim lighting of the hall, Tau's hunched form enters, the muted taupe from his tactical poncho swallowed immediately by shadow. Rho swiftly follows, leaving me as the last to enter. Shoulder pressed firmly to the wall, I peek around the doorframe before sliding in after my teammates.

The change in lighting is immediately remedied as my visor automatically switches to a mix of night vision and infrared, though I'm quick to cancel the latter. As I suspected, the room's label wasn't just for show. A massive server farm stretches before us—row upon row of high-density rack cabinets filling the space in a precisely aligned grid pattern. They hum quietly in the dark expanse, all aglow with lime green status LEDs that blink in hypnotic patterns as they process data. The heat signature each machine puts off confirms they're not just operational but running significant workloads. Yet another question to add to the mix: Why is the UF still powering an abandoned site, and what the hell is it processing?

The other two Zeta remain just within the doorway, both studiously avoiding the sliver of light that followed us in from the hallway. To be cautious, I reach back and carefully reset the door. It's possible whoever is within has already detected our entrance, but I'd like to avoid advertising our position if they missed it.

The area is far larger than I anticipated. Far larger. A rough estimate would be the size of a football field, with cooling systems and power distribution units interspersed throughout the server racks. It's simply massive. Obviously, the schematics provided to us left off some significant details. It makes me wonder what else they've kept from us.

"Well, fuck," I mutter.

"*You're telling me,*" Rho empathizes. Shit, I didn't intend to broadcast that.

Sighing, I shake my head in resignation. Clearing this space is going to be painful, but we have no choice but to do so. Before I can despair, I recall what I can't believe I nearly forgot. The Alpha.

"We need to find them and fast. Tau." I turn to face him directly. "You knew they were in here. Can you narrow down their location?"

With a silent nod of the helmet, he allows his rifle to hang across his chest before reaching up to release the catch on the upper half of his helm. With a soft snick and hiss of air, his bare face is revealed. Unphased by the lack of direct lighting, his head performs a methodical scan of our surrounding space.

With bated breath, I wait for his gaze to stop, eyes narrowed in focus. Unblinking, he continues the forty-yard stare. After a minute, he blinks rapidly, giving himself a slight shake while a frown of displeasure forms. Practically glaring at nothing, Tau tilts his shaved head, straining to hear something more than the ambient drone of cooling fans and our controlled breathing. Whatever confirmation he was seeking, he must get it as his face relaxes back into a more neutral expression, nodding to himself before turning to me.

"There are at least six in the northern corner. Spread out but not moving from their current positions. This many machines are throwing off my senses." Eyes narrowing, he pauses, and the break adds unintended weight to his last point. "Human and armed."

Sucking in a breath through my teeth, I curse mentally. There's no accounting for this scenario in our planning. A bitter and gross oversight on my part. Zee? Why, yes. Of course, there's always the chance of some poor sap-turned-monster hanging about. Unknown civilians breaking into a supposedly secret and secure UF facility while carrying? Fuck, no.

"Maybe just sentries?" I venture.

"Perhaps. There are no other lifeforms I detect in the immediate area."

"Okay. Change of plan. Let's hope they're not expecting company and see if we can catch them off guard. The goal is to capture, not kill, but your life is priority one when it comes down to it." Nodding to the Alpha, I take another step into the deep end and give him the reins. "Tau, lead the way."

Face stern and mouth pulled in a grim line, the Alpha acknowledges with a short nod. Without wasting another word, he readies his weapon and moves on hushed feet, slipping between the first row of server racks. Rho and I follow in perfect sync, our movements silent and deadly as we stalk through the digital forest toward whoever the hell is about to receive a very unpleasant surprise.

The racks tower over us like steel monoliths, each one housing dozens of blade servers stacked in perfect alignment. The narrow paths between them force us into single-file formation, increasing our vulnerability but also providing cover. The ambient noise masks our approach—a constant symphony of fans, drives, and cooling systems that drown out any minor sound infraction we might create.

As we navigate deeper into the maze of technology, the temperature rises noticeably. Even with environmental controls, the heat generated by this many active systems creates pockets of warmth that my helmet's sensors register immediately. Sweat beads at my hairline as we press forward, the server room's artificial climate working against our stealth approach.

Tau signals us to halt with a raised fist, then points toward a more open area ahead. The northern corner, where the control terminals would logically be positioned. That's where our unexpected company waits, unaware they're no longer alone.

I nod at Tau, giving the silent command to proceed with extreme caution. Whatever we're about to walk into, I have a sinking feeling it's going to complicate our already problematic mission. Nothing about this facility has been what it seemed, and I doubt these armed intruders will be the exception.

—Ω—

NOT ALL KNOWLEDGE SHOULD BE EMPOWERED

[OMICRON]

"This cannot be right."

Chi's incredulous voice breaks the charged silence. Her face is practically glued to one of the thin, curved pieces of glass displayin' whatever information the scout was tasked with downloadin'. I take a glance at whatever concerns her, but I can't make sense of it. I also have little depth on what it exactly is, as only the Sergeant and Chi know the finer details of this job.

There's a rustle and some new warmth at my side as Mu's slighter form comes to stand by me. I imagine she's more curious than anythin'. Turnin' her bright eyes to me, I shake my head once, at a loss as to any of this. I've been more concerned with Omega's intruders. Things could get a whole lot uglier if they end up bein' a bigger problem.

"What is it, Chi?" I prod when she says nothin' further. She's already been sucked back into the data.

"Hmm? Oh, Omicron. The timestamps on these entries...they cannot be right."

"Why's that?" I ask, more than a little intrigued now.

"Well, for one, the oldest so far is more than four decades old." She offers, not takin' her eyes off the glowin' screens.

"There's gotta be a mistake. The United Forces weren't around then. The Armed Forces, yes. Could it be old military?" I question, more to myself than the other two. There were six branches of the military, each distinct and separate from the other. I should know.

I served right up until they were all but wiped out.

"What?!" Mu cries out a little louder than necessary. She quickly covers her mouth with both hands, cheeks reddened in shame.

I smile wanly at her, and not unkindly. Her honest reactions are one of the more refreshin' things about havin' her on the team. I can't say that I've come across anyone as open as she is in the service—still so genuine despite what we've seen.

Rubbin' my chin in thought, I try recallin' when this all began. When was the first time I heard the name 'United Forces'? When did that become the norm? I just don't know. What I do know is that, for now, it doesn't make a difference. At this point, we can go through the data later to figure out what's missin'. We gotta get this info downloaded and outta here safely.

This place isn't right. I know it's not just me thinkin' that. Things have been off from the start. I'm no scientist, but I've never been to a place like this. All the bases I've known, includin' the intake facility, were your standard army base, right down to the gray walls and lack of empathy.

This, though... It's somethin' on a whole 'nother level. I know everything the Forces do, and the Army before that isn't exactly above board. But there's no use in bringin' that up now.

Glancin' over to Mu, I know that girl's scared. She's doin' her best to be a good soldier, back in position by the door, but the tells are there if you're lookin'. Those blue eyes don't miss much and are hard to miss, even across this dim room. They flick toward me for an instant, and I do my best to stay relaxed and smile for her. She's quick to do the same with a warm smile of her own before pullin' herself up and doin' her best to look focused.

I feel a bit better about our youngest teammate, so I opt to give Chi another check. Now, she's someone you don't have to worry about focusin'. I think the trouble with her is she's puttin' out too much of it. There's not much space between her and those screens, lookin' about as intense as I've ever seen her. That says a lot, and none of it is good.

With a deep sigh, I ease myself behind her chair. This narrow room makes for a tight squeeze, and I'd rather not crowd her, but there's no havin' it. My closeness gets me a bit of a side-eye from Chi, but not much else. I didn't expect otherwise.

A brief look is all it takes to tell what she's downloadin' ain't right. Over Chi's shoulder, I catch terms like *"early experiments"* and *"genetic adaptations,"* and my favorite, *"possible military application."* That's about as far as I'm goin'. Anythin' more, and my stomach turns. Instead, I give Chi a nudge.

"Why don't you just get it downloaded for now? If we've time later, you can look at what's in there. You don't need that added pressure now."

She's twirlin' one of the twin locks of long hair, usually framin' her face around a finger. There's some serious doubt in that look. Odd behavior for her—nerves maybe—but this entire mission has been Tango Uniform. With narrowed eyes, Chi releases a harsh breath before straightenin' up to apply herself once again to the task at hand.

"I suppose you are right," she concedes, her crisp tone carrying a rare note of uncertainty. "The encryption is unusually complex. I have never encountered something this...layered before."

I have to say it's fascinatin' watchin' her type faster, causin' more screens to pop open, then closed. She moves through each of them without pause or hesitation. Faster than my eyes or mind wants to follow. The girl's on a mission now.

Mu shifts, gettin' a little uneasy behind me. She's far back enough to be out of the loop but not so much that she hasn't caught on to what's goin' on.

"It's okay, Mu. We're wrappin' up. Why don't you keep an ear open for Omega and the others?"

She nods once, hurriedly. Glad to have somethin' to occupy herself with.

"Okay! I'll listen super carefully," she whispers, brightenin' at having a specific task. "Do you think they found those people Tau heard? I hope they're okay."

"I'm sure they can handle themselves just fine," I reassure her with a gentle smile. Mu's concern for the team is always genuine, even when she's scared herself.

The words keep comin' back to me. *Early experimentation. Possible military application.* Those are some ominous and heavy words. A part of me is scared of where they'll lead us. The rest hopes we'll never find out.

Chi's fingers pause momentarily over the keyboard. "The data transfer is at sixty-seven percent," she reports clinically, though I catch the slight tightening around her eyes. "But there is something else." Her voice drops lower. "These files…they contain personnel records. Test subjects."

"Test subjects?" I echo, keepin' my voice even despite the chill that runs down my spine.

Chi nods once, her usual aloofness broken by what I can only ascribe as disgust. "Of varying ages, Omicron. Perhaps even children."

226

Mu gasps softly from her position by the door, her enhanced hearing picking up our hushed conversation. I catch her eyes widen with horror and give her a reassurin' nod, though there's nothin' reassurin' about what we're discoverin'.

"Just get what you need," I tell Chi, restin' a steady hand on her shoulder. "We'll sort through it all later, somewhere safer than here."

She nods once, resumin' her work with renewed intensity, fingers flying across the interface. I straighten up, rollin' my shoulders to release some tension and move back toward Mu.

The weight of whatever secrets this facility holds settles around us like a shroud. I've seen a lot in my years of service, both before and after the Zeta program, but somethin' tells me we're just scratchin' the surface of somethin' much darker than any of us are prepared for.

—O—

AND WHO IS THIS TRAP FOR?

[OMEGA]

The path from my brain to my body is positively lit with adrenaline. My heart hammers double-time while I fight the instinct to breathe shallowly, every muscle locked down to keep movements measured and controlled. With hostile contact likely imminent, there can be no mistakes. As point in our three-person squad, I set both pace and tempo for the other two. Dwarfed by towering pillars of metal and microchips, we're nothing but intrusive vermin in this digital forest, winnowing our chances of engagement with each row that's cleared.

At the next break in the grid, I halt, risking a look around the corner down the next darkened aisle. The flickering neon casts everything in an eerie, inconsistent glow. I wave Rho forward, gesturing concisely.

You go. We'll cover.

With our comms silenced to prevent unplanned broadcasts, we've reverted to hand signals exclusively. The gunner flashes an 'okay' before positioning himself in front of me to execute our next leapfrog. I sense the Alpha drawing closer, crouched and still covering our six as I prepare to watch our front. With a burst of speed and motion, the gunner sprints across the exposed space between our position and the next server bank.

Blood surges through my system as I cross the limbo between positions next, pivoting at the final step to cover Tau as he brings up our rear. Still no sign of hostiles, but I trust the Alpha's instincts. If his senses say there are intruders, I'm game. Hell, I'm eager for it. I've been itching for a good, straightforward fight. The last altercation we dealt with has left a lingering bitterness and moroseness that I'd just as well leave behind. These trespassers might provide exactly the therapy I need.

Slinking along the next server bank, I refocus on the task at hand. Tau taps my shoulder in warning as the Alpha overtakes me, swapping positions in our column. He's about to swap again with Rho when the gunner's hand flashes up in a tight fist at shoulder height. We freeze instantly as his right hand forms an inverted 'L,' pointing to the space ahead. Enemy sighted.

Rifle gripped one-handed, I tap the Alpha's shoulder to gain his attention. With his upper helm still off, Tau's irritation is evident, as is the downturn of his thin lips and a narrowed gaze aimed at me. I point directly at him with specific instructions: *You listen. Numbers.*

His mouth tightens, but he acknowledges with a single nod, visible through our HUDs. Rho slides back, allowing the shorter soldier the best access to ascertaining our enemy. Head cocked once again, the Alpha does whatever he's been doing. Both my de facto second and I are as still as possible. I don't want to screw up whatever magic he's packing with an errant noise. With a sharp nod, he slides back to our huddle and holds up his palm with all fingers and thumb extended. Five, huh? Not bad odds.

I flash the 'okay' symbol before tapping the crown of my helmet. I ease past both men to lay eyes on the junction separating us from our targets. A hasty peek around the corner confirms five bodies clustered around an open terminal. Four form a loose circle while the fifth works feverishly at the keyboard, riveted to the screen before them. The entire setup reeks of convenience. How the hell did they even get into this base, let alone a room that we were uninformed about?

The two nearest targets face away, oblivious to the impending danger. The remaining three pose a minimal threat of early detection. The unknown quantity is the weapons casually displayed and the potential for reinforcements. They may not be Zeta, but give any idiot a gun, and he'll think himself unstoppable. I'm neither bulletproof nor inclined to have Omicron extract lead from my tissue later. Our attack calls for precision rather than brute force.

Several scenarios flash through my mind in quick succession, varying in violence and outcome, before I settle on the most direct solution. I'm a one-woman wrecking ball for a reason. My teammates observe my silent planning, and at the very least, Rho recognizes the calculated violence I'm intending to unleash. Calling the taller soldier to my position, I form a loose bridge with my hands and mime him giving me a leg up onto the servers.

The gunner slings his rifle, dropping to one knee with hands ready for the boost. I ensure that I have the attention of both males as I convey my last set of non-verbal orders. *Cover me. Engaging.* I deliberately grasp my throat. *Comms active.* The element of surprise is about to become defunct anyway.

Following my own directive, I activate my comms, the initial crackle of static a welcome intrusion into the oppressive quiet. I don't bother with any of my firearms. This action requires a fluid and controlled response. In one smooth motion, I step into the gunner's cupped hands as he rises. He effortlessly has me up and onto the servers in the blink of an eye. I brace myself on all fours. The smooth surface beneath my extended fingertips radiates a mild warmth. Drawing both batons, my eyes remain locked on our unsuspecting targets.

A first proper look at the group leaves me underwhelmed. New scents lay heavy in the air—warm metal, stale perspiration, and the distinct odor of unwashed bodies. They don't hold themselves like well-trained militia expecting a confrontation— more like a small pack of nervous teenagers. Their mismatched, loose clothing and lax stance only reinforce this assessment. It makes what comes next almost too easy.

For one suspended moment, I'm airborne, my form concealed in deep shadow before I descend with intent. The solid weight of my left stick catches the guy closest to my position on the back of the neck, dropping him instantly. The rightmost hostile hasn't completed his turn before my follow-up strike to his jaw renders him unconscious. No telltale crack of bone, so he's likely salvageable. Probably.

I remind myself: incapacitate, don't terminate. A helpful rhyme for when instinct drives me toward permanently eliminating threats. I'm preventing these intruders from becoming a problem for my team later. The abrupt assault startles the remaining three, who pivot as one, unprepared for my blatant and direct assault.

Now, at ground level, I drive the hard edge of my shoulder guard into the diaphragm of the nearest guy. He folds without resistance, too surprised to do more than release an *'oof'* of displaced air. With unbroken momentum, I bulldoze through the other two, leaving a messy heap of collateral damage. Exploiting their disorientation, I swing the dense wood of my baton across the face of the first to recover. The sharp crack accompanies my backhanded strike to the next, catching him across the nasal bridge. Both collapse back into their useless pile.

The final instigator scrambles in a crab walk away from me. Even with the dim lighting, it's easy to see his eyes blown wide, stark fear etched into his bloodless pallor. With greasy locks of unkempt hair falling into his face, the younger male scoots back inelegantly on his rear, palms raised in desperate supplication.

"No, wait. Don't!"

I wag an admonishing finger before delivering a right cross to lay him out, "You didn't say please."

Stepping back to assess my handiwork, I find myself humming with residual excitement but underwhelmed by the encounter's brevity. After a quick check that everybody's down and nobody's dead, I gradually downshift from combat readiness. It's easier to interrogate the living.

Rho and Tau converge on my position, the former whistling appreciatively before lifting his faceplate. "Nice work, Sarge. How about saving at least a couple of them for us next time?"

I offer a casual shrug. "You should've gone first."

He grins, stowing his rifle to retrieve gray zip ties from his tactical vest. Without prompting, he hands a couple off to Tau before trussing up the hands and ankles of the unconscious. Tau mirrors his actions with mechanical precision.

With all unexpected and unwelcome guests in secure custody, I allow my body to return to a state of normalcy and breathe a little easier. My initial impressions were disappointingly spot on. Barely older than boys, dressed in bizarre amalgamations of desert nomad and countercultural styling—utterly human. Definitely not United Forces material. So, who are they?

"Check them over for anything suspicious. Any UF property or souvenirs."

With my team executing their tasks, I maintain a loose grip on my weapon and a sharp eye on the space surrounding us. The unlikelihood that they came alone is overpowering, and I'm loath to allow another breach of our space.

With nothing better to do during their methodical processing, I switch to my scout's dedicated channel, interrupting what's likely critical data extraction. She'll be thrilled.

"Chi. We've secured some bogeys, over."

There's a millisecond of calculated hesitation that precedes her response.

"*Is that so, Sergeant?*" Her words are laced with the pain of chewing on glass shards. She's probably spiraling with all of the information she's had to parse through. Almost makes me regret the interruption. Almost.

"Can you confirm if they breached any data?

"*And why, pray tell, do you not ask them?*"

"I'd rather not tip my hand. Plus, your method is faster."

Her sigh resonates with cosmic weariness.

"*Give me...a moment.*"

"Take your time. We're expecting more company. Hate for them to miss the party."

Another sharp hiss of exasperation spits across the channel before silence stretches between us. It goes on long enough that I check my display to verify the connection's still active. I needn't worry, as what can only be a few minutes later, she returns to the line.

"*Sergeant. They penetrated initial security layers and accessed multiple files. Downloaded them as well, if I am not mistaken, and I rarely am.*"

"Shit. Okay. Note which files were compromised. We'll need to report that up-chain."

"Roger. Will do, Omega."

"How much longer do you think?"

"Ten minutes maximum. Provided there are no further interruptions."

"Got it. Wrap up and signal when ready to extract. We still need to process our friends. Omega, out."

A collection of confiscated items accumulates near my boots while I was mentally away—worn walkie-talkies, mismatched weapons, and some circular, brightly-colored items I'm not keen on handling. They remind me of poppers that you would use during Independence Day—all flash and minimal function.

The Alpha straightens first, gem-hued eyes flashing in the minimal lighting their few errant flashlights provide. My gunner, however, needs a lesson on frisking, with how excessively thorough he's being with the final subject.

"Dude, you two need a room or something? Wrap that shit up and get your ass over here." I step to grab his collar, but I halt midstride as something glints, catching my peripheral vision from beneath a server tower. With a narrowed focus, I point out the anomaly to the shorter of the two Zeta.

"Tau. What's behind you? Under that end tower?" His expression inverts as he turns, quickly identifying the object before kneeling to retrieve it.

"It is a computer of some kind." He tilts the notebook-sized device from side to side. "It appears damaged. The screen is cracked." He passes it to me without hesitation, and I grunt a *'thanks.'*

After a brief examination, I'm inclined to agree with his assessment. A jagged fracture bisects the display, likely from impact with the concrete floor. But it's light and shows minimal wear. The device refuses to activate through conventional inputs, prompting me to give up quickly and set it aside for later analysis. There'll be time later to figure out what it is and why these guys have it. The tech is a far cry from our older, utilitarian equipment, which begs the question of why these amateurs possess such technology.

Shaking my head, I address the other two. "Let's see which one of these sleeping beauties rouses first."

Rho nods before going down the line, shaking and lightly slapping the less-damaged captives until one appears to stir. The most senior-looking person, and I use that term loosely, has bleached blonde hair and a filthy red handkerchief tied loosely around his throat. I'm tempted to call him 'Fred,' for simplicity's sake. He lets out some groaning and grumbling, hissing a little in apparent discomfort.

Gray eyes blink open drowsily before widening at our proximity. The captive recoils violently against the metal housing behind him in a futile escape attempt.

Rho winces with a sympathy he doesn't deserve. "Hey, man. You're okay."

He attempts to calm the blithering fool, even as the guy starts hyperventilating. Obviously, he wasn't planning on getting ambushed, even though he did the ambushing to begin with. Turnabout is fair play, they say.

"Who are you? What are you doing here?"

"You know, that's funny. I was about to ask you the same thing." I counter shrewdly.

The guy clams up, his mouth shut with theatrical determination.

I chuckle at their amateur tradecraft. These are not seasoned operatives.

Rho crouches at a calculated distance—close enough for psychological effect but beyond the subject's reach.

"Look, we're not here to cause harm, and I'd be happy to let you go. You need to tell us what you're doing in this facility. That's trespassing at minimum, but maybe there's something more worth sharing?"

Rho tilts his head with practiced disarmament as if he couldn't easily break this guy's neck in one move. Yeah, he's as harmless as a wolf eyeballing a rabbit.

The subject shakes his head, still unwilling to say anything. I crack my knuckles with deliberate audibility.

"Okay, that's fine. Perhaps our friend here needs a bit more encouragement. What do you think?"

The young man, barely more than a boy, finally notices me leaning against the wall and visibly pales. I guess he remembers who decked him earlier.

"Look. I...I can't tell you guys. I have nothing to say." He begins what promises to be the start of some fantastic lies, but we're interrupted quite rudely by the sharp crackle of a radio.

"*Thomas? What is your status?*" An older male voice crackles through some hidden communication on the guy's person. He pales even more.

I fix "Thomas" with a predator's smile. The situation just evolved.

"*Thomas, what is your team's status? Have you secured the data yet?*"

I trace gloved fingers along his collar, locating a compact device no larger than my palm pinned to his shirt. Minimal effort is required to remove it.

I extract and examine it—another piece of advanced tech. The mystery compounds exponentially.

I glance at Tau and Rho, an eyebrow raised in silent inquiry. Rho offers an unhelpful shrug while Tau nods decisively toward the device. His unspoken meaning registers clearly. Our silent communication appears to have improved.

There doesn't appear to be any ON/OFF button for the device. Likely voice-activated. Going with that hunch, I hold it up to my mouth and respond, "Thomas is temporarily unavailable. However, if you'd provide your authorization, I'd be happy to inform you of his whereabouts and where you can shove it."

Our hostage's jaw drops while Rho facepalms dramatically. Tau's expression of stunned amazement completes the tableau. Still got the touch. Whoever's on the other end of the line starts sputtering but seems to think better of it.

"Who is this? How did you access this frequency?"

"I believe that's secondary to your current predicament." All humor evaporates from my tone. "We have multiple personnel in custody for unauthorized access to United Forces property. You will provide proper authorization and disclose your location to us, or they will be remanded into custody."

Dead silence fills the channel. It's impossible to determine if this controller is on-site or remote. Their technology suggests distance, but operational security demands we consider all possibilities.

The voice returns, tone shifting to something ceremonial and outright strange. *"We are Shepherds of the Light. We stand between the dark that devours and those who will be saved."*

With this cryptic declaration, all power and illumination cease abruptly. The omnipresent electronic hum vanishes, plunging us into absolute darkness.

Things just got interesting.

—Ω—

MORE WHYS THAN WHEREFORES

"Shit!"

For once, someone else beats me to one of my favorite words. I'll have to correct Rho's usurpation later. As it is, we're plunged into absolute darkness—not even the faint indicator lights from the servers remain. I sense my compatriots shifting anxiously, along with our restrained captive.

We aren't the intended target. We're collateral damage at best. So why cut the power? It undermines their purpose if data extraction is the sole intent. There must be another objective, perhaps even their primary goal, that we disrupted.

Almost simultaneously, our comms crackle to life. Chi's voice cuts through with palpable urgency, her words clipped and staccato in measure.

"Omega! We have a breach! A group of at least a dozen armed individuals is moving toward this level. Mu spotted them on surveillance before the blackout hit."

"Chi!" I nearly shout. "Are you compromised? What's your status with the data?"

"We are presently secure with physical locks engaged. The main power is offline, but local backup systems are running. I am in the final ten percent of the extraction."

That could be uplifting, except the last tenth often takes longer than the first ninety percent.

"We're locked in for now, Sarge." Omicron's rich voice flows through the connection. *"But if they head our way, we're cornered. There's no other way outta here."*

His tone alone tells me he's wearing that deeply displeased expression reserved for dire situations. Muffled conversation filters through in the background. As I wait impatiently, my eyes grow more accustomed to the lack of proper lighting. Several of our other captives are beginning to stir. I glance down at our talkative one just as he attempts to wriggle away. A swift boot to his chest pins him back to the floor.

"Don't worry about that. We'll move to your position and clear any hostiles we encounter along the way. You keep yourself secure and finish that download."

I tap Tau on his shoulder, signaling for him to replace his helm and prepare to move. Pass it on.

I take a moment to seal my helm completely, creating a barrier against prying eyes and ears. I hail Chi specifically, hoping she has her headset active.

"*Yes, Sergeant?*"

"Wipe all data from this site. Set fire to it if necessary. We can't let these hostiles access any of this historical information. No matter what."

"*Understood, Omega.*" She confirms gravely.

Switching over to general comms, I begin outlining the plan to the other two soldiers. I manage to get a single sentence out when a searingly bright flash blinds my HUD and, by extension, me. It's closely followed by a series of piercing cracks and pops. For a moment, I fear my eardrums have ruptured. The assault leaves me disoriented with a ringing that drowns out all other peripheral sounds for what might be seconds or minutes. My world contracts to this packing foam headspace.

Then comes a series of muffled impacts, including Tau's shoulder colliding with mine. Not intentional, judging by his posture—he's hunched inward, trying to escape the cacophony of sensory information. I doubt his helmet was secured entirely when the flashbang detonated.

Despite his disorientation, the Alpha manages to direct my attention to our next complication, not that we needed any more. Through blurry sight, I make out the telltale beams of tactical lights from a brand-new wave of interlopers. Unlike their predecessors, this group displays actual situational awareness. That could be a problem.

"We've got to move!" I growl, shoving Tau ahead of my crouched position while snagging Rho's rigid collar to drag him along.

We barely make it around the corner as high-velocity rounds ping off the server banks behind us. It's a good thing I worked to put solid metal between us and them.

There's muffled cursing that follows the exchange, thankfully not from our side. I almost laugh as our former hostages howl in pain, miserably caught in the crossfire. But this isn't the time for celebration. There's a battle to win. I was looking for a challenge. Should've been more specific.

My heart thuds deep and steady within my chest, distributing blood and oxygen all over my body as muscles tense in joyful preparation for what's to come. "Tau. How many?"

He releases the latches to the top of his helm, removing it entirely and wincing as he rubs ineffectually at a temple. Trauma from the blast appears to be affecting him more than Rho and me.

"Give me a moment," he rasps, ceasing his fidgeting to concentrate intensely on our surroundings. Through my HUD, I catch his eyes illuminated with their own infrared glow. Well, that's another interesting development.

"Eight in this room, not counting our five captives." He tilts his head, blind to everything but whatever frequencies he perceives. "Perhaps five or six more in the hallway, moving away from us." Finally, he turns to address me directly. "All civilians and armed similarly to the first group."

"Considering that they're firing on us, I'd say their intent is lethal. If they try to take you out, you take them out first. No hesitation, no excuses. Clear?"

Tau's mouth compresses into a thin line, but he nods. I get the sense that he's not as willing as I am to use lethal force against this enemy. Glancing at Rho, his lowered head suggests a similar reservation despite his sealed helmet.

No matter. Survival takes precedence.

"On my mark, we clear the room. Rho left. Tau right. I'm going up, over, and right into their center. Let's neutralize these assholes."

They both nod without further comment. Tau replaces his helm and shifts sideways, preparing to round the corner. I notice that one of the jawbreaker-sized balls that we seized earlier has rolled to my feet. Without hesitation, I retrieve it, examining what appears to be the same device that disoriented us moments ago. It's not a grenade, but it's still a concussive device. After a quick inspection, I address my team.

"One distraction coming up. You guys might want to look away for a moment. On my mark. Three. Two." I press down the tiny button sitting dead center in the middle of the orb. "One." And I toss it in the direction of the incoming.

A brief sizzle precedes another godawful pop, followed by immediate cries of distress. Light erupts like a miniature firework, accompanied by searingly disorienting noise—you don't need enhanced senses to be affected. The momentary confusion provides our window, and I make good use of the moment to dart around the server bank, rifle at the ready.

The first combatant is targeted upon landing. With feet planted solidly, my opening shot pierces one of the intruder's knees. They go down in a spray of crimson, screaming hysterically. The next turns toward me, one hand still shielding his face. I duck low, sweeping his legs from under him before delivering a decisive strike to his face. Two down.

Tau enters the field of combat, not with his rifle but with an unsheathed and fully extended sword. A delicate swoosh follows its smooth arc as it slices through the air, cleaving a civilian's rifle in half while narrowly missing their fingers. Shocked, the guy doesn't react fast enough, and Tau's side kick to the jaw sends him into an inelegant sprawl.

Rho deals with the intruders with the least finesse as he plants his foot into the gut nearest to him, swinging his rifle like a club and clocking the guy over the head. Target neutralized.

If Tau's correct, we're halfway through their numbers without a minute having passed. I don't celebrate that victory either. Bullets whiz past my faceplate—close enough to feel a bit of drag from them. Hunkering down, I barrel toward the shooter, catching them in the midsection with my shoulder before slamming them to the ground.

More whistling sounds through the air as Tau's blade finds two more targets, one of which I'm certain will not be getting back up.

The final intruder stands transfixed, frozen between us and visibly trembling. Rho releases a hoarse battle cry, swinging his short axe at their weapon. The man moves at the last minute in precisely the wrong direction. The strike not only finds home in the gun but also deflects, biting into his arm as well. There's a screech as he falls, clutching the deep rent in his body, feebly trying to stop the blood flow. Rho's posture radiates horror at the unintended severity.

It's unavoidable that someone would get maimed. Amateurs shouldn't attempt to be professionals when it comes to killing. Don't initiate deadly force without expecting in-kind retribution.

"We need to move. There's not much time."

Without ensuring my teammates follow, I turn to make my way to the remainder of our team and stop cold. A flash of movement catches my eye as an unaccounted-for hostile emerges from the shadows. They're slighter than the other enemy but dressed the same and equally eager to thrust the business end of their rifle our way.

Their appearance is briefly illuminated by errant emergency lighting, and my attention is no longer where it should be. For a moment, however brief, a vaguely familiar face with a mocha hue reflects at me. But it can't be. That girl. That young woman from before. The one who nearly got my team killed after we agreed to shelter them. It can't be her.

Kari.

What the hell is she doing here?

My hesitation lasts only a fraction of a second, but it's enough. Her jade eyes widen in recognition, mirroring my own shock.

Before I can react, her face screws up as she hurls something small and cylindrical between us.

"Fire in the hole!" I shout, diving sideways. Hopefully, the others follow my lead as well, as a secondary flashbang detonates.

When my vision clears, she's gone—vanished into the labyrinth of server stacks and maintenance corridors. I curse my momentary lapse, but there's no time to pursue. The distant sound of gunfire indicates that the second half of my team is already engaged in more of the same.

My retaliation and ire erupt in a savage kick to a struggling hostile near me, knocking them the hell out. What lingers in the silence is the distinct sensation of a trap closing around us. Every instinct screams to charge directly toward our comrades and whatever chaos awaits.

The girl's presence here can't be a coincidence. These *Shepherds*, the data breach, and Kari—all connected pieces of a puzzle we're only beginning to see. Why is she with them?

Questions for later. Right now, we have a team to reach and an extraction to complete.

"Tau, Rho—on me. We're moving to Chi's position. Stay tight, stay alert."

—Ω—

MU KNOWS BEST

[CHI]

The steady flow of my typing falters before ceasing altogether. Speed reading—or at least my adaptation of it—proved a valuable tool during my collegiate years. On occasion, it still provides value, even beyond its originally intended function. My parents had meticulously planned my trajectory toward a private practice, a future that seemed inevitable when they invested a decade of collective income into my Ivy League education.

A mercy, perhaps, that they didn't survive to witness prestigious institutions collapse upon themselves. Indeed, my fall from grace to such a lowly station as a soldier would have horrified them. I briefly grasp that thought in an attempt to uncover some fragment of sympathy for them, maybe even empathy, but my emotional canvas remains blank. This absence of sentiment suits my current circumstances, as more pressing matters demand attention.

Origo.

A term I have never encountered, at least not throughout this second existence of mine. It lingers as an oddity in this missive. The report makes multiple mentions of the term intertwined with something called "Dux" or "Apex Protocol." I have a decent enough foundation in the English vernacular to identify a Latin word when I see it. Lamentably, my education lacked fluency in dead language—what exposure I did have left me predictably disinterested. Nevertheless, I commit the term to memory for future inquiry, assuming such an opportunity presents itself.

I observe that this record predates our current timeline by nearly four decades. In my unsolicited assessment, perhaps some historical fragments are better left buried in obscurity.

"Chi. How much longer?" Omicron calls from his position by the door.

He has not resorted to physically barricading the door but is vigilantly monitoring the goings-on directly outside. A lime-green emergency light casts his stern features in eerie relief—broad planes and sharp drops into dark chasms. I am growing increasingly concerned about the reliability of our auxiliary power systems.

"Almost complete. I am processing the final portion of the files. Can we maintain our position a few minutes longer?" I respond, my determination to complete this mission overwriting any apprehension that arises.

"Yeah. I don't think we gotta worry about those folks gettin' in. It's us gettin' out that's the problem," the medic drawls with a touch of grim humor.

"Don't worry!" Mu pipes up cheerfully from beside me, breaking her previous silence. "Omega and the others are totally on their way!"

"That's exactly what I'm worried about," Omicron corrects our azure-haired colleague with a shake of his head. "I don't much like the idea of them comin' down that long hallway with nothin' to hide behind."

His fatalistic assessment aligns with my own. The hallway offers absolutely no protective positioning. The imagery of 'shooting fish in a barrel' surfaces unbidden—a trite expression I attribute to Omega's unfortunate influence on my lexicon with her predilection for colloquialisms.

"They won't have to," Mu states with bright confidence, bouncing slightly on her toes. Her unwavering optimism, while admirable, seems unlikely to alter our tactical reality. I consider myself neither pessimistic nor pragmatic.

"Oh? Elaborate," I prompt, dividing my attention between the sniper and my primary objective. I anticipate little value in her response and am, therefore, genuinely surprised by it.

"We can bail through the glass." I pause, gaze following her extended finger. "There's another way out through there."

Perplexed, I momentarily pause to seek confirmation from Omicron. His confusion mirrors my own, prompting an exasperated huff from Mu as she approaches the seamless black glass extending from floor to ceiling. She raps her knuckles decisively against its surface.

"I mean, they had to get people in there somehow, right? And it wasn't through here." I blink slowly as my mind absorbs this new facet of information, conducting a rapid analysis.

"Dear Lord, she's right."

That, thankfully, is not voiced by me. I could never forgive myself for such an admission. However, I must agree with our medical expert. Nevertheless, Mu's deduction, while retrospectively obvious, remains entirely valid.

"Clever, Mu," I concede, permitting myself a slight smile at this revelation. Our resourcefulness in identifying an egress route infuses me with calculated optimism. Returning to my task with renewed efficiency, I complete the data extraction and immediately activate Omega's communication channel.

"Omega, are you presently engaged?" Her response arrives as a terse grunt followed by labored breathing.

"*Were you thinking otherwise, Chi?*"

"In that case, I shall dispense with pleasantries. Mu found us a back door, in a manner of speaking."

"Back door?" She pauses breathlessly, and I hear the distant report of gunfire from her end. I visualize her mental review of the room's configuration. *"Where exactly is this mysterious passageway?"*

"Through the looking glass, of course. The one-way observation panel and its adjoining antechamber should suffice. As Mu astutely noted, facility personnel required the means to transport subjects. According to structural schematics, that room's exit should position us adjacent to the northern elevator and stairwell, assuming either remains operational."

There is a moment of silence as she processes this information. *"Holy shit, she's right."*

"Yes, we have already progressed beyond disbelief," I inform her, not wanting this to drag out any longer than it has. "The relevant point is that we now possess a viable extraction route without requiring your intervention. I would suggest that you use your newfound freedom from obligation to discover an optimum evacuation path for yourselves."

"No shit," Omega deadpans flatly, her tone devoid of humor and heavy in annoyance. *"That we can manage."* Her vocal quality improves measurably, at least for the Sergeant. *"Are you done with the data?"*

"Affirmative. I am initiating a comprehensive system purge." My final keystrokes activate what amounts to a complete network sanitization, rendering it inoperable without fundamental reconstruction. Warning tones emanate from ceiling-mounted speakers as the system executes its terminal sequence. "We will rendezvous at the surface, Sergeant."

"Acknowledged. Omega, out."

Rising from my position, I retrieve my rifle from where it hangs across Mu's shoulder.

"We are all done here. Omicron, if you would please."

I gesture toward the glass barrier as I step aside to provide adequate clearance. The imposing medic unslings his close-combat weapon and advances two measured steps before executing a precise arc directly at the panel's center. A single, expertly delivered strike from his 'god-hammer' shatters the reinforced glass, which collapses into a cascade of minute crystalline fragments. I signal approval before vaulting over the now-dormant console into the revealed chamber.

"Come. I believe it is time for us to vacate these premises."

—X—

GET OUT OF DODGE AND THIS PLACE TOO

I'm more than ready to get the hell out of this decrepit freak show and leave its twisted memory behind. Rho, Tau, and I remain positioned in the server room, awaiting Chi's signal that her team is clear—our cue to move and cover their six.

Our exit strategy is direct and straightforward, avoiding unnecessary backtracking. After a quick assessment of our latest batch of captives, I'm convinced we're facing a coordinated effort from a well-organized group. That last cryptic radio transmission raises critical questions: Who are these '*Shepherds*,' and how did they know about this facility, let alone breach it?

My initial theory was they'd tailed us in, but the first group we encountered looked too comfortable nestled among the servers. Without question, they were here before us, possibly by hours. The second group, likewise. Given its undisturbed state when we entered, they didn't use the main entrance either. A military installation like this wouldn't have just one access point—there'd be alternate routes carefully concealed to minimize attention during personnel and equipment transfers.

If they're after the same intel as us, Chi's system purge has at least prevented further breaches. This place is dead to the UF now, but I'm hesitant to execute the final portion of our orders. With civilians present, even hostile ones, I can't bring myself to authorize mass casualties for the sake of operational cleanliness. There's a stark difference between combat kills and cold-blooded execution.

"*Omega. Do you read me, over?*"

Chi's precise voice cuts through the comms.

"Yes, Chi, go ahead." I raise my hand, signaling the others to prepare for movement.

"*We are clear of the base, Sergeant. However, we encountered a significant number of operational vehicles outside, along with several armed civilians. The personnel have been neutralized.*"

"Where are their transports relative to our bikes?"

"*Directly in front of the entrance—they did not attempt to conceal their presence.*" Her derisive sniff speaks volumes. "*I believe the remaining individuals were posted as sentries, though they clearly weren't expecting Zeta soldiers. Disarmament was executed without alerting their associates.*"

"Good. Let's maintain that advantage."

I tap my chin, weighing our options. We're not demolishing the facility—that's non-negotiable. But we can't risk these hostiles following us back to base either. I'd rather not complete a seven-month deployment by delivering enemies to our doorstep.

"*Your orders?*" Chi prompts me when I fail to continue.

"Give me a minute, Chi," I snap back.

Rho shifts impatiently, practically in the hallway, if not for the remnants of his self-preservation keeping him in check. Through my peripheral vision, I notice Tau backing away from his position by the doorframe to stand beside me.

"*What is the concern?*" he asks directly. His sharp tone bristles my nerves, but I suppress the reaction. There'll be time to put him in his place later, assuming we survive.

"The hostiles have vehicles at ground level, likely belonging to a third wave rather than the teams we've engaged. I won't risk leading them back to base."

"*Why not prevent their pursuit?*" The Alpha questions with unexpected simplicity.

"I'm trying to avoid executing civilians despite their armed status," I retort, heavy on the sarcasm.

He shakes his head once. "*No, I mean immobilize their vehicles from functioning.*" The implication now registers. Perhaps I'm too used to lethal solutions.

"That'll work." I pause to grit out. "Thanks." Tau acknowledges with a slight nod, but I've already moved on.

"Omicron, do you read me, over?" I broadcast to the entire team, but I need his specific expertise.

"*Yeah, Sarge? What can I help you with, over?*" His drawl comes through steady and calm.

"Need you to decommission those vehicles. Make them inoperable enough to prevent pursuit. Can your team handle it?"

"*Without a doubt, Omega.*"

"Good. Do it and report completion. We should be topside in fifteen minutes at the most. Work with what time you have. We're using the back stairwell."

"*You got it, Boss. Don't go doin' anything reckless now.*"

"Not likely. Over and out."

I quickly move to join Rho with Tau on my heels.

"Contact assessment?" I ask quietly as I reach the position. Rho peers around the doorframe again.

"*At least seven hostiles attempting to breach the control room.*"

The repeated metallic impacts confirm his report.

"There must be more to their operation," I mutter, then shake it off. "If we time this right, we can flank to the nearest stairwell and exfil." Turning to the other two, I continue. "I'll take point and clear the door. Tau follows. Rho covers our six."

"*Why am I always last?*" Rho's whine carries enough volume to make me wince.

"Shut it," I hiss. I can practically feel the gunner rolling his eyes behind his helmet, but there's no time for his bullshit. "Move out."

Ducking low, I advance around the corner directly toward the stair access. The handle predictably resists—locked. No surprise and no longer a concern given the facility's compromised status. Tau taps my shoulder, signaling his position. I nod once, then apply my enhanced grip to the mechanism, wrenching until something gives with a metallic crunch and loud *pop*.

The door swings inward, but the noise alerts our unwelcome guests down the hall. Damn it. I was hoping to avoid this confrontation. A curse escapes as I shove the door fully open. My teammates rush through as bullets begin peppering our position.

Rho slides in last, slamming it shut behind him with considerable force before collapsing against it with a relieved sigh. His optimism is misplaced—we've only traded one problem for another. The stairwell is a kill box, and now we've stepped in it, trading one tactical nightmare with another. The lighting in here is dismal at best, but at least the emergency lighting doesn't impede our vision. I only hope there aren't hostiles above us as well, or we're completely fucked. I've no interest in attempting to breach solid steel.

"Rho, secure that door. I don't care how. Buy us time."

"Wow. How about asking for something really challenging, like a fully accessible extraction route?"

I roll my eyes at his lip. "Just do it and stop wasting carbon."

Scanning our position reveals something far worse than pursuing hostiles. Bodies—dozens of them, scattered across every surface. They drape over railings, sprawl across stairs, and are contorted in positions that suggest exceptionally violent ends. Military personnel, technicians in lab coats torn and stained, office workers in the tattered remains of business attire. All beyond recognition and desiccated to leather-like husks. Many are eviscerated or mutilated beyond identification as human, if not for clothing remnants.

Tau appraises the scene with clinical detachment as he maneuvers around the remains, edging along the wall to the next flight, checking the upper level. A sizzling burst of heat and chemical stench announces Rho's return before either of us advances further.

"I welded the door edge to the frame. Not lasting, but it'll slow them down," He brushes his hands together, rolling his shoulders reflexively.

"We've got multiple floors to clear before reaching viable exit points. I'll take below, Tau middle, Rho above. Standard clearing procedures, but at one and a half speed. We don't have long."

I lead with Tau close behind, his poncho brushing against me at regular intervals. At the next turn, I shift laterally to check the landing between stair flights. The area is corpse-laden but shows no movement. Cautiously, I edge out, maintaining visual contact with the upper level while avoiding debris. The others are covering adjacent zones, but minimizing noise remains critical.

"Rho," I call quietly. "Advance to the next landing. I'll follow your move. Tau, take the rear. We'll leapfrog between positions."

"*Roger, Boss.*" The gunner jogs past and up the next flight, stopping at the landing. He gives no all-clear or follow signal. After thirty seconds of silence, I growl in frustration and take the stairs two at a time to his position.

His towering frame creates an effective blockade. Expecting him to make way, I nearly collide with his back before catching myself and cursing his name. Whatever he's fixated on has completely immobilized him. I follow his line of sight up the stairs and immediately understand.

A child, no more than ten years old, or what remains of one, lies broken across the upper steps. The lower torso rests flat while the upper portion spills downward, remnants of dark hair cascading over each step like a macabre waterfall.

There's an unsettling resemblance to another young girl we recently encountered, though she was very much alive when we last saw her. Electric blue eyes burning with raw hatred. The memory leaves me momentarily speechless.

I imagine Rho feels similarly affected. He formed an almost brotherly bond with Megan in that short span of time. It makes me wonder about his life before Zeta. Perhaps he had siblings—a younger sister? It would explain his protective instincts toward the team... when he's not being an insufferable ass.

Regardless, we can't afford to linger. I deliver a firm nudge to the tall soldier's side.

"Rho, we have to move. Our pursuers won't wait."

He inhales sharply, coming back to himself with a terse nod.

"*Yeah. Okay.*" Not another word passes as we clear the remaining steps.

We reach the next narrow landing with Tau positioned between us and press through the corner in a tight crouch. The next flight appears equally abandoned, save for the scattered remains frozen mid-flight. We've nearly cleared this level when the door below crashes open, the rhythmic pounding culminating in splintered metal.

Rho shouts a warning, but not about our pursuers. Somewhere above, a screech reverberates—organic and high-pitched yet distinctly inhuman. It pauses briefly before resuming its ear-splitting wailing.

Heart hammering, I advance despite every instinct screaming retreat. The source is unlike any Zee I've encountered. Its mass spans two or three human widths but lacks muscular definition— more amorphous blob than a predator. It occupies two-thirds of the landing. A hairless, bloated head sits nestled in the center of a mass of quivering, pale flesh layers. An at odds skeletal hand extends toward us with desperate intent. Rust-colored gore coats everything from its gaping maw to the floor beneath. But it's virtually immobile and, therefore, not the most immediate threat.

Shouts erupt behind us, distinctly human and closing fast, followed by sporadic gunfire. After evaluating our limited options, I make a reckless decision without consulting the others. I sprint directly at the nightmare, pushing off and dodging right at the final moment. Grip faltering, my rifle nearly slips from my grasp during landing, surprising me, but a desperate reflex secures it. Not dwelling on the almost, I wave the others forward without breaking momentum.

"Keep moving!"

They neatly sidestep the creature and continue their advance, boots pounding against metal stairs without hesitation. The Zee poses a minimal danger in its current state—too damaged to pursue but still baring its teeth in frustrated rage.

I rush to rejoin my team, lungs burning as I clear the next series of landings. Behind us, terrified screams erupt as our pursuers encounter the creature. Gunfire punctuates the chaos, followed by the monster's inhuman howls and human screams intermingling in a horrific concert.

Grimacing in reluctant sympathy, I find Rho and Tau waiting at the final door, its black signage clearly marked with "L" for "Lobby" in a reassuringly large font. This stairwell should have provided an adequately secure alternate egress if the primary route was compromised by structural damage or *Other Hazards*. We hadn't accounted for third-party infiltration—a significant tactical error. Regardless, we can't remain in the stairwell. The creature will only delay our pursuers temporarily.

"Tau, open and center. Rho, high right. I'll take low left."

"Sure you don't want the opposite? I can go low, and you go high," Rho snickers.

"Fuck off and do your job," I snarl, in no mood for height jokes. Not that I ever am.

I sense his desire to continue needling me, but I ignore it in favor of following Tau's bronze helmet into whatever awaits us. Ducking low with rifle raised, I position myself behind the Alpha. Both flanks appear clear of threats. Miraculously, we've reached our intended extraction point.

The corridor is blissfully empty. Emergency lighting flickers from our position to the far end, roughly ten yards distant. That should mark our exit to the exterior, where our bikes and teammates await. Tau pivots slowly from the doorway, equally surprised by the absence of resistance.

I seize the opportunity without hesitation.

"Move toward the eastern exit. Chi and the others should be there."

"*And if they're not?*" Rho questions.

"Then we locate them. We leave no one behind. That shouldn't require explanation."

The gunner raises his palms defensively. "*Got it. Just asking about contingencies. Sheesh.*"

"We'll address that once we're clear. No sense fixating on hypotheticals."

Tau intervenes, positioning himself between us. "*The corridor is secure. May I suggest we proceed as planned?*"

I scowl at his presumption, but can't fault his attempt to defuse what would have ended with my fist through Rho's faceplate. That doesn't mean I appreciate the Alpha's unsolicited mediation.

Directing a withering glare at Tau, I seal my faceplate before planting my palm firmly between Rho's shoulder blades. With a forceful shove, I propel him into the hallway. A thick layer of orange dust coats every surface, accumulating in drifts along the floor. Rho's boots disturb one such pile, sending particles billowing upward. My patience with both him and the Alpha wears dangerously thin.

"Watch your movement, Rho," I growl.

For once, he complies without commentary, perhaps unwilling to lose face in front of Tau. Or recognizing he's one misstep from joining the facility's body count. With rifle at the ready position, he navigates the remaining distance with surprising grace. Tau and I follow in formation, maintaining vigilance despite the apparent lack of threats. The absence of resistance feels suspicious—missions rarely conclude without chaotic finales.

Within minutes, we clear the hallway, exit point, and immediate exterior. The only missing elements are our remaining teammates. I prepare to contact them when movement at the edge of my vision draws attention.

One of the intruders' vehicles sits unattended at the perimeter. As we approach cautiously, their battered fleet of rust-bucket trucks and cars comes into view. There beneath one vehicle lies Omicron, his substantial frame wedged under the chassis. Mu crouches nearby, rifle ready. She lowers it immediately upon recognizing us.

With a nudge to Rho's shoulder, I lead toward the prone medic.

"Mu. Om. Status report?"

"*Almost finished, Omega! Chi's waiting with the bikes.*" Mu waves enthusiastically. Even with her faceplate sealed, her excitement radiates outward. Perhaps she's just relieved to see us intact.

Tilting to observe Omicron's work, I ask, "How many remain?"

The large man continues his work uninterrupted, clearly aware of our arrival. "Just two more after this one."

Surveying the small fleet, I marvel at his efficiency. "These guys clearly skipped the carpool lane."

"Need backup, brother?" Rho crouches near Omicron's position. The medic peers out from beneath the chassis.

"Sure thing. Finish splicing these cables." He extends several wires for Rho to trace to their connections. "I'll handle the last vehicle."

"No problem." Rho passes his rifle to me as Omicron extracts himself. The lankier soldier slides into the vacated position.

"Tau. Cover Omicron." The bronze helmet nods, already turning to shadow the medic to the remaining truck.

I assess our sniper with a quick head motion toward our concealed bikes. "Mu, join Chi and prepare for immediate departure. I'll remain with Rho."

We maintain low profiles, attempting to blend with the terrain. I divide my attention between the door we exited and the bend concealing the main entrance. We've secured both the stairwell and exterior access, but nothing's guaranteed. I refuse to lose the intel or personnel at this stage.

Rho works with surprising competence, requiring minimal supervision. I need to remember his aptitude for mechanical systems extends beyond basic familiarity. He's no match for Chi's technical expertise, but he clearly understands fundamental hardware manipulation.

The midday sun beats mercilessly overhead, baking everything within reach. Sweat traces the ridge of my spine as it collects and trickles downward. The heat and stillness feel suffocating, too quiet. My instincts scream imminent complication.

But then Rho slides from beneath the matte blue sedan. His spine cracks audibly as he rises from the prone position. Absently, he attempts to brush endemic dust from his gloves and body armor with limited success. At some point, he removed his helmet— his angular face appears haggard beneath a layer of grime that's settled into every crease and pore. Not that I look any better, likely.

I return his rifle, which he accepts readily, then check our remaining team members. Omicron rolls clear of the final truck, with Tau hovering nearby and monitoring the facility entrance. Surprisingly, no alarm has sounded, and no pursuit materializes. It feels wrong—that persistent itch between my shoulder blades intensifies. I'm anxious to put significant distance between us and this place.

With a sharp gesture, I summon Omicron and Tau to our position before shouldering my rifle and setting pace toward our remaining squadmates. Mu and Chi stand ready, acknowledging our approach with curt nods.

"Data secure?" I ask the latter.

She taps a small pouch above her left breast. "*Completely. Thoroughly encrypted and protected. All system traces were eliminated. I do not leave loose ends.*"

I smirk. "Never doubted it. We've neutralized their transportation capabilities. Let's return to base before HQ springs additional surprises." With my entire team, plus one, assembled and safe, I deliver a final order I'm grateful to give. "Mount up and move out. Mu, Rho on point. Chi, Tau center. Omicron, follow with me on rear guard."

The formation appears random, but it serves a specific purpose—Chi and Tau represent our highest-value assets for this final segment. Without prompting, Mu accelerates forward like a bolt, followed closely by Rho, Chi, and Tau. Omicron and I complete the formation. Within minutes, the abandoned facility diminishes to a pale smudge in my rearview. I have zero desire ever to see it again.

—Ω—

WHAT FOLLOWED AFTER

[KARI]

The warmer hues of the day begin to give way to the cool blues and violets that herald the night. I sit among twenty or so of our people outside the dilapidated structure, watching over those in various states of wellness. The worst off were laid out on old, green and brown tarps that had seen better days spread across the hard-packed desert floor. We'd tended to the injured as best we could with our limited resources without leaving this place. Not that any of us wouldn't prefer to be anywhere else—hence waiting outside in the growing dark instead of inside that flickering gloom with its shroud of death hanging over.

I hear the engines first, from some distance off. A genuine fear grips me—what if whoever approaches isn't who we're expecting? Could those soldiers we'd encountered earlier, seemingly out of nowhere, be returning for something they forgot? Or worse, had they been ordered to finish the job?

But no, it doesn't sound like motorcycles or whatever those machines are. Grabbing the binoculars to confirm, relief washes over me. It's them. Ragged cheers go up around me, though I make sure everyone keeps their voices down, mindful of wandering Zee that could be in the area. An absent joy infuses our group, making even our failure seem less crushing. A small group of vehicles becomes visible to the naked eye just outside the parking lot, comprising sedans, four-wheel drives, and SUVs.

We're thoroughly energized now, eager to meet our arriving companions as they slow, then stop altogether. The sharp click of doors opening and closing punctuates the sudden silence. Booted feet cross the few yards to the concrete steps in front of the facility's entrance. At the end of the new group, a figure follows, careful and deliberate in their steps. A curling wooden cane accompanies their movement, muted clacks against the hard-packed earth chronicling their slightly slower progress.

Father. I'd know that silhouette anywhere.

He reveals himself in the waning light—middle-aged at the minimum, though older in the body than by his face. His age is evident in how he holds himself. His pale green eyes reflect the few spotlights we'd set up in our makeshift camp, providing basic luminosity without attracting attention. A short, scraggly beard covers the lower half of his face, charcoal gray and white mixed with a smattering of burnt orange. It might match whatever hair remains on his head, but that's impossible to tell with the wide-brimmed Panama Jack-style hat pulled snugly over his crown.

Father surveys us with a subdued smile and nod. "Things did not go according to plan, did they?" he asks, not unpleasantly and with little judgment. More of an observation than anything.

"Yes, Father," Micah pipes up immediately, his forehead sporting a broad swath of white gauze curled tightly around it. "We weren't expecting to run into soldiers...or anything else in there."

I wince slightly. I should have anticipated the possibility.

"And yet, we must do so at all times. Not just now, but in the future. Do not assume that we are alone in this, my children," Father gently chides.

Heads nodded slowly in agreement around me. Humbled but not ashamed. I feel the weight of responsibility firmly settle upon my shoulders—I'd led this mission, after all.

Father gazes upon us, lowering his bushy eyebrows as he considers our numbers before his sight stops on me. "How many did we lose?" His voice is barely above a whisper, but we all hear him well. Everyone is so eager to know his words that he might as well have shouted the question.

I step forward. "Six altogether, Father," I keep my voice steady despite the hollow ache in my chest. "There's maybe a seventh if Elijah can't hold on until we return to camp."

A few speak amongst themselves, their voices low and mournful. Father nods in understanding but doesn't push for more details, at least not yet. There'll be time for that later. Instead, he shifts his attention to our dormant transports, hobbling slowly to the nearest automobile, taking time to run a scarred hand along its dusty hood.

"And what happened here?"

"They severed something under all the cars, Father," answers Nathan from beside me, draped in his drab gray poncho with fraying edges. "We haven't been able to correct it yet." He pauses before looking up almost shyly under his fringe of dirty blonde hair. "We were hoping someone in your group might have an answer. None of us really know much about cars."

I'd tried my best with the vehicles, but mechanics has never been my strong suit. Instead, I focused on keeping everyone calm and organizing a defensive perimeter in case those soldiers returned.

Father nods absently, toeing the shifted dirt with his shoe's tip, nudging the parts and pieces commingled with it. Something catches his eye—from where I stand, I can't tell what. Whatever it is, Father's old aches and discomforts don't prevent him from reaching down to retrieve whatever he found. Cradling it within his palm, he turns it over in thoughtful inspection. Clearly, he's interested, but he doesn't bother to share, nor does he need to.

"No matter," he states firmly. His fist carefully closes around his discovery as he gently leverages back to standing. "Matthew. We'll need the duct tape and whatever spare motor oil we have."

"Yes, Father." Matthew hurries to comply, his khaki trench coat flying in the wake of his departure.

Father's gaze is steady as he follows Matthew's departure, but not his path. Instead, he turns toward the horizon. As I step beside him, mindful of my proximity, I scan the same distant line. We both know that although we won't find evidence of them, those soldiers are out there somewhere, continuing their journey.

I can't shake the image of Omega's face when our paths had crossed earlier. That momentary flicker in her eyes—did she recognize me from when her Zeta team had taken us in? I accidentally unleashed that trapped horde of Zee on their camp, leaving them to deal with the bloody aftermath while we escaped. The guilt of that still gnawed at me, though I'd never admitted it to Father or the others. I'm trying to earn my place as a leader now rather than dwelling on past mistakes.

Omega's team might not have known who we were then, but they'll have a slightly clearer idea now. We aren't exactly on the same side. Still, I wonder if they'll report this to their superiors, as they must have previously. It's doubtful Omega kept her team's interaction with us private. No matter. Our paths are destined to collide once more, and though today is a setback, something tells me I'll face that team again before this is over. Whether it be as enemies or something else, only fate will determine.

But what did they miss? A glance at Father's closed fist leaves me wondering what piece of the puzzle he'd found and what use it'll be to us. To end the Zee.

—⊙—

ACT 5
THE ALLURE OF ENDINGS

ARRIVALS AND DEPARTURES

Traveling between missions. Those long stretches of empty desert and clear skies. There's no other person to be seen and no activity beyond the forward momentum of the ATCs. It's the closest to serenity that I experience these days.

Many on my team bitch and moan about the journey from one site to another. The continuous repetition of setting up and breaking down a campsite. Of tensed backs over metal monstrosities, eyes vigilant for a stray Zee or the thin plumes of marauders on the move. We tend to avoid, or at a minimum ignore, the other beings out here. Most Zee are in no state to give chase or cause problems. Hell, I wonder if we move so fast they can't track us. We try not to engage the one-offs and smaller hordes unless there's a risk of them showing up at our doorstep later.

The marauders are different. We may have more on them in terms of strength and ability, and our equipment is pretty formidable to be on the wrong end of. Where they cause problems comes down to two things: numbers and territoriality. Marauders choose a site, sometimes an abandoned one, or they overtake the existing living spaces of civvies and acquire captives. From there, they become territorial and claim as much of the surrounding area as they can defend. This usurpation gives them a central base from which to operate. Of course, this stability allows them to accrue additional people who lack scruples and definitely outnumber us.

So far, they're not stupid enough to challenge the full strength of the UF, but that doesn't stop them from coming after smaller teams like mine. That's my difficulty—I'd rather shoot first, second, and third time between the eyes than give them any opportunity to harm my people. It's a gray area for the UF. Technically, we shouldn't engage them first. Nor should we shoot to kill.

Shoulda, woulda, coulda. My team comes first.

After that craziness with the abandoned UF site and the cultists—Ah, right. They have a name—one that I made sure to sear into my memory to inform our superiors and aid in putting the fear of their God in them. The Shepherds of Light...SOL. How utterly disappointing in originality. Like they played spin the bottle with religious terms and randomly paired a couple. Voila! Instant cult, complete with T-shirts. With the acronym version of their name, I'm betting someone with a prior life in marketing or IT had a hand in the naming.

All joking aside, they were better informed about the building than we were. Somehow, guarded knowledge of how deep the site ran and the type of work being done there was common knowledge. Something's amiss in all of this. Add that to the list, along with how well-organized they were and how handy they were with taking out the Zee. Seriously, WTF?

Now that I've managed to rev myself up over something I have zero control over, I focus on the horizon ahead. The sun's already a few hours into its daily odyssey across the sky. We are as well, simply on a smaller scale, as we head straight for the base. Having left right as the sun crested, we made good time on the last leg of our journey. That's good and bad. A somber tone has taken over my team, even the plus one. There's hesitation in completing our goal as it implies an end to this new dynamic we've found. That feeling of loss only strengthens as we near the base.

The last hour of riding has been in complete radio silence. The level of internalizing around me is blatant compared to how this team typically operates. Rho's annoying music isn't blasting through the comms, for one. No back and forth between Chi and Omicron, with Mu piping in to add her two cents. Tau acts like a man on a death march. Since our impromptu chat at the fireside several nights ago, he hasn't said a word to me beyond basic soldier pleasantries. Can't tell if he's spoken to anyone else. All I know is that once we reach base, we'll be back down to five, and if we're lucky, we'll get some green Zeta added to our team in his place.

I realize he was never on my team. I understand this, as does everyone else. Gods can't tell me why I don't want that asshole to leave, but it's all I can think about. I should be glad. Hell, grateful, at least. Tau, the arrogant prick that he is, is a superb soldier who is seasoned and skilled, but his integration hasn't been seamless. Over the last four months, he's gone from an unplanned outsider to an indispensable comrade. One who can be relied upon to execute an order, similar to Rho or Chi. He's become an invaluable asset.

The difficulty lies in assigning a member of the Alpha Squadron to Beta. I can't blame him for being eager to be reassigned and for things to return to normal for him. He'll join a new team, but his role should remain the same. No one to compete with for leadership. His burden of guilt remains his to carry, as I'm sure he will. Perhaps this is where we overlap most. Where we are equals. I'm responsible for all those under my command. What happened to Epsilon was my fault. The review panel may have ruled it an unfortunate accident, but I don't see it that way.

To permanently lose any more of my team is a pain I can't define or wish to. Having already experienced that destruction of my world, I'm not looking forward to knowing it ever again. That devastation will wreak havoc on my soul until I give my last breath. Even if Tau's stay was temporary, the feeling of loss still exists.

I can't believe myself either. How could I have gotten attached to that smug, sharp-tongued aristocrat when my instinct is to keep my sentiments tightly reined in? Emotions are the enemy of logic and not worth the trouble they bring. But I digress, and not a moment too soon. With no small amount of awe, our destination is finally in sight. Hell, it's hard to miss with monolithic walls of a height not seen since humans were into building megaliths.

It's been over six months since I last saw this gate, though I was on an exit path then. It makes our training base look like a low-budget film set. The outer walls are completely smooth and built from a combination of steel framing and concrete. They slope outward slightly from bottom to top, making scaling them by hand impossible, especially for Zee. The amount of concrete required was on a scale previously unvisited by modern man. However, the situation presented itself, and the remaining engineers rose to the challenge.

To make entry even more complicated, a deep trench surrounds the base, measuring no less than thirty feet across and fifteen feet deep and ending in a bell-bottom space that makes escape highly formidable. On our side of the trench, a metal security fence encircles it, interspersed with guard towers every fifty feet. The main entrance is watched over by a pair of towers equipped with Zeta and some nasty-looking large-caliber guns. The last piece of the puzzle is a barbed wire anti-personnel trap about ten feet out from the fence line that serves as a first layer of defense, and that's where we halt. The protocol now is to wait while someone from one of the guard towers verifies our identities via ID chips.

I've no clue how far back they can begin verification, but it still takes forever to get approval to come inside. If I'm ever pressed to get to safety due to some threat, I'll not be coming through the front door of this base. I'd be a pile of bones long before someone decided I was on the up and up and should be let in. Not that I expect difficulty being let in—the base has been expecting us. We've been in near constant contact with HQ over the last week, both to submit a SITREP for the latest mission and to inform them of our imminent arrival.

That's one benefit of being near a major outpost. Communications are damn near perfect—still not as clear as a pure satellite signal, but beggars aren't choosers. It'll be good to have access to maintenance, supplies, and R&R, which is another bonus of being back on base. Of course, there's a downside too. Much easier to keep control of your mutt when they're right by your side. We give up the freedom enjoyed in the field and go back to being pawns at their beck and call. But I'm not bitter.

In less time than expected, a woman's tinny voice comes through a speaker set somewhere incongruously in the landscape.

"Beta Team 226 and Alpha Squadron 42 Staff Sergeant Tau, you are cleared for entry. Please proceed directly to intake."

With that command, a section of the anti-personnel trap slickly pulls back and to the sides, clearing a pathway just wide enough for an ATC to run single file through. The cleared path meets with the massive outer security gates as they creak and grind on their hinges, pulled apart by invisible mechanisms. Beyond that, a massive bridge extends forth, covering the gaping abyss of the inescapable trench.

Turning in my seat to the others, I give a brief nod before kicking my bike into gear and proceeding at a steady, slow pace. My neck cranes up briefly to take in the guard towers, wondering, as always, who the gatekeepers are of our enclosure. I can't focus on it too long as I pick up speed, and my tires switch from the constant crunch of organic material to the smooth surface of a human-made road. No guardrails or warnings about going over the side of the bridge. It's wide enough for several tanks to cross simultaneously, but there's always that bottleneck once they pass either gate. Not the best design, in hindsight.

Another little bump and we clear the inner gate, past the enormous charcoal walls of the inner perimeter. It's as though we just left. Everything is placed, as I recall, down to the finest details. I'm sure the soldiers manning it are the same as well. A single soldier flags us with a lit wand, glowing brightly fuchsia even in the midday sun. We follow the unspoken direction, parking each of our ATCs in an orderly fashion just within the gates. They'll be scanned and searched for any foreign signals or contraband, while the same is, in essence, done to us. There isn't exactly tremendous trust between the brass and its subordinates. Oh well. Worse things.

Upon dismounting, a relief settles across my shoulders that hasn't been there for half a year: *security*. Above all else, this place offers safety and freedom from the worries of survival. Stretching my arms high above my head, I embrace the feeling of finally being back— and successful at that. Between the Alpha's retrieval and the information we pulled from the defunct site, I am incredibly proud of my team. Yes, Tau is included. Fuck.

I won't bore you with the rigmarole that is intake. By the time we've all cleared it, the sun has well passed its zenith and is making a steep descent. At one point in the process, we are shepherded in one direction to debrief while Tau is led in another. I imagine he now has to recall and recount everything that befell his team in gruesome detail. I feel a pang of sympathy as I've endured a similar thing, granted, only for one soldier, but the trauma of that experience is inescapable.

The Alpha's haunted eyes and pale expression when we finally cross paths again only confirm this. Rho goes so far as to clap his shoulder with a companionable sort of half-hug. Tau, surprisingly, accepts the gesture and, in fact, leans into it, however briefly. Damn. Making eye contact with him, I'm surprised to see the regret I feel mirrored in his face. We've yet to shower and get cleaned up, but the Alpha's face is clear of dirt and blemishes, smooth and tanned by our lifestyle.

"Tau," I comment dumbly.

"Omega." He intones in reply. No derision this time.

"So, I imagine you are in line for team reassignment?" I hedge.

He shakes his head, though I imagine it's more in the unbelievable nature of all this. Lose five close companions? No therapy needed! The United Forces will provide new team members lickety-split. There's something very wrong about that.

"Yes. I have R&R for now, but it sounds like the intent is for me to lead a new Alpha squadron."

I try not to let my disappointment show. Somehow, I was hoping that Tau would decide to...what? Self-demote, not once but twice? Become a gunner on a Beta Squad? Definitely ridiculous and unrealistic on my part.

"That's great." I try to channel some of Mu's enthusiasm. The rest of the team is quick to follow with praise and support. This transition is rough for everyone.

"Yes." He ducks his head almost in embarrassment. "I am in the Alpha barracks for now until that happens. Where are you headed to?" As if he doesn't already know.

Rubbing the back of my neck, I confirm, "We're on to Beta barracks. We've at least graduated to a private building for the team, so that's a plus." Tau smiles weakly in response. "There's the potential for getting an additional squadmate assigned to round out the team prior to the next deployment as well."

"Excellent." He smiles genuinely at that, although there's a pinch to his expression. I recognize that this is the point where we part ways and go our separate ways. I do my best to handle the transition with all the decency I can manage, even while my head screams that this is an opportunity lost.

"Well. I think this is where we part, Staff Sergeant Tau. I wish you the best of luck in your future assignments. The team will miss *y...*" Here, I struggle with what to say versus the truth. "Your skills and experience in the field."

Genially, I offer my hand to him. All that I can offer. He grasps my extended hand, and I almost gasp at the skin-to-skin contact. I'd forgotten that I'd removed my gloves earlier. Apparently, Tau did as well. The hand that clasps mine is warm and dry, but soft and clear of the rough calluses you expect in our line of work. I don't know what to think. Blankly, I complete the handshake but am quick to drop his hand for the next member of my team.

As they say their farewells and well-wishes, I turn my back on them all. It's not my intention to make a big scene or draw attention away from Tau's departure. I need to get out of here. I'm fully intent on leaving this space, this place, and after debriefing, making my way to the first bar I can find.

—Ω—

A MISERABLE WAY TO START THE DAY

I'm halfway to the Tactical Operations Center when I realize I've left behind the one person essential for this debrief. Thankfully, my data analyst-slash-scout-slash-demolition expert remembered far sooner than I did.

As I turn to backtrack, I find her ten steps behind me, hurrying to catch up. I pause and wait until she's beside me. Her narrow face shows a light pink flush from exertion, but not a hair out of place. Chi's perfect order stands in stark contrast to the chaos that radiates from me.

She offers me a minimalist smile of acknowledgment.

"Finally realized you forgot someone important?"

I snort but don't disagree. No sense pretending otherwise.

"Yeah, sorry. Head's in the clouds a bit."

"I cannot imagine why that would be the case." Her lofty expression matches her tone perfectly.

"Well, between gaining an Alpha, preventing said Alpha from self-destruction, falling into a literal pit where Rho and I nearly died, leaving a child in a Zee-infested mall, entering a questionable base with even more questionable data, running into second-rate zealots, and finally offloading the Alpha…Oh, yeah, I'm *fine*."

"Is that all?" She asks, serious despite her dry delivery. She knows the gravity of what I've just glossed over.

"Those are the pertinent points, though I'm not sure how much I want to share with the brass."

She nods once, contemplating. Her long strides slow to match my pace. I'm in no hurry to sit in a room for hours, rehashing every detail of our time away. That's where Chi comes in handy— her memory is invaluable, particularly for visuals. She is less reliable with audio or names, but her visual recall is unmatched.

"There is little to be done regarding most of what has transpired. You know what was reported during our rotation, particularly about the Alpha and the retrieved data."

"Yeah...about that data," My steps slow to a halt even as my mind turns. "Omicron shared some thoughts on what we found."

The scout stops, scanning our surroundings subtly. So subtle, I'd have missed it if I hadn't been right beside her. Satisfied with our security, she continues. "Ah, yes. Do tell me what your take is on what he imparted?"

Rubbing my neck out of habit, I reflect. "That facility, while United Forces-run, it isn't your typical abandoned site."

I pause to gather my thoughts, and Chi prompts, "Continue."

"Beyond standard research and development, the timestamps go back at least four decades. Additionally, tests of some sort were conducted on people, including children. Any highlights I'm missing?"

She hums. "There is one additional piece that may interest you. Something called *Origo*."

"Origo," I repeat. I remember it, but the name didn't stick.

Chi taps her pointer finger against her lower lip, musing aloud. "That one gave me considerable trouble. It's not as straightforward as other archives. The timing of Origo spanned those four decades, including up to when the facility was decommissioned."

"So, what is it? An experiment? A person, place, or thing?"

"It is quite possible," she interjects, "that Origo describes either a test data set or a hypothesis—something requiring long-term tracking." I open my mouth to say more, but am quickly cut off.

"To answer your next question, Origo means '*origin*' or '*beginning*.'"

"Not ominous at all. But why would the UF leave important data sitting around unattended for over a decade? Conversely, why the sudden interest in retrieving the data?"

"And for that matter," Chi adds sharply, "how would interlopers with no known UF affiliation find a backdoor into the base and know to steal that precise information?"

"You mean those 'Shepherds of Light'?"

"Precisely. There are too many intersecting points. One wonders what has transpired." She sighs into the warm morning air.

I almost follow suit before catching myself, rubbing my hand across my face, likely leaving dirt streaks, but not caring.

"The data you found went directly to HQ, right?"

She nods.

"Then, not much more we can do. I'll have to explain how these cultists accessed the base and data, why we didn't terminate them, and why I let them go."

Arms crossed, eyes shuttered, she responds, "We executed within mission parameters. Data was retrieved and wiped. We lacked resources and time to capture the intruders."

"Plus, our original objective was getting the Alpha back in one piece. We're in the clear."

Chi hums again—agreement, or perhaps her usual disdain for civilians. Never can tell.

"Did we miss anything? Something about those Shepherds that was overlooked?" she asks, more curious than concerned.

Looking skyward, I think aloud. "One thing," I hesitate, not to save face but because it involves omitted details from a prior report. "Remember that group of women we sheltered? I might have run into one of them."

"What?" Chi's response and perplexed expression almost make admitting this worth it.

"Yeah. Pretty sure I saw Kari at the site, dressed and armed like those server room guys."

"They did seem vaguely familiar." She rubs her pointed chin thoughtfully. "Their attire was too similar for coincidence, matching how those women dressed."

I nod. "Hell of a coincidence."

"Indeed. As coincidental as those women appearing near a Zee-infested office complex."

The day's heat intensifies. I wipe sweat from my brow with gloved fingertips. With no immediate threats and relative base safety, my self-awareness returns—the itch of unwashed fabric, dirt embedded in my scalp, even the base's usually comforting scents masked by my body odor. I exhale, trying not to breathe deeply.

"That's my thinking, too. Do we tell Command or let them connect the dots?"

The scout frowns ever so slightly. "Perhaps that is one area we should not focus on presently."

"Agreed."

Chi starts forward, then pauses, sensing my hesitation without any obvious tell.

"What is it, Omega?" Her question comes low and quiet.

I shake my head, considering how much to share. There's no point avoiding it—Chi will extract it eventually. She's good at that.

"Is it the child, Megan?" Chi asks directly, already knowing.

"Yeah. Can't stop thinking about her trapped with those monsters." I see her heart-shaped face dark hair framing those piercing blue eyes. "I failed her. We failed her."

Chi tilts her head, purple forelocks shifting as she processes my words.

"As you stated, the girl has survived alone in that buried mall for some time. Perhaps even thrived."

"That's how it seemed. But how does a kid survive active hordes?"

Chi's eyes narrow in thought. "How old would you estimate she was?"

I snort. "Worst question for me. Ten? Eleven? Preteen, anyway."

"I see." Her speech slows deliberately. "Yet it must have been apparent that the structure was buried for more than a few years. That mall's condition—the desert's consumption of it."

It's obvious where she's going. It's occurred to me, too, but I've been sidestepping this particular ugliness.

"I understand what you're saying, but it's impossible. She must have ended up there later somehow. That's the only explanation that makes sense."

"Truly?" The lilt in Chi's voice accentuates my naivety. "The simplest answer is often correct."

"But it doesn't make sense, Chi." I know why I can't accept it. I don't want to face that truth.

With a dancer's grace, she pivots to face me fully.

"Was there anything in her demeanor that seemed off? Any behavior inconsistent with your mental model of a child?"

I know the answer to that. Chi's words weigh on me as doubt grows into something more disturbing. With so many unknowns, it's hard to be sure about anything. The scout takes my silence as confirmation, nodding in agreement with some unspoken fact. But how could she be anything but the child we saw? Who interacted with us as any child would?

I offer nothing more, and Chi lets the subject drop for now. She's not finished with me, but maybe later, I'll feel like exploring this rabbit hole.

"All right," I straighten my shoulders, projecting confidence I don't feel. "Let's get this over with."

Chi's currant eyes close briefly in acceptance before falling in beside me as we move toward TOC.

"And Chi," I say without breaking stride or making eye contact, "Let's keep that mall business between us."

—Ω—

PATIENCE IS A VIRTUE I CARE LITTLE FOR

The weight of the cool metal bar presses down upon me with unrelenting force. Thin rivulets of sweat carve paths down my forehead, sliding along my brow, then nose, until dropping behind me. But I don't falter. I won't.

With arms locked and muscles tensed, I push the bar away from my face. The slow but steady pressure has my sides heaving with each breath. I give a final shove and extend my arms fully, placing the bar back in its rack before collapsing against the padded bench. Above my head, a large fan churns slowly in its endless rotation, circulating artificially cool air throughout the room.

I blink away the annoyingly dull white ceiling before a long-chinned, goateed face blocks my vision. Garnet eyes appear below hair, a few shades darker.

"Well, that was impressive." Rho grins cheekily, and I resist the urge to smack him on principle.

"How impressive?" My eyes dart to the side, attempting to see the numbers on the screen, but its surface is turned away from me.

Glancing to the side as well, Rho smirks but doesn't help by actually turning the device so that I can read it. Ass.

"Let's just say you beat your last record by fifteen percent."

He offers me a gloved hand up, which I grasp quickly, squeezing initially too hard before letting him leverage me into a sitting position. Half-joking, he shakes his hand as if in pain. I ignore both him and his dramatics in favor of wrapping up my routine.

The soft terry cotton of the towel draped over my shoulder feels great as I swipe away the remaining moisture from my brow.

Reaching below my seat, I snag my canteen and take a swig, expecting tepid water but pleasantly surprised when it still has the subtle clink of ice cubes. Yet another luxury of being back in the pen. Real, honest to God, ice.

Taking in my de facto second, I notice he's wearing a steel gray long-sleeve shirt along with his gloves. Innocuous in design, it does an excellent job covering his upper torso. I raise an eyebrow at this—it's well over a hundred degrees outside. Noticing my appraisal, Rho shrugs, unrepentant. It doesn't bother any of us that he has a military-grade prosthetic. However, for whatever reason, he always gets like this around crowds. I've never taken Rho for the self-conscious type, more like the not-so-secretly nudist kind. Then again, he's probably doing it more for others' comfort than his own. He can be considerate like that.

Shaking drips of perspiration clinging to the short ends of my hair, a few land on the taller soldier, eliciting a "Hey!"

I smile in response to his protest, but the expression quickly drops. It's been over a week of downtime, and I'm still in the same mental state. If anything, I'm anxious and cagey, and I can be outright irritable with anyone attempting to interact with me. I seem unable to shake off my irritation with Tau or my frustration with things in general.

I shouldn't have expected anything different from him, but I did. I thought I'd witnessed greater depth and understanding in the Alpha. One that would lend itself to a different path, a merger of sorts, of his world and ours, where the balance would be struck, benefiting all of us.

How totally wrong I was. No matter. It's happened, and life has proceeded in its never-ending forward march, as always. I'm grateful for my team, but they're driving me insane. Between Mu's sympathetic remarks and Chi's knowing looks, I'm this close to either stabbing one of them or running away screaming. Instead, I'm going to take the grown-up soldier route and occupy myself productively elsewhere.

A clang of metal on metal brings me back to the present. Rho has moved on and is working out on his own using a weight machine. Even with his robotic limb, he still needs to exercise the muscles and tendons that support it or risk tearing something permanently. Looks like he doesn't need a spotter.

"Hey, Rho. I'm gonna wash up and head to Personnel."

"Okay." He grunts mid-rep before pausing to ask, "What for?"

Shifting to avoid eye contact, I continue grabbing my stuff but don't respond immediately. He doesn't move, waiting for me to continue.

"I'm going to see if there are any solo assignments I can grab. I need to do something, and it might as well be something useful."

"Really? You want some company?" He asks cautiously.

Probably worried I'm going to bite his head off. I have my sights set elsewhere, though, so as long as he stays out of my crosshairs, he'll survive.

"Nah, don't bother. Assuming I don't come back from Personnel, can you let the team know I'll be gone for a couple of days?"

Sighing, I finally work up the nerve to take in his expression. He looks disappointed, and there's that damn sympathy permeating his face. At least he has the intelligence not to voice it.

"Fine. Just message me the specs so we know what's up."

"Okay." I nod, already halfway out the nearest door. I'm unsure if he sees the gesture, but I have little desire to linger. There's an itch under my skin to move and move now. It's hard to believe that others don't have the same driving urge. They certainly don't act like it.

"Omega, wait up."

I pause at the door but don't turn around. "What?"

"Look, I get that you're pissed about the whole Tau situation, but—"

"It's not about Tau." The rebuke comes too quickly, too sharply.

"Right." His tone suggests he's not buying it. "So, what did the brass say about SOL?"

I finally turn to face him. "Not much. They took the intel and filed their reports. Business as usual."

"And the fact that these cultists knew exactly where to find classified data in an abandoned UF facility?"

"Above my pay grade, apparently." The bitterness in my voice surprises even me.

Rho sets down his weights and walks closer. "What about Megan?"

My jaw tightens. "What about her?"

"Did you mention her? The odd Zeta kid trapped in that mall?"

I shake my head. "No point. What would they do? Send a retrieval team for one quasi-civilian? Waste resources on a maybe?"

"So you just left it out."

"I left it out." The admission tastes sour.

Rho studies my face for a long moment. "That's what's really eating at you, isn't it? Not Tau. The kid."

I don't answer, but I don't need to. He's known me for too long.

"You can't save everyone, Omega."

"Don't." I hold up a hand, my voice going flat and dangerous. "Just don't."

He raises both hands in surrender. "Alright. But maybe taking off solo right now isn't the best—"

"It's exactly what I need." I turn back toward the door. "Two days. Maybe three. I'll be back before our next rotation."

"And going solo when you're this wound up?"

I pause, grateful he doesn't know about the real issues—the way my hands sometimes shake now, the brief moments where my enhanced strength has failed me entirely. I thought I'd have recovered at this point.

"Nothing's going to happen." I attempt to change my approach, trying to placate him.

"You don't know that. You're not exactly thinking clearly right now."

I finally look back at him, and for a moment, the apparent concern almost breaks through my resolve. Almost.

"I'll be fine, Rho. I just need some space to think."

He nods slowly, clearly not happy about it but recognizing a losing battle when he sees one. "Just… be careful out there. And check in."

"Will do."

As I push through the door into the corridor, I catch his parting shot in the gap between.

"And Omega? Tau's an idiot for not staying."

I don't respond, but something tight in my chest loosens just a fraction. Maybe that's why I keep Rho around—even when he's being a pain in the ass, he somehow knows exactly what I need to hear.

—Ω—

AN INTERIM ARRANGEMENT

It really is my fault. I'm clear on that.

The aide behind the counter shuffles through another thin stack of papers for the fifth time. I pray to whatever god or demon is listening for patience to not end this person. Patience and perhaps a halfway decent mission.

The swishing of old paper pauses, and in that gap of silence, I'm lulled into hopeful anticipation. Then, further disappointment as her sorting continues, along with whatever protocol she's following. Of course, I'm assuming that's what this soldier is doing. Beyond a halo of dark black curls, I can't see who I'm dealing with over the counter. I'm assuming it's female based on the hair and voice, but that's a big assumption.

Far be it from me to say anything about the inaccessibility of UF-regulation countertops. I'd rather silently sulk than draw attention to it. Not that there's much else to stimulate my visual cortex, or at least distract me. Like every other building not inhabited by soldiers, the walls here are depressingly blank and painfully white. Except for those made of steel instead of concrete— those are just gray. Zero personality—like this soldier who's yet to find an assignment that a solo Zeta could be useful for. Great inefficiency.

"Oh!" The exclamation causes my head to pop up eagerly.

A round face joins the hair as the soldier peers down at me from on high. Her bright smile reminds me of another soldier, but only in its openness. The rest of Private 'Whoever' is as different from Mu as I can compare them to.

"Yes, Sergeant. I've found something that could work. It arrived a couple of days ago—general maintenance and engineering. It was somehow misfiled under Alpha-level assignments, but it's intended for Beta. You're good with machine diagnosis and repair, right?"

I'm positive my expression flatlined, and not intentionally. Nothing like being reminded of one's shortcomings. Her face drops in reaction to mine. Sucking on my teeth, I give her my most pleasant smile, given the situation.

"Yeah. That's doable. Sign me up."

Her returning smile is tentative as she fumbles on. "I mean... It's fairly straightforward—one of the few we get. A UF township nearby is having trouble with its communication array. They're requesting support to resolve the issue, hopefully without requiring an entire team and all the time and materials that implies."

My less-than-thrilled dead stare adds to the soldier's nervousness. Her fidgeting spikes, rolling one of the pens along the worn white surface. The fact that this woman has sole responsibility, along with the ability to deny me work, let alone decent work... I take a step back, closing my eyes briefly to reduce stimuli as my breathing slows.

It's not this soldier's fault I'm relegated to low-end repair work outside my team's assignments. Hell, I should be grateful for the opportunity to do anything other than skulk around the base and avoid starting fights.

"Fine." I grit out, slapping my palm to the cool surface a few inches from where the private leans. The abrupt gesture startles her, causing her to jump out of her chair, which she nervously giggles over. That uncomfortable behavior is worse than if she hadn't said anything at all.

My hand flips over and makes little 'gimme' grabbing motions. Her smile wanes, almost breaking. She delicately hands over the mission specs before pulling her extended hand back sharply as if expecting a bite. My eyebrow flips up at the behavior, but I hold back from commenting. Unhooking my helm to have it loose and ready, I abruptly turn on my heel.

Without another word to the quasi-helpful soldier, I exit the Personnel building and don't look back. It's easy to scoff at the admin and her apparent ineptitude. I try not to judge her too strongly. Not everyone who serves in the UF is warrior material. Some are just trying to make it to the end. End of what? Who knows? It sure as hell isn't this base in the ass end of nowhere. Yeah, it's relatively safe and sane, but is there truly a place one can consider 'safe'? Flesh-eating humans wander around, grabbing a nibble here and there like one long buffet line.

The first step outside shifts the temperature by twenty degrees. It'll be another warm one. The ideal climate for spending half a day on a communication array, running basic functionality tests.

Whoopee.

The crunch of loose gravel beneath my treads transitions to the hushed texture of asphalt. With my eyes closed, I could still find where the bikes were stored. Follow the black line of tar to the land of plenty. Or at least the base parking lot. A brisk pace has me moving double time to get on my way. I don't want any excuse to get in the way of me leaving.

With the covered grounds dead ahead, I queue up Rho's line from my gauntlet. Hopefully, he's not in the middle of doing something or someone.

"Rho, you read me, over?"

"Reading you loud and clear, Megs, over."

"Good. I've got a half-day mission underway. Heading out to a nearby civvie safe zone to check on their comms equipment. Should be back by dinner."

The line lapses into silence, accompanied by the light crackle of static from an open mic. More than likely, Rho's near the rest of our teammates and conveying what I just told him.

"*Yeah, we'll hold you to that. I have it on good authority that they're serving lasagna tonight, so don't miss it.*"

"Not likely to," I chuckle lowly. "That's a meal worth coming back to."

"*Damn straight!*" As the gunner pauses again, I catch the tail end of some side conversation going on wherever he is. Barracks, maybe? Mu's voice dominates the tone of the discussion.

"I'll be back soon, Rho. Keep an eye on everyone for me, will you?"

"*You know I will. See you in a few. Over and out, Sarge.*"

"Over and out."

In a laughable amount of time, I'm back astride my beast and rolling through the gates under the sentries. My bike practically purrs, moving just as smoothly as it can without a paved path beneath its tires. After a week of retooling and repairs, our machines are back to spec.

As I head to my destination, miles of open and empty terrain and a midday sun are my companions. One hundred miles of this, I can manage. Almost cheerfully. Anything's better than sitting on my ass and moping about what might have been and what never could be.

—Ω—

COMMUNICATION IS A TRICKY THING

The communications array rises like a cream-colored bowl balanced on a monolith in the middle of the desert. Like everything else the UF builds out here, it's functional and lacking in artistic flair. At the very least, it provides me with a clear destination to head toward.

There's an unpaved dirt track running parallel to the array. Its smoother surface is carved through the surrounding desert and is well-worn enough to imply regular traffic. My guess is it leads to the civilian township.

I've never been out this far in this direction for United Forces work, so it's an interesting experience. Thankfully, maintenance and functionality checks on these terminals are relatively low-tech and don't require a high level of expertise. If you're in the field, you're taught basic maintenance of typical UF machinery. As a general rule, we can be called upon to provide assistance wherever needed, even if it's only five percent of our duty statement.

As expected, the location is flat, innocuous, and utterly dull. I opt to park my bike directly next to the array. Attempting to find a decent hiding spot provides little value other than forcing me to hoof it the extra distance. The likelihood of encountering hostiles is low this close to the base. Marauders tend to keep a wide berth from UF-protected spaces, and any stray Zee are regularly cleared from the area.

Beneath the wide, curved bottom of the dish is the array's interface. Nothing fancy. Actually, it's pretty straightforward—the first portion of my assignment is equally so.

Calling up my gauntlet's interface, I hold my forearm close to the largest panel and let the two antiquated pieces of tech have a conversation. It takes thirty seconds of flickering code, along with a smattering of tinny chirps and beeps, for the two to agree they know each other and allow me access. The hatch creaks shrilly as the rusty hinge opens the panel door outward. Gazing into the mess of wires and connections, I'm overwhelmed for a moment by the seemingly chaotic layout. But I'm no green private.

Extending one of the built-in interface cables from its housing within my gauntlet, I push it into a matching port.

"Okay. Let's see what the problem is," I mutter to myself, already focused.

Swiping through menu options on my local interface, I select the built-in tests for self-diagnostics. The simplest way to identify obvious issues is by querying the system to do it for you. Rudimentary, I know, but it's why just about any operator can perform the basic maintenance these terminals require. The tests can rapidly identify up to ninety percent of terminal issues.

As the diagnostic runs, I idly take in the relatively vacant scenery surrounding me. Though in the dish's shadow, I'm already sitting warm in my gear. Fifty-plus pounds of armor, weaponry, and standard tactical gear will do that. The arid atmosphere, even combined with a slight breeze, is stifling. But there's something about the scent of sun-warmed desert sand, perfumed by the various oils hardy lowland vegetation secretes. Almost pleasant. Homey, in fact.

But this isn't my home, nor are the base and its barracks. I could wax philosophical about how my team is where my home lies, but that isn't quite true either. Home, either technically or in some transcendental sense, has no grounding in my life.

A bright flash from my gauntlet's inset screen signals completion.

The tests have all come back green. Based on their analysis, everything appears to be in order with the unit. Not a single damn issue.

That rules out the easy route for figuring out the problem. Moving on to more manual processes, I inspect the power, cables, generator, and all associated components, even verifying the antenna's alignment. But there's nothing. At least, nothing I can pick out with the tools at hand. At most, the array needs a good wipe-down of the antenna. The rest of the routine maintenance was completed a couple of months ago, according to the system's logs.

Gazing up at the apparatus, sweat gathering along my collar, I again run through the standard protocol in my mind, searching for a missed step. But nope. I may not have a photographic memory, but I can recall the procedures for servicing these Ground Mobile Force terminals. My focus shifts to the road ahead, where I know the dependent outpost lies, just out of visual range but within range of short-wave radio communications. I should be able to connect with their local communications array with this proximity.

Jogging back to my bike, I pop the curved storage area just beneath my ATC's instrument panel and rifle through its contents. The loose blue missive sheet is easy to locate among the various hardware and tools I keep on hand. There it is, in the upper left corner, in bold, blocky type—the frequency of the requesting outpost, alongside contact information for the outpost's senior officer, a Malone character.

Keying in the six-digit code to my gauntlet, I wait for the call to go through. There's static...and then more, and then more. A minute of white noise is about what I can handle. Twice more, I try. At this point, it's to verify nobody's answering and that I didn't just miskey or perhaps not give them enough time to respond.

The latter is least likely, as these towns or outposts always have someone staffing their lines, regardless of time or day. The last thing the UF wants to hear is radio silence. But that's what I'm getting, along with a deepening sense of unease in my gut.

Shielding my eyes from the unobstructed midday sun, I appraise that I have at least six to seven hours of daylight remaining. More than enough to make direct contact with whoever's manning the fort and find out what happened to their system. There's always a chance that the equipment malfunctioned for whatever reason. Nothing in use today has been manufactured for at least a couple of decades.

With that decided, I drop my helm into place, securing the leads to the lower jaw portion before radioing back to base.

"Base Command, this is Sergeant Omega Two Two, over."

This close to base, the response is clear and immediate. A sharp, nasal woman's voice assaults my ears.

"*Sergeant, this is Base Foxtrot Yankee Communications reading you loud and clear. Proceed, over.*"

"Base, I've completed diagnostics of GMF terminal One Seven and have not identified any issues through BIT, environmental, or physical inspections. A subsequent short-wave communications test with the affected outpost has also yielded negative results. Requesting permission to proceed to the site to confirm in person their comms issue for further assessment, over."

As is typical with UF command, I'm left in the gray limbo of non-communication while someone, somewhere, reviews my request and probably runs it by a committee. Then, they'll get back to me once the request is documented and processed in triplicate. Or, at minimum, that's my take on the ridiculous delay.

They can tell me to pound sand and get my ass back to base if I'm asking too much.

I'm about to do just that when my line comes to life, and a new voice is on the other end. Male this time, older, and not as by the book about comms protocol as radio operators typically are.

"*Sergeant Omega. You're cleared to proceed to Outpost Charlie Alpha Zero Seven. Confirm with the outpost the nature of their communication difficulties and rectify them if possible. I'd rather not send someone else out. If you can't resolve it, return to base and report your findings.*"

"Yes, sir. Estimating no more than three hours for contact and to diagnose the problem. I'll contact base if I discover anything additional, over."

"*Roger that. Good luck, Sergeant. Base Command, out.*"

Well, if that wasn't a bit odd. Sighing to myself, I shake it off. This base has always been more casual in its adherence to protocol than others I've been stationed at. Probably part of why Rho enjoys it so much. Open orders like this aren't so out of line.

I've direction enough to know where I'm going next and what my goal is. That's all I need. Turning to mount my bike, I dismiss the slight urge to check in with my team. This little side adventure should still have me back in time for chow. There's no sense in getting the team worked up over nothing.

—Ω—

CLANG, CLANG, CLANG GOES THE DINNER BELL

At least my sense of direction isn't off. I was right in assuming the path running past the array led to the outpost. Well-worn grooves, crushed rocks, and sparse vegetation pave a clear path between desolate nothing and the high walls of the sanctuary.

The outpost appears normal at first glance—reinforced walls, security fencing, and watchtowers positioned at regular intervals. Standard UF construction, built to withstand both Zee hordes and marauder attacks. But as I approach the outer perimeter, something feels off. No movement on the walls. No response to my radio calls.

Erring on the side of caution, I park my bike a quarter mile out and approach on foot, keeping low. Flipping my comms on, I again attempt to hail the outpost, but unsurprisingly, I don't manage to connect to anybody. More out of morbid curiosity and perhaps a desire to be proven wrong, I key my radio in an attempt to pick up the UF's general comms line. It's not beyond the limits of my system, and the chance that someone's monitoring is high.

"This is Sergeant Omega Two Two. Anybody reading me, over?"

Static. Complete communications blackout outside the walls, just like the relay station. Something is actively jamming signals here. No communications are getting out, including my own. If that isn't strange enough, this area's a dead zone to any life. And I mean any. I haven't seen a single weed, let alone anything from the Kingdom Animalia. That's just bizarre—and unsettling.

Now, more than a little frustrated. I'm not quite sure how to proceed. On one hand, I can consider this all to be a crapshoot, head back to base, and find out what happens next. Or, since I'm here, I can continue with my original plan, take a peek over the wall, and do a quick investigation of my own before heading back. I hate to say it, but the latter appeals to me more than the former.

Scaling the outer wall isn't difficult with my enhanced strength. A sprinter's dash at the wall provides enough momentum to get me more than halfway up. My fingers find purchase in the concrete joints, and I haul myself up the remaining portion of the twenty-foot barrier with relative ease, making short work of what would challenge a regular soldier. I pause at the top, scanning the interior below.

Empty. Completely empty.

No guards on patrol. No movement in the compound. The silence is absolute except for the whisper of desert wind through the structures. I drop down into the outpost proper, landing in a crouch with my rifle ready.

The wrongness hits me immediately. Not just the absence of people—everything is too perfect. Too undisturbed. Doors closed. Equipment is stored correctly. No signs of struggle, no blood, no indication of what happened to an entire outpost's worth of civilians and personnel. It's as if everyone simply vanished mid-activity.

Moving through the compound, I check building after building. Homes: beds made, personal effects in place. Mess hall: tables clean, chairs pushed in. Armory: locked tight, no signs of forced entry. Administrative building: paperwork stacked neatly on desks, coffee cups placed at the ready to be filled.

This *isn't* a thriving outpost.

That nagging thought can't be avoided any longer. Stopping short in the middle of the road, I glower at nothing in particular. The midday heat has me sweltering in my gear, and I'm wasting my damn time on a fool's errand. This place has been uninhabited for quite some time, if it ever was. What am I supposed to report to Command?

Hey, yeah, your outpost is empty. Did you remember to put actual people in it, or did that slip your mind?

Scuffing my toe in the dirt and sending up a mini plume, a frustrated growl rises in my throat. What the fuck am I doing here? Turning in disgust, I decide to try salvaging this entire stupid day by at least getting back to base early. I've backtracked more than halfway when I hear the sharp rattle of wood banging into wood.

I approach the source cautiously, rifle up, finger on the trigger. The civic center sits at the heart of the compound—a large, multipurpose building used for briefings, community gatherings, and emergency shelter. Its front entrance stands slightly ajar when everything else is sealed tight.

The wrongness intensifies as I near the building. My heightened senses pick up something—a scent underneath the desert air. Sweet. Cloying. The smell of decay, masked by something else.

Inside, the building appears as empty as the rest. Long hallways stretch past administrative offices, all doors closed, and all rooms dark. But there's a sound deeper in the structure—the rhythmic rustle and shuffle of bodies moving. Faint but persistent.

I follow the sound through the maze of corridors, my boots silent on the polished floors. The sound of bodies brushing against each other grows louder as I approach what looks like an auditorium or meeting hall. Double doors stand at the end of the hallway, and the sound emanates from beyond them.

Something is wrong with this entire situation. An outpost doesn't just empty out. People don't simply disappear. And that smell— I recognize it now. The sweet-sick stench of turned flesh. Of rot. Of the *Zee*.

But how? How does an entire fortified outpost fall to Zee without a single sign of struggle? Without distress calls? Without any indication of what happened?

I reach for the door handle, every instinct screaming that I should turn around and get the hell out. But I need to know. The UF needs to know what happened here.

The handle turns easily under my grip. Not locked. Merely shut. I push the door open just a crack and peer inside. The hairs on the back of my neck stand up in warning, but I'm too drawn in to stop now.

The entire population of the outpost is in there—all ages, all types, and all in their Sunday best. All of them. Packed into the auditorium like sardines, standing shoulder to shoulder in perfect, silent rows.

In my shock, the handle slips out of my hand, and the door creaks, the gap unintentionally widening as one of them—a blonde woman with red-lined blue eyes—turns toward me. Her vacant stare fixes on mine, neither of us quite comprehending what we're looking at until her mouth quivers, and she releases a sound that chills my blood. A lusty, heady moan of delight and despair.

Fresh Zee. An entire outpost of them.

The sound triggers the rest. Fifty-plus bodies surge toward the door as one, a wave of newly turned undead rallying to escape their makeshift prison and get their ravenous claws on their next meal.

I slam the door shut and throw my weight against it, but there's no way to hold back this many. My heart thunders frantically against my ribs, practically breaking through in my exertion to hold back the rising wave of bodies. They hit the barrier like a tsunami, pressing through with inhuman strength. I'm not outlasting them. There's not enough in me to stand unmoving against this many Zee.

The screech of my heels dragging adds to the cacophony as I'm slowly forced back. My abilities let me hold them for a few seconds longer, but it's not enough. Fingers, hands, and worse thrust through the growing gap. Fingernails paw and claw at my helmet and arms, pulling, tugging, trying to get a piece of me.

And then it happens again. My strength flickers, almost like a dying light bulb about to burn out.

In that brief hesitation, I fail completely. The door bursts open, and I find myself beneath it all, crushed by a throng of advancing Zee. They're so excited by their victory that they don't even realize they've won. As they tumble over and around me in their eagerness, the fractured door further pins me to the floor like a bug as one after another clamber over and off, searching for their lost meal.

For once, my height comes in handy as the door serves to shelter and hide my presence, at least for the moment. I'm also being crushed to death, so that's a problem. Everything hurts, particularly my right arm, where it's pinned against my chest. My leg twisted wrong when I fell—if I didn't pull something, I sure as hell broke the bone. Even my head takes another hit.

After what's probably only minutes but stretches in my mind to far longer, the press and rattle of movement peters off and then ceases. I hold my breath, listening, straining for signs they're still close. In the narrow gap between the door and floor, I manage to turn my helmet enough to make out the still-open doorway behind me. Daylight filters in, illuminating a few pairs of shuffling feet in the space beyond. Without an obvious target in sight, they've settled into aimless wandering, none of it in my direction.

I could cry from the relief. I probably am, actually. The side of my face feels wet where it's pressed to the smooth composite beneath my cheek. Although tasting the bitterness of copper mixed with salt...there's probably blood in there as well.

I don't bother moving for the next few minutes. I'm too focused on ensuring my lungs continue their pattern of expansion and contraction, keeping my blood oxygenated. That, and there's a lingering high-pitched ringing that I'm reasonably certain isn't my comms and is screwing with my ability to sense anything.

Breaths ragged and uneven, it takes several whimpered gulps of air to allow me to hold off the rising panic and take stock. Severely screwed covers it, but that's a vast understatement. I've no doubt that there's no way in hell I'm walking out of here, let alone riding back to base. If I can just last a couple of days, UF protocol will send a backup team to retrieve my missing ass and, hopefully, return whatever's left of me.

The minor break in action serves its purpose, and I can finally determine it's about as safe as it's going to get. Gingerly, I push against the hardwood holding me captive. I nearly scream the first time I try to shift things—my arm gives out immediately when I put pressure on it. Instead, I have to be smart the second time, using my left arm and right shoulder to brace the slow progress.

I manage to push the door up enough to slither out as quietly as possible, one-quarter of me at a time, until finally, I'm free. But now I'm exposed where any wandering Zee can lay eyes on me. Lying flat and panting as pain threatens to overwhelm my senses, I do my best to move minimally while still taking in the immediate area.

What stands out the most is one of the cubicle quads, with chairs still pushed in and desktops empty. It's not far, but I'll be exposed getting there.

Gritting my teeth, I push up, relying heavily on my elbows to avoid my injured forearm. I drag myself across the floor, the carpet catching roughly against my gear. A slithering sound follows as

I awkwardly make my way to the closest desk, pushing myself back into the corner until I'm braced against the junction of four cubicle spaces.

My left arm hooks around a support post as I ease my unresponsive leg in, pulling it closer and attempting to tuck it under. It may just be an awkward sprain—something nerve-related that temporarily numbed the area. No bone is poking out, but that doesn't mean much, and I'm not holding out hope for something minor. No matter. I'm able to hitch up my other leg, though it's equally uncomfortable, until I'm as compressed and unobtrusive as possible.

The entire operation can't have taken more than ten minutes, as I can still make out light from outside spreading its rays within. But I'm left winded and haggard. Everything hurts, and I haven't yet figured out what to do about it.

For now, I'm just so damn tired.

—Ω—

HOW TO MAKE FRIENDS AND PISS OFF EVERYONE ELSE

Approximately 10 years after the widespread incursion of Zee.

[OMEGA]

I wasn't expecting this.

I should have been expecting this.

That mantra loops endlessly inside my skull, even as the pavement rushes up to greet my face. The solid crack to the back of my head—courtesy of standard-issue metal pipe—assisted my ungraceful descent. The attack came so swiftly that I barely managed to turn my head and brace for impact. My hands? Useless appendages that failed to deploy when needed most. Hitting concrete is no less excruciating than the last time I found myself eating pavement. Not a habit I cultivate, but one with which I'm regrettably familiar. We'll leave it at that.

No time to dwell. Teeth gritted in a facsimile of a smile, I push up from my faceplant. Gravel and shattered rock crumble free from the myriad of indentations they've carved into the soft flesh of my unprotected face, leaving behind constellations of tiny wounds. Ignoring the initial discomfort, I tense my stomach in anticipation of the inevitable follow-up—a swift kick to the gut. It comes right on cue, precision-timed like everything in this godforsaken military.

"Where do you think you're going?"

The moment the Alpha completes his rib-cracking kick, I'm coiled and ready. As he retracts for another strike, I pivot my left leg in a calculated arc. The kick misses his important bits but connects with

307

magnificent efficiency against the side of his knee. There's a satisfying succession of sounds—crunch, pop, snap—followed by the soldier collapsing into a pained lump. His howls pierce the night air at precisely the decibel level guaranteed to draw unwanted attention. Tactical advantage: mine.

"Shut up!" another hisses at his writhing comrade. His eyes never leave me for more than a microsecond.

"Think you're smart, little girl, do you?"

"If you're my comparison..." I manage through a groan that vibrates through my cracked ribs. Forget the damage to my torso. My skull feels bisected, pressure building behind my eyes until— without preamble or warning—I empty my stomach rather fantastically across soldier number two's meticulously polished boots. Concussion protocol initiated. He curses with inventive ferocity before executing a rapid backward maneuver, giving me a healthier amount of personal space. Can't fault his instinct for self-preservation. I do, however, fault him for the attempted cranial fracturing.

Again, it's tactically unsound of me not to have anticipated this. It's irrelevant now. The immediate threat has been neutralized, and I'm claiming this round.

Dragging my sleeve across my acid-bitter mouth, I force my body vertically despite every muscle fiber protesting the change in orientation. Standing unsteadily, I assess the tactical situation. They've doubled their numbers, minus one temporarily decommissioned Alpha, who won't be bearing weight on that knee anytime soon. The whisper of displaced air triggers my reflexes— I shift right, avoiding a glancing strike to my zygomatic arch. Seizing the generously offered wrists, I weaponize his forward momentum, yanking his arm and attached torso directly into my rising knee. The impact reverberates through both our bodies, but only one of us was prepared for it. Following through, I execute two additional precision strikes to his solar plexus before disengaging with a calculated shove, leaving another soldier incapacitated.

My attention lingers on one of my last opponents for a second too long. A thick forearm locks across my trachea from behind as another Alpha exploits my lapse in attention. His muscular arm constricts against my windpipe as he leverages his superior height. My boots lose contact with solid ground, leaving me balanced on the tips of my toes like some macabre ballet. Boot soles scrape uselessly as I struggle for leverage. The flat planes of his solid chest against my back confirm what I already know—another male Zeta, this one with enhanced upper body strength, as he jerks his arm upward.

I choke on my own saliva, nearly severing my tongue as my teeth slam together. Supernova explosions detonate behind my eyelids, and I realize quite profoundly that if I don't do something now, I will be blacking out. Using my brain for half a second, I abandon attempts to pry away his forearm—the only way to break that hold would be to snap his radius and ulna, which would terminate my UF career as definitively as turning Zee.

I retain one tactical advantage despite compromised footing. There's enough raw strength in my form to mete out severe damage with any strike that I can land successfully. Currently, I maintain two free arms and one sharp and dense elbow, all backed by considerable brute force. With a calculated wind-up, I brace one fist against the other and drive that bony protrusion into his unprotected side. He grunts in pain but doesn't give up his grip just yet. Black spots encroach on my peripheral vision, threatening to overtake the prevailing light. That's not happening. I manage three more precisely targeted blows before his grip incrementally loosens.

He bellows to his remaining operational teammates, his voice laced with pain.

"Shit! She's getting loose. Help me."

Apparently, the universe favors his request over mine.

A fist materializes, connecting perfectly with my partially rotated face. The punch delivers kinetic energy sufficient to snap my head rightward, a crimson mist spewing out from between my parted lips. My last attacker knocks my head in the opposite direction with another cross-strike of equal force. There's a sick dread creeping into my mind that I'm not getting out of this.

That realization, coupled with an unbidden image of Epsilon's disappointed face, paralyzes me. Involuntarily, my muscles disengage as consciousness begins to fade, even as additional blows connect with my now-exposed midsection. The chokehold has relaxed, but oxygen remains a luxury I can't obtain.

Breathe. Fuck.

Just breathe air.

The dark spots multiply and merge into a gray void. Then, an unmistakable crack reverberates in the dead space of our alley, and my unwanted support system abruptly withdraws. Boneless, I drop, hitting the dirt-coated floor like a sack of rocks. Another sharp report follows, acoustically similar to gunfire yet lacking the characteristic percussion of standard ammunition. One of my attackers releases a howl that would make a banshee envious. Another wails as his footwear executes a rapid retreat from my limited field of vision. I force my eyelids to separate a bit more, creating visual slits through which I perceive a reality both weightless and crushingly heavy. Either way, I'm in no position to significantly alter my perception or perspective.

Silence descends with the same abruptness that characterized the assault's initiation. Long legs bisect my visual field, their limbs encased in non-standard issue fatigues. Specialist classification, perhaps? A high-level operator who's fortuitously positioned to intervene. From the fetal position I landed in and have thoroughly embraced, I register hands, distinct from my own, conducting a preliminary field assessment of my injuries, applying pressure at strategic points, and withdrawing when my response is a warning hiss. The contact heightens my awareness momentarily before the seductive pull of oblivion reclaims dominance.

"You are safe, soldier. We have you." Female voice. That's unexpected. The tone is well-articulated and level, but abrupt and perfunctory in their remarks.

I wonder who…becomes my final coherent thought before I figure the hell with it and let go completely, vaguely optimistic I might wake again.

—Ω—

THIS STEW NEEDS MEAT

Present Day

[TAU]

The persistent scratch of a pen tip dragging steadily against paper is a familiar and welcome sound. The ordinary simplicity of the activity transforms the space into an illusion of this being just another day at the office. With my helm tucked securely under my arm and standing at parade rest, I wait for the secretary at the front desk to finish my transfer papers. The Personnel building is as austere and non-descript inside as it is on the outside.

As much as I've wanted nothing more than to be on a proper Alpha team and back among my 'peers,' I now find myself precisely in that position, but rethinking the decision entirely. Something about that strange team and its sergeant has grown on me during our last four months of travel and tribulation. I have never been particularly fond of people in general. There were those few I was close to in my life prior to the United Forces—primarily family— but beyond that, I was never a very sociable individual, and it suited me just fine.

With everything and everyone I knew no longer as it was, initially, I found myself challenged by living in this world where survival means a level of codependency. It has been a difficult transition, but now I find the changed circumstances strangely welcome and comforting. It does not matter much at present, though, as I will shortly be assigned to a new squad as their commander. A new team means building relationships from scratch once again, earning their trust, and hoping that they will earn mine—a point I appear to have reached with Omega's team.

Shaking my head in a feeble attempt to dislodge that circular thinking, I focus again on the unhurried sounds of the admin writing my paperwork. I attempt to let the white noise consume my thoughts and for my mind to go blissfully blank.

I may have been successful, too, if someone had not chosen to enter the building quite loudly a moment later. The resounding '*twang*' of the metal door slamming back to its starting position is enough of a distraction to derail my attempts at low-grade meditation. Apparently, the new addition requires attention. I do my best not to react and give them that satisfaction. From my peripheral vision, I can make out a taller man garbed in the standard deep blue uniform of a Beta-level Zeta soldier. For some reason, his unique scent pulls at my senses momentarily, but I ignore that twinge of familiarity. Studiously, I face forward and ignore the interloper until the voice that breaks the silence captures my attention immediately.

"I need to speak to the Colonel!" A gloved hand slams flat against the sparse stone counter with the resounding clang of metal, rattling a plain blue mug filled with precisely sharpened pencils. Startled, I turn to see Rho positively seething at the poor administrator who had been helping me a moment ago. She seems shell-shocked, and I cannot say that I am too far off from her, although for a different reason. I have never heard Rho speak in such a tone and with that much force, not once during my time with his squad. His face perfectly mirrors his voice—dark eyebrows drawn sharply down, red eyes narrowed and frowning nastily. A different facet of the easy-going and joking Rho, whom I assumed I had figured out.

Hair tightly pulled back into an immaculate auburn bun, the admin shifts uncomfortably in her seat before answering him. "The Colonel isn't on base at the moment."

"Great. Terrific. *Wonderful.* And do you know how long the Colonel will be gone?"

The secretary leans as far away from the larger soldier as she can while seated, giving ground to Rho as he leans in dangerously, his voice too sweet to be sincere. It is then that I also notice he is completely decked out in field attire as if he is prepared to head out on a mission. That is entirely wrong, though, as he and the rest of Omega's team should currently be on mandatory leave. They just returned from a six-month assignment in the field. The team was promised at least two weeks of downtime. Even the United Forces know when to let their soldiers rest, or else they would indeed have a mutiny on their hands—one they might be ill-prepared to handle.

"We're not apprised of that, but if you need to speak with him, you can request a wire be sent from the Communications branch. He'll probably be able to retrieve it within the week."

"A week? Damn, that's too long." The last part is commented on lowly, but my hearing easily picks up on the words.

"Major Ewing is acting as base commander for the Colonel. Have you tried speaking with him?"

"Yes, and that did me a hell of a lot of good."

Pinching the bridge of his nose in frustration, Rho lets loose a sharp huff of air before straightening to his full height.

"You know what? Never mind. I know what needs to be done."

Without waiting for the admin's reply, he turns to stalk out as dramatically as he had entered, and consequently makes eye contact with me as he turns to leave.

"Tau?" He stutters to a halt. He must have truly been oblivious to his surroundings if he missed my presence mere feet away.

"Rho." I incline my head slightly in response.

"What are you doing here?"

"I am putting in for my transfer." Seeing realization dawn in his eyes, I continue. "And you? What business do you have here?" *Scaring the desk staff*, I add on mentally but do not bother to verbalize that particular thought.

"That's right. You wouldn't have heard." He frowns, troubled.

Confused by his response, I prompt the gunner to complete his cryptic statement. "Heard what?"

His eyes flick to the staff behind the counter before leaning in slightly to speak in low tones.

"Omega is late checking in from a solo assignment. She should've been back yesterday. We haven't been able to raise her on the comms yet, and you know how by-the-book Sarge is on these kinds of missions. The base protocol requires a minimum of two days of silence before anyone questions anything. Two days is a lot of time for things to go wrong."

A part of me clenches, and the air leaves my lungs in a barely contained gasp as if I have been punched. I do not understand my reaction.

"I see. Is that why you were asking to speak with the Colonel?" My voice sounds unconcerned, even to my ears—too controlled. I am not feeling either of these things at the moment, but I suppose a lifetime of suppressing emotions serves me well.

"Yeah, but he's not on base, and his temp replacement flat out refused to break protocol and allow for a second scout to enter the site at minimum, let alone an entire Zeta team rescue party. Thinks Meg's just hanging out at the outpost or some other shit. Fucking worthless stooge, if you ask me."

The last part is practically spat out. Attempting to keep the conversation reasonable and to redirect Rho's attention, I interrupt. "Then, what will you do?"

"The same thing that we always do when command staff won't listen to reason." There's a hint of the Rho I have become familiar with in his flippant response. Devious, unafraid, and slightly combative.

"And that is?"

His wolf-like grin is all the confirmation I need. They are going to disobey a direct "stay" order and run off to find their sergeant. I sigh ruefully, but I am already mentally accepting the violation far quicker than I would have. The impulse to report the infraction is lacking as well, as is my common sense, it would seem.

"I am coming with you." A voice that sounds like my own states firmly before my brain catches up with my mouth and realizes I spoke those words.

"What?!"

That captures his attention. The lanky man's 'tough guy' mode drops for a moment, leaving him to blink owlishly at me in shock. I cannot say that I blame him—I have surprised myself as well.

"I said..." I begin again slowly, as if speaking to a small, dim, and particularly inattentive child. He may not be small or a child, but being dim might not be so far-fetched. He cuts me off quickly with a dismissive wave of his hand.

"I heard what you said, just…are you sure? You know this goes against at least a manual or two of regulations, right?"

"Of course."

"…And you know this will probably cost you your Alpha status, or at least the command position when they get a hold of us." He regards me expectantly now, and yet there is a glimmer of hope in his expression.

"I am prepared to face the consequences of my actions," I state pragmatically.

And I am.

Shaking his head in amusement, I get a hearty slap between the shoulder blades that nearly propels me forward from Rho's 'good arm,' followed by a bark of laughter. Typical.

"In that case, what are we wasting time here for?" His eternal optimism seems to have returned and is once again shining through in great abundance.

Smiling tightly, I meet his eager expression, and just like that, something clicks into place inside me. Right here and now is where I need to be.

"Lead the way."

The walk to Beta barracks passes in relative silence, both of us lost in our own thoughts. I find myself over-analyzing my decision, searching for the logical reasoning behind such an impulsive choice. There is none, of course. This is purely emotional—a response I would have criticized in any other soldier under my command.

Yet here I am.

The Beta quarters are smaller than the Alpha accommodations, but they are far more personal. Individual touches that speak to the team's cohesion—colorful photos of wildlife taped to walls, precisely organized technical manuals, the faint scent of medical supplies, a worn stack of playing cards on top of an even more weathered bible, and what looks like a sketchbook and a plain white mug filled with pencils—a handwritten "*#1 Boss*" in faded black scrawl on its side. It feels lived-in in a way Alpha barracks never did.

The remaining team members are gathered in the common area when we enter. Chi looks up from a tactical map spread across the table, her purple-streaked hair catching the light. Mu sits cross-legged on the floor, cleaning her rifle with methodical precision—the care of someone whose life depends on the weapon's reliability. Omicron stands near the window, his massive frame blocking most of the light.

"Well?" Chi asks without preamble, her precise gaze shifting between Rho and me, though not outwardly surprised by my appearance.

"No dice," Rho reports. "Colonel is off-base, and Major Ewing will not authorize anything until we hit the forty-eight-hour mark."

"Bureaucratic stupidness," Mu mutters, not looking up from her rifle. "Omega wouldn't just disappear. She said she'd be back for lasagna." She pauses in her cleaning, glancing up with a slight smile. "I had a feeling you might bring backup, Rho. Hi, Tau!"

I can only nod at her overly cheerful but seemingly genuine greeting.

"Zeta do not simply vanish," Chi comments, her tone clinical but with an undercurrent of genuine concern. "Particularly not soldiers of Omega's caliber."

Omicron's rumbling voice carries from the window. "Y'all know she would come for us without hesitation."

The simple statement settles over the room like a weight. They are right, of course. During the months I have served alongside them, Omega's unwavering loyalty to her team is unquestionable. She would never leave them to wonder, to worry.

"So, what is the plan?" I find myself asking.

Four sets of eyes turn to me with varying degrees of interest. Chi's eyebrows rise marginally—her equivalent of shock.

"So, you're helping?" Mu asks, her enthusiasm barely contained.

"It would appear so."

Rho grins. "I told him he'd probably lose his Alpha status for this."

"Probably?" Chi interjects dryly. "Certainly. Command does not look favorably upon officers who abandon their posts to participate in unauthorized rescue operations."

I incline my head. "I understand the risks."

"Then you understand this is likely a one-way ticket back to grunt status," Omicron observes, not unkindly.

"Perhaps. But some things are worth the risk."

The words surprise me as much as they do the others. When did I become someone who made decisions based on emotion rather than reason? When did this team—Omega—become worth sacrificing my career for?

Mu bounces to her feet, rifle forgotten. "So, we're really doing this? Going after her?"

"We are," Rho confirms. "Question is, how do we get off base without authorization?"

All eyes turn to me, and I realize they're looking for leadership. Not because I'm Alpha—because technically, I am the one with the clearance and access codes that will get us through the gates.

"Leave that to me," I say. "If we are doing this, we do it right. Full gear, coordinated approach. We find Omega and bring her home."

Chi begins rolling up her maps with clinical precision. "I will gather intelligence on her last known location and mission parameters."

"I'll prep the bikes," Rho adds.

"Medical kit and trauma supplies," Omicron states simply.

Mu's grin is brilliant as she carefully secures her rifle. "This is gonna be fun."

As the team disperses to prepare, I find myself standing alone in their common area, surrounded by the evidence of their bond. For the first time since losing my original team, I feel like I'm exactly where I belong.

Even if it costs me everything.

—T—

CAGED PREDATORS ARE NO GAME

[OMEGA]

Drip.

Drip.

Drip.

With morbid detachment, I contemplate the bulbous red droplets as they make their slow progression, sliding to the absolute edge of the ceiling tile before hesitating. For the briefest moment, each lingers, surface shimmering in indecision before relinquishing control to gravity, plummeting nine feet to splash against the faux wood flooring below.

Each drop is a lost bit of my life's essence that I'm not getting back. Small bulbs of liquid are counting down my remaining moments. Liquid granules of sand making their methodical descent without the aid of an hourglass.

I probably should be worried—or at least vaguely concerned. That's my time ticking away. But I can't. I lack the motivation or clear head to do anything more than act as a passive observer from some distant place in my muddled mind.

The ductwork I managed to squeeze onto before passing out remains solid beneath my aching back. I'm not worried about falling through the ceiling, and I'm positioned just high enough in this sealed-off space that the wandering undead below can't reach me. Hell, they don't even look up. Zee really are as dumb as fuck. Thank whatever God for that. Being eaten to death isn't high on my list of preferred ways to exit this life.

It appears that I've found where the outpost's population went. Go me. One mystery solved, but it won't do me any good if I can't manage to pull myself out of this hellhole. My strength hasn't entirely left my body, though I doubt it'll remain that way much longer. I have a few bars and a cylinder of water but beyond that...?

Remaining carefully detached from my predicament, grunts and the rasps of motion below are amplified in this space above, but at least it serves as an early warning. Through a tile that shifted during my haphazard ascent, I spy a lone Zee shuffling by in a lovely brown and yellow flowered dress. Obviously not finding the meal she was searching for, the Zee continues with her vague search pattern. How can any creature be so utterly empty of existence and yet be so yearnful?

Climbing into this overhead gap yesterday evening cost me several good hours of consciousness. Essential hours—ones I should have used to bind my injuries and come up with some fantastic plan to save my ass. Of course, when my body decided to wake up, I made the delightful discovery that, actually, both of my legs were more than likely damaged courtesy of being crushed by a newly minted throng of Zee. The brilliant white of bone glistening through a tear in my gauntlet strap was the next dead giveaway, adding to the list of 'things wrong with me.' I managed to wrap a torn strip of my poncho around it in a makeshift field dressing, but only to pass out briefly afterward. I suppose doing that sort of thing, combined with severe blood loss, can do that. Go figure.

I might be in shock.

At least I'm in a better position to assess my surroundings and accidental prison. The space up here isn't exactly luxury living. I have maybe a foot and a half between the ceiling tiles, sprinkler system, and lighting below my ass, and the girders above that lead to the roof. My primary weapon is missing—the strap snapped when I first went down and became trapped beneath the door. With hands that refused to cooperate, I had to prioritize my life over my rifle. Another mistake at this point, but who's keeping track?

Lying up here has kept me semi-cool, but the aridness drains you dry. I've yet to quell my thirst, and there's no way I'm depleting my canteen just yet. With nothing better to do, I attempt to reach my knife's hilt, where it's strapped to my left leg. The crossover is awkward with a busted right arm, and my first attempt to get a grip fails miserably, as does the second. By the third unsuccessful try, I'm more than frustrated with my lack of progress, which only serves to aggravate my delicate condition. Settling back, I take a few breaths—as deep as I can manage—before once again attempting to grasp my Ka-Bar.

It takes a few fumbled tries, but I succeed. Finally! I grip the handle, leather washers cool and smooth in my hand. The action leaves me gasping as parts of my body protest vehemently against the movement. With the metal tang of the blade exposed, I clutch it close to my rapidly beating heart. The press of its smooth surface centers me, granting me a small measure of control since this cluster fuck began.

At least now, if one of those undead bastards manages to climb its way up to my hiding spot, I can deal with it. That's the extent of preparation I can manage, and there's nothing more for me to do than play the waiting game. This entire situation is my own damn fault, really.

I let everything occurring around the base put me into a state of distraction. My team was either moping around or begging me to convince Tau to stay. To join the team. That's not my call to make. That arrogant, wannabe ninja warrior is more than capable of making his own decisions. He made that abundantly clear from day one when we rescued his sorry ass from that hellhole, risking our lives just for him. Continued to risk and protect him even as he floundered.

Well, fuck you, Tau.

Huh. I guess my attitude is still intact. God...even on the verge of oblivion, that guy still manages to vex me. I have never met a person who vexes me. Irritates? Yes. Try having Rho under your command for more than five seconds. Aggravates? Oh yeah. Colonel Stick-Up-the-Ass has given me and my team more grief than we ever fully deserved. But therein lies the problem and why I've landed myself in this mess. I allowed my emotions to get the best of me. Became too attached and irrational. I've worked pretty damn hard during my short life to keep that side of me in check.

Once I joined the UF, I learned to keep a dependable lock on that little black box. How else can I make the decisions that I do in an instant? There's no room to emote or regret a course of action. What needs to be done is done. Don't linger on what-ifs—there's no benefit in doing so. I wouldn't be here if I hadn't chosen to dwell on the past. Big mistake. Probably my last.

These loose thoughts are troubling, if not slightly dizzying. Or maybe that's the room moving around me. I release a sigh and abruptly cut off the deep breath that follows with a sharp wince. Damn. I must have busted a few ribs, too. How do you not notice something like that? Shifting to ease the weight away from lingering pain and move into a more comfortable position becomes pointless. Resigned to my less-than-optimum position, I settle as the underlying symphony of moans lulls me.

My team will look for me, and I have no doubt about that. However, protocol requires that the UF won't send out a second scout for forty-eight hours after a missed check-in. It isn't uncommon in our line of work for missions to run longer than expected. Even with all the training Zeta soldiers receive, no amount of anticipation can prepare you for the unknown. It's a bonus that our communication system is incredibly delicate and fickle in this rather indelicate environment.

Two days of waiting won't guarantee approval to perform a Search and Rescue. That'll require additional discussions, evaluations, and, finally, more paperwork. How can everything go to shit, and we still find time for policy and bureaucratic nonsense? It doesn't matter. I just hope my team doesn't blame themselves for my death. They don't deserve to bear that burden.

I'm not being a fatalist or pessimist—this is me being a realist. I've been gone more than a day now, which means the soonest they'll come for me is two days after my missed forty-eight-hour check-in tomorrow morning. Four days. Four days of little food and water, one-hundred-degree temperatures, internal injuries, and blood loss don't add up to a happy ending. Just an end.

I must have a concussion because the need to sleep is overwhelming. But really, what's stopping me? Or who?

Sighing in resignation, I settle more solidly against the sheet metal supporting my lower half and let my heart rate slow, and what's left of me drift. I've been saved from my own stupidity before. Maybe this time won't be different.

—Ω—

ENDINGS BECOME BEGINNINGS

Approximately 10 years after the widespread incursion of Zee.

[OMEGA]

Living can be such a son of a bitch.

I'm regretting my return to consciousness almost before I'm actually aware. What begins as throbbing in cadence with my slowly pulsing heart evolves into the merciless impact of a phantom mallet on repeat. You'll forgive me if the lure of sleep tempts me back into its rapturous embrace for a few minutes more.

When the task of avoiding whatever awaits becomes too dull, I finally decide to open my eyes. I'm underwhelmed, at the very least. Kind of predictably, brilliant white surfaces shine in their clinical cleanliness. The stench of something more than antiseptic invades my nostrils, burning a path in its wake with the intensity of the aroma. How medical-grade air purifiers can run 24/7, and yet this place still reeks of cleanser, is a mystery. Last on my list of things I despise about Medical—as I might as well list my grievances—is that ever-present hum underlying everything. How can anyone with enhanced senses be expected to rest and recover with that kind of racket?

Something I push aside as I catch movement from the corner of my eye. One of the attending physicians is making his steady and deliberate way through the berths toward me. I note that Theta still occupies the same spot as when I last visited him. The bushy tops of my eyebrows nearly reach my hairline when I catch sight of two of the newer occupants of the space. It may have been dark when I last encountered them, but I recognize their ugly mugs just the same. What I don't recall is the vivid purple blooming around the nearly swollen-shut eyelid of one or the obviously reset broken nose of the other. It's the latter's puce-colored hair that comes to my memory first, looking like a lousy juice box dye job. The two are situated close enough to each other that they're able to actively whisper back and forth, too engrossed in whatever conversation they're having to notice little ol' me.

Probably for the better.

I'm apparently at the top of this medic's list for being checked on. That wisp of conversation with Rho filters up, and I wonder if this broad man is the one he mentioned. Nothing about the soldier's countenance seems anything less than affable. He's hard to miss both from the physical space he occupies and the deep color of his skin. It's a marked contrast with the sterile white of everything here, including his uniform. There isn't long to wait in suspense as he's suddenly right next to my bedside, seeming genuinely pleased as he takes in my awakened state.

With a low hum, he taps something into the tablet-sized pad he clutches in one hand before turning his full attention to me. Let me say it's no fun being prone when somebody much larger looms over you. My impulse is to throw the first punch, which…I actually do. Probably not my best thought in hindsight, but I blame the drugs still addling my brain for that one. He catches my pathetic excuse for a hit easily as if he knew my instinct before I did.

It's improbable but not wholly implausible. I've come across stories of Zeta who, for all intents and purposes, have unlocked some higher power of intuition. Psychic is too strong a term. It pushes my boundaries of reality. There is no way in hell a person can predict events that have not happened or see into the future. Thank you very much. Given how many soldiers these medics see in any given week, I'm sure I'm not the first to be that kind of stupid. The medic's smile tightens just so.

Back to the present. I wait idly, with little more to do than flex my toes intermittently to keep the anxiety at bay. Thankfully or not, this medic is possessed of a level of common sense and proceeds to cut right to the chase.

"This is becomin' a regular occurrence for you and me, isn't it, Omega?"

I grimace at not only his recollection of our past couple of crossovers, but now he has a name to go with my misdeeds. Clearing my throat of the crud built up in it, I realize this soreness can't just be from being almost choked to death. I must have been intubated, however briefly. That thoroughly derails my first reply as I lead with a different question instead.

"What day is it?" I can't help but wince at the hoarse sound of my voice and the sensation of sandpaper that accompanies my speaking.

"It's Thursday." The medic smiles indulgently at my question. "You've been under sedation for two days and were admitted almost three days ago."

Sedation? I find myself confused. Why would you sedate someone with a concussion? Before I can ask the medic the whys and hows of it, he moves away from directly addressing me to busying himself with the readings on his tablet, absently adjusting something associated with the drip lines. With his broad back to me, I'm hard-pressed to catch his eye, but it appears I don't have to as he elaborates after a minute has passed.

"We decided to sedate you as a precaution. You had bleedin' on the brain, and your body needed time to reduce the inflammation and swellin' to minimize any long-term impact on your cognitive skills. It was a risk, but a safer option than surgery. Better than lettin' you rouse naturally and do somethin' stupid. Like, leave before you're fully recovered."

"Nice to know you had my best interest in mind," I mumble petulantly.

"You know, you can drop that face you're makin'. Believe it or not, we probably saved your life. After a stupid stunt like that, I'd think you'd have a bit more gratitude, if not to me, than to the soldier who stepped in and prevented somethin' permanent from happenin' to you."

"Stepped in?" What's he talking about?

He leans back from his imposing loom with an almost pleased grin, the move giving me a touch more light in my quadrant.

"I suppose you thought that miraculously, you dragged your unconscious carcass here, and all was fine and forgotten, right?" I get an expectant look on that one.

"Not exactly." I hedge. "More like some poor sucker tripped over my unconscious carcass and decided to drag me here because they'd had nothing better to do."

"Try again." The medic states expectantly. As if I actually knew my savior's identity. This isn't a game for me. Besides my head having been nearly split open, I was more focused on my aggressors than some white knight. His expectant look transforms into one of exasperation as he takes pity on my readily apparent knowledge gap.

"Her name's Chi." He rumbles pleasantly. I'm familiar enough with the Greek alphabet that his hard "k" pronunciation doesn't skew my mental picture of the symbol. "She's a demolition specialist and quite handy with a knife."

"Fascinating…" I begin, but I'm cut off by a coughing fit that runs my airways ragged.

A metal cup is thrust without warning into my face. Reluctantly, I take the proffered gift from the medic's giant mitt. With a cursory glance, I pick up on a network of minute, lighter-hued marks running the circumference of his hand. I'm curious why a doctor would have a multitude of cuts and burns on one of his primary tools. I don't ask, though. I'm not one to solicit unnecessary conversation.

After a good, long chug of icy water sans the cubes, I can't help but needle the man a little. "What? No straw?"

"If you're well enough to ask for damn room service, then you can get the hell out of my med bay. I'm not in the business of treatin' divas."

"But I thought you wanted my delightful presence here a while longer to heal properly. Right?"

Scoffing, he shakes his head.

"I need another body here like I need a hole in my head. Speakin' of which…"

He's about to continue when the far door slides open, admitting a solitary figure. Even from where I lie, I can tell they're an officer of sorts. When the medic stiffens into attention, salutes, and waits, immediately allowing them access to me once being saluted back, I have no doubt. The formerly relaxed medic holds himself differently in an instant, ramrod straight and at attention. That, more than anything, brings me to full alertness as I carefully watch the senior officer's approach.

"At ease, Doc."

"Yes, sir." The medic makes quick work of finishing whatever checkup he was midstream on. His movements are measured and to the point as he examines my vitals, then passes a small handheld device with a shiny metal ball at the end from temple to temple. It chirps in a quiet and pleased manner for an inanimate device. The physician seems glad with whatever results it provides to his ever-present tablet.

With a succinct nod at who I now recognize as the Base Commander, Colonel Adams, the medic, Omicron, removes his six-foot-plus bulk in a hurry. I'm left alone with the quiet rhythmic beeps of machines, my superior, and a weighty chunk of foreboding. The officer is no less of a towering man than the medic, although his broad shoulders drop to a more pronounced 'V' in the waist. He's obviously formidable and a powerhouse. From the crisp starch of his suit jacket lapels, I raise my eyes and inadvertently meet his. It leaves me slack-jawed and stunned to silence at a sight I'm not expecting. The man's eyes are vibrant red. Brilliantly light enough to be almost mistaken for orange.

He's Zeta. Holy shit.

Let me explain. Throughout my combined tenure, including conversion, basic, and advanced training, I've never encountered any members of the command staff exhibiting apparent signs of Zeta mutation. I'd assumed that officers did not go through conversion. Perhaps because of the risk, or maybe it has more to do with the irreversible, less-than-human result? I don't know. Maybe there's a rule against it. What I do know is that my guard is up. And as the Colonel concludes his visual assessment of me, I think it's warranted. This soldier is a danger and a threat to me. I have no idea how he's been enhanced, but intuitively, I know I'm not at his level. And he knows it as well. Damn.

"Sergeant Omega, I assume?" He intones sternly.

"Yes, sir," I respond on automatic, with a sharp nod. The best reply I can give to him while lying flat on my back.

"Good. Glad to see you up, soldier." He cocks his head to the side ever so slightly, seeming to size me up. "I imagine you're wondering what my presence here means for you." Although his voice is low, its sonorous quality fills the near-empty room, compelling my complete attention. His words, more so as I fixate on what precisely he's getting at.

"Yes, sir. What am I charged with?" No sense in pretending to be obtuse about what has transpired. If there's some disciplinary action or worse to be had, I have no choice but to deal with it.

I catch what sounds like a low chuckle in amusement before he audibly clears his throat. The Colonel rubs his chin in apparent thought. The sharp crackle of stubble across gloved fingers is cringeworthy to my enhanced hearing. It's an odd and trite thing to focus on, but the fact that he's not as freshly shaven as one would expect adds another layer of intrigue to the Colonel. Who is he really? And why would what I suspect is a highly lethal Zeta soldier play overseer to a base full of trainees?

Most of the ones I've dealt with are in no way ready to face the actual enemy in open engagement. My team's almost lackluster performance is a testament to this.

"Charged with? Now, there's your first missed assumption. If you were to have any correction, it would not come from me." His eyes harden, and I understand without further discussion the punitive side of the UF he's referring to.

"No, fortunately for you, the soldiers you assaulted have chosen not to report the incident formally."

My jaw flops open, whether to protest the implication that I started any of this mess or that it's not being pursued in spite of it being known to the higher-ups. Regardless, it wasn't my fault that they chose the wrong trainee to teach a lesson to. They had it coming to them.

"However," he sharply cuts off any protest that was arising, dead on arrival. "However. One of the soldier's parents is a senior officer here and has logged a formal complaint with the personnel board regarding your behavior and breach of base conduct."

My throat suddenly goes dry and tightens in preparation for the last hit to strike me down. The Colonel continues, either oblivious or unconcerned with the news he's delivering.

"As it stands, there are no prior complaints or grievances on your record. Additionally, your exemplary performance throughout basic and advanced training exercises, as well as your capacity to take on a more leadership-oriented role, positions you well for Alpha Squadron placement."

Okay, now I'm just confused. There's no clear direction this bus is heading, except maybe sideways with a barrel roll off a cliff. My perplexity must broadcast blatantly across my face as the Commander chuckles once again. Almost warmly, but definitely at the expense of my sanity.

"In light of all that I've stated, we're in a quandary as to how best to handle the situation. Clearly, you have the potential to be a fine asset to the United Forces. That being said, no good deed goes unpunished. It is our judgment, then, to recommend you be given command of a small team."

A single, leather-wrapped finger is raised to emphasize whatever point follows. Not that this soldier needs to emphasize anything, given how rapt my attention is on him.

"A Beta team. As for the time being, you're clearly not ready for assignment to the Alpha Squadron."

With those final heavy words, my mind abruptly halts for a moment. Caught in a loop of white noise and the lyrics of my soured fate. A demotion of sorts. And without having officially been an Alpha soldier for at least twenty-four hours. I realize I should be grateful for being allowed not only to continue but also to command rather than being expelled or assigned to low-level cleaning duties. However, that would somehow imply that I'm accepting of a B-level, especially after being told twice now that I'm Alpha material.

"Think of this as your final test. An opportunity to prove your capabilities and redeem yourself of any potential behavioral shortcomings."

Bowing my head in capitulation, I have to agree even if I don't want to. I understand that this will be my only chance. The only way to climb to the top from here on out. Anything less will keep me right where I am indefinitely.

"Yes, sir. Thank you for the opportunity to prove myself to you and the Board."

"Very good. Ensure that our decision is not in vain. We could use someone of your talents."

But you'd better play by the rules and toe that clearly demarcated line, is inferred in the silence that pervades afterward. "Your team and field assignments await you in Personnel. You will proceed there once you've been released from medical. Any questions?"

Mutely, I shake my head negatively, mind already wandering to five steps down the line.

"All right. In that case, I will take my leave. Good day, Sergeant. I look forward to following your career."

"Thank you, sir. I won't disappoint." My voice is strong and sure even if I've been dealt a shit hand. I'm going to come out of it smelling of lavender and mother-effing victory.

Without another word or glance back, the imposing form of our base commander exits my space and the medical building, moving onto whatever the brass are inclined to do with their days. This time, the medic's approach doesn't escape my notice. Slumping back into my raised bed, I swivel my head in his general direction, not bothering to react. He says nothing, even once he knows my coherent self is keyed into him. With measured motions, he deliberately rechecks my vitals, adjusting tubes and other paraphernalia to his satisfaction. I'm almost lulled into a doze by his motions until the medic opts to speak.

"You know, rank ain't the only way to be effective, right? What you did for that other trainee—people take notice of that. There's more damn respect to be earned in how you act at any given time."

I can't help but snort at his seeming naivety. Not that this medic strikes me as some newbie.

"Respect doesn't do a whole lot of good without the gravitas to back it up. You can't say I can do the same whether I'm Alpha or Beta. Or else what's the point of having the different classifications?"

"Now that's where I'm gonna disagree. I've ridden on the military carousel for a while now. I've worked under and with all different ranks and supposed elites. I can say with conviction that it all comes down to the individual. Who they are and how they act dictate their path and how they affect those around them." He stares intently at me now, no longer the pretense of beating around the bush.

I get what he's saying, honestly. And maybe it's a mark of maturity on my part that I actually listen to his poignant ideas instead of dismissing them outright. Wearily, I rub a hand over my face, clearing sleep from my eyes and giving me a few more seconds to respond. Maybe wisely.

"Okay, let's say you're right, medic. That still leaves my effectiveness and impact dependent on five other soldiers. Five strangers who, for all I know, couldn't care less about doing more than the bare minimum to stay on this side of the fence line."

"Then that's your true path. Convincin', no, *inspirin'* others to follow your lead and soldier like you will. Think you're up to the challenge of that?"

"Fuck if I know," I smirk, half-deprecating. "But I'll be damned if I don't try."

The medic returns my smirk wholeheartedly. "That's all any of us can do. I'll tell you now, I believe you can."

Such simple words and phrases shouldn't affect me, but I find that this soldier has created an unavoidable sense of purpose in me.

Later, once I've been released with a clean bill of health, I make my way over to Personnel (I don't pass "Go" or collect my $200). Instead, I collect a crew of Zeta soldiers to 'lead and inspire.' Staring at that list of five names and the roles they'll fill, I'm met with a sense of déjà vu. *Epsilon, Rho, Chi, Mu,* and *Omicron.*

I guess we'll all have something to prove.

—Ω—

LOST AND CERTAINLY NOT UNFOUNDED

Present Day

[TAU]

The scenery flows by in a stream of muted colors as we steadily make our way across the desert. The terrain is easily managed by our ATCs, and as such, the pace that I have set pushes the upper limits of our machines' performance. I am framed by Omega's team— Rho on my right, Chi mirroring him in placement on the left, and Mu and Omicron bringing up the rear. Our formation is tighter than usual, more apt for heading into a battle than collecting a missing squad leader. The possibility of conflict is high. It is strange to be in the lead position once again, though it has not been that long since I last occupied it. More than that, I have become accustomed to the Beta Sergeant holding it without question. I do not know what I have done to earn this spot, let alone what has led me to be here in the first place.

No, that is not entirely true.

Once Rho informed me that Omega was missing in action, the compulsion to provide aid to him and the team was immediate. I owe them a life debt—my life would have long been forfeit if not for them. That sense, at least in part, drove me to ignore standard protocol and simply act. This team is a challenge, but that may just be what I need in this life.

They are as essential to Omega as she is to them. Why else would they risk so much for her sake?

And I...I find myself risking my future for them...for her.

I lost my team. Omega brought me into hers.

"We're ten miles out."

Rho's crisp tenor resounds over the comms, breaking me from my reverie. Typically, there is some measure of trite and meaningless chatter being exchanged when this team is on the move. The past couple of hours have been spent in silence, each team member deeply immersed in their thoughts.

"Affirmative." My reply is succinct. I have no doubt about my ability to lead. Stepping back into this role is like a well-worn glove sliding perfectly into place.

Chi prompts, more than likely plotting our course, *"Tau, where do you want to start? The array?"*

"I suggest we start at Omega's last assumed location. Chi, you were able to confirm that she performed a check-in from there, correct?"

"Yes. Although I was unable to access either the audio or the transcript of the transmission to verify that it was the Sergeant. I can only affirm that a transmission broadcast from a Zeta soldier was received from the array's location at 1430 yesterday."

"Then that is our starting point. Approach with caution—plan to drop to half our speed once we are within a mile of the array."

My audio rings with their affirmatives before collapsing into dead silence once more.

It seems like no time passes, though it can't be less than twenty minutes later, when the communications array rises solid and lone amongst the lowly plains surrounding its base. It's distinctly inorganic and foreign in its form. Having seen one of these in the past, I am familiar with its general design and operation.

I begin to decelerate once we're within a mile or so of the array. Whenever in the field, one must always expect to encounter the enemy, and therefore, our approach is with the utmost caution. It seems unlikely there are any threats nearby, as between the built-in scanners of our ATCs and the lack of places to hide, we would have spotted anything amiss by now. As it is, I angle my bike toward the communications device, intent on placing us as close to the array as possible.

Once at a complete stop, along with Omega's teammates, it only takes a five-second glance to know that the Sergeant's bike is nowhere in the immediate vicinity. There are tire tracks pressed into the soft, ground-down earth. However, there are far too many to distinguish one set from another, given that many weeks, months, and years of personnel vehicles have driven through here. Outposts like these typically take at least six months to a year to form before they become habitable. This means a fair share of traffic to set up and secure the site.

Glancing over to where Chi has already dismounted her bike, I call to her, my faceplate flipped up.

"Chi, I need you to check the logs for a record of Omega's last transmission. Find out what was completed and when."

Chi nods without another word and breezes by me, already accessing the panel and going to work on the system inside. The others close in, not wanting to miss out.

Rho, scuffing a boot as he glances around this place, approaches me first. With his faceplate up, the deep frown etched into his countenance is difficult to miss. "No Omega, huh?"

I nod. "I will say I was not expecting a different scenario than this. It would be far too easy for Omega to escape or, at the minimum, anticipate danger from this location."

"Logs accessed," Chi cuts in, voice monotone and unemotional. "According to the last entry, Omega completed the standard maintenance protocol of the machine. The results are indicative of no issue locally with the system." Her eyes rise to meet mine, sparking ruby with curiosity and perhaps a bit of suspicion—more than a healthy amount of suspicion.

"Wait, so you're telling me that nothing's wrong with this comm system?" Rho interjects sharply, apparent signs of his frustration growing.

"It would appear so," Chi remarks loftily. "No sign of any alterations to the array."

"Hardware looks like it's the same—untouched." Omicron remarks from over my shoulder. I catch his nod toward the dish itself.

"So where does that leave us?" Mu pipes up finally, anxiety-laden in spades by her tone.

"Chi, do you recall what her communication to base stated?"

With a sharp clang, Chi seals the panel door before straightening from her kneeling position, face pulled tight in frustration. "The communications log was unavailable. I could not get the transcript of their last exchange, and yes, I would surmise that there were multiple messages based on the beginning and ending time stamps."

"That seems unusual," Rho adds, head tilted in confusion and voice laced with suspicion.

"Indeed," I respond dryly. I am inclined to agree that the picture we are presented with is clearly riddled with gaps.

With a deep sigh, I take another look around, attempting to put myself in Omega's position. What would I do? Report my findings to base and return? No, the mission was to fix communications between the outpost and base. My actions would continue along that route.

Nodding to myself, I am more certain than ever, and I share my findings with the team. "Omega's next course of action should have been to go to the outpost and confirm if the communication issue originates from there. We have a few knowns: We know she was here. We know she completed a standard maintenance operation. We know that she communicated with the base. That leaves us with a primary unknown: what occurred after that last communication."

"All right, then." Rho claps his hands together, dust flying up from the action. "Guess that means we're heading over to the outpost."

I nod, accompanying the gesture with a verbal affirmation. "Yes." Something else occurs to me. If a trap has been laid, the last thing I want to do is feed this team into its gaping maw. The plan forms smoothly in my mind, as it always has—my thoughts are once again that of a leader, not a follower. "We will continue our formation and approach from the eastern side of the town, avoiding the main road— we don't know what we are heading into."

—T—

COMPROMISING POSITIONS ARE WE

[TAU]

"Well, shit. That's going to be a problem." Rho's sarcasm fills the space around us.

Gazing down at where his sight is centered, I feel compelled to agree. From our position atop the outpost wall, we have an unobstructed view of the entire compound—its basic grid of roads and buildings laid out before us. What we are seeing is not good news. A whole town of Zee wander aimlessly, though I can almost perceive an underlying pattern to their behavior. The space is filled with their muted grunts and shuffling gaits. Their movements are smooth and energetic, which leads me to suspect they are newly mutated.

It does not bode well for us, but more so for Omega. Her bike, stationed outside in plain view, leaves no other conclusion. She came to this outpost and is more than likely still here.

Crouching down, I sink back into my mind to assess the situation. This is not a time to be rash and unplanned in our actions. It is paramount to focus on the goal at hand—obtaining Omega through the most direct and safest approach we can.

Turning toward the medic, I call out lowly. Our comms are unusable here, so we have had to resort to actual face-to-face communication, upper helms off. We entered a dead zone the moment we hit the perimeter of this site.

"Will your medical scanners work without active communications?"

"Yeah, they should. They don't require any connections. It's all local to my scanner."

There is a rush of relief for me, knowing that we still have the capability of finding the Sergeant without conducting a door-to-door search.

"All right then. Can you get a reading from Omega's ID chip?"

Shifting his primary weapon over his shoulder, Omicron pulls a smaller device in front of him and starts toggling through settings. I have never had much need to interact with medical devices, so I am not familiar with their interface. An oversight on my part.

"There," he releases a sigh. "Yep, got her beacon loud and clear. She is here and not too far off."

"Can you get a reading on her vital signs as well?"

"That one may be a little harder," he grimaces. "Any comms interference degrades the quality of what I see, so it might give me a false negative—maybe even a false positive."

"Do your best," I nod.

He fiddles with his device again before his brows draw together in a sharp line. "Shit."

The harsh sound does not inspire much confidence in Omega's situation.

"How bad is it?" Mu peeks over his broad shoulder guard.

"Not good." He shakes his head. "Blood pressure is too low. Heart rate is all over the board. She is alive, but she is not functionin' at her best."

"That is where we will focus our efforts," I interrupt before things can get more dire sounding. I need this team focused and not reactive. "How far from our location is she?"

"Looks to be about an eighth of a mile from us. Damn near the center of the outpost."

"And the Zee? How many are we dealing with?"

"Hard to read them when they cluster, but there are at least a few dozen, probably more. Some areas seem a bit more dense than others."

"What areas?"

"Probably won't surprise you, but I'd say it's right around Omega's beacon."

"Then that is where we need to go," I nod decisively.

With a team of enhanced soldiers at my disposal, I am not limited in options. It is merely a matter of determining who is best suited for which role.

"Omega's signal is within the center of this outpost. Correct?"

Without breaking eye contact, he nods emphatically. "Yeah. Her signal hasn't moved in the last half day. Her vitals aren't stable, so we need to figure out what we're doin' soon. She needs medical attention now."

"I understand. We will need to pull at least some of the Zee away from that location." I scan the team. "Mu, Chi, I need you to create a distraction to draw them out and pick off as many as you safely can."

"What type of distraction?" Chi questions. "I assume you mean something of the explosive variety?"

"Yes, but not too forceful. We need to keep the Zee contained here as much as possible. What happened here needs to be documented and understood. I would also rather not unleash a new horde into the surrounding area."

"I see." She dips her chin. "Then attract but not release. A reasonable request."

"Excellent. Mu, you will act as Chi's extra set of eyes. Support and eliminate whatever Zee you can while maintaining your position from the wall. I do not want either of you two down below if it can be helped."

"And what will you three be doing?" Mu questions, her eyes darting between us and then toward where Omega is supposed to be. From her fidgeting, it is not difficult to surmise that her worry is peaking.

"Once you and Chi have pulled enough Zee to your side of the outpost, Rho, Omicron, and I will proceed to track down the Sergeant. We will enter from the rear of the center, hopefully avoiding most of the lingering Zee. Once we have Omega secure, we will exfiltrate the same path—up the wall, back to this position."

Turning to address the two females, I instruct, "With our comms down, we will signal via flare. You can respond in kind to let us know that you are ready as well. Once hear your distraction, we will proceed to infiltrate the center. If we encounter issues, we will signal for assistance with a flare. However, our gunfire may be the only alert you receive. Is that clear?"

The team all nods, their faces taut and serious but prepared.

"All right. Then let us move out."

It does not take the three of us long to get into position. Rho pulls one of the flares, aiming up and out as he sends it arcing over the open town center. Its colored tail of purple catches some of the Zee's attention, stopping them in their tracks as they gaze blankly at the newest aspect of their environment.

Less than a minute later, a duplicate flare streams into the sky from the opposite direction. All are in position and ready.

I count down: "Five, four, three, two, one..."

Boom. A plume of dirt, rock, and debris shoots upward like a geyser, suspended for a breath before careening back to the earth. The explosion shakes the ground briefly, but most importantly, it gets the attention of the creatures below.

Like magic, the ambling Zee pick up their pace, coalescing toward the source of the disturbance. They follow each other without deviation.

We wait until the last few are out of sight, the distant pings and thuds of sniper fire confirming contact with the second half of the team before our group descends into the now-empty space.

Once all three of us have boots on the ground, I provide succinct instructions. Rho will lead, Omicron will follow, directing with his bio scanner, and I will cover the rear. There is a definite possibility that Chi and Mu will be unable to keep the Zee population engaged indefinitely.

A light breeze brings with it the scent of warm wood from the buildings around us and a sweet, sick stench that is unmistakably that of decay. We slowly but surely pick our way toward Omega's beacon.

"She's not too far ahead. Beacon's static, but I am still gettin' fluctuation on her vitals."

"And what does that mean?" Rho hisses reflexively. I shush

him, and the taller soldier straightens immediately.

"It means she still ain't movin', so we need to move our collective butts," Omicron cuts in.

The medic's focus is entirely on his device...until it is not. His stop is abrupt, accompanied by a sharp exhale that echoes in the silence.

"Shit, it's gone." He turns sharply, moving his device to and fro. "I lost Sarge's signal."

"Why would that occur?" My stomach clenches painfully.

"I don't know." The big man growls, giving his scanner a solid hit to the side before releasing a heavy sigh. "I'm not gettin' any readings now."

That perks me up instantly. "No readings. How about for any of us?"

Omicron dutifully checks the tablet, touching it multiple times before pulling back, eyes wide in surprise. "Nothin'. I'm not pickin' up on anyone or anythin'."

Rho steps closer, forming an impromptu huddle. "So now local dead zone as well, not just satellites." He rubs his goatee chin in thought. "I can get on board with the satellite comms being less than stellar at a new outpost. But local tech isn't working— not just our radios, but the medical scanner as well. Yeah, that smacks of intentional sabotage and setup."

Anger roils beneath the soldier's laid-back tone, but none of that matters at the moment.

"Omega is our mission," I remind them. "Everything else is secondary."

I make sure to get a look of comprehension from both men before reevaluating the town. It is noticeably vacant of signs of previous activity. Windows and doors are firmly closed, and roads are clear of debris, except for one location.

What must be the outpost's primary center is the lone anomaly with its front doors ajar and hanging slightly off their hinges— evidence of a forceful exit. The upset earth before its entrance is a strong indicator of Zee activity.

Without a word to the other two, I close the several yards of ground and instinctively know I am right. The loose ground is a maze of tracks, most of which lead out and away from each other. But that is not the most encouraging piece of evidence. The prevailing rot is now cut by the sharp tang of metal, specifically iron, fresh enough to lack that edge of rust that old blood emits.

Taking a step closer to the gaping entrance, the space within is notably cooler and darker. A chill rushes up my spine, but my intuition encourages me forward.

"We're gonna have to clear room by room without my scanner," the broad medic growls lowly.

I am shaking my head before he even finishes his statement. "That will not be necessary."

Holstering my weapon, I take a deep breath, then another shallower one. My senses are flooded with the scents lingering in the stale air: wood glue, paper, rotting flesh, blood, and, just below it, a different scent that is an amalgamation of several— leather, gun oil, and lavender.

"Omega is in there." Drawing my sword without hesitation, I turn from the others. "Short-range weapons only. Let us avoid alerting the other Zee to our presence for however long we can."

Rho grins ferally as he pulls out a tomahawk-like ax from his belt. "You got it. Let's get her."

We move as quickly and quietly as possible into the dimly lit interior. Each careful step releases a loud crunch of glass crystals regardless of how light the tread is. As my eyes adjust, I am taken aback by the mess we have wandered into. In contrast to the sterile landscape, this building's interior screams chaos.

Doing a careful sweep, I note row upon row of desks, some overturned, some not, and none with any signs of usage. The place is as empty and new as if it had just been completed, waiting for tenants.

Bypassing a set of doors laid flat on the floor, I nearly miss the rifle, almost entirely buried beneath it. Without a word, I lean down, grab it, and hand it over to Rho, who slings it across his chest. I avoid commenting on the bloodstain across its handle.

Speaking of blood, it now saturates the air. Browning red splotches decorate the floor in uneven patterns, starting with the disconnected double doors and flowing to a nearby cubicle. There, the spots gather into a spreading swath only to break up and scatter down a different path—a macabre trail leading further into the building.

"Fuck. That's a lot of blood," Rho curses lowly. At this point, it should be apparent that Omega's health has been compromised.

Painstakingly, we follow the sporadic trail until it comes to an end in a smaller conference room. Here, brighter red patterns are brushed along the walls and floor. Besides what amounts to a visceral crime scene, the room is empty of life.

"Did we miss somethin'?" Omicron breaks his silence. He moves to peer out into the hallway again while Rho goes so far as to peek under the table.

"Fuck!" A Zee slithers out after him. Its mouth opens and closes in silent clicks each time its teeth connect. Pink-tinged foam sprays from parted lips. A portion of its throat appears to be collapsed, preventing it from making noise and alerting others.

Lip curled in disgust, I take two swift strides before stabbing the length of my blade down into its skull. The rapid motion cuts off any further movement abruptly. I immediately withdraw my sword and clean the edge.

"Thanks, man." Rho gives me a weak smile.

I do not follow their actions any further as the faintest sound demands my attention. My breathing halts as I focus entirely on whatever my hearing has locked onto. A faint, wet rasp of displaced air. It is all I need to pinpoint the source. Other indicators pile on: a splash of burgundy on the ceiling's gray crossbeams, the more pungent scent of fresh blood, and lastly, a ceiling tile slightly misaligned.

"Holy shit." Rho follows the path of my eyes. "She's up there."

Sheathing my sword, I motion to the other two. "Let us get this table out of the way."

With our combined strength, that massive piece of hardwood slides effortlessly into the far wall. The *thunk* of impact is overly loud.

"Omicron, stand guard. Rho, a lift up, please."

A pair of gloved hands, fingers interlocked tightly, are presented to me just under the off-kilter tile.

I step into the gunner's lift and easily reach the tile, shifting it up and to the side. The opening is barely wide enough for me to fit through, and I am forced to hand over both rifle and katana to the medic before squeezing into the musty plenum space above.

The shallow space around me stands out in sharp grayscale clarity thanks to my enhanced vision. At first, it is what you would expect: a space no more than a couple of feet high, filled with ductwork, support structures, and piping. But there is an anomaly. In the corner, a slumped form is propped up in a graceless heap, braced by a cross-section of beams.

Omega.

Even with my enhanced sight, it is difficult to decipher where her injuries lie. More immediately, I cannot tell if she is alive. I take a deep breath and am hit with the pungent aroma of death. Cool sweat breaks out across my forehead as I fumble to remove my right gauntlet.

I search for a pulse at her throat. The skin my fingers make contact with is chilled and unmoving. For a moment, there is despair, but then a flutter yields under my fingertips. It is faint and thready but discernible.

A flash of silver in my peripheral vision is all the warning I have to jerk back. Even then, the blade manages to score a thin line below my right eye. Never underestimate a soldier's first instincts. Not daring to move, I regard the knife pointed steadily at my throat and patiently wait.

Awareness is slow to reach the other soldier, but eventually, I am rewarded with a pair of dark eyes staring at me, albeit not wholly coherently.

"Omega." I breathe her name into the quiet between us.

Muzzily, her head shifts to focus on my voice, but I can see the energy it is taking her to recognize me.

"Tau?"

Her voice is hard to recognize and even harder to hear. It is weak and throaty. I slowly wrap my fingers around the extended hand, tightly clutching the knife. With my remaining hand, I brush aside a few gore-caked locks from where they are obscuring her view.

"Yes, I am here. *We* are here." I emphasize.

She seems to relax then. A twitch of dark lips gives way to a tired smile. Satisfied that she is indeed alive, I call calmly down to the others below.

"I found her. She is alive."

"She is? Thank God." Rho's voice almost cracks with relief.

Omicron quickly overlaps with his own question. "What's her condition?"

"Injured and badly. I do not know the extent as of yet."

"We need to get her down, man." Rho is emphatic.

"Not yet." Omicron resolutely interrupts. "Tau, I need you to check her for any signs of trauma to her spine."

With a frown, I look Omega over more meticulously. Deciding on the direct approach, I lightly brush my fingertips along her body, starting at the ankles. Her feet look correctly aligned. Her lower legs seem intact as well, but as I assess above her kneecaps, it becomes clear that something is wrong with one of her femurs. Beneath thick muscle, the leg gives at the wrong place.

Carefully and as clinically as possible, I feel under Omega's poncho along her sides and chest. Her breathing remains ragged throughout. Her right forearm shows the most obvious damage—

a three-inch gash gives way to the protrusion of bone beneath a makeshift bandage. That, and a nasty blow to the head.

"Omega? Omega!"

"*Hmm...*" She is awake but definitely battling for awareness.

"From what I can tell, there are no injuries to her back. However, at least one of her legs looks to be compromised. She has a fully fractured right arm and some kind of head injury. She is disoriented, and I am having difficulty keeping her conscious."

"All right. That's about as good as I can expect. Get her down here."

I do not bother wasting any more time, shifting and dropping the closest four tiles out of the way. As I turn to gather Omega, I find that she is awake again and looking more lucid than initially. She wears a faintly bemused expression.

"Your team is waiting for you. Are you ready for them?"

"Sure." She exhales tiredly. "Why not? This place is starting to get a little dull anyway."

Gingerly, I slide one arm behind her upper back and the other underneath the backs of her knees. She is already clenching her teeth from the pain.

"Just do it," she grits out.

I comply and am mildly surprised at the weight I am hefting. With her gear and muscle, she is not lightweight.

Two sets of hands are already reaching up, ready to receive their leader.

"Incoming," I warn. "Careful of the left thigh and right forearm."

No sooner do I lower her legs through the gap than her weight is no longer supported by me alone. Once her body is completely removed from my possession, I am quick to drop through the gap myself.

Now that she is out, both soldiers fight to speak with or touch her. Omicron sets Rho to rights, firmly telling him to back off. I reinforce the request with an order for him to keep watch.

With more light, I can see the extent of her injuries in full color. Omega is paler than usual but flushed in the cheeks—probably a fever. The arm is her most noticeable physical injury, besides the liberal coating of dried blood from her forehead down. She is entirely too docile—almost listless. It is painful to see her reduced to this state.

Omicron moves from crown to heel, assessing wounds, prioritizing treatment, and applying various methods he has at his disposal. I rotate between watching the medic's movements and extending my senses at the doorway for any unplanned visitors.

Finally, the large specialist seems satisfied enough with his fieldwork for the four of us to exfiltrate. A well-maintained facility with an abundance of resources is Omega's best bet for a full recovery.

The only thing that seems to go right is our clear pathway out. When we begin stepping around a decent amount of dead Zee that were not here when we entered, it becomes obvious the other two decided to ignore the second half of my orders.

This is confirmed when a rope is helpfully dropped from the outer wall. It seems fair to let the misconduct slide as their help allows Omicron to ascend quickly first, before pulling Rho with Omega in a fireman's carry up and out, then finally, myself.

Once we are all safely atop the wall, Chi and Mu rush to Omega's side. The relief on their faces is palpable—their squad leader is alive, battered but breathing.

"Decent work down there," Chi says quietly, her precise tone carrying genuine gratitude.

Mu bounces on her toes, tears threatening to spill. "I knew you would find her. I just knew it."

Rho carefully adjusts Omega in his arms, mindful of her injuries. "Let's get her home."

As we prepare to descend the outer wall toward our bikes, I catch Omega's eye for a moment. Even in her weakened state, there is something in her gaze—recognition, perhaps even gratitude. For the first time since becoming Zeta, I feel like I am exactly where I belong.

"Team," I call out quietly, ensuring everyone's attention. "Well done. All of you."

The words are simple, but they carry weight. We worked as a cohesive unit today, with each member's strengths complementing one another. Chi's tactical precision, Mu's intuitive insights, Rho's unwavering loyalty, Omicron's medical expertise—and somehow, my leadership brought it all together.

As we make our way back toward the bikes and safety, Omega secure in our care, I realize this is what true teamwork feels like.

Not the rigid hierarchy of Alpha Squadron, but something more profound. Something worth sacrificing everything for.

—T—

SENSELESS AND NOT QUITE RIGHT

[OMEGA]

My dream recedes with a knife-edge sharpness as an unmistakable sensation crawls across my skin—someone's watching me. I can always tell. My body responds at a subconscious level. Goosebumps erupt like an invading army of phantom ants marching double-time up my vertebrae.

Unwilling to surrender to wakefulness yet, I attempt to ignore the sensation and settle back into oblivion's embrace. If someone wants to kill me, go for it. The coolness of the sheets whispers against my bare skin, and their crisp, clean scent is some excellent salve on my weary body. I might have succeeded in my retreat— might being the operative term here—if not for a deliberate flick against the tip of my nose. Fury sparks forth behind my eyelids as I pry them open, the full strength of my glare taking precious seconds to initialize, combat systems coming online one by one.

Of course, it's Rho, his insufferable grin hovering at my bedside like some demented guardian angel. Just beyond his shoulder, I spot a sapphire-blue head of hair catching the sterile light. Mu's barely contained energy vibrates through the air between us, and she is barely keeping herself from pouncing on me. All it takes is Rho's infinitesimal nod before she launches herself, all unrestrained happiness and bubbling over joy. With no other option, I reluctantly submit to the crushing embrace she delivers. How someone so lithe can compress my ribcage with the force of a hydraulic press remains one of life's great mysteries.

I fucking hate Rho. Have I mentioned that?

The traitorous bastard gives me a theatrical thumbs-up from behind her shoulder, dissolving into exaggerated kissing gestures.

My middle finger rises in a universal salute, which he has little trouble interpreting.

A sharp smack intercepts my digit mid-air, and I finally register Chi and Omicron standing at the periphery. The dark-haired demolition expert smirks, her dark eyes glinting with warning beneath her perfectly manicured brow, as Chi's composure never quite hides the predator within. Meanwhile, Omicron's massive frame hunches over my medical readout, thick fingers scrolling through what I'm certain is a comprehensive encyclopedia of my physical failures. The psychological ones, thankfully, won't be listed until my next psych exam—mandatory after near-death flirtations.

Mu finally releases me from her evil clutches, my busted ribs sighing in relief. Awkwardly, I give her a pat on the arm as she sniffles and rubs red-rimmed eyes made all the more vivid against her brilliant blue irises. The gunny looks terrible. Hell, they all look as though they could use a week's worth of rest, not to mention a good scrub in the shower. Even the ever-immaculate Chi looks slightly less than perfect, a couple of strands of hair out of place and defying gravity.

"So...?" I manage to pass through the constriction of a throat that's still raw and swollen. A straw materializes before my chapped lips, and I'm too thirsty to give a damn as Omicron chuckles in amusement over my attempt to drain the cup in one go. My body is sorely lacking hydration, and it's as if I've spent a week wandering the Sahara. Which, come to think of it, isn't far from the truth.

"So, that was cutting it kind of close, don't you think, Sarge?" Rho's voice carries none of its usual levity, instead weighted with something foreign rippling beneath the solemn surface. I'm hard-pressed to categorize it, but I'd swear it was anger.

"Hmm. Is that why everyone looks like you've been to a wake?"

I deflect, attempting to lighten the atmosphere. It doesn't work.

"Who said 'been'?" One delicate eyebrow of Chi's rises ever so slightly. "You still look worse off than the Zee you scrapped with, *Sarge*."

I would have deigned to stick my tongue out if I had the energy. Right now, it's a misshapen lump of flesh partially glued to the bottom of my mouth. Smacking my lips a few times to moisten them, I attempt to speak again. My eyes slide to the disturbingly quiet medic.

"What's the damage?" I hazard and almost shrink back into my extra fluffy pillow at the beady-eyed look he gives me. Okay. I could've phrased that better.

"The damage is three fractures, one per leg and your right ulna, cracked ribs—though miraculously none fully separated—dehydration, lacerations, contusions, and yet another concussion." Omicron drags his broad palm across his face, from forehead to chin, raw concern beyond medical inquiry behind the gesture.

"Is that all?" I half-joke before my drug-addled brain catches up. "Wait. I have another concussion?"

His eyes roll skyward, seeking divine patience. "Yes. Another, and don't be askin' me how many your total count's up to. I don't want to think about how your brain's functionin' right now. You're lookin' at several weeks of recovery, minimum."

I nod mechanically, recalling at that moment what the attending physician told me prior to the ill-fated solo mission. The neurological scans had shown "anomalies"—something about degradation in certain neural pathways. He'd dismissed it. Both assuming and assuring me that it's probably related to my particular Zeta enhancement. A side effect of the beyond-human strength. "We see similar patterns in other strength-enhanced Zetas," he'd said casually. "Nothing concerning."

I wanted to ask how many strength-augmented soldiers he'd treated. I've never encountered another soldier with my specific mutation expression. My performance during the Combat Readiness Test, or the CaRT as it's affectionately called, definitely highlighted something's wrong—I'm tracking twelve percent below my established baseline for combat fitness. It might not sound catastrophic until you're facing down a Zee, and that fraction of a second determines whether you end the day as the predator or the prey.

From the foot of my bed, I catch Omicron studying me with an unsettling intensity. I wonder if he's accessed my previous records. The man has the clearance, and I wouldn't put it past him to dig through my files. At least he won't find anything psych-related. That information is heavily restricted. But his expression reveals nothing, and I maintain my mask of indifference.

"Fair enough." I manage to keep my voice steady. With another scan of the surrounding space, I search for a face that should be here but isn't. Maybe I hallucinated his presence during my extraction. Rho ferrying me out seems more likely than any other explanation.

Chi reads something in my face as her demure expression warps to a more devious edge. Licking narrow lips, she prepares to interject something ominous and personal. I fear the next words to come out of her mouth.

"Oh, Omega. You missed Tau earlier. We had to forcibly eject him from his bedside vigil to bathe and get some rest. I imagine he will return presently to check on your current condition. I doubt if he can be kept away long. Do not worry yourself."

I frown darkly at her. If Omicron weren't here, monitoring my every twitch, I'd be testing her notoriously sharp reflexes. Or at least making a good attempt at it. She has the audacity to chuckle at my expense before tossing her hair over a shoulder and turning to leave.

"And where are you going?" I demand, injecting as much authority as one can muster while horizontal and half-broken.

"I figure that I might as well treat myself to lunch and a little rest of my own. Now that we know you intend to stay among the living, I have more pressing matters to attend to." With a dismissive nod and a flash of violet hair, the scout is gone, leaving the rest of us stunned.

"I want to say I can't believe she just did that, but…" Mu sighs, exasperation threaded with undeniable fondness. I wouldn't expect any less, as well. My demolitionist has never been one for emotional scenes, and this was probably as close as she'd ever get to one without breaking out in hives.

I offer Mu a wan smile in agreement, and the minimalist gesture earns me a beaming look infused with disproportionate joy and warmth. There are worse things than a bit of kindness, I suppose.

The room clears gradually after that, Rho practically dragging Mu away upon Omicron's insistence on my needing rest, before he follows as well. As the door slides shut behind them, I allow myself a moment—just one—of pure, undiluted fear. It coils heavy and disconcerting in my gut like a venomous viper, leaving my mouth sour, breathing ragged, and a dangerously overfull mind. I can't stop replaying that moment at the outpost—my hand refusing commands, my weapon suddenly foreign in my grip. A momentary lapse that nearly cost me everything.

Twelve percent below baseline, and there's no guarantee it's at its limit of impact. I could continue to deteriorate until…what end? Something messy and burdensome. In our line of work, that's not just a handicap—it's a death sentence. I haven't confided in anyone yet—not Rho, not Chi, not even Omicron. They need their squad leader to be solid and uncompromised, especially with whatever comes next.

I press the heels of my palms into my eye sockets until stars explode behind my lids, then force myself to focus. There are more immediate concerns, such as why HQ sent me alone into what was clearly an ambush, but more likely a death trap.

Even before that, there's been too much going sideways of late, starting with Tau's extraction if we're looking for the linchpin. That strange child with her inexplicable connection to the Zee. Those Shepherds, their breach of a UF facility, and whatever it was they were after. I'm trying to assemble these random, fragmented pieces into a whole, but my battered brain won't cooperate, and the last few days haven't fixed much.

With a huff, I thump the back of my head against the softer fluff of the pillow. A useless gesture, but for the moment, it feels helpful. As I stare outward at the bare achromatic walls, there's nothing worth noting to focus on, either above or beyond me. It serves to aid my spiraling into a void of my mind's creation. As I've done so many times before, my fingers find the raised brand on my neck, where it lies barely visible beneath my hairline and behind my right ear. I gently trace the elegant curve that's both a symbol of my Zeta batch and my designation—*Omega*. What did they really do to us in that conversion process? And, more importantly, why? Do I genuinely want the answers?

The door slides open on a whisper of movement, and I drop my hand to find Tau standing on the threshold, his usually impassive face betraying the slightest hint of relief when our eyes meet. He's cleaned up, but the bruising under his eyes tells me he hasn't slept much.

"You look like shit," I offer by way of greeting.

A ghost of a smile touches his lips. "A sentiment I could return with interest, Sergeant."

He enters, allowing the door to seal behind him. Instead of claiming the visitor's chair, he remains standing, his posture military-precise even though we're alone.

"I've been officially reassigned," he announces without preamble. "To Beta Squadron. Your squadron, specifically."

I blink, at a loss to comprehend. "Command demoted you? For what reason?"

"They didn't." He shifts very slightly, but I don't miss the discomfort he attempts to smooth over. "I requested the transfer."

My jaw slackens. "You...*what*?"

"I requested permanent assignment to your team." His voice is more assertive and matter-of-fact, though I catch something else lurking beneath the words. "It took some convincing, but Command eventually conceded."

"Why the downgrade?"

Garnet eyes lock with mine, unguarded in that brief exchange. A complexity of emotions I can't half name lay bare there. He seems to debate how much to say before offering a partial truth, along with a hitch of his shoulder.

"The mission effectiveness of this unit speaks for itself."

But there's more. I can feel it hanging low in the air between us. Our time together has been brief but intensely concentrated. After everything we've faced, I've learned some of those subtle shifts in Tau's expression. The tightening around his eyes and the almost imperceptible tension in his jaw betray him. He's discovered something in our team that the Alphas couldn't provide. Something authentic. Trust. Dependability. Maybe even belonging. I doubt he'd admit to any of it directly. That would be too easy.

He pauses to scan the eaves of the room, his eyes tracking to the sealed door, before stepping closer to my bed, his voice barely a whisper as he folds into my space.

"That civilian outpost you were sent to check? Chi cross-referenced UF records. The communication disruption was logged less than a week ago, but as you undoubtedly observed, the settlement has been out of communication significantly longer. A month minimum."

"There was no running water or electricity, and dust accumulated everywhere. No signs of dishes used or homes lived in—not even a struggle or the remains of victims. Nothing recently active, except for the Zee," I murmur, connecting dots that form an increasingly disturbing pattern.

"Yes. And you were sent there alone, despite protocol requiring a minimum three-person team for settlement checks." That particular point seems to stick in Tau's craw as someone as by-the-book as he is. His jaw muscles bunch visibly. "It was not a standard comms check, Omega. It was something else entirely."

I process this silently. He's right. The entire mission was flawed, from the poorly constructed structures to the lack of signs indicating that people had actually lived there. Someone at Command knew precisely what they were sending someone into, but why?

Was it a deliberate test? Maybe not necessarily to kill me, but… to observe something? The thought sends a discordant chill through me despite the balmy seventy-two degrees in here.

"There's more," he continues, voice hardly audible. "Chi reviewed the data she extracted from the facility, at least what she could recall. There were references to experiments spanning at least four decades. Genetic manipulation, behavioral conditioning…experiments… possibly concerning children."

"Children?" The word emerges hollow, as empty as that thought leaves me. "Why would they use children?"

"That was not explicitly stated in the files. It is also unclear who was running the facility, as it predates the inception of the United Forces. The data Chi assessed was high-level and fragmented—mostly project codes, subject identification numbers, and clinical outcomes."

The silence between us grows dense, almost suffocating.

"What exactly are you suggesting, Tau?" I need him to be clear and direct at this moment. No sidestepping or bullshit.

He hesitates, weighing the risk. "I am saying we need to exercise caution. There is far more to the UF and perhaps what preceded it. You survived, your team recovered what appears to be vital data, and now Command is aware of your collective capabilities."

As much as I can, I straighten. My voice is still low and raspy, but I do my best to enunciate my response with deliberate precision. "And I'll tell you what I know. Our last few missions have been way above our pay grade and assigned with an insufficient amount of intelligence, putting us in some really shitty situations. None of this feels right."

Before he can respond, the door slides open again. It's Mu, her heart-shaped face flushed with excitement rather than her earlier distress. A thin line of sweat traces along the edge of her hairline. I imagine she sprinted all the way here from wherever she just came from.

"Omega! Oh—sorry, I didn't realize—" Breathless, she halts, registering Tau's presence with obvious surprise.

"It's fine," I assure her. My team was obviously apprised of Tau becoming a more permanent add-on. "What's up?"

"We've got new orders," she announces, glancing between us with barely contained excitement. "They're sending us to retrieve a person of interest. Someone who's a civvie and…" She lowers her voice, "supposedly *immune* to the Zee."

I exchange a look with the Alpha…er, former Alpha. Damn. I guess I can't keep calling him that. "Immune?"

"That's what they're claiming. One of our reconnaissance teams identified this individual but lost contact before extraction. We're being deployed to locate and bring in whoever they are. Well…us and a few other teams." Her face splits into a grin. "And guess what? Those other teams are all Alpha-level. They're trusting us with an Alpha-class mission!"

"Us?" I echo skeptically. "I'm not exactly combat-ready." I hold up my bandaged limbs for emphasis.

"Two weeks," she declares, holding up two fingers either as the number or a sign of victory. I'm betting on the latter. "You'll be healed enough by then. The rest of us begin preparations tomorrow, between serving our disciplinary duties for going temporarily AWOL. Which was completely justified, by the way." The last bit is puffed out as a defiant pout.

"And I'm profoundly grateful for that insubordination, Mu. Truly. All of you saved my life when I was thoroughly fucked."

"Any time, Omega. Just don't make a habit of it. We all need to make it to the end." With that oddly cryptic parting shot, she delivers a jaunty salute before practically dancing from the room.

After her departure, I turn back to Tau, unease crystallizing into something sharper. "An Alpha-level retrieval mission assigned to a Beta team immediately after we uncover classified data?"

"And directly following being assigned a deliberate suicide mission," Tau adds grimly.

"That's one hell of a coincidence." I sink back into my pillows, mind racing despite the medication slowing my thoughts. "A civilian immune to the Zee..."

"If such a person exists, they would be invaluable."

I study him closely, searching for any hint of duplicity. "This isn't what you signed up for when you joined the United Forces, is it?"

"No," he admits with a slow shake of his shaved head. "But I am beginning to wonder if any of us understood what we were committing to." His words settle between us with the weight of a funeral shroud.

"Fear and trauma have a way of hijacking critical thinking," I observe quietly.

Whatever conspiracy we've stumbled into runs deeper than any of us can fathom. And soon, we'll be wading back into its murky epicenter. The quiet stretches languidly between us for several minutes before Tau breaks the silence.

"So, what is our strategy?" He asks, apropos of anything.

I try not to give him the side eye. For someone who was looking for hidden surveillance in our space a handful of minutes ago, this feels like a 180-degree turn from his straight-laced persona. Not to mention, the guy voluntarily demoted himself to a team that he admits is mucking about in the UF's dirty business. I want to believe that he can be trusted and that he's joined us because of what we offer, but I'm not stupid. Survival demands skepticism. I'm not assuming I know him or whatever hidden drivers he may have.

"We do as ordered. Locate the immune civilian, if they exist, and bring them in. We maintain awareness." I don't voice my other thoughts. They border on sedition. Then again, the old me—me from before being sent on a suicide mission to rescue a lone Alpha soldier, prior to that facility and its damning data, those Shepherds…before being sent to die—would have rejected that line of thinking instantly. But now…if anything's amiss, and I do mean anything, I'm not above intentionally sabotaging the mission or neutralizing a perceived threat. Even a Zeta-shaped one.

"Understood," he agrees with unsettling immediacy, nodding as he turns to leave. There's something like respect flickering in his eyes, an unquestioning acceptance of my judgment that feels both powerful and dangerous. The new dynamic is heady and entirely unexpected. "Two weeks. Focus on recovering fully. I will investigate what is known about this immune civilian and perhaps enlist Chi's assistance. Better to have whatever intelligence on our side before we're exposed again."

As he reaches the threshold, I call after him. "Tau." He pauses, looking back. "Why did you really choose my team?"

He considers this for a moment, weighing his response and how much to reveal. "Your squad operates differently," he finally elaborates. "You trust each other. You…" he pauses, searching for the right words. "You function as something more integral than a military unit."

There's more he's not saying, but I understand the core truth. After witnessing how we fight for each other and risk everything to leave no one behind, he wants to belong to something genuine and meaningful. Something the Alphas, for all their elite status and superior resources, couldn't give him.

After he's gone, I stare at the ceiling, fingers unconsciously drifting to my temple, where the headaches have been getting worse. My mind churns with unanswered questions. Forty years of experiments. Children as test subjects. Suicide missions disguised as routine assignments. And now, this new objective. What spun web are we caught in, and what awaits us in its center?

FIN

Acknowledgments

Continuing the story of Omega and her team has been a great joy and a lovely challenge for me to immerse myself in.

First and foremost, I want to thank my husband and de facto accountability buddy. If I didn't quite know what I was getting into when I opened this mystery box, I'm fairly certain he *really* didn't know either. Maybe we both still don't know, but regardless it's a fun journey. Thank you for letting me fling ideas your way, helping me to poke holes in the feasibility of scenarios, and allowing my post-it notes and scribbles to multiply and take over random spaces. Your steadfast support and acceptance of this storytelling drive of mine is immeasurable.

An enormous thank you and warm hug to my developmental editor. Her feedback and intuition with my story, as well as the questions she posed, helped me to evolve this tale into something far broader and more intriguing, and I cannot thank you enough.

To my family: My parents for supporting this creative place in my heart and mind, and my father specifically for fact-checking me on military behaviors and tactics. My mama-san for loving and encouraging me no matter which direction the wind and I go. My sister for believing in me and bringing me into the book club world, exposing me to so many new stories. And my kids for understanding and living with a distractable mother trying to do all of it at once—and not always succeeding.

And, of course, I appreciate my friends and readers who have given this story and its characters a chance. As much as I enjoyed writing this book, your accolades and not-so-gentle prompts for the next book in the series gave me the courage to carry on. I hope that you have enjoyed this team and their shenanigans and trials. More to come, of course, and, as always, hopefully sooner than last!

Excerpt from:

Zombie Girl Omega – Insurrection
Book Three of the Zeta Wars

AS IT RENDS

[MU]

I wake tasting ash and the sweet char of burnt flesh.

A stifling, all-encompassing heat follows, suffocating, holding me captive. Pain sings along nerve endings, warping the composition of my perception to where it's difficult to determine the individual parts of me. It's all that I can comprehend, amassing into a chaotic symphony of agony.

And I'm not alone.

Strange dark mounds surround me. Their shapes twisted and contorted, but not so much so that I can't recognize what they are. Who they were. Some faces stare blankly up, vaguely familiar beneath the gore. I can put a name to their still forms. Many more are distributed among them, sprawled, limbs akimbo, and faces down. I don't know them. Not really. They're not Zeta—they lack the obvious uniform and gear, let alone general care. The clothes resting atop the piles are haphazard, dirty, and torn. And not a one of them is moving. That truth is unavoidable, no matter how hard I try to shy away from it.

Something's gone so terribly wrong. What led us to this? There's only a white void where my memories should be. Understanding why is futile, like grasping at wisps of shadow and smoke with trembling fingers. And the pounding cadence within my head continues unbothered.

I've been stripped of all senses, blanketed by white noise and the stillness of a tomb. My hands drag up to my chest—too slow, too numb. They skim the loose ground, cradling it, before finally remembering how to work. Even then...even then, I can't bring myself to apply the pressure needed to separate my battered self from where I'm resting.

Can't. Or don't want to. I don't want to see what's left. Find the empty faces of my colleagues, my friends. So empty. I can't do that again. It's too much, too often. They never survive. I'm always the only one left.

A crackle and a sharp pop from near my upturned ear surprise me enough to raise my chin enough to peer through the haze. The noise resolves into fire lapping at the edges of my world. Hungry, uncaring of what it consumes, gnawing relentlessly like the Zee. And beyond that, cries and wails of pain and uncertainty. People are hurting, being hurt.

Panting, each inhale tastes of char and the burnt flesh of my tongue, robbing me of breath. Dirt and debris abrade my throat, lingering, coating my insides. I'm sure it runs through to my stomach, shards piercing me from the inside out.

As I brace my palms and press against the cool, flat earth, I gingerly remove myself from its embrace. A deep ache in my chest, falling along the side of my rib cage, chases the movement. It shocks a harsh bark of a cough from my lips, spittle and blood flying with it. But I keep at it and grit my teeth, muscles shaking, sweat dripping, as I finally rise up, blinking past the loose tears streaming unhindered from the corners of my eyes.

Blood-red skies burn hatefully above a ground blackened with death. The familiarity of that shade of red strikes me at my core, a shock of electric heat. I see scarlet irises burning with defiance above a sharp nose and a downturned mouth. Someone who should be here...who was right beside me. Omega!

That moves me more than anything else. Clutching at the soil beneath my fingertips, it gives without resistance. Furrows are left in the wake of my grip as, finally, I press away from the Earth. There's a light crunch as granules slide through the leather of my gloves, cascading away from me, uncaring. Sands through a bottomless hourglass. Time never adheres to me long enough to make a difference.

It all hurts to the point that there is little left of me not wrapped in the sharp yet numbing ache of fragility. Light and dark war and warp around each other, forming shapes as they flicker along the edges of my vision. Cries and screams echo against the darkening sky. I can't make out who they are. Do I know them? Only carnage and fading afterimages remain. Smudges carelessly splattered against the landscape, dripping infinite pools of ichor.

Finally, I gain enough sense to shakily get my feet under me, bent over, and huffing air in and out of my body like semi-automated bellows. I almost overlook the state of my boots humbly waiting below me as I stare listlessly past them. Their firm rubber treads, usually unremarkable and therefore unnoticed, have changed drastically in shape. A slight tilt of one foot reveals that the regular, perfectly patterned ridges and valleys have been transformed into the gentle roll of uneven hills.

Disbelief lingers, albeit shallowly, along the fringes of my mind. Along with it, a bit of delirium and the barely stifled start of a giggle. Could be worse—at least I still have my feet in them.

Enough.

The voice echoes harshly in my mind, foreign and unwelcome in my distressed state. But it's right. I have to stop focusing on myself. Where's Omega? I have to find her. She was here, right?

The agonized screams of others—people—are sporadically interrupted by the cannibalistic screeching of the Zee. Their addition to the recently dialed-up cacophony only serves to amplify the chaos surrounding me so much that I can't tell where they're coming from. It sounds like I'm surrounded by a horde, but through the plumes of smoke dancing sinuously around me, I'm met with no one. Nothing substantial or evident. There could be a few or a few hundred, and they couldn't care less about me.

Then, as though some greater being exhaled across the battlefield, a breeze crosses the blotched plain. It exposes the fallout in its wake— vivid and raw, and what I feared confronting. But it confirms everything about my story.

Bodies everywhere—Zeta, Zee, strangers. So many. Scattered like dolls flung in a toddler's tantrum, immortalized in macabre poses and still as corpses. Although it may be a trick of my mind, I think some do shift here and there.

And then one cadaver, a little closer to me, catches my attention. The fire's wind ripples across coarse, short crimson locks, dancing untethered in the stirred-up air. That mane of hair is as vivid as the flames surrounding us, its owner remaining conversely motionless, rooted to the ground. Her face is turned away—the smaller figure lacking poncho or helm as it lies chest-down.

My heart seizes. Forgets to start. A fist grasps it firmly and unyieldingly as my eyes burn with unshed tears. Lungs suddenly incapable of breathing, I force out a cry, calling out to her, my mind screaming.

"Omega!!"

"A single crack ruptures the silence—then, my heart stops."

ABOUT THE AUTHOR

O. T. Riesen started life as an Army brat, beginning on the East Coast of the United States and finishing on the West Coast with her parents and younger sister. A Jill of all trades, she's an avid reader, writer, and artist who enjoys expressing her overactive imagination in whatever form it takes. She calls Northern California home, where she lives with her family.

For more information about current and future work by O. T. Riesen, events, and subscriber-only content, join her newsletter at:
https://bit.ly/otrnews

Visit the author's website at:
https://otriesen.com

www.ingramcontent.com/pod-product-compliance
Lightning Source LLC
Chambersburg PA
CBHW070902260626
47162CB00007B/2537